St. Winifred's, or The World of School

Frederic W. Farrar

St. Winifred's, or The World of School

Table of Contents

St. Winifred's, or The World of School..1
    Frederic W. Farrar..1
PART ONE..2
    CHAPTER ONE. WALTER'S HOME..2
    CHAPTER TWO. ST WINIFRED'S...6
    CHAPTER THREE. NEW BOYS..9
    CHAPTER FOUR. FRIENDS AND FOES..16
    CHAPTER FIVE. SCHOOL TROUBLES..25
    CHAPTER SIX. A BURST OF WILFULNESS..35
    CHAPTER SEVEN. VOGUE LA GALERE..43
    CHAPTER EIGHT. THE BURNT MANUSCRIPT......................................51
    CHAPTER NINE. PENITENCE..59
    CHAPTER TEN. UPHILLWARDS..67
    CHAPTER ELEVEN. HAPPIER HOURS..79
    CHAPTER TWELVE. MY BROTHER'S KEEPER......................................87
    CHAPTER THIRTEEN. DAUBENY..95
    CHAPTER FOURTEEN. APPENFELL..102
    CHAPTER FIFTEEN. IN THE CLOUDS..110
    CHAPTER SIXTEEN. ON THE RAZOR..116
    CHAPTER SEVENTEEN. THE GOOD RESOLVE....................................124
    CHAPTER EIGHTEEN. THE MARTYR−STUDENT................................129
    CHAPTER NINETEEN. THE SCHOOL−BELL..136
    CHAPTER TWENTY. FAREWELL...144
    CHAPTER TWENTY ONE. KENRICK'S HOME..148
    CHAPTER TWENTY TWO. BIRDS OF A FEATHER...............................160
    CHAPTER TWENTY THREE. A BROKEN FRIENDSHIP........................171
    CHAPTER TWENTY FOUR. EDEN'S TROUBLES..................................178
    CHAPTER TWENTY FIVE. EDEN'S TROUBLES....................................186
    CHAPTER TWENTY SIX. A TURBULENT SCHOOL MEETING...............192
    CHAPTER TWENTY SEVEN. THE MONITORS.......................................203
    CHAPTER TWENTY EIGHT. FALLING AWAY...212
    CHAPTER TWENTY NINE. WALTER'S HOLIDAYS.................................217
PART TWO...222
    CHAPTER THIRTY. OLD AND NEW FACES..222
    CHAPTER THIRTY ONE. AMONG THE NOELITES.................................232

St. Winifred's, or The World of School

Table of Contents

St. Winifred's, or The World of School

    CHAPTER THIRTY TWO. DISENCHANTMENT..242
    CHAPTER THIRTY THREE. MARTYRDOM..252
    CHAPTER THIRTY FOUR. A CONSPIRACY FOILED................................262
    CHAPTER THIRTY FIVE. THE FINAL FRACAS..271
    CHAPTER THIRTY SIX. IN THE DEPTHS..285
    CHAPTER THIRTY SEVEN. THE RECONCILIATION AND THE
      LOSS..300
    CHAPTER THIRTY EIGHT. THE STUPOR BROKEN................................311
    CHAPTER THIRTY NINE. ON THE DARK SEA..324
    CHAPTER FORTY. WHAT THE SEA GAVE UP..330
    CHAPTER FORTY ONE. L'ENVOI..336

St. Winifred's, or The World of School

Frederic W. Farrar

Kessinger Publishing reprints thousands of hard-to-find books!

Visit us at http://www.kessinger.net

- PART ONE

  - CHAPTER ONE. WALTER'S HOME.
  - CHAPTER TWO. ST WINIFRED'S.
  - CHAPTER THREE. NEW BOYS.
  - CHAPTER FOUR. FRIENDS AND FOES.
  - CHAPTER FIVE. SCHOOL TROUBLES.
  - CHAPTER SIX. A BURST OF WILFULNESS.
  - CHAPTER SEVEN. VOGUE LA GALERE.
  - CHAPTER EIGHT. THE BURNT MANUSCRIPT.
  - CHAPTER NINE. PENITENCE.
  - CHAPTER TEN. UPHILLWARDS.
  - CHAPTER ELEVEN. HAPPIER HOURS.
  - CHAPTER TWELVE. MY BROTHER'S KEEPER.
  - CHAPTER THIRTEEN. DAUBENY.
  - CHAPTER FOURTEEN. APPENFELL.
  - CHAPTER FIFTEEN. IN THE CLOUDS.
  - CHAPTER SIXTEEN. ON THE RAZOR.
  - CHAPTER SEVENTEEN. THE GOOD RESOLVE.
  - CHAPTER EIGHTEEN. THE MARTYR-STUDENT.
  - CHAPTER NINETEEN. THE SCHOOL-BELL.
  - CHAPTER TWENTY. FAREWELL.
  - CHAPTER TWENTY ONE. KENRICK'S HOME.
  - CHAPTER TWENTY TWO. BIRDS OF A FEATHER.
  - CHAPTER TWENTY THREE. A BROKEN FRIENDSHIP.
  - CHAPTER TWENTY FOUR. EDEN'S TROUBLES.
  - CHAPTER TWENTY FIVE. EDEN'S TROUBLES.

- CHAPTER TWENTY SIX. A TURBULENT SCHOOL MEETING.
- CHAPTER TWENTY SEVEN. THE MONITORS.
- CHAPTER TWENTY EIGHT. FALLING AWAY.
- CHAPTER TWENTY NINE. WALTER'S HOLIDAYS.

- PART TWO

  - CHAPTER THIRTY. OLD AND NEW FACES.
  - CHAPTER THIRTY ONE. AMONG THE NOELITES.
  - CHAPTER THIRTY TWO. DISENCHANTMENT.
  - CHAPTER THIRTY THREE. MARTYRDOM.
  - CHAPTER THIRTY FOUR. A CONSPIRACY FOILED.
  - CHAPTER THIRTY FIVE. THE FINAL FRACAS.
  - CHAPTER THIRTY SIX. IN THE DEPTHS.
  - CHAPTER THIRTY SEVEN. THE RECONCILIATION AND THE LOSS.
  - CHAPTER THIRTY EIGHT. THE STUPOR BROKEN.
  - CHAPTER THIRTY NINE. ON THE DARK SEA.
  - CHAPTER FORTY. WHAT THE SEA GAVE UP.
  - CHAPTER FORTY ONE. L'ENVOI.

"ST. WINIFRED'S" BY DEAN F.W. FARRAR

A TALE OF A YOUNG MAN'S SEARCH FOR HIS SISTER AND HIS IDENTITY

PART ONE

CHAPTER ONE. WALTER'S HOME.

The merry homes of England!
Around their hearths by night,
What gladsome looks of household love,
Meet in the ruddy light!—*Mrs Hemans.*

St. Winifred's, or The World of School

"Good-bye, Walter; good-bye, Walter dear! good-bye;" and the last note of this chorus was "Dood-bye," from a blue-eyed, fair-haired girl of two years, as Walter disengaged his arms from his mother's neck, and sprang into the carriage which had already been waiting a quarter of an hour to convey him and his luggage to the station.

It is the old, old story: Mr Evson was taking his son to a large public school, and this was the first time that Walter had left home. Nearly every father who deigns to open this little book has gone through the scene himself; and he and his sons will know from personal experience the thoughts, and sensations, and memories which occupied the minds of Walter Evson and his father, as the carriage drove through the garden gate and the village street, bearing the eldest boy of the young family from the sacred and quiet shelter of a loving home to a noisy and independent life among a number of strange and young companions.

If you have ever stood on the hill from which Walter caught a last glimpse of the home he was leaving, and waved his final farewell to his mother, you are not likely to have forgotten the scene which was then spread before your eyes. On the right-hand side, the low hills, covered with firs, rise in gentle slopes one over the other, till they reach the huge green shoulder of a mountain, around whose summits the clouds are generally weaving their awful and ever-changing diadem. To the left, between the road and a lower range of wooded undulations, is a deep and retired glen, through which a mountain stream babbles along its hurried course, tumbling sometimes in a noisy cataract and rushing wildly through the rough boulder stones which it has carried from the heights, or deepening into some quiet pool, bright and smooth as glass, on the margin of which the great purple loosestrife and the long fern leaves bend down as though to gaze at their own reflected beauty. In front, and at your feet, opens a rich valley, which is almost filled as far as the roots of the mountains by a lovely lake. Beside this lake the white houses of a little village cluster around the elevation, on which the church and churchyard stand; while on either shore, rising among the fir-groves that overshadow the first swellings of the hills, are a few sequestered villas, commanding a prospect of rare beauty, and giving a last touch of interest to the surrounding view.

In one of these houses—that one with the crowded gables not a hundred feet above the lake, opposite to which you see the swans pluming their wings in the sunlight, and the green boat in its little boathouse—lived the hero of our story; and no boy could have had a dearer or lovelier home. His father, Mr Evson, was a man in easy, and almost in affluent circumstances, who, having no regular occupation, had chosen for himself this quiet retreat, and devoted all his time and care to the education of his family, and the ordinary duties of a country gentleman.

Walter was the eldest child, a graceful, active, bright-eyed boy. Up to this time—and he was now thirteen years old—he had had no other teaching but that of his father, and of a tutor, who for the last year had lived in the house. His education, therefore, differed considerably from that of many boys of his own age, and the amount of book knowledge which he had acquired was small as yet; but he was full of that intelligent interest in things most worth knowing which is the best and surest guarantee for future progress.

Let me pause for a moment to relate how a refined and simple-hearted gentleman had hitherto brought up his young boys. I do not pronounce whether the method was right or wrong; I only describe it as it was; and its success or failure must be inferred from the following pages.

The positive teaching of the young Evsons did not begin too early. Till they were ten or twelve years old nearly all they did know had come to them either intuitively or without any conscious labour. They were allowed almost to live in the open air, and nature was their wise and tender teacher. Some object was invented, if possible, for every walk. Now it was to find the shy recesses of the wood where the wild strawberries were thickest, or where the white violets and the rarest orchis flowers were hid; or to climb along the rocky sides of the glen to seek the best spot for a rustic meal, and find mossy stones and flower- banks for seats and tables near some waterfall or pool.

When they were a little older their father would amuse and encourage them until they had toiled up even to the very summit of all the nearest hills, and there they would catch the fresh breeze which blew from the far-off sea, or gaze wonderingly at the summer lightning flashing behind the chain of hills, or watch, with many playful fancies, the long gorgeous conflagration of the summer sunset. And in such excursions their father or mother would teach them without seeming to teach them, until they were thoroughly familiar with the names and properties of all the commonest plants, and eagerly interested to secure for their little collections, or to plant in their gardens, the different varieties of all the wild flowers that were found about their home. Or, again, when they sat out in the garden, or wandered back in the autumn twilight from some gipsy party, they were taught to recognise the stars and planets, until Mars and Jupiter, Orion and Cassiopeia, the

St. Winifred's, or The World of School

Pleiads and the Northern Crown, seemed to look down upon them like old and beloved friends.

It was easy, too, and pleasant, to teach them to love and to treat tenderly all living things—to observe the little black-eyed squirrel without disturbing him while he cracked his nuts; to watch the thistle-thrush's nest till the timid bird had learned to sit there fearlessly, and not scurry away at their approach; and to visit the haunts of the moorhen without causing any consternation to her or her little black velvet progeny. Visitors who stayed at the house were always delighted to see how all creatures seemed to trust the children; how the canary would carol in its cage when they came into the room; how the ponies would come trotting to the boys across the field, and the swans float up and plume their mantling wings, expecting food and caresses, whenever they came in sight.

The lake was a source of endless amusement to them; summer and winter they might have been seen bathing in its waters till they were bold swimmers, or lying to read their books in the boat under the shade of the trees, or rowing about till the little boy of six years was allowed to paddle himself alone to the other side, and even when the waves were rough, and the winds high, the elder ones were not afraid to venture out. In short, they were healthy and manly mountain-boys, with all their senses admirably exercised, and their powers of observation so well trained, that they sometimes amazed their London cousins by pointing to some falcon poised far-off above its prey, which was but a speck to less practised eyes, or calling attention to the sweetness of some wood-bird's note, indistinguishable to less practised ears.

Even in such lessons as these they would have made but little progress if they had not been trained in the nursery to be hardy, modest, truthful, unselfish, and obedient. This work had effectually been done when alone it *can* be effectually done, in the earliest childhood, when the sweet and plastic nature may acquire for all that is right and good the powerful aid of habit, before the will and the passions are fully conscious of their dangerous and stubborn power.

Let no one say that I have been describing some youthful prodigies. There are thousands such as I describe in all happy and well-ordered English homes; there might be thousands more if parents spent a more thoughtful care upon the growth of their children; there will be many, many thousands more as the world, "in the rich dawn of an ampler day," in the gradual yet noble progress of social and moral improvement, becomes purer and holier, and more like Him who came to be the ideal of the loftiest yet the lowliest, of the most clear-sighted yet the most loving, of the most happy and yet the most humble manhood.

CHAPTER TWO. ST WINIFRED'S.

> Gay Hope is theirs by Fancy led,
> Less pleasing when possess'd,
> The tear forgot as soon as shed,
> The sunshine of the breast.—*Gray*.

Walter's destination was the school of St Winifred. Let me here say at once that if any reader set himself to discover what and where the school of St Winifred is, he will necessarily fail. It is impossible, I suppose, to describe *any* school without introducing circumstances so apparently special as to lead some readers into a supposed identification. But here, and once for all, I distinctly and seriously repudiate all intention of describing any particular foundation. I am well aware that for some critics this disclaimer will be insufficient. But every *honourable* reader and critic may rest assured that in describing St Winifred's I have not intended to depict any one school, and that no single word dictated by an unworthy personality will find a place in the following pages.

St Winifred's School stands by the seaside, on the shores of a little bay embraced and closed in by a range of hills, whose sweeping semicircle is only terminated on either side by the lofty cliffs which, in some places, are fringed at the base by a margin of sand and shingle, and in others descend with sheer precipices into the ever-boiling surf. Owing to the mountainous nature of the country, the railroad cannot approach within a distance of five miles, and to reach the school you must drive through the dark groves which cover the lower shoulder of one of the surrounding mountains. When you reach the summit of this ascent, the bay of St Winifred lies before you; that line of white houses a quarter of a mile from the shore is the village, and the large picturesque building of old grey stone, standing in the angle where the little river reaches the sea, is St. Winifred's School.

The carriage stopped at the grand Norman archway of the court. The school porter—the Famulus as they classically called him— a fine-looking man, whose honest English face showed an amount of thought and refinement above his station, opened the gate, and, consigning Walter's play-box and portmanteau to one of the school servants, directed Mr Evson across the court and along some cloisters to the house of Dr Lane, the head-master. The entering of Walter's name on the school books was soon accomplished, and he was assigned as private pupil to Mr Robertson, one of the tutors. Dr Lane then spoke a word of encouragement to the young stranger, and he walked back with his father across the court to the gate, where the carriage was still waiting to take Mr Evson to meet the next train.

"Please let us walk up to the top of the hill, papa," said Walter; "I shan't be wanted till tea-time, and I needn't bid good- bye to you here."

Mr Evson was as little anxious as Walter to hasten the parting. They had never been separated before. Mr Evson could look back for the rare period of thirteen years, during which they had enjoyed, by God's blessing, an almost uninterrupted happiness. He had begun life again with his young children; he could thoroughly sympathise alike with their thoughts and with their thoughtlessness, and by training them in a manner at once wise and firm, he had been spared the greater part of that anxiety and disappointment which generally spring from our own mismanagement. He deeply loved, and was heartily proud of his eldest boy. There is no exaggeration in saying that Walter had all the best gifts which a parent could desire. There was something very interesting in his appearance, and very winning in his modest and graceful manners. It was impossible to see him and not be struck with his fine open face, and the look of fearless and noble innocence in his deep blue eyes.

It was no time for moral lectures or formal advice. People seem to think that a few Polonius-like apophthegms delivered at such a time may be of great importance. They may be, perhaps, if they be backed up and enforced by previous years of silent and self-denying example; otherwise they are like seed sown upon a rock, like thistle-down blown by the wind across the sea. Evson spoke to Walter chiefly about home, about writing letters, about his pocket-money, his amusements, and his studies, and Walter knew well beforehand, without any repetitions *then*, what his father wished him to be, and the principles in accordance with which he had endeavoured to mould his thoughts and actions.

St. Winifred's, or The World of School

The time passed too quickly for them both; they were soon at the top of the hill where the carriage awaited them.

"Good-bye, Walter. God bless you," said Evson, shaking hands for the last time, and throwing deep meaning into those simple words.

"Good-bye, papa. My best love to all at home," said Walter, trying to speak cheerfully, and struggling manfully to repress his rising tears.

The carriage drove on. Walter watched it out of sight, and, turning round, felt that a new phase of his life had begun, and that he was miserably alone. It was natural that he should shed a few quiet tears, as he thought of the dear friends with whom he had parted, and the four hundred strangers into whose society he was about to enter. Yet being brave and innocent he feared nothing, and, without any very definite religious consciousness, he had a clear and vivid sense that One friend was ever with him.

The emotions of a boy are as transient as they are keen, and Walter's tears were soon dried. As he looked round, the old familiar voice of the mountains was in his ears. He gazed with the delight of friendship on their towering summits, and promised himself many an exhilarating climb up their steep sides. And now too for the first time—for hitherto he had not much noticed the scenery around him—a new voice, the great voice of the sea, broke with its grand but awful monotony upon his listening ear. As he gazed upon the waves, glowing and flashing with the golden network of autumnal sunbeams, it seemed to dawn upon him like the discovery of a new sense, and he determined to stroll down to the beach before re-entering the gates of Winifred.

He wandered there not only with a boy's delight, but with the delight of a boy whose eyes and ears have always been open to the beauty and wonder of the outer world. He longed to have his brother with him there. He picked up handfuls of the hard and sparkling sand; he sent the broad flat pebbles flying over the surface, and skimming through the crests of the waves he half filled his pockets with green and yellow shells and crimson fragments of Delessaria Sanguinea for his little sisters; and he was full of pleasurable excitement when the great clock of Winifred's, striking five, reminded him that he had better go in, and learn something, if possible, about the order of his future life.

St. Winifred's, or The World of School

CHAPTER THREE. NEW BOYS.

Parolles.—I find my tongue is too foolhardy.
All's Well that Ends Well, Act 4, Scene 1.

The Famulus—"familiar"—as the boys called him, directed Walter across the court to the rooms of his Housekeeper, who informed him about the places where his clothes and his play–boxes would be kept, and the dormitory where he was to sleep. She also gave him a key of the desk in the great schoolroom, in which he might, if he chose, keep his portable property. She moreover announced, with some significance, that she should be glad to do anything for him which lay in her humble power, and that the day after to–morrow was her birthday. Walter was a little puzzled as to the relevancy of the latter piece of information. He learnt it at a subsequent period, when he also discovered that Mrs Higgins found it to her interest to have periodical birthdays, recurring two or three times at least every half–year. The years which must have passed over that good lady's head during Walter's stay at St Winifred's—the premature rapidity with which old age must have subsequently overtaken her, and the vigour which she displayed at so advanced a period of life—were something quite extraordinary of their kind.

Towards the great schoolroom Walter accordingly directed his steps. The key turned out to be quite superfluous, for the hasp of the lock had been broken by Walter's predecessor, who had also left the trace of his name, his likeness, and many interesting though inexplicable designs and hieroglyphics, with a red–hot poker, on the lid. The same gentleman, to judge by appearances, must have had a curious entomological collection of spiders and earwigs under his protection, and had bequeathed to Walter a highly miscellaneous legacy of rubbish. Walter contemplated his bequest with some dismay, and began busily to dust the interior of the desk, and make it as fit a receptacle as he could for his writing–materials and other personal possessions.

While thus engaged he could not help being secretly tickled by the proceedings of a group of boys standing round the large unlighted stove, and amusing themselves, harmlessly for the most part, with the inexperience and idiosyncrasies of various newcomers. After tiring themselves with the freaks of a mad Irish boy who had entered into the spirit of his own cross–examination with a high sense of buffoonery which refused to grow ill– tempered, they were now playing on the extreme gullibility of a heavy, open-mouthed, bullet-headed fellow, named Plumber, from whom the most astounding information could extract no greater evidence of sensation than a little wider stare of the eyes, and an unexcited drawl of "Really though?" One of the group, named Henderson, a merry-looking boy with a ceaseless pleasant twinkle of the eyes, had been taxing his own invention to the uttermost without in the least exciting Plumber's credulity.

"You saw the fellow who let you in at the school gates, Plumber?" said Henderson.

"Yes; I saw some one or other."

"But did you notice him particularly?"

"No; I didn't notice him."

"Well, you should have done. That man's called `The Familiar.' Ask any one if he isn't. But do you know why?"

"No;" said Plumber.

"It's because he's got a familiar spirit which waits on him," said Henderson mysteriously.

"Really though," said Plumber, and this time he looked so frightened that it was impossible for the rest to avoid bursting into a fit of laughter, during which Plumber, vaguely comprehending that he was considered a very good joke, retired with discomfiture.

"You fools," said Henderson; "if you'd only given me a little more time I'd have made him believe that Lane had a tail, and wore his gown to conceal it, except when he used it to flog with; and that before being entered he would have to sing a song standing on his head. You've quite spoilt my game by bursting out laughing."

"There's another new fellow," said Kenrick, one of the group. "Come here, you new fellow," called two or three of them.

St. Winifred's, or The World of School

Walter looked up, thinking that he was addressed, but found that the summons was meant for a boy, rather good-looking but very slender, whose self-important attitude and supercilious look betrayed no slight amount of vanity, and who, to the apparent astonishment of the rest, was surveying the room and its appurtenances with a look of great affectation and disdain.

"So you don't much seem to like the look of St Winifred's," said Kenrick to him, as the boy walked up with a delicate air.

"Not much," lisped the new boy; "everything looks so very common."

"Common and unclean to the last degree," said Henderson, imitating his manner.

"And is this the only place you have to sit in?"

"Oh, by no means," said Henderson; "each of us has a private apartment furnished in crimson and gold, according to the simple yet elegant taste of the owner. Our meals are there served to us by kneeling domestics on little dishes of silver."

"I suppose you intend that for wit," said the new boy languidly.

"Yes; to do you, to wit," answered Henderson; "but seriously though, that would be a great deal more like what you have been accustomed to; wouldn't it, my friend?"

"Very much more," said the boy.

"And would you politely favour this company," said Henderson, with obsequious courtesy, "by revealing to us your name?"

"My name is Howard Tracy."

"Oh, indeed!" said Henderson, with an air of great satisfaction, and making a low bow.

"I am called Howard Tracy because I am descended lineally from both those noble families."

St. Winifred's, or The World of School

"My goodness! are you really?" said Henderson, clasping his hands in mock transport. "My dear sir, you are an honour to your race and country! you are an honour to this school. By Jove, we are proud, sir, to have you among us!"

"Perhaps you may not know that my uncle is the Viscount George," said Tracy patronisingly.

"Is he, though, by George!" said Henderson, yawning. "Is that George who

"Swinged the dragon, and e'er since
Sits on his horseback at mine hostess' door?"

but finding that the boy's vanity was too obtuse to be amusing any longer, he was about to leave him to the rest, when Jones caught sight of Walter, and called out:

"Halloa, here's a new fellow grinning at the follies of his kind. Come here, you dark–haired chap. What's your name?"

"Evson," said Walter, quietly approaching them. Before getting any fun out of him it was necessary to see what kind of boy he was; and as Jones hardly knew what line to take, he began on the commonest and most vulgar tack of catechising him about his family and relations.

"What's your father?"

"My father is a gentleman," said Walter, rather surprised at the rudeness of the question.

"And where do you live?"

"At Semlyn."

"And how old are you?"

"Just thirteen."

"And how many sisters have you?"

St. Winifred's, or The World of School

Walter rather thought of asking, "What's that to you?" but as he saw no particular harm in answering the question, and did not want to seem too stiff-backed, he answered—"Three."

"And are they very beautiful?"

"I don't know; I never asked them. Are yours?"

This last question was so perfectly quiet and unexpected, and Jones was so evidently discomfited by it, that the rest burst into a roar of laughter, and Henderson said, "You've caught a tartar, Jones. You can't drop salt on this bird's tail. You had better return to Plumber, or George and the dragon. Here, my noble Viscount, what do you think of your coeval? Is he as common as the rest of us?"

"I don't think anything about him, if you mean me by Viscount," said Tracy peevishly, beginning at last to understand that they had been making a fool of him.

"Quite right, George; he's beneath your notice."

Tracy ran his hand through his scented hair, as if he rather implied that he was; and being mortified at the contrast between his own credulous vanity and Walter's manly simplicity, and anxious if possible to regain his position, he said angrily to Walter—

"What are you looking at me for?"

Not wishing to be rude, Walter turned away, while some one observed, "A cat may look at a king."

"Ay, a cat at a king, I grant you," answered Henderson; "but not a mere son of Eve at any Howard Tracy."

"You are laughing at me," said Tracy to Walter again, in a still angrier tone, seeing Walter smile at Henderson's remark.

"I've not the slightest wish to laugh at you," said Walter.

"Yes he has. Shy this at him," said Jones, putting a great bit of orange peel into Tracy's hand.

Tracy threw it at Walter, and he without hesitation picked it up, and flung it back in Tracy's face.

"A fight! a fight!" shouted the mischief-making group, as Tracy made a blind blow at Walter, which his antagonist easily parried.

"Make him fight you. Challenge him," said Jones. "Invite him to the milling-ground behind the chapel after first school to-morrow morning."

"Pistols for two, coffee for four, at eight to-morrow," said Henderson. "Trample on the Dragon's tail, some one, and rouse him to the occasion. What! he won't come to the scratch? Alack! alack!

"What can ennoble fools or cowards?
Not all the blood of all the Tracys, Dragons, and Howards!"

he continued mischievously, as he saw that Tracy, on taking note of Walter's compact figure, showed signs of declining the combat.

"Hush, Henderson," said Kenrick, one of the group who had taken no part in the talk; "it's a shame to be setting two new fellows fighting their first evening."

But Henderson's last remark had been too much for Tracy. "Will you fight?" he said, walking up to Walter with reddening cheeks. For Tracy had been to school before, and was no novice in the ways of boys.

"Certainly not," said Walter coolly, to everybody's great surprise.

"What! the other chap showing the white feather too. *All* the new fellows are cowards it seems this time," said Jones. "This'll never do. Pitch into him, Tracy."

"Stop," said Kenrick; "let's hear first why he won't fight?"

St. Winifred's, or The World of School

"Because I see no occasion to," said Walter; "and because, in the second place, I never could fight in cold blood; and because, in the third place—"

"Well, what in the third place," said Kenrick, interested to observe Walter's hesitation.

"In the third place," said Walter, "I don't say it from conceit, but that boy's no match for me."

To any one who glanced at the figures of the two boys this was obvious enough, although Walter was a year the younger of the two. The rest began to respect Walter accordingly as a sensible little man, but Tracy was greatly offended by the last remark, and Jones, who was a bully and had a grudge against Walter for baffling his impertinence, exclaimed, "Don't you be afraid, Tracy. I'll back you. Give him something to heat his cold blood."

Fired at once by taunts and encouragements, Tracy did as he was bid, and struck Walter on the face. The boy started angrily, and at first seemed as if he meant to return the blow with compound interest, but suddenly changing his intention, he seized Tracy round the waist, and in spite of all kicking and struggling, fairly carried the humiliated descendant of the Howards and Tracys to a far corner of the room, where, amid a shout of laughter, he deposited him with the laconic suggestion, "don't you be a fool."

Walter's blood was now up, and thinking that he might as well show, from the very first, that he was not to be bullied, or made a butt with impunity, he walked straight to the stove, and looking full at Jones, (who had inspired him already with strong disgust), he said, "You called me a coward just now; I'm not a coward, though I don't like fighting for nothing. I'm not a bit afraid of *you*, though you forced that fellow to hit me just now."

"Aren't you? Saucy young cub! Then take that," said Jones, enforcing the remark with a box on the ear.

"And you take that," said Walter, returning the compliment with as much energy as if he had been playing at the game of *Gif es weiter*.

Jones, astonished beyond measure, sprung forward, clenched his two fists, squared, and blustered with great demonstrativeness. He was much Walter's senior, and was utterly taken by surprise at his audacity, but he seemed in no hurry to avenge the insult.

"Well," said Walter, heaving with indignation, "why don't you hit me again?"

Jones looked at his firm and determined little assailant with some alarm, slowly tucked up the sleeves of his coat, turned white and red, and—didn't return the blow. The tea-bell beginning to ring at that moment gave him a convenient excuse for breaking off the altercation. He told his friends that he was on the point of thrashing Walter when the bell rang, but that he thought it a shame to fight a new fellow:—"and in cold blood too," he added, adopting Walter's language, but not his sincerity.

"Don't call me a coward again then," said Walter to him as he turned away.

"I say, Evson, you're a regular brick, a regular stunner," said young Kenrick, delighted, as he showed Walter the way to the Hall where the boys had tea. "That fellow Jones is no end of a bully, and he won't be quite so big in future. You've taken him down a great many pegs."

"I say, Kenrick," shouted Henderson after them, "I bet you five to one I know what you're saying to the new fellow."

"I bet you don't," said Kenrick, laughing.

"You're saying—it's a quotation you know, but never mind— you're saying to him, `A sudden thought strikes me; let's swear an eternal friendship.'"

"Then you're quite out," answered Kenrick. "I was saying come and sit next me at tea."

"And go shares in jam," added Henderson: "exactly what I said, only in other words."

CHAPTER FOUR. FRIENDS AND FOES.

He who hath a thousand friends hath not one friend to spare,
And he who hath one enemy shall meet him everywhere.

St. Winifred's, or The World of School

Already Walter had got some one to talk to, some one he knew; for in spite of Kenrick's repudiation of Henderson's jest, he felt already that he had discovered a boy with whom he should soon be friends. It doesn't matter how he had discovered it; it was by animal magnetism; it was by some look in Kenrick's eyes; it was by his light-heartedness; it was by the mingled fire and refinement of his face which spoke of a wilful and impetuous, yet also of a generous and noble nature. Already he felt a sense of ease and pleasure in the certainty that Kenrick—evidently no cipher among his schoolfellows—was inclined to like him, and to show him the ways of the school.

They went into a large hall, where the four hundred had their meals. They sat at a number of tables arranged breadth-wise across the hall; twenty or thirty sat at each table, and either a master or a monitor, (as the sixteen upper boys were called), took his place at the head of it.

"Now, mind you don't begin to smoke," said Henderson, as Walter went in, and found most of the boys already seated.

"Smoke?" said Walter, taking it for a bit of good advice; "do fellows smoke in Hall? I never have smoked."

"Why, you're smoking now," said Henderson, as Walter, entering among the crowd of strange faces and meeting so many pairs of eyes, began to blush a little.

"Don't tease him, Flip," said Kenrick; "smoking is the name fellows give to blushing, Evson; and if they see you given to blushing, they'll stare at you for the fun of seeing the colour mount up in your cheeks."

Accordingly, as he sat down, he saw that numerous eyes were turned upon him and upon Tracy, who happened to sit at the same table. Tracy, unaccustomed to such very narrow scrutiny, blushed all over; and, as he in vain looked up and down, this way and that, his cheeks grew hotter and hotter, and he moved about in the most uneasy way, to the great amusement of his many tormentors, until at last his eyes subsided finally into his teacup, from which he did not again venture to raise them until tea was over. But Walter was at once up to the trick, and felt thoroughly obliged to Henderson and Kenrick for telling him of it. So he waited till he saw that a good dozen fellows were all intently staring at him; and then looking up very simply and naturally, he met the gaze of two or three of them steadily in succession, and stared them out of countenance with a quiet smile. This turned the laugh against them; and he heard the remark, that he was "up to snuff, and no mistake." No one ever tried to make Walter smoke again, but for some time it used to be a regular joke to pass round word at tea-time, "Let's make Tracy smoke;" and as Tracy always *did* smoke till he got thoroughly used to it, he was generally glad when tea-time was over.

In spite of Henderson, who poked fun at them all tea-time, (till he saw that he really embarrassed them, and then he desisted), Kenrick sat by Walter, and took him more or less under his protection; for an "old boy" can always patronise a newcomer at first, even if they are of the same age.

From Kenrick Walter learnt, rather to his dismay, that he really would have no place to sit in except the big schoolroom, which he would share with some fifty others, and that he would be placed in a dormitory with at least five or six besides himself.

"Have you been examined yet?" asked Kenrick.

"No; but Dr Lane asked me what books I had read; and he told me that I was to go and take my chance in Mr Paton's form. What form is that?"

"It's what we call the Virgil form. Have you ever read at least only a few easy bits."

"I wish you joy, then."

"Why? what sort of a fellow is Mr Paton?"

"Mr Paton? he's not a man at all, he's a machine; he's the wheel of a mill; he's a cast-iron automaton; he's—"

"The abomination of desolation spoken of by Daniel the prophet," observed Henderson, who had caught a fragment of the conversation; "I'm in his form too, worse luck!"

"Hush! shut *up*, Henderson, and don't be profane," said Kenrick. "Well, Evson, you'll soon find out what Mr Paton's like; anything but `a paten of bright gold,' at any rate."

St. Winifred's, or The World of School

"Oh! oh! turn him out for his bad pun," said Henderson, hitting him with a pellet of bread; for which offence he immediately received "fifty lines" from the master at the other end of the table.

"Don't abuse Mr Paton," said a boy named Daubeny, which name Henderson had long ago contracted into Dubbs; "I always found him a capital master to be under, and really very *kind*."

"Oh, *you*; yes," answered Kenrick, "if we were all gifted with your mouselike stillness in school, my dear old Dubbs—"

"And your metallic capacity of grind, my dear old Dubbs," added Henderson.

"And your ostrich-like digestion of crabbed rules, my dear old Dubbs; why, then," said Kenrick, "we should all be boys after Mr Paton's heart."

"Or Mr Paton's pattern," suggested Henderson; so it was now Kenrick's turn to shudder at a miserable attempt at a pun, and return Henderson's missile, whereupon he got a *hundred* lines, which made him pull a very long face.

"Who's to be your tutor, Evson?" he asked, after this interlude.

"I suppose you're going to pick him to pieces, now," said Daubeny, smiling; "don't you believe half they say of him, Evson."

"Oh, if you're sharp, and successful, and polite, and gentlemanly, and jolly, and all that sort of thing, he'll like you very much, and be exceedingly kind to you; but if you are lazy, or mischievous, or stupid, or at all a pickle, he'll ignore you, snub you, won't speak to you. I wish you'd been in the same pupil-room with me."

"Depends on who he is, O virtuous Dubbs," said Henderson; "his end shall be `pieces,' as Punch says, if he deserves it."

"He told me I was to be Robertson's pupil," said Walter.

"Hum-m!" observed Kenrick.

St. Winifred's, or The World of School

"Why, what sort a person is he?"

"Some of his pups detest him, others adore him."

"Why?"

"Who's your tutor, then?"

"Percival; there, the master who is chatting and laughing with those monitors. He's a regular brick. *plinthos estin*! as we say in Greek," said Kenrick. "Halloa! tea's over."

"And you've been chattering so much that the new fellow's had none," said Henderson, as a bell rang and one of the monitors read a short Latin grace.

The boys streamed out, and Kenrick helped his new friend to unpack his books and other treasures, and put them in his desk, for which they ordered a new lock. The rest of the evening was occupied with "Evening Work," a time during which all the boys below a certain form sat in the schoolroom, and prepared their lessons for the next day, while a master occupied the desk to superintend and keep order. As other boys who were in the same form with himself were doing no work, Walter did not suppose that any work would be expected of him the next morning, and he therefore occupied his time in writing a long letter home. When this was over he began talking to Henderson, of whom he had a thousand questions to ask, and whose chief amusement seemed to consist in chaffing everybody, and whom, nevertheless, everybody seemed to regard as a friend. At nine a bell rang, the whole school went to chapel, where a short evening service was held, and then all but the higher forms, and the boys who had separate rooms, went to bed. As Walter lay down to sleep, he felt at least a century older than he had done that morning. Everything was marvellously new to him, but on the whole he was inclined to take a bright view of things. Two of the things which had happened to him gave him special delight; the sight of the sea, and the happy dawn—for as such he regarded it—of a genuine hearty boyish friendship, both with Henderson and Kenrick. When the gas was turned off, tired out with his journey and his excitement, he quickly fell asleep.

And, falling asleep, he at once passed into the land of dreams. He was out on the sea with Kenrick and Henderson in a row-boat, and all three of them were fishing. First there was a pull at Henderson's line, and, tugging it up, he caught not a fish, but Jones, who, after a few flounderings, lay down in the fish-basket. As this did not in the least surprise any of them, and excited no remark whatever, they set to work again, and Kenrick had a bite this time, which proved to be Howard Tracy, whom they laid quietly in the bottom of the boat, Jones assisting. The third time Walter himself had a tug, and was in the act of hauling up Dubbs, when he became conscious that the boat was rocking very violently, and he felt rather surprised that he was not sea-sick. This seemed to give a new current to his thoughts, for all of a sudden he was out riding with some one, and his horse began to rear in the most uncomfortable manner, right on his hind legs. He kept his seat manfully,—but no! that last rear was too much, and, suddenly waking, he was at once aware that his bed was rising and falling in a series of heavy shakes and bumps, whereby he was nearly flung off the mattress. He instantly guessed the cause, for, indeed, Kenrick had given him a hint of such a possibility. He knew that some one, wishing to frighten him, had got under the bed, and was heaving it up and down with his back. All that he had noticed when he undressed, was that there were several big fellows in the dormitory, and he knew that the room had rather a bad reputation for disorder and bullying.

Being a strong little fellow, brave as a lion, and very active, Walter was afraid of no one, so springing up during a momentary cessation of the mysterious upheavals, he instantly made a dash under the bed, and seized some one by the leg. The leg kicked violently, and as a leg is a particularly strong limb, it succeeded in disengaging itself from Walter's hands, not however, till it had left a slipper as a trophy; and with this slipper Walter pursued a dim white figure, which he could just see scuttling away through the darkness to the other side of the room. This figure he overtook just in time to give it some resounding smacks with the sole of the slipper; when the figure clutched a counterpane off the nearest bed, flung it over Walter, and made good an escape, while Walter was entangled, Agamemnon-like, in the voluminous folds. Walter, however, still kept possession of the slipper, and was determined next morning to discover the owner. He knew that it was probably some bigger fellow who had been playing this game, and his common sense told him that it was best to take it good-humouredly as a joke, and yet at the same time to make it as little pleasant as possible for the perpetrator, even if he got thrashed himself. A bully or a joker of practical jokes is not likely to do things which cause himself a certain amount of discomfort, even if he succeeds in causing a still greater amount to some one else.

Walter cared very little for this adventure. It certainly annoyed him a little, and it showed him that some of the others in his dormitory must be more or less brutes, if they could find it amusing to break the sleep and play on the fears of a new boy the very night of his arrival among them. But he thought no more about it, and was quite determined that it should not happen often.

Far different was the case with poor little Arthur Eden, another new boy—who, as Walter had observed, occupied the bed next to him. He had been roused from his first sweet sleep in the same way, about the same time as Walter. But no one had prepared him for this annoyance, and as he was a very timid child, it filled him with terror; he was even so terrified that he did not know what it was. He lay quite still, not daring to speak, or make a sound, only clinging to his mattress with both hands in an agony of dread. He was already worn and bewildered with the events of the day. He had fallen among the Philistines; at the very moment of his arrival he had got into bad hands, the hands of boys who made sport of his weakness, corrupted his feelings, and lacerated his heart. He was very young—a mere child of twelve—and in the innocence of his simplicity he had unreservedly answered all their questions, and prattled to them about his home, about his twin sister, about nearly all his cherished secrets. In that short space of time he had afforded materials enough for the coarse jeers of the brutal, and the poignant ridicule of the cruel, for many a long day. Something of this derision had begun already, and he had found no secret place to hide his tears. That they would call him a milksop, a mollycoddle, and all kinds of horrid names he knew, and he had tried manfully to bear up under persecution. It was not until after many hot and silent drops had relieved the fever of his overwrought brain that sleep had come to him; and now it was broken thus.

O parents and guardians—anxious, yet unwise class—why, tell me why, knowing all that you must know, do you send such children as this to school? Eden's mother, indeed, had opposed the step, but his guardian, (for the boy's father was dead), seeing that he was being spoilt at home, and that he was naturally a shrinking and timid lad, had urged that he should be sent to St. Winifred's, with some vague notion of making a man of him. He might as well have thrown a piece of Brussel's lace into the fire with the intention of changing it into open iron-work. The proper place for little Eden would have been some country parsonage, where care and kindliness might have gradually helped him, as he grew older, to acquire the faculties which he had not; whereas, in this case, a public school only impaired for a time in that tender frame the bright yet delicate qualities which he had.

St. Winifred's, or The World of School

The big, clumsy ne'er-do-well of a boy, Cradock by name, who was choking with secret laughter as he tilted little Eden's bed— leaving a pause of frightful suspense now and then to let him recover breath and realise his situation—was as raw and ill- trained a fellow as you like, but he had nothing in him wilfully or diabolically wicked. If he had been similarly treated he would have broken into a great guffaw, and emptied his water-jug over the intruder; and yet if he could have seen the new boy at that moment, he would have seen that pretty little face—only meant as yet for the smiles of childhood—white with an almost idiotic terror, and he would have caught a staring and meaningless look in the glassy eyes which were naturally so bright and blue. But he really did not know—being merely an overgrown stupid fellow —the mischief he was doing, and the absolute horrible torment that his jest (?) was inflicting.

Finding that his joltings produced no apparent effect, and thinking that Eden might, by some strange somnolence peculiar to new boys, sleep through it all, he tilted the bed a little too high, and then indeed a wild shriek rang through the room as the mattress and clothes tumbled right over the foot of the bed, and flung the child violently on the floor. Fortunately the heap of bedclothes prevented him from being much hurt, and Cradock had just time to pick him up and huddle him into bed again, and jump back into his own bed, when the lamp of one of the masters, who had been attracted by Eden's cry, appeared through the door. The master, finding all quiet, and having come from a distant room, supposed that his ears had deceived him, or that the cry was some accidental noise outside the building. He merely walked round the room, and seeing Eden's bedclothes rather tumbled, kindly helped the trembling child to replace them in a more comfortable order, and left the room.

"I say, that's quite enough for one night," said the voice of one of the boys, when the master had disappeared. "You new fellows can go to sleep. Nobody'll touch you again to-night." The speaker was Franklin, rather a scapegrace in some respects, but a boy of no unkindly nature.

The light and the noise had revealed to Walter something of what must have taken place. In his own case, he cared very little for the assurance that he would not be molested again that night, feeling quite sure that he could hold his own against any one, and that his former enemy at any rate would not be likely to assault him again. But he was very, very glad for poor little Eden's sake, having caught a momentary glimpse of his scared and pitiable look.

St. Winifred's, or The World of School

Walter could not sleep for a long time; not till long after he heard from the regular breathings of the others that they were all in deep slumber. For there were sounds which came from Eden's bed which disturbed his heart with pity. His feelings bled for the poor little fellow, so young and fresh from home, a newcomer like himself, but evidently so little accustomed to this roughness and so little able to protect his own interests. For a long time into the night he heard the poor child crying and sobbing to himself, though he was clearly trying to stifle the sound. At last Walter could stand it no longer, and feeling sure that the rest were sound asleep, he whispered in his kindest tone, for he didn't know his neighbour's name:

"I say, you little new fellow."

The sound of sobbing was hushed for a moment, but the boy seemed afraid to answer; so Walter said again:

"Are you awake?"

"Yes," said a weak, childish voice.

"Don't be afraid; I'm a new fellow, too. Tell me your name."

"Eden," he whispered tremulously, though reassured by the kindly tone of voice. "Hush! hush! you'll awake some one."

"No, I won't," said Walter; "here I'll come and speak to you;" and stepping noiselessly out of bed, he whispered in Eden's ear, "Never mind, my poor little fellow; don't be frightened, the boy didn't mean to hurt you; he was only shoving your bed up and down for a joke. Some one did the same to me, so I jumped up and licked him with a slipper."

"But I got so frightened. Oh, do you think they'll do it again to-night?"

"No, certainly, not again to-night," said Walter, "they're all asleep; and if any one does it again another night, you must just slip out of bed and not mind it. It doesn't hurt."

"Thank you," whispered Eden; "you're very kind, and nobody else has been kind to me here. Will you tell me *your* name?"

"My name's Walter Evson. Do you know your voice and look remind me of my little brother. There," he said, tucking him up in bed, "now good-night, and go to sleep."

The little fellow pressed Walter's hand hard, said good-night, and soon forgot his misery in a sleep of pure weariness. I do not think that he would have slept at all that night, but for the comforting sense that he had found, to lean upon, a stronger nature and a stronger character than his own. Walter heard him breathing peacefully, and then he too fell asleep, and neither woke nor dreamt, (that he was aware of), until half-past seven the next morning, when a servant roused the boys by ringing a large hand-bell in their ears.

CHAPTER FIVE. SCHOOL TROUBLES.

> The sorrows of thy youthful day
> Shall make thee wise in coming years;
> The brightest rainbows ever play
> Above the fountains of our tears.—Mackay.

Walter jumped up and began to dress at once; Eden, still looking pale and frightened, soon followed his example, and recognised him with a smile of gratitude. None of the other five boys who occupied the room thought of stirring until the chapel bell began to ring, which left them the ample space of a quarter of an hour for their orisons, ablutions, and all other necessary preparations!

Walter, who was now half-dressed, glanced at them as they got up, to discover the owner of the slipper, which he still kept in his possession. He watched for the one-sandalled enemy as eagerly as Pelias may be supposed to have done. First Jones tumbled out of bed, not even deigning a surly recognition, but Jones had his right complement of slippers. Then two other fellows, named Anthony and Franklin, not quite so big as Jones; their slippers were all right. Then Cradock, who looked a little shyly at Eden, and, after a while, told him that he was only playing a joke the night before, and was sorry for having frightened him; and last, Harpour, the biggest of the lot. Harpour was one of those fellows who are to be found in every school, and who are always dangerous characters: a huge boy, very low down in the forms, very strong, very stupid in work, rather good-looking, generally cut by the better sort, unredeemed by any natural taste or accomplishment, wholly without influence except among little boys, (whom he alternately bullied and spoilt), and only kept at school by his friends, because they were rather afraid of him, and did not quite know what to do with him. They called it "keeping him out of mischief," but the mischief he did at school was a thousandfold greater than any which he could have done elsewhere; for, except at school, he would have been comparatively powerless to do any positive harm.

By the exhaustive process of reasoning, Walter had already concluded that Harpour must have been his nocturnal disturber; and, accordingly, after thrusting a foot into a slipper, Harpour began to exclaim, "Hallo! where's my other slipper? Confound it, I shall be late; I can't dress; where's my other slipper?"

Wishing to leave him without escape from the necessity of betraying himself to have been the author of last night's raid, Walter made no sign, until Harpour, who had not any time to lose, said to him:

"Hi! you new chap, have you got my slipper?"

"I've got a slipper," said Walter blandly.

"The deuce you have. Then give it here, this minute."

"I captured it off some one's leg, who was under my bed last night," said Walter, giving it into Harpour's hand.

"The deuce you did!"

"Yes; and I smacked the fellow with it, as I will do again, if he comes again."

"The deuce you will! Then take that for your impudence," said Harpour, intending to bring down the slipper on his shoulder; but Walter dodged down, and parrying the blow with his arm, sent the slipper in a graceful parabola across the washhand-stand into Jones' basin.

"So, so," said Harpour, "*you're* a pretty cool hand, you are. Well, I've no time to settle accounts with you now, or I should be late for chapel. But—"

St. Winifred's, or The World of School

A significant pantomime explained the remainder of the sentence, and then Harpour, standing in his one slipper, hastily adjourned to his toilet. Walter being dressed in good time, knelt down for a few moments of hearty prayer, helped poor Eden, who was as helpless as though he had been always dressed by a servant, to finish dressing, and ran across the court into the chapel just as the bell stopped. There were still two minutes before the door was shut, and he occupied them by watching the boys as they streamed in, many of them with their waistcoats only half buttoned, and others with the water-drops still dangling from their hastily combed hair. He saw Tracy saunter in very neat, but with a languid air of disapprobation, blushing withal as he entered; Eden, whose large eyes looked bewildered until he caught sight of Walter and sat down beside him; Kenrick, beaming as ever, who nodded to him as he passed by; Henderson, who, not withstanding the time and place, found opportunity to whisper to him a hope that he had washed his desirable person in clear water; Plumber looking as if his credulity had been gorged beyond endurance; Daubeny with eyes immovably fixed in the determination to know his lessons that day and lastly, Harpour, who had just time to scuffle in hot, breathless, and exceedingly untidy, as the chaplain began the opening sentence.

"Where am I to go now?" asked Eden, when chapel was over.

"Well, Eden, I know as little as you. You'd better ask your tutor. Here, Kenrick," said Walter, "which of those black gowns is Mr Robertson?—this fellow's tutor and mine."

Kenrick pointed out one of the masters, to whom Eden went; and then Walter asked, "Where am I to go to Mr Paton's form?"

"Here, let me lead the victim to the sacrifice," said Henderson; "Oh for a wreath of cypress or funeral yew, or—"

"Nettles?" suggested Kenrick.

"Observe, new boy," said Henderson, "your eternal friend's delicate insinuation that you are a donkey. Here, come with me and I'll take you to be patted on." Henderson's exuberant spirits prevented his ever speaking without giving vent to slang, bad puns, or sheer good-humoured nonsense.

"Aren't you in that form, Kenrick?" asked Walter, as he saw him diverging to the right.

St. Winifred's, or The World of School

"Oh no! dear me, no!" said Henderson; *I* am, but the eternal friend is at least two forms higher; he, let me tell you, is a star of no ordinary magnitude; he's in the Thicksides'—meaning the Thucydides' class. "You'll require no end of sky-climbing before you reach *his* altitude. And now, victim, behold your sacrificial priest," he said, placing Walter at the end of a table among some thirty boys who were seated in front of a master's desk in the large schoolroom, in various parts of which other forms were also beginning work under similar superintendence. When all the forms were saying lessons at the same time it may be imagined that the room was not very still, and that a master required good lungs who had to teach and talk there for hours.

Not that Mr Paton's form contributed very much to the quota of general noise. Although Henderson had chaffed Daubeny on his virtuous stillness, yet all the boys sat very nearly as quiet as Dubbs himself during school hours. Even Henderson and such mercurial spirits were awed into silence and sobriety. You would hardly have known that in that quarter of the room there was a form at all. Quicksilver itself would have lost its volatility under Mr Paton's manipulation.

It was hard at first sight to say why this was. Certainly Mr Paton set many punishments, but so did other masters who had not half his success. The secret was, that Mr Paton was something of a *routinier*, and that was the word which, if he had known it, Kenrick would have used to describe him. If he set an imposition, the imposition must be done, and must be done at a certain time, without appeal, and *causa indicta*. Mr Paton was as deaf as Pluto to all excuses, and as inexorable as Rhadamanthus in his retributive dispensations. Neither Orpheus nor Amphion would have moved him. Orpheus might have made all the desks and forms dance round as they listened to his song, but he could never have got Mr Paton to let of fifty lines; and Amphion would have been equally unsuccessful even if the walls of the court had come as petitioners in obedience to his strains. As for remitting a lesson, Mr Paton would not have done it if St Cecilia had offered him the whole wreath of red and white roses which the admiring angels twined in her golden hair.

Mr Paton's rule was not the leaden rule of Lesbos; it could not be bent to suit the diversities of individual character, but was a rule iron and inflexible, which applied equally to all. His measure was that of Procrustes; the cleverest boys could not stretch themselves beyond it, the dullest were mechanically pulled into its dimensions. Hence some fared hardly under it; yet let me hasten to say that, on the whole, with the great number of average boys, it was a success. The discipline which he established was perfect, and though many boys winced under it at the time, it was valuable to all of them, especially to those of an idle or sluggish tendency; and as it was rigidly just as well as severe, they often learned to look back upon it with gratitude and respect.

After a time the form went up to say a lesson. Each boy was put on in turn. When it came to Walter's turn Mr Paton first inquired his name, which he entered with extreme neatness in his class–book—a book in which there was not a single blot from the first page to the last. He then put him on as he had put on the rest.

"I had no book, sir, and didn't know what the lesson was," said Walter.

"Excuses, sir, excuses!" said Mr Paton sternly; "you mean that you haven't learnt the lesson."

"Yes, sir."

"A bad beginning, Evson; bring me no excuses in future. You must write the lesson out." And an ominous entry implying this fact was written by Walter's freshly–entered name. Most men would have excused the first punishment, and contented themselves with a word of admonition; but this wasn't Mr Paton's way. He held with Escalus that—

   Mercy is not itself that oft looks so;
   Pardon is still the nurse of second woe?

Now it happened that Walter hated excuses, and had always looked on them as first cousins to lies, and he determined never again to render to Mr Paton any reason which could by any possibility be construed into an excuse. He therefore had to undergo a large amount of punishment, which he flattered himself could not by any possibility have been avoided.

On this occasion Henderson was also turned, and with him a boy named Bliss. It was quite impossible for Henderson to be unemployed on some nonsense, and heedless of the fact that he was himself Bliss's companion in misfortune, he opened a poetry–book, and taking Lycidas as his model, sat unusually still, while he occupied himself in composing a "Lament for Blissidas," beginning pathetically—

St. Winifred's, or The World of School

>Poor Blissidas is turned; turned ere his prime
>Young Blissidas, and hath not left his peer;
>Who would not weep for Blissidas? He knew
>Himself to say his Rep.—but give him time—
>He must not quaff his glass of watery beer
>Unchaffed, or write, his paper ruled and lined,
>Without the meed of some melodious jeer.

"I'll lick you, Flip, after school," said the wrathful Bliss, shaking his fist, as Henderson began to whisper to him this monody.

"Why do they call you Flip?" asked Walter, laughing.

"Short for Flibbertygibbet," said Bliss.

"Bliss, Henderson, and Evson, do me two hundred lines each," said Mr Paton; and so on this, his first morning in school, a second punishment was entered against Walter's name.

"Whew–w–w ... abomination of ... spoken of by ... hush!" was Henderson's whispered comment. "I call that hard lines." But he continued his "Lament for Blissidas" notwithstanding, introducing St Winifred and other mourners over Bliss's fate, and ending with the admonition that in writing the lines he was—

>To touch the tender tops of various quills,
>And mind and dot his quaint enamelled i's.

When Walter asked his tutor for the paper on which to write his punishment, Mr Robertson said to him, "Already, Evson!" in a tone of displeasure, and with a sarcasm hardly inferior to that Talleyrand's celebrated "Deja." "Two hundred lines and a lesson to write out *already!*" Bitter; with no sign of sympathy, without one word of inquiry, of encouragement for the future, or warning about the past—no advice given, no interest shown; no wonder that Walter never got on with his tutor.

The days that began for Walter from this time were days of darkness and disappointment. He was not deficient in natural ability, but he had undergone no special training for St. Winifred's School, and consequently many things were new to him in which other boys had been previously trained. The practice of learning grammar by means of Latin rules was particularly trying to him. He could have easily mastered the facts which the rules were intended to impress, but the empirical process suggested for arriving at the facts he could not remember, even if he could have construed the crabbed Latin in which it was conveyed. His father, too, had never greatly cultivated his powers of memory, and hence he felt serious difficulty at first with the long lessons that had to be learnt by heart.

Mr Paton's system was simply this: If a boy failed in a lesson from any mundane cause whatever, he had to write it out; if he failed to bring it written out, he had to write it twice; if he was turned in a second lesson he was sent to detention, *i.e.* he was kept in during play hours; if this process was long continued he was sent to the head-master in disgrace, and ran the chance of being flogged as an incorrigible idler. Mr Paton, who was devoted to a system, made no allowance for difference of ability, or for idiosyncrasies of temperament; he was a truly good man, at bottom a really kind-hearted man, and a genuine Christian; but the system which he had adopted was his "idol of the cave," and, as we said before, the justice of flexible adaptation was unknown to him.

Now, the way the system worked on Walter was this:—He failed in lessons because they were so new to him that he found it impossible to master them. He was not accustomed to work in such a crowded and noisy place as the great schoolroom, and the early hour for going to bed left little time for evening work. Accordingly he often failed, and whenever he did, the impositions or detentions, or both, took away from his available time for mastering his difficulties, and as this necessitated fresh failures, every single punishment became frightfully accumulative, and, alas! before three weeks were over, Walter was "sent up for bad" to the head-master. By this he felt degraded and discouraged to the last degree. Moreover, harm was done to him in many other ways. Conscious that all this disgrace had come upon him without any serious fault of his own, and even in spite of his direct and strenuous efforts, he became oppressed with a sense of injustice and undeserved persecution. The apparent uselessness of every attempt to shake himself free him these trammels of routine rendered him desperate and reckless, and the serious diminution of his hours for play and exercise made him dispirited and out of sorts. And all this brought on a bitter fit of home-sickness, during which he often thought of writing home and imploring to be removed from the school, or even of taking his deliverance into his own hands, and running away himself. But he knew that his father and mother were already distressed beyond measure to hear of the mill-round of punishment and discredit into which he had fallen, and about which he frankly informed them; so for their sakes he determined to bear up a little longer.

Walter was getting a bad name as an idler, and was fast losing his self-respect. And when that sheet-anchor is once lost, anything may happen to the ship; however gay its trim, however taut its sides, however delicate and beautiful the curve of its prow, it may drive before the gale, it may be dashed pitilessly among the iron rocks, or stranded hopelessly upon the harbour bar. A little more of this discipline, and a boy naturally noble- hearted and capable, might have been transformed into a mere moon- calf, like poor Plumber, or a cruel and vicious bully, like Harpour or Jones.

Happily our young Walter was saved by other influences from losing his self-respect. He was saved from it by one or two kindly and genial friendships; by success in other lines, and by the happy consciousness that his presence at St Winifred's was a help and comfort to some who needed such assistance with sore need.

One afternoon he was sitting disconsolately on a bench which ran along a blank wall on one side of the court, doing absolutely nothing. He was too disgusted with the world and with himself even to take up a novel. It was three o'clock, and the court was deserted for the playground, as a match had been announced that afternoon between the sixth-form and the school, at which all but a very few, (who never did anything but loaf about), were either playing or looking on. To sit with his head bent down, on a bench in an empty court doing nothing while a game was going on, was very unlike Walter Evson of six weeks before; but at that moment Walter was weary of detention, which was just over; he was burdened with punishments, he was half sick for want of exercise, and he was too much out of spirits to do anything.

Kenrick and Henderson had noticed and lamented the change in him. Not exactly knowing the causes of his ill-success, they were astonished to find so apparently clever a boy taking his place among the sluggards and dunces. With this, however, they concerned themselves less than with the settled gloom which was falling over him, and which rendered him much less available when they wanted to refresh themselves by talking a little nonsense, or amusing themselves in any other way. On this day, guessing how it was likely to be, Kenrick had proposed not to join the game until detention was over, and then to make Evson come up and play; and Henderson had kindly offered to stay with him, and add his persuasions to his friend's.

St. Winifred's, or The World of School

As they came out ready dressed for football they caught sight of him.

"Come along, old fellow; you're surely going to fight for the school against the sixth," said Kenrick.

"Isn't it too late?"

"No; any one is allowed a quarter of an hour's grace."

"Excuse number one bowled down," said Henderson.

"But I'm not dressed, I shan't have time to put on my jersey."

"Never mind, you'll only want your cap and belt, and can play in your shirt-sleeves."

"There goes excuse number two; so cut along," said Henderson, "and get your belt. We'll wait for you here. Why, the eternal friend's getting as wasted with misery as the daughter of Babylon," said Henderson, as Walter ran off.

"Yes," said Kenrick; "I don't like to see that glum look instead of the merry face he came with. Never mind; the game'll do him good; I never saw such a player; he looks just like the British lion when he gets into the middle of the fray; plunges at everything, and shakes his mane. Here he is; come along."

They ran up and found a hotly contested game swaying to and fro between the goals; and Walter, who was very active and a first-rate runner, was soon in the thick of it. As the evenness of the match grew more apparent the players got more and more excited. It had been already played several times, and no base had been kicked, except once by each side, when the scale had been turned by a heavy wind. Hence they exhibited the greatest eagerness, as school and sixth alike held it a strong point of honour to win, and a shout of approval greeted any successful catch or vigorous kick.

Whenever the ball was driven beyond the bounds, it was kicked straight in, generally a short distance only, and the players on both sides struggled for it as it fell. During one of these momentary pauses Kenrick whispered to Walter, "I say, Evson, next time it's driven outside I'll try to get it, and if you'll stand just beyond the crowd I'll kick it to you, and you can try a run."

"Thanks," said Walter eagerly, "I'll do my best."

The opportunity soon occurred. Kenrick ran for the ball; a glance showed him where Walter was standing; he kicked it with precision, and not too high, so that there was no time for the rest to watch where it was likely to descend. Walter caught it, and before the others could recover from their surprise, was off like an arrow. Of course the whole of the opposite side were upon him in an moment, and he had to be as quick as a deer, and as wary as a cat. But now his splendid running came in, and he was besides rather fresher than the rest. He dodged, he made wide detours, he tripped some and sprang past others, he dived under arms and through legs, he shook off every touch, wrenched himself free from one capturer by leaving in his hands the whole shoulder of his shirt, and got nearer and nearer to the goal. At last he saw that there was one part of the field comparatively undefended; in this direction he darted like lightning—charged and spilt, by the vehemence of his impulse, two fellows who stood with outstretched arms to stop him—seized the favourable instant, and by a swift and clever drop-kick, sent the ball flying over the bar amid deafening cheers, just as half the other side flung him down and precipitated themselves over his body.

The run was so brilliant and so plucky, and the last burst so splendid, that even the defeated side could hardly forbear to cheer him. As for the conquerors, their enthusiasm knew no bounds; they shook Walter by the hand, patted him on the back, clapped him, and at last lifted him on their shoulders for general inspection. As yet he was known to very few, and "Who's that nice-looking little fellow who got the school a base?" was a question which was heard on every side.

"That's Evson; Evson; Evson, a new fellow," answered Kenrick, Henderson, and all who knew him, as fast as they could, in reply to the general queries. They were proud to know him just then, and this little triumph occurred in the nick of time to raise poor Walter in his own estimation.

"Thanks, Kenrick, thanks," he said, warmly grasping his friend's hand, as they left the field. "They ought to have cheered *you*, not me, for if it hadn't been for you I should not have got that base."

"Pooh!" was the answer; "I couldn't have got it myself under any circumstances; and even if I could, it is at least as much pleasure to me that *you* should have done it."

Of all earthly spectacles few are more beautiful, and in some aspects more touching, than a friendship between two boys, unalloyed by any taint of selfishness, indiscriminating in its genuine enthusiasm, delicate in its natural reserve. It is not always because the hearts of men are wiser, purer, or better than the hearts of boys, that "summae puerorum amicitiae saepe cum toga deponuntur."

CHAPTER SIX. A BURST OF WILFULNESS.

> Nunquamne reponam
> Vexatus toties?—Juvenal 1, 1.

Although Walter's football triumphs prevented him from losing self-respect and sinking into wretchedness or desperation, they did not save him from his usual arrears of punishment and extra work. Besides this, it annoyed him bitterly to be always, and in spite of all effort, bottom, or nearly bottom, of his form. He knew that this grieved and disappointed his parents nearly as much as himself, and he feared that they would not understand the reason which, in his case, rendered it excusable—viz, the enormous amount of purely routine work for which other boys had been prepared by previous training, and in which, under his present discouragements and inconveniences, he felt it impossible to recover ground. It was hard to be below boys to whom he knew himself to be superior in every intellectual quality; it was hard for a boy, really clever and lively, to be set down at once as an idler and dunce. And it made Walter very miserable. For meanwhile Mr Paton had taken quite a wrong view of his character. He answered so well at times, construed so happily, and showed such bright flashes of intelligence and interest in parts of his work, that Mr Paton, making no allowance for new methods and an untrained memory, set him down, by an error of judgment, as at once able and obstinate, capable of doing excellently, and wilfully refusing to do so. This was a phase of character which always excited his indignation; and it was for the boy's own sake that he set himself to correct it, if possible. On both sides, therefore, there was some misunderstanding, and a consequent exacerbation of mind which told injuriously on their daily intercourse.

St. Winifred's, or The World of School

Walter's vexation and misery reached its acme on the receipt by his father of his first school character, which document his father sent back for Walter's own perusal, with a letter which, if not actually reproachful, was at least uneasy and dissatisfied in tone.

For the character itself Walter cared little, knowing well that it was founded throughout on misapprehension; but his father's letter stirred the very depths of his heart, and made them turbid with passion and sorrow. He received it at dinner-time, and read it as he went across the court to the detention-room, of which he was now so frequent an occupant. It was a bright September day, and he longed to be out at some game, or among the hills, or on the shore. Instead of that, he was doomed for his failures to two long weary hours of mechanical pen-driving, of which the results were torn up when the two hours were over. He had had no exercise for the last week; all his spare time had been taken up with impositions; Mr Robertson had given him a severe and angry lecture that morning; even Mr Paton, who rarely used strong language, had called him intolerable and incorrigible, and had threatened a second report to the head-master, because this was the tenth successive Greek grammar lesson in which he had failed. Added to all this, he was suffering from headache and lassitude. And now his father's letter was the cumulus of his misfortunes. A rebellious, indignant, and violent spirit rose in him. Was he always, for no fault of his own, to be bullied, baited, driven, misunderstood, and crushed in this way? If it was of no use trying to be good, and to do his duty, how would it do to try the other experiment—to fling off the trammels of duty and principle altogether; to do all those things which inclination suggested and the moral sense forbade; to enjoy himself; to declare himself on the side of pleasure and self-indulgence? Certainly this would save him from much unpleasantness and annoyance in many ways. He was young, vigorous, active; he might easily make himself more popular than he was with the boys; and as for the authorities, do what he would, it appeared that he could hardly be in worse disrepute than now. Vice bade high: as he thought of it all, his pen flew faster, and his pulse seemed to send the blood bounding through his veins as he tightened the grasp of his left hand round the edge of the desk.

Hitherto the ideal which he had set before him, as the standard to be attained during his school life, had been one in which a successful devotion to duty, and a real effort to attain to "godliness and good learning," had borne the largest share. But on this morning a very different ideal rose before him; he would abandon all interest in school-work, and only aim at being a gay, high-spirited boy, living solely for pleasure, amusement, and self-indulgence. There were many such around him—heroes among their schoolfellows, popular, applauded, and proud. Sin seemed to sit lightly and gracefully upon them. Endowed as he was with every gift of person and appearance, to this condition at least he felt that he could easily attain. It was an ideal not, alas! unnatural to the perilous age

> Which claims for manhood's vice the privilege
> Of boyhood—when young Dionysus seems
> All joyous as he burst upon the East
> A jocund and a welcome conqueror;
> And Aphrodite, sweet as from the sea
> She rose, and floated in her pearly shell
> A laughing girl; when lawless will erects
> Honour's gay temple on the Mount of God,
> And meek obedience bears the coward's brand;
> While Satan in celestial panoply
> With Sin, his lady, smiling by his side,
> Defies all heaven to arms.

Yes; he would follow the multitude to do all the evil which he saw being done around him; it looked a joyous and delightful prospect. He gazed on the bright vision of sin, on the iridescent waters of pleasure; and did not know that the brightness was a mirage of the burning desert, the iridescence a film of corruption over a stagnant pool.

The letter from home was his chief stumbling–block. He loved his father and mother with almost passionate devotion; he clung to his home with an intensity of concentrated love. He really had tried to please them, and to do his best; but yet they didn't seem to give him credit for it. Look at this cold reproachful letter; it maddened him to think of it.

There was only one thing which checked him. It was a little voice, which had been more silent lately, because other and passionate tones were heard more loudly; but yet even from a child poor Walter had been accustomed to listen with reverence to its admonitions. It was a voice behind him saying—"This is the way, walk ye in it;" now that he was turning aside to the right hand or to the left. But the noble accents in which it whispered of patience were drowned just now in the clamorous turbulence of those other voices of appeal.

St. Winifred's, or The World of School

The two hours of detention were over, and the struggle was over too. Walter drew his pen with a fierce and angry scrawl over the lines he had written, showed them up to the master in attendance with a careless and almost impudent air, and was hardly out of the room before he gave a shout of emancipation and defiance. Impatience and passion had won the day.

He ran up to the playground as hard as he could tear to work off the excitement of his spirits, and get rid of the inward turmoil. On a grass bank at the far end of it he saw two boys seated, whom he knew at once to be Henderson and Kenrick, who, for a wonder, were reading, not green novels, but Shakespeare!

"I'll tell you what it is, Henderson," he said; "I *can't* and I *won't* stand this any longer. It's the last detention breaks the boy's back. I hate St Winifred's, I hate Dr Lane, I hate Robertson, and I *hate, hate, hate* Paton," he said, stamping angrily.

"Hooroop!" said Henderson; "so the patient Evson is on fire at last. Tell it not to Dubbs!"

"Why, Walter, what's all this about?" asked Kenrick.

"Why, Ken," said Walter more quietly, "here's a history of my life: Greek grammar, lines, detention, caning—caning, detention, lines, Greek grammar. I'm sick of it; I *can't* and I *won't* stand it any more."

"Whether," spouted Henderson, from the volume on his knee—

"Whether 'twere nobler for the mind to suffer
The slings and arrows of outrageous fortune,
Or to take arms against a sea of troubles,
And by opposing end them!"

"End them I will," said Walter; "somehow, I'll pay him out, depend upon it."

"Recte si possis si non quocunque modo," said Somers, the head of the school, whose fag Walter was, and who, passing by at the moment, caught the last sentence; "what is the excitement among you small boys?"

St. Winifred's, or The World of School

"The old story, pitching into Paton," said Kenrick indifferently, and rather contemptuously; for he was a protege of Somers, and felt annoyed that he should see Walter's unreasonable display; the more so as Somers had asked him already, "why he was so much with that idle new fellow who was always being placed lag in his form?"

"What's it all about?" asked Somers of Kenrick.

"Because he gets lines for missing his grammar, I suppose." There was something in the tone which was especially offensive to Walter; for it sounded as if Kenrick wanted to show him the cold shoulder before his *great* friend, the head of the school.

"Oh, *that* all? Well, my dear fellow, the remedy's easy; work at it a little harder;" and Somers walked on, humming a tune.

"I wonder what he calls *harder*," said Walter, shaking his fist; "when I first came I used to get up quite early in the morning, and learn it till I was half stupid; I wonder whether he ever did as much?"

"Well, but it's no good abusing Paton," said Kenrick; "of course, if you don't know the lesson, he concludes you haven't learnt it."

"Thank you for nothing, Kenrick," said Walter curtly; "come along, Flip."

Kenrick was vexed; he was conscious of having shown a little coolness and want of sympathy; and he looked anxiously after Henderson and Walter as they walked away.

Presently he started up, and ran after them. "Don't be offended, Walter, my boy," he said, seizing his hand. "I didn't mean to be cold just now; but, really, I don't see why you should be so very wrathful with Paton; what can a master do if one fails in a lesson two or three times running? he must punish one, I suppose."

"Hang Paton," said Walter, shaking off his hand rather angrily, for he was now thoroughly out of temper.

"Oh, very well, Evson," said Kenrick, whose chief fault was an intense pride, which took fire on the least provocation, and which made him take umbrage at the slightest offence;

St. Winifred's, or The World of School

"catch me making an advance to you again. Henderson, you left your book on the grass;" and turning on his heel, he walked slowly away— heavy at heart, for he liked Walter better than any other boy in the school, and was half ashamed to break with him about such a trifle.

Henderson, apart from his somewhat frivolous and nonsensical tone, was a well-meaning fellow. When he was walking with Walter, he had intended to chaff him about his sudden burst of ill-temper, and jest away his spirit of revenge; but he saw that poor Walter was in no mood for jokes, and he quite lacked the moral courage to give good advice in a sober or serious way, or to recommend any course *because* it was right. This, at present, was beyond Henderson's standard of good, so he left Walter and went back for his book.

And Walter, flinging into the schoolroom, found several spirits seven times more wicked than himself, and fed the fire of his wrath with the fuel of unbounded abuse, mockery, and scorn of Mr Paton, in which he was heartily abetted by the others, who hailed all indications that Walter was likely to become one of themselves. And that evening, instead of attempting to get up any of his work, Walter wasted the whole time of preparation in noise, folly, and turbulence; for which he was duly punished by the master on duty.

He got up next morning breathing, with a sense of defiance and enjoyment, his new atmosphere of self-will. He of course broke down utterly, more utterly than ever, in his morning lessons, and got a proportionately longer imposition. Going back to his place, he purposely flung down his books on the desk, one after another with a bang; and for each book which he had flung down, Mr Paton gave him a hundred lines, whereupon he laughed sarcastically, and got two hundred more. Conscious that the boys were watching with some amusement this little exhibition of temper and trial of wills, he then took out a sheet of paper, wrote on it, in large letters, the words, TWO HUNDRED LINES FOR MR PATON, and, amid the tittering of the form, carried it up to Mr Paton's desk.

This was the most astoundingly impudent and insubordinate act which had ever been done to Mr Paton for years, and it was now his turn to be angry. But mastering his anger with admirable determination, he merely said, "Evson, you must be beside yourself this morning; it is very rarely, indeed, that a new boy is so far gone in disobedience as this. I have no hesitation in saying that you are the most audacious and impertinent new boy, with whom I have ever had to deal. I must cane you in my room after detention, to which you will of course go."

"Thank you, sir," said Walter, with a smile of impudent *sang froid*; and the form tittered again as he walked noisily to his seat. But Mr Paton, allowing for his violent frame of mind, took no notice of this last affront.

Whereupon Walter, taking another large piece of paper, and a spluttering quill pen, wrote on it, with a great deal of scratching:

> Due from Evson
> to
> Mr Paton.

For missing lesson	100 lines
For laying down books	300 lines
For laughing	200 lines
For writing 200 lines	A caning

> Detention, of course.
> Thank you for nothing.

And on the other side of the sheet he wrote in large letters— "NO GO!" Which being done, he passed the sheet along the form *pour encourager les autres*.

"Evson," said Mr Paton quietly, "bring me that paper."

Walter took it up—looking rather alarmed this time—but with the side *"No go!"* uppermost.

"What is this, Evson?"

St. Winifred's, or The World of School

"Number ninety, sir," said Walter, amid the now unconcealed laughter of the rest, who knew very well that he had intended it for "No go."

Mr Paton looked curiously at Walter for a minute, and then said, "Evson, Evson, I could not have thought you so utterly foolish. Well, you know that each fresh act *must* have its fresh punishment. You must leave the room now, and *besides all your other punishments* I must also report you to the head-master. You can best judge with what result."

This was a mistake of Mr Paton's—a mistake of judgment only— for which he cannot be blamed. But it was a disastrous mistake. Had he been at all a delicate judge or reader of the phenomena of character, he would have observed at once that at that moment there was a wild spirit of anger, a rankling sense of injustice and persecution in Walter's heart, which no amount of punishment could have cowed. Walter just then might without the least difficulty have been goaded into some act of violence which would have rendered expulsion from the school an unavoidable consequence. So easy is it to petrify the will, to make a boy bad in spite of himself, and to spoil, with no intentions but those of kindliness and justice, the promise of a fair young life. For when the will has once been suffered to grow rigid by obstinacy— a result which is very easy to avoid—no power on earth can bend it *at the time*. Had Mr Paton sent Walter out of the room before, had he at the end said, "Evson, you are not yourself to- day, and I forgive you," Walter would have been in a moment as docile and as humble as a child. But as it was, he left the room quite coolly, with a sneer on his lips, and banged the door; yet the next moment, when he found himself in the court alone, unsupported by the countenance of those who enjoyed his rebelliousness, he seated himself on a bench in the courtyard, hung his head on his breast, and burst into a flood of tears. If any friend could have seen him at that moment, or spoken one word in season, how much pain the poor boy might have been saved! Kenrick happened to cross the court; the moment Walter caught sight of him he sat with head erect and arms folded, but Kenrick was not to be deceived. He had caught one glimpse of Walter first; he saw his eyes wet with tears, and knew that he was in trouble. He hung on his foot doubtfully for one moment—but then his pride came in; he remembered the little pettish repulse in the playground the day before; the opportunity was lost, and he walked slowly on.

And Walter's heart grew as hard within him as a stone.

CHAPTER SEVEN. VOGUE LA GALERE.

Ah! Diamond, thou little knowest what mischief thou hast done.
Life of Sir Isaak Newton.

That afternoon Mr Paton, going into the Combination Room, where the masters often met, threw himself into one of the arm-chairs with an unwonted expression of vexation and disgust on his usually placid features.

"Why, what's the matter with you, Paton?" asked Mr Robertson. "Is to-day's *Times* too liberal for your notions, or what?"

"No," said Mr Paton; "but I have just been caning Evson, a new boy, and the fellow's stubborn obstinacy and unaccountable coolness annoy me exceedingly."

"Oh yes; he's a pupil of mine, I'm sorry to say, and he has never been free from punishment since he came. Even your Procrustean rule seems to fail with him, Paton. What have you been obliged to cane him for?"

Mr Paton related Walter's escapade.

"Well, of course you had no choice but to cane him," replied his colleague, "for such disobedience; but how did he take it?"

"In the oddest way possible. He came in with punctilious politeness, obviously assumed, with sarcastic intentions. When I took up the cane he stood with arms folded, and a singularly dogged look; in fact, his manner disarmed me. You know I detest caning, and I really could not do it, never having had occasion for it for months together. I gave him two cuts, and then left off. `May I go, sir?' he asked. `Yes,' I said, and he left the room with a bow, and a `Thank you, sir.' I am really sorry for the boy; for as I was obliged to send him to Dr Lane, he will probably get another flogging from him."

"What a worthless boy he must be," answered Mr Robertson.

"No, not exactly worthless; there's something about him I can't help liking; but most

St. Winifred's, or The World of School

impudent and stubborn."

"Excuse me," said Mr Percival, another of the masters, who had been listening attentively to the conversation. "I humbly venture to think that you're both mistaken in that boy. I like him exceedingly, and think him as promising a lad as any in the school. I never knew any boy behave more modestly and respectfully."

"Why, how do you know anything of him?" asked Mr Robertson in surprise.

"Only by accident. I had once or twice noticed him among the *detenus*, and being sorry to think that a new boy should be an *habitue* of the extra schoolroom, I asked him one day why he was sent. He told me that it was for failing in a lesson, and when I asked why he hadn't learned it, he said, very simply and respectfully, `I really did my very best, sir; but it's all new work to me.' Look at the boy's innocent, engaging face, and you will be sure that he was telling me the truth.

"I'm afraid," continued Mr Percival, "you'll think this very slight ground for setting my opinion against yours; but I was pleased with Evson's manner, and asked him to come and take a stroll on the shore, that I might know something more of him. Do you know, I never found a more intelligent companion. He was all life and vivacity; it was quite a pleasure to be with him. Being new to the sea, he didn't know the names of the commonest things on the shore, and if you had seen his face light up as he kept picking up whelk's eggs, and mermaid's purses, and zoophytes, and hermit-crabs, and bits of plocamium or coralline, and asking me all I could tell him about them, you would not have thought him a stupid or worthless boy."

"I don't know, Percival; you are a regular conjuror. All sorts of ne'er-do-wells succeed under your manipulation. You're a first- rate hand at gathering grapes from thorns, and figs from thistles. Why, even out of that Caliban, old Woods, you used to extract a gleam of human intelligence."

"He wasn't a Caliban at all. I found him an excellent fellow at heart; but what could you expect of a boy who, because he was big, awkward, and stupid, was always getting flouted on all sides? Sir Hugh Evans is not the only person who disliked being made a `vlouting-stog'."

St. Winifred's, or The World of School

"You must nave some talisman for transmuting boys if you consider old Woods an excellent fellow, Percival. I found him a mass of laziness and brute strength. Do give me your secret."

"Try a little kindness and sympathy. I have no other secret."

"I'm not conscious of failing in kindness," said Mr Robertson dryly. "My fault, I think, is being too kind."

"To clever, promising, bright boys—yes; to unthankful and evil boys, (excuse me for saying so)—no. You don't try to descend to their dull level, and so understand their difficulties. You don't suffer fools gladly, as we masters ought to do. But, Paton," he said, turning the conversation, which seemed distasteful to Mr Robertson, "will you try how it succeeds to lay the yoke a little less heavily on Evson?"

"Well, Percival, I don't think that I've consciously bullied him. I can't make my system different to him and other boys."

"My dear Paton, forgive my saying that I don't think that a rigid system is the fairest *summa lex, summa crux*. Fish of very different sorts and sizes come to our nets, and you can't shove a turbot through the same mesh that barely admits a sprat."

"I'll think of what you say; but I must leave him in Dr Lane's hands now," said Mr Paton.

"Who, I heartily hope, won't flog him," said Mr Percival.

"Why? I don't see how he can do otherwise."

"Because it will simply drive him to despair; because, if I know anything of his character, it will have upon him an effect incalculably bad."

"I hope not," said Mr Paton.

The conversation dropped, and Mr Percival resumed his newspaper.

St. Winifred's, or The World of School

When Walter went to Dr Lane in the evening, the Doctor inquired kindly and carefully into the nature of his offence. This, unfortunately, was clear enough, and Walter was far too ingenuous to attempt any extenuation of it. Even if he had not been intentionally idle, it was plain, on his own admission, that he had been guilty of the greatest possible insubordination and disrespect. These offences were rare at St Winifred's, and especially rare in a new boy. Puzzled as he was by conduct so unlike the boy's apparent character, and interested by his natural and manly manner, yet Dr Lane had in this case no alternative but the infliction of corporal punishment.

Humiliated again, and full of bitter anger, Walter returned to the great schoolroom, where he was received with sympathy and kindness by the others in his class. It was the dark part of the evening before tea-time, and the boys, sitting idly round the fire, were in an apt mood for folly and mischief. They began a vehement discussion about Paton's demerits, and called him every hard name they could invent. Walter took little part in this, for he was smarting too severely under the sense of oppression to find relief in mere abuse; but, from his flashing eyes and the dark scowl that sat so ill on his face, it was evident that a bad spirit had obtained the thorough mastery over all his better and gentler impulses.

"Can't we do something to serve the fellow out?" said Anthony, one of the boys in Walter's dormitory.

"But *what* can we do?" asked several.

"What, indeed?" asked Henderson mockingly; and as it was his way to quote whatever he had last been reading, he began to spout from the peroration of a speech which he had seen in the paper— "Aristocracy, throned on the citadel of power, and strong in—"

"What a fool you are, Henderson," observed Franklin, another of the group; "I'll tell you what we can do; we'll burn that horrid black book in which he enters the detentions and impositions."

"Poor book!" said Henderson; "what pangs of conscience it will suffer in the flames; give it not the glory of such martyrdom. Walter," he continued in a lower voice, "I hope that you'll have nothing to do with this humbug?"

"I will though, Henderson; if I'm to have nothing but canings and floggings, I may just as well be caned and flogged for *something* as for *nothing*."

"The desk's locked," said Anthony; "we shan't be able to get hold of the imposition–book."

"I'll settle that," said Walter; "here, just hand me the poker, Dubbs."

"I shall do no such thing," said Daubeny quietly, and his reply was greeted with a shout of derision.

"Why, you poor coward, Dubbs," said Franklin, "you *couldn't* get anything for handing the poker."

"I never supposed I could, Franklin," he answered; "and as for being a coward, the real cowardice would be to do what's absurd and wrong for fear of being laughed at or being kicked. Well, you may hit me," he said quietly, as Franklin twisted his arm tightly round, and hit him on it, "but you can't make me do what I don't choose."

"We'll try," said Franklin, twisting his arm still more tightly, and hitting harder.

"You'll try in vain," answered Daubeny, though the tears stood in his eyes at the violent pain.

"Drop his arm, you Franklin," indignantly exclaimed Henderson, who, though he was always teasing Daubeny, was very fond of him— "drop his arm, or, by Jove, you'll find that two can play at that. Dubbs is quite right, and you're a set of asses if you think you'll do any good by burning the punishment–book. I've got the poker, and you shan't have it to knock the desk open. I suppose Paton can afford sixpence to buy another book; and enter a tolerable fresh score against you for this besides."

"But he won't remember my six hundred lines, and four or five detentions," said Walter; "here, give me the poker."

"Pooh! pooh! Evson, of course he'll remember them; here, I'll help you with the lines; I'll do a couple of hundred for you, and the rest you can write with two pens at a time; it

St. Winifred's, or The World of School

won't take you an hour. I'll show you the two-pen dodge; I'll admit you into the two-penetralia. Like Milton, you shall 'touch the slender tops of various quills.' No, no," he continued in a playful tone, in order not to make Walter in a greater passion than he was, "you can't have the poker; any one who wants that must take it from me *vi et armis*."

"It doesn't matter; this'll do as well; and here goes," said Walter, seizing a wooden stool. "There's the desk open for you," he said, as he brought the top of the stool with a strong blow against the lid, and burst the lock with a great crash.

"My eyes! we *shall* get into a row," said Franklin, opening his eyes to illustrate his exclamation.

"Well, what's done's done; let's all take our share," said Anthony, diving his hand into the desk. "Here's the imposition- book for you, and here goes leaf number one into the fire; you can tear out the next if you like, Franklin."

"Very well," said Franklin; "in for a penny in for a pound; there goes the second leaf."

"And here the third; over ankles over knees," said Burton, another of those present.

"Proverbial Fool-osophy," observed Henderson contemptuously, as Burton handed him the book. "Shall I be a silly sheep like the rest of you, and leap over the bridge because your leader has? I suppose I must, though it's very absurd." He wavered and hesitated; sensible enough to disapprove of so useless a proceeding, he yet did not like to be thought afraid. He minded what fellows would *think*.

"Do what's right," said Daubeny, "and shame the devil; here, give me the book. Now, you fellows, you've torn out these leaves, and done quite mischief enough. Let me put the book back, and don't be like children who hit the fender against which they've knocked their heads."

"Or dogs that bite the stick they've been thrashed with," said Henderson. "You're right, Dubbs, and I respect you; ay, you fellows may sneer if you like, but I advised you not to do it, and I won't make myself an idiot because you do."

St. Winifred's, or The World of School

"Never mind," drawled Howard Tracy; "I hate Paton, and I'll do anything to spite him;" whereupon he snatched the book from Daubeny, and threw it entire into the flames. Poor Tracy had been even in more serious scrapes with Mr Paton than Walter had; his vain manner was peculiarly abhorrent to the master, who took every opportunity of snubbing him; but nothing would pierce through the thick cloak of Tracy's conceit, and fully satisfied with himself, his good looks, and his aristocratic connections, he sat down in contented ignorance, and despised learning too much to be in the least put out by being invariably the last in his form.

"What, is there nothing left for me to burn?" said Walter, who sat glowering on the high iron fender, and swinging his legs impatiently. "Let's see what else there is in the desk. Here are a pack of old exercises apparently, they'll make a jolly blaze. Stop, though, *are* they old exercises? Well, never mind; if not, so much the better. In they shall go."

"Stop, what *are* you doing, Walter?" said Henderson, catching him by the arm; "you know these can't be old exercises. Paton always puts *them* in his waste-paper basket, not in his desk. Oh, Walter, what *have* you done?"

"The outside sheets were exercises anyhow," said Walter gloomily; "here, it's no good trying to save them now, whatever they were," (for Henderson was attempting to rake them out between the bars); "they're done for now," and he pressed down the thick mass of foolscap into the reddest centre of the fire, and held it there until nothing remained of it but a heap of flaky crimson ashes.

A dead silence followed, for the boys felt that now at any rate they were "in for it."

The sound of the tea-bell prevented further mischief; and as Henderson thrust his arm through Walter's, he said, "Oh, Evson, I wish you hadn't done that; I wish I'd got you to come away before. What a passionate fellow you are."

"Well, it's done now," said Walter, already beginning to soften, and to repent of his fatuity.

"What can we do?" said Henderson anxiously.

"Take the consequences; that's all," answered Walter.

St. Winifred's, or The World of School

"Hadn't you better go and tell Paton about it at once, instead of letting him find it out?"

"No," said Walter; "he's done nothing but bully me, and I don't care."

"Then let me go," said his friend earnestly. "I know Paton well; I'm sure he'd be ready to forgive you, if I explained it all to him."

"You're very good, Flip; but don't go; it's too late."

"Well, Walter, you mustn't think that I had no share in this because of being afraid. I was one of the group, and I'll share the punishment with you, whatever it is. I hope for your sake it won't be found out."

But if Henderson had seen a little deeper he would have hoped that it would be found out, for there is nothing that works quicker ruin to any character than undiscovered sin. It was happy for Walter that his wrong impulses did *not* remain undiscovered; happy for him that they came so rapidly to be known and to be punished.

It was noised through the school in five minutes that Evson, one of the new fellows, had smashed open Paton's desk, and burned the contents. "What an awful row he'll get into," was the general comment. Walter heard Kenrick inquiring eagerly about it as they sat at tea; but Kenrick didn't ask *him* about it, though they sat so near each other. After the foolish, proud manner of sensitive boys, Walter and Kenrick, though each liked the other none the less, were not on speaking terms. Walter, less morbidly proud than Kenrick, would not have suffered this silly alienation to continue had not his attention been occupied by other troubles. Neither of them, therefore, liked to be the first to break the ice, and now in his most serious difficulty Walter had lost the advice and sympathy of his most intimate friend.

The fellows seemed to think that he must inevitably be expelled for this *fracas*. The poor boy's thoughts were very, very bitter as he laid his head that night on his restless pillow, remembered what an ungovernable fool he had been, and dreamt of his happy and dear-loved home. How strangely he seemed to have left his old, innocent life behind him, and how little he would have believed it possible, two months ago, that he could by any conduct of his own have so soon incurred, or nearly incurred, the penalty of expulsion from St Winifred's School.

He had certainly yielded very quickly to passion, and he felt that in consequence he had made his position more serious than that of other boys who were in every sense of the word twice as bad as himself. But what he laid to the score of his ill-luck was in truth a very happy providence, by which punishment was sent speedily and heavily upon him, and so his evil tendencies, mercifully nipped in the bud, crushed with a tender yet with an iron hand before they had expanded more blossoms and been fed by deeper roots. He might have been punished less speedily had his faults been more radical, or his wrong-doings of a deeper dye.

CHAPTER EIGHT. THE BURNT MANUSCRIPT.

> All
> All my poor scrapings, from a dozen years
> Of dust and desk-work.—*Sea Dreams.*

It may be supposed that during chapel the next morning, and when he went into early school, Walter was in an agony of almost unendurable suspense; and this suspense was doomed to be prolonged for some time, until at last he could hardly sit still. Mr Paton did not at once notice that his desk was broken. He laid down his books, and went on as usual with the morning lesson.

At length Tracy was put on. He stood up in his usual self-satisfied way, looking admiringly at his boots, and running his delicate white hand through his scented hair. Mr Paton watched him with a somewhat contemptuous expression, as though he were thinking what a pity it was that any boy should be such a little puppy. Henderson, with his usual quick discrimination, had nicknamed Tracy the "Lisping Hawthornbud."

"Your fifth failure this week, Tracy; you must do the usual punishment," said Mr Paton, taking up his key to unlock the desk.

"Now for it," thought all the form, looking on with great anxiety.

The key caught hopelessly in the broken lock. Mr Paton's attention was aroused; he pushed the lid off the desk, and saw at once that it had been broken open.

St. Winifred's, or The World of School

"Who has broken open my desk?"

No answer.

He looked very grave, but said nothing, looking for his imposition–book.

"Where is my imposition–book?"

No answer.

"And where is my—?"

Mr Paton stopped, and looked with the greatest eagerness over every corner of the desk.

"Where is the manuscript I left here with my imposition–book?" he said in a tone of the most painful anxiety.

"I do hope and trust," he said, turning pale, "that none of you have been wicked enough to injure it," and here his voice faltered. "When I tell you that it was of the utmost value, I am sure that if any of you have concealed or taken it, you will give it back at once."

There was a deep silence.

"Once again," he asked, "where is my imposition–book?"

"Burnt, sir; burnt, sir," said one or two voices, hardly above a whisper.

"And my manuscript?" he asked in a louder voice, and in still greater agitation. "Surely, surely, you cannot have been so thoughtless, so incredibly unjust as to—"

Walter stood up in his place, with his head bent, and his face covered with an ashy whiteness. "I burnt it, sir," he said in an almost inaudible voice, and trembling with fear.

"Come here," said Mr Paton impetuously; "I can't hear what you say. Now, then," he continued, as Walter crept up beside his desk.

St. Winifred's, or The World of School

"I burnt it, sir," he said in a whisper.

"You—burnt—it," said Mr Paton, starting up in uncontrollable emotion, which changed into a burst of anger, as he gave Walter a box on the ear which sounded all over the room, and made the boy stagger back to his place. But the flash of rage was gone in an instant; and the next moment Mr Paton, afraid of trusting himself any longer, left his desk and hurried out, anxious to recover in solitude the calmness of mind and action which had been so terribly disturbed.

Mr Percival, who taught his form in another part of the room, seeing Mr Paton box Walter so violently on the ear, and knowing that this was the very reverse of his usual method, since he had never before touched a boy in anger, walked up to see what was the matter, just as Mr Paton, with great hurried strides, had reached the door.

"What is the matter with Mr Paton?" he asked.

There was a general murmur through the form, out of which Mr Percival caught something about Mr Paton's papers having been burnt.

Anxious to find him, to ask what had happened, Mr Percival, leaving the room, caught sight of him pacing with hasty and uneven steps along a private garden walk which belonged to the masters.

"I hope nothing unpleasant has occurred," he said, overtaking him.

"Oh, nothing, nothing," said Mr Paton with quivering lip, as he turned aside. And then, suppressing his emotion by a powerful effort of self-control: "It is only," he said, "that the hard results of fifteen years' continuous labour are now condensed into a heap of smut and ashes in the schoolroom fire."

"You don't mean to say that your Hebrew manuscripts are burnt?" asked Mr Percival in amazement.

"You know how I have been toiling at them for years, Percival; you know that I began them before I left college, that I regarded them as the chief work of my life, and that I devoted to them every moment of my leisure. You know, too, the pride and pleasure which I took in their progress, and the relief with which I turned to them from the vexations and anxieties of one's life here. To work at them has been for years my only recreation and delight. Well, they were finished at last; I was only correcting them for the press; they would have gone to the printer in a month, and I should have lived to complete a toilsome and honourable task. Well, the dream is over, and a handful of ashes represents the struggle of my best years."

Mr Percival knew well that his coadjutor had been working for years at a commentary on the Hebrew text of the Four Greater Prophets. It had been the cherished and chosen task of his life; he had brought to it great stores of learning, accumulated in the vigour of his powers, and the enthusiasm of a youthful ambition, and he had employed upon it every spare hour left him from his professional duties. He looked to it as the means of doing essential service to the church, of which he was an ordained member, and, secondarily, as the road to reputation and well– merited advancement. And in five minutes the hand of one angry boy had robbed him of the fruit of all his hopes.

"If they wanted to display the hatred which I well know that they feel," said Mr Paton bitterly, "they might have chosen any way, literally *any way*, but that. They might have left me, at least, that which was almost my only pleasure and object in life, and which had no connection with them or their pursuits." And his face grew haggard as he stopped in his walk, and tried to realise the extent of what he had lost. "I would rather have seen everything I possess in the whole world destroyed than that," he said slowly, and with strong emotion.

"And was it really Evson who did this?" asked Mr Percival, filled with the sincerest pity for his colleague's wounded feelings.

"It matters little who did it, Percival; but, yes, it was your friend Evson."

"The little, graceless, abominable wretch!" exclaimed Mr Percival, with anger, "he must be expelled. But can't you recommence the task?"

"Recommence?" said Mr Paton in a hard voice; "and who will give me back the hope and vigour of the last fifteen years? how shall I have the heart again to toil through the same long trains of research and thought? where are the hundreds of references which I had sought out and verified with hours of heavy midnight labour? how am I to have access again to the scores of books which I consulted before I began to work? The very thought of it sickens me. Youth and hope are over. No, Percival, there is no more to be said. I am robbed of a life's work. Leave me, please, alone for a little, until I have learnt to say less bitterly, `God's will be done.'"

> "He needeth not
> Either man's work or his own gifts; who best
> Bear his mild yoke they please Him best,"

said Mr Percival in a tone of kind and deep sympathy, as he left him to return to the schoolroom.

But once in sight of Mr Paton's open and rifled desk, Mr Percival's pent-up indignation burst forth into clear flame. Stopping in front of Mr Paton's form, he exclaimed, in a voice that rang with scorn and sorrow:

"You boys do not know the immense mischief which your thoughtless and worthless spite and folly have caused. I say boys, but I believe, and rejoice to believe, that one only of you is guilty, and I rejoice too, that *that* one is a new boy, who must have brought here feelings and passions more worthy of an ignorant and ill-trained plough-boy than of a St Winifred's scholar. The hand that would burn a valuable manuscript would fire a rick of hay."

"Oh, sir," said Henderson, starting up and interrupting him, "we were all very nearly as bad. It was the rest of us that burnt the imposition-book; Evson had nothing to do with that." Henderson had forgotten for the moment that he at least had had no share in burning the imposition-book, for his warm quick heart could not bear that these blows should fall unbroken on his friend's head.

But his generous effort failed; for Mr Percival, barely noticing the interruption, continued: "The imposition-book? I know nothing about that. If you burnt it you were very foolish and reckless; you deserve no doubt to be punished for it, but that was *comparatively* nothing. But do you know, bad boy," he said, turning again to Walter, "do you know what *you* have done? Do you know that your dastardly spitefulness has led you to destroy writings which had cost your master years and years of toil that cannot be renewed? He treated you with unswerving impartiality; he never punished you but when you deserved punishment, and when he believed it to be for your good, and yet you turn upon him in this adder-like way; you break open his desk like a thief, and, in one moment of despicable ill-temper, you rob him and the world of that which had been the pursuit and object of his life. You, Evson, may well hide your face,"—for Walter had bent over the desk, and in agonies of shame and remorse had covered his face with both hands;—"you may well be ashamed to look either at me or at any honest and manly and right-minded boy among your companions. You have done a wrong for which it will be years hence a part of your retribution to remember, that nothing you can ever do can repair it, or do away with its effects. I am more than disappointed with you. You have done mischief which the utmost working of all your powers cannot for years counterbalance, if, instead of being as base and idle as you now appear to be, you were to devote your whole heart to work. I don't know what will be done to you; I, for my part, hope that you will not be suffered to remain with us; but if you are, I am sure that you will receive, as you richly deserve, the reprobation and contempt of every boy among your schoolfellows who is capable of one spark of honour or right feeling."

Every word that Mr Percival had said came to poor Walter with the most poignant force; all the master's reproaches pierced his heart and let blood. He sat there not stirring, stunned and crushed, as though he had been beaten by the blows of a hammer. He quailed and shuddered to think of the great and cruel injustice, the base and grievous injury into which his blind passion had betrayed him, and thought that he could never hold up his head again.

Mr Percival's indignant expostulation passed over the other culprits who heard it like a thunderstorm. There was a force and impetuosity in this gentleman's manner, when his anger was kindled, which had long gained for him among the boys, with whom he was the most popular of all the masters, the half- complimentary soubriquet of "Thunder-and-lightning." But none of them had ever before heard him speak with such concentrated energy and passion, and all except generous little Henderson were awed by it into silence. But Henderson at that moment was wholly absorbed in Walter's sorrows.

"Tell him," said he in Walter's ear, "tell him it was all a mistake, that you thought the papers were old exercises. Dear Walter, tell him before he goes."

But Walter still rested with his white cheeks on his hands upon the desk, and neither moved nor spoke. And Mr Percival, turning indignantly upon his heel, with one last glance of unmitigated contempt, had walked off to his own form.

"Walter don't take it to heart so," said Henderson, putting his arm round his neck; "you couldn't help it; you made a sad mistake, that's all. Go and tell Paton so, and I'm sure he'll forgive you."

A slight quiver was all that showed that Walter heard. Henderson would have liked to see his anguish relieved by a burst of tears; but the tears did not come, and Walter did not move.

At last a hand touched him, and he heard the voice of the head– boy say to him, "Get up, Evson, I'm to take you to Dr Lane with a note from Mr Percival."

He rose and followed mechanically, waiting in the head–master's porch, while the monitor went in.

"Dr Lane won't see you now," said Somers, coming out again. "Croft," (addressing the school Famulus), "Dr Lane says you're to lock up Mr Evson by himself in the private room."

Walter followed the Famulus to the private room, a little room at the top of the house, where he knew that boys were locked previous to expulsion, that they might have no opportunity for doing any mischief before they went.

The Famulus left him here, and returned a few minutes after with some dry bread and milk, which he placed on the deal table, which, with a wooden chair, constituted the sole furniture of the room; he then locked the door, and left Walter finally to his own reflections.

Then it was that flood after flood of passionate tears seemed to remove the iron cramp which had pained his heart. He flung himself on the floor, and as he thought of the irreparable cruelty which he had inflicted on a man who had been severe indeed, but never unkind to him, and of the apparent malignity to which all who heard it would attribute what he had done, he sobbed and sobbed as though his heart would break.

St. Winifred's, or The World of School

At one o'clock the Famulus returned with some dinner. He found Walter sitting at a corner of the room, his head resting against the angle of the wall, and his eyes red and inflamed with long crying. The morning's meal still lay untasted on the table.

He looked round with a commiserating glance. "Come, come, Master Evson," he said, "you've no call to give way so, sir. If you've done wrong, the wrong's done now, and frettin' won't help it. There's them above as'll forgive you, and make you do better next time, lad, if you only knew it. Here, you must eat some of this dinner, Master Evson, and leave off cryin' so; cryin's no comfort, sir."

He stood by and waited on Walter with the greatest kindness and respect, till he had seen him swallow some food, not without difficulty, and then with encouraging and cheerful words left him, and once more locked the door.

The weary afternoon wore on, and Walter sat mournfully alone with nothing but miserable thoughts—miserable to whatever subject he turned them, and more miserable the longer he dwelt on them. As the shades of evening drew in he felt his head swimming, and the long solitude made him feel afraid as he wondered whether they would leave him there all night. And then he heard a light step approach the door, and a gentle tap. He made no answer, for he thought he knew the step, and he could not summon up voice to speak for a fit of sobbing which it brought on. Then he heard the boy stoop down, and push a note under the door.

He took it up when he heard the footsteps die away, and by the fast failing light was just able to make it out. It ran thus—

"Dear Walter,

"You can't think how sorry, how very very sorry I am for you. I wish I could be with you and take part of your punishment. Forgive me for being cold and proud to you. I have been longing to speak to you all the time, but felt too shy. It was all my fault. I will never break with you again. Good–bye, dear Walter, from your ever and truly affectionate,

"Harry Kenrick."

"He will never break with me again," thought Walter. "If I'm to go to-morrow I'm afraid he'll never have the chance." And then his saddest thoughts reverted to the home which he had left so recently for the first time, and to which he was to return with nothing but dishonour and disgrace.

At six o'clock the kind-hearted Famulus brought him a lamp, some tea, and one or two books, which he had no heart to read. No one was allowed to visit the private room under heavy penalties, so that Walter had no other visitor until eight, when Somers, the monitor who had taken him to Dr Lane, looked in and icily observed, "You're to sleep in the sick-room, Evson; come with me."

"Am I expelled, Somers?" he faltered out.

"I don't know," said Somers in a freezing tone; "you deserve to be."

True, O lofty and pitiless Somers! But is that all which you could find to say to the poor boy in his distress? And, if we *all* had our deserts...

"At any rate," Somers added, "I for one won't have you as a fag any longer, and I shouldn't think that any one else would either."

With which cutting remark he left Walter to his reflections.

CHAPTER NINE. PENITENCE.

> If hearty sorrow
> Be a sufficient ransom for offence,
> I tender it here; I do as truly suffer
> As e'er I did commit.
> *Two Gentlemen of Verona, Act 5, Scene 4.*

Next morning Walter was reconducted to the private room, and there, with a kind of dull pain in head and heart, awaited the sentence which was to decide his fate. His fancy had left St. Winifred's altogether; it was solely occupied with Semlyn, and the dear society of home. Walter was rehearsing again and again in his mind the scene of his return; what he should say to his father; how he should dry his mother's tears; and how he should bear himself, on his return, towards his little brothers and sisters. Would he, expelled from St Winifred's, ever be able to look any one in the face again at home?

While he was brooding over these fancies, some one, breathless with haste, ran up to his room, and again a note was thrust underneath the door. He seized it quickly, and read:

"Dear Walter,

"I am so glad to be the first to tell you that you are not to be expelled. Paton has begged you off. No time for more. I have slipped away before morning school to leave you this news, and can't stay lest I should be caught. Good-bye, from your ever affectionate friend,

"H.K."

The boy's heart gave one bound of joy as he read this. If he were not expelled he was ready to bear meekly any other punishment appointed to his offence. But his banishment from the school would cause deep affliction to others besides himself, and this was why he had dreaded it with such a feeling of despair.

Alone as he was in the little room, he fell on his knees, and heartily and humbly thanked God for this answer to his earnest, passionate, reiterated prayer; and then he read Kenrick's note again.

"Paton has begged you off." He repeated this sentence over and over again, aloud and to himself, and seemed as if he could never realise it. Paton—Paton, the very man whom he had so deeply and irreparably injured—had begged him off, and shielded him from a punishment which no one could have considered too severe for his fault. Young and inexperienced as Walter Evson was, he could not of course fully understand and appreciate the *amount* of the loss, the nature and degree of the injury which he had inflicted; but yet, he *could* understand that he had done something which caused greater pain to his master than even the breaking of a limb, or falling ill of a severe sickness. And he never prayed for himself without praying also that Mr Paton's misfortune might in some way be alleviated; and even, impossible as the prayer might seem, that he, Walter, might himself have some share in rendering it more endurable.

St. Winifred's, or The World of School

It may seem strange that Walter should be apparently excessive in his own self-condemnation. A generous mind usually is; but Walter, it may be urged, never intended to do the harm he had done. If he mistook the packet for a number of exercises the fault was comparatively venial. Comparatively—yes; for though it will be admitted that to break open a private desk and throw its contents into the fire is bad enough in a schoolboy under any circumstances, still it would be a far less aggravated sin than the wilful infliction of a heavy damage out of a spirit of revenge. But here lay the gravamen of Walter's fault; he knew— though he had not said so—in his inmost heart he *knew* that the packet did not, and could not, consist merely of old exercises, like the outer sheets, which were put to keep it clean. When he threw it into the fire and thrust it down until it blazed away, he felt sure—and at that wicked moment of indulged passion he rejoiced to feel sure—that what he was consuming was of real value. Henderson's voice awoke in a moment his dormant conscience; but then, however keen were the stings of remorse, what had been done could never be undone. And "Paton had begged him off." It was all the more wonderful to him, and he was all the more deeply grateful for it, because he knew that, in Mr Paton's views, the law of punishment for every offence was as a law of iron and adamant—a law as undeviating and beneficial as the law of gravitation itself.

A slow and hesitating footstep—the sound of the key turning in the door—a nervous hand resting on the handle—and Mr Paton stood before him.

In an instant Walter was on his knees beside him, his head bent over his clasped hands; "Oh, sir," he exclaimed, "please forgive me; I have been longing to see you, sir, to implore you to forgive me; for when you have forgiven me I shan't mind anything else. Oh, sir, forgive me, if you can."

"Do you know, Evson, the extent of what you have done?" said Mr Paton, in a constrained voice.

"Oh, sir, indeed I do," he exclaimed, bursting into tears; "Mr Percival said I had destroyed years and years of hard work; and that I can never, never, never make up for it, or repair it again. Oh, sir, indeed I didn't know how much mischief I was doing; I was in a wicked passion then, but I would give my right hand not to have done it now. Oh, sir, can you ever forgive me?" he asked, in a tone of pitiable despair.

St. Winifred's, or The World of School

"Have you asked God's forgiveness for your passionate and revengeful spirit, Evson?" said the same constrained voice.

"Oh, sir, I have, and I know God has forgiven me. Indeed, I never knew, I never thought before, that I could grow so wicked in a day. Oh, sir, what shall I do to gain your forgiveness; I would do anything, sir," he said, in a voice thick with sobs; "and if you forgave me, I could be almost happy."

All this while Walter had not dared to look up in Mr Paton's face. Abashed as he was, he could not bear to meet the only look which he expected to find there, the old cold unpitying look of condemnation and reproach. Even at that moment he could not help thinking that if Mr Paton had understood him better, he would not have seemed to him so utterly bad as then he must seem, with so recent an act of sin and folly to bear witness against him.

He dared not look up through his eyes swimming with tears; but he had not expected the kind and gentle touch of the trembling hand that rested on his head as though it blessed him, and that smoothed again and again his dark hair, and wiped the big drops away from his cheeks. He had not expected the arm that raised him up from his kneeling position, and the fingers that pushed back his hair from his forehead, and gently bent back his head; or the pitying eyes, themselves dim, as though they were about to well over with compassion—that looked so sorrowfully, yet so kindly, into his own. He could not bear this. If Mr Paton had struck him, as he did in the first moment of overwhelming anger; if he had spurned him away, and ordered him any amount of punishment, it would have been far easier to bear than this Christian gentleness; this ready burying in pity and oblivion of the heaviest and most undeserved calamity which the master had ever undergone at the hands of man. Walter could not bear it; he flung himself on his knees again in a passion of weeping, and clasped Mr Paton's knees, uttering in broken sentences, "I can never make up for it, never repair it as long as I live."

For a moment more the kind hand again rested on the boy's head, and gently smoothed his dark hair; and then Mr Paton found voice to speak, and lifting him up, and seating him upon his knee, said to him:

"I forgive you, Walter; forgive you freely and gladly. It was hard, I own, at first to do so, for I will not disguise from you that this loss is a very bitter thing to bear. I have been sleepless, and have never once been able to banish the distress of mind which it has caused since it occurred. And yet it is a loss which I shall *not* feel fully all at once, but most and for many a long day when I sit down again, if God gives me strength to do so, to recover the lost stores and rearrange the interrupted thoughts. But I too have learnt a lesson, Walter; and when you have reached my age, my boy, you too, I trust, will have learnt to control all evil passions with a strong will, and to bear meekly and patiently *whatever* God sends. And you too, Walter, learn a lesson. You have said that you would give anything, do anything, to undo this wrong, or to repair it; but you can do nothing, my child, give nothing, for it cannot be undone. Wrong rarely can be mended. Let this very helplessness teach you a truth that may remain with you through life. Let it check you in wilful impetuous moments; for what has once been done remains irrevocable. You may rue for years and years the work of days or of moments, and you may *never* be able to avoid the consequences, even when the deed itself has been forgotten by the generous and forgiven by the just."

And all this so kindly, so gently, so quietly spoken; every word of it sank into Walter's heart never to be forgotten, as his tears flowed still but with more quiet sadness now.

"Yes, Walter, this occurrence," continued Mr Paton in a calm low voice, "may do us both good, miserable as it is. I will say no more about it now, only that I have quite forgiven it. Man is far too mean a creature to be justified in withholding forgiveness for any personal wrong. It is far more hard to forgive oneself when one has done wrong. I have determined to bury the whole matter in oblivion, and to inflict no punishment either on you or on any of the other boys who were concerned in this folly and sin. I will not forgive by halves. But, Walter, I will not wrong you by doubting that from this time forward you will advance with a marked improvement. You will have something to bear, no doubt, but do not let it weigh on you too heavily; and as for me, I will try henceforth to be your friend."

What could Walter do but seize his hand and clasp it earnestly, and sob out the broken incoherent thanks which were more eloquent than connected words.

"And now, Walter, you are free," said Mr Paton. "From *us* you will hear no more of this offence. It is nearly dinner-time. Come; I will walk with you to Hall."

He laid his hand on the boy's shoulder, and they walked downstairs and across the court. Walter was deeply grateful that he did so, for he had heard rumours of the scorn and indignation, with which the news of his conduct had been received by the elder and more influential portions of the school. He had dreaded unspeakably the first occasion when it would be necessary to meet them again, but he felt that Mr Paton's countenance and kindness had paved the way for him, and smoothed his most formidable trial. It had been beyond his warmest hopes that he should be able to face them so. He had never dared to expect this open proof, that the person who had suffered chiefly from his act would also be the first to show that he had not cast him off as hopeless or worthless, but was ready to receive him into favour once again.

The corridor was full of boys waiting for the dinner-bell, and they divided respectfully to leave a passage for Mr Paton, and touched their hats as he passed them with his hand still on Walter's shoulder, while Walter walked with downcast eyes beside him, not once daring to look up. And as the boy passed them, humbled and penitent, with Mr Paton's hand resting upon him, there was not one of those who saw it that did not learn from that sight a lesson of calm forgiveness as noble and as forcible as any lesson which they could learn at St Winifred's School.

Walter sat at dinner pale and crying, but unpitied. "Alas for the rarity of Christian charity under the sun!" the worst construction had assiduously been put upon what he had done, and nearly all the boys hastily condemned it, not only as an ungentlemanly, but also as an inexcusable and unpardonable act. One after another, as they passed him after dinner, they cut him dead. Several of the masters, including Mr Percival, whom Walter had hitherto loved and respected more than any of them, because he had been treated by him with marked kindness, did the same. Walter met Mr Percival in the playground and touched his cap; Mr Percival glanced at him contemptuously for a moment, and then turned his head aside without noticing the salute. It may seem strange, but we must remember that to all who hear of any wrong act by report only, it presents itself as a mere naked fact—a bare result without preface or palliation. The subtle grades of temptation which led to it—the violent outburst of passion long pent-up which thus found its consummation—are unknown or forgotten, and the deed itself, isolated from all that rendered it possible, receives unmitigated condemnation. All that any one took the trouble to know or to believe about Walter's scrape was, that he had broken open a master's private desk, and in revenge had purposely burnt a most valuable manuscript; and for this, sentence was passed upon him broadly and in the gross.

St. Winifred's, or The World of School

Poor Walter! those were dark days for him; but Henderson and Kenrick stuck fast by him, and little Arthur Eden still looked up to him with unbounded gratitude and affection, and he felt that the case was not hopeless. Kenrick indeed seemed to waver once or twice. He sought Walter and shook hands with him at once, but still he was not with him, Walter fancied, so much as he had been or might have been, till, after a short struggle, his natural impulse of generosity won the day. As for Henderson, Walter thought he could have died for him, so much he loved him for his kindness in this hour of need; and Eden never left his side when he could creep there to console him by merry playfulness, or to be his companion when he would otherwise have been alone.

The boys had been truly sorry to hear of Mr Paton's loss; it roused all their most generous feelings. That evening as they came out of chapel they all gathered round the iron gates. The intention had been to groan at poor Walter. He knew of it perfectly well, for Henderson had prepared him for it, and expressed his determination to walk by his side. It was for him a moment of keen anguish, and that anguish betrayed itself in his scared and agitated look. But he was spared this last drop in the cup of punishment. The mere sight of him showed the boys that he had suffered bitterly enough already. When they looked at him they had not the heart to hurt and shame him any more. Mr Paton's open forgiveness of that which had fallen most severely on himself changed the current of their feelings. Instead of groaning Walter they let him pass by, and waited till Mr Paton came out of the chapel door, and, as he walked across the court, the boys all followed him with hearty cheers.

Mr Paton did not like the demonstration, although he appreciated the kindly and honourable motives which had given rise to it. He was not a man who courted popularity, and this external sign of it was, as he well knew, the irregular expression of an evanescent feeling. So he took no further notice of the boys' cheers than by slightly raising his cap, and by one stately inclination of the head, and then he walked on with his usual quiet dignity of manner to his own rooms. But after this he every now and then took an opportunity to walk with Walter; and almost every Sunday evening he might have been seen with him pacing, after morning chapel, up and down the broad walk of the masters' garden, while Walter walked unevenly beside him, in vain endeavours to keep step with his long slow stride.

A letter from Dr Lane brought Walter's father to St Winifred's the next day. Why dwell on their sad and painful meeting? But the pain of it soon wore off as they interchanged that sweet and frank communion of thoughts and sympathies that still existed as it had ever done between them. They had a long, long walk upon the shore, and at every step Walter seemed to inbreathe fresh strength, and hope, and consolation, and Mr Evson seemed to acquire new love for, and confidence in, his unhappy little son, so that when in the evening he kissed him and said "good-bye," at the top of the same little hill where they had parted before, Mr Evson felt more happily and gratefully secure of his radical integrity, now that the boy had acquired the strength which comes through trial, through failure, and through suffering, than he had done before when he left him only with the strength of early principle and untested innocence of heart.

But long years after, when Walter was a man, and when he had been separated for years from all intelligence of Mr Paton, there emanated from a quiet country vicarage a now celebrated edition of the *Major Prophets*; an edition which made the author a high reputation, and secured for him in the following year the Deanery of ——-. And in the preface to that edition the reader may still find the following passage, which, as Walter saw even then, those long years after, he could not read without a thrill of happy, yet penitent emotion. It ran thus:

"This edition of the *Major Prophets* has been the chosen work of the author's leisure, and he is almost afraid to say how many of the best years of his life have been spent upon it. A strange fortune has happened to it. Years ago it was finished, it was written out, and ready for the press. At that time it was burnt— no matter under what circumstances—by a boy's hand. At first, the author never hoped to have the courage or power to resume and finish the task again. But it pleased God, who sent him this trial, to provide him also with leisure, and opportunity, and resolution, so that the old misfortune is now at last *repaired*. It is for the sake of one person, and one person only, that these private matters are intruded on the reader's notice; but that person, if his eye should ever fall on these lines, will know also why the word `repaired' has been printed in larger letters. And I would also tell him with all kindness, that it has pleased God to bring out of the rash act of his boyhood nothing but good. The following commentary is, I humbly trust, far more worthy of its high subject, now that it has received the maturer consideration of my advancing years, than it would have been had it seen the light at St Winifred's long ago. I write this for the sake of the boy who then wept, for what seemed an *irreparable* fault; and I add thankfully, that never for a moment have I retracted my then forgiveness; that I think of his after efforts with kindliness and affection; and that he has, and always will have, my best prayers for his interest and welfare.

"H. PATON."

CHAPTER TEN. UPHILLWARDS.

But that Conscience makes me firm,
The boon companion, who her strong breastplate
Buckles on him that feels no guilt within,
And bids him on and fear not.
Dante, Inferno 100, 28.

"Qui s'excuse s'accuse." "If a character can't defend itself, it's not worth defending." "No one was ever written down, except by himself." These, and proverbs like these, express the common and almost instinctive feeling, that self–defence under calumny is generally unsuccessful, and almost always involves a loss of dignity. Partly from this cause, and partly from penitence for his real errors, and partly from scorn at the malice that misrepresented him, and the Pharisaism of far worse offenders that held aloof from his misfortune, Walter said nothing to exculpate his conduct, or to shield himself from the silent indignation, half real and half affected, which weighed heavily against him.

The usual consequences followed; the story of his misdoing was repeated and believed in the least mitigated form, and this version gained credence and currency because it was uncontradicted. The school society bound his sin upon him; they retained it, and it was retained. It burdened his conscience with a galling weight, because by his fellows it remained long unforgiven. At the best, those were days of fiery trial to that overcharged young heart. He had not only lost all immediate influence, but as he looked forward through the vista of his school life, he feared that he should never entirely regain it. Even if he should in time become a monitor, he felt as if half his authority must be lost while this stigma was branded so deeply on his name.

Yet it was a beautiful sight to see how bravely and manfully this young boy set himself to re–establish the reputation he had destroyed, and since he could not "build upon the *foundations* of yesterday," to build upon its *ruins*; to see with what touching humility he accepted undeserved scorn, and with what touching gratitude he hailed the scantiest kindness; to see how he bore up unflinchingly under every difficulty, accepted his hard position among unsympathising schoolfellows, and made the most of it, without anger and without complaint. He could see in after years that those days were to him a time of unmitigated blessing. They taught him lessons of manliness, of endurance, of humility. The necessity of repairing an error and recovering a failure became to him a more powerful stimulus than the hope of avoiding it altogether. The hour of punishment, which was bitter as absinthe to his taste, became sweet as honey in his memory. Above all, these days taught him, in a manner never to be forgotten, the invaluable lesson that the sense of having done an ill deed is the very heaviest calamity that an ill deed ensures, and that in life there is no single secret of happiness comparable to the certain blessing brought with it by a conscience void of all offence.

Perhaps the strain would have been too great for his youthful spirits, and might have left on his character an impress of permanent melancholy, derived from thus perpetually being reminded that he had gone wrong, but for a school sermon which Mr Paton preached about this time, and which Walter felt was meant in part for him. It was on the danger and unwisdom of brooding continually, on what is over; and it was preached upon the text, "I will restore to you the years which the locust hath eaten, the canker-worm, the caterpillar, and the palmer-worm, my great army." "The past is past," said the preacher; "its sins and sorrows are irrevocably over; why dwell upon it now? Do not waste the present, with all its opportunities, in a hopeless and helpless retrospect. The worst of us need not despair, much less those who may have been betrayed into sudden error by some moment of unguarded passion. There lies the future before you;—onwards then, and forwards! it is yet an innocent, it may be a happy future. Take it with prayerful thankfulness, and fling the withered part aside. Thus, although thus only, can you recover your neglected opportunities. Do this in hope and meekness, and God will make up to you for the lost past; He who inhabiteth eternity will stretch forth out of His eternity a forgiving hand, and touch into green leaf again the years which the locust hath eaten." How eagerly Walter Evson drank in those words! That day at least he felt that man doth not live by bread alone, but by every word that proceedeth out of the mouth of God.

If Walter had been old enough to be an observer of character, he might have gathered out of his difficulties the materials for some curious observation on the manner, in which he was treated by different boys. Many, like Harpour and Cradock, made, of course, no sort of difference in their behaviour towards him, because they set up no pretence of condemnation; others, like Anthony and Franklin, had been nearly as bad as himself in the matter, and therefore their relations to him remained quite unaltered. But there were many boys who, like Jones, either cut him or were cold to him, not because they really

St. Winifred's, or The World of School

felt any moral anger at a fault which was much less heinous in reality than many which they daily committed, but because he was, for the time, unpopular, and they did not care to be seen with an unpopular boy. On the other hand, through a feeling, which at the time they could not understand, a few of the very best boys, some of the wisest, the steadiest, and noblest, seemed drawn to him by some new tie; and in a very short time he began to know friends among them, in whose way he might not otherwise have been thrown. Daubeny, for instance, than whom, although the boys chose to make him something of a butt, there was no more conscientious fellow at St Winifred's, sought Walter out on every possible occasion, and when they were alone spoke to him, in his gentle and honest way, many a cheering and kindly word. Another friend of this sort (whom Walter already knew slightly through Kenrick, who was in the form below him), was a boy named Power. There was something in Power most attractive; his clear eyes, and innocent expression of face, his unvarying success in all school competitions, his quiet and graceful manners, and even the coldness and reserve which made him stand somewhat aloof from the herd of boys, mixing with very few of them, firmly and unobtrusively assuming an altogether higher tone than theirs, and bestowing his confidence and friendship on hardly any—all tended to make him a marked character, and to confer on his intimacy an unusual value. Walter, to whom as yet he had hardly spoken, thought him self- centred and reserved, and yet saw something beautiful and fascinating even in his exclusiveness; he felt that he could have liked him much, but, as he was several forms lower than Power, never expected to become one of his few associates. But during his troubles Power so openly showed that he regarded him with respect and kindness, and was so clearly the first to make advances, that Walter gladly and gratefully accepted the proffered friendship.

It happened thus: One day, about a fortnight after his last escapade, Walter was amusing himself alone, as he often did, upon the shore. The shore was very dear to him. I almost pity a boy whose school is not by the seaside. He found on the shore both companionship and occupation. He never felt lonely there. He could sit there by the hour, either in calm or storm, watching the sea-birds dip their wings which flashed in the sunlight, as they pounced down on some unwary fish; or listening to the silken rustle and sweet monotony of the waves plashing musically upon the yellow sands on some fine day. On this evening the tide was coming in, and Walter had amused himself by standing on some of the lumps of granite tossed about the shore until the advancing waves encroached upon and surrounded his little island, and gave him just room to jump to land. He was standing on one of these great stones watching the sunset, and laughing to himself at the odd gambols of two or three porpoises that kept rolling about in a futile manner across the little bay, when he heard a pleasant voice say to him:

"I say, Evson, are you going to practise the old style of martyrdom—tie yourself to a stake and let the tide gradually drown you?"

Looking round he was surprised to see Power standing alone on the sands, and to see also that his little island was so far surrounded that he could not get to shore without being wet up to the knees.

"Hallo!" he said; "I see I must take off my shoes and stockings, and wade."

But on the slippery piece of rock upon which he was standing he had no room to do this without losing his balance and tumbling over; so Power had in a moment taken off his own shoes and stockings, turned up his trousers above the knees, and waded up to him.

"Now," he said, "get on my back, and I'll carry you in unwetted."

"Thanks, Power," he said, as Power deposited him on the sand; "I'm much obliged."

Not knowing whether Power would like to be seen with him or not, he looked at him shyly, and was walking off in another direction, when Power, who was putting on his stockings again, said to him playfully:

"What, Walter; haven't you the grace to wait for me, after my having delivered you from such a noyade? Excuse my calling you Walter; I hear Kenrick and Henderson do it, and somehow you're one of those fellows whom one meets now and then, whose Christian name seems to suit them more naturally than the other."

"By all means call me Walter, Power; and I'll wait for you gladly if you like," said Walter, blushing as he added, "I thought you might not like to walk with me."

"Not like? Nonsense. I should like it particularly. Let's take a turn along the shore; we shall just have time before roll-call."

St. Winifred's, or The World of School

Walter pointed out to him the droll porpoises which had absorbed his attention, and while they stood looking and laughing at them, Henderson came up unobserved, and patting Walter on the back, observed poetically:

> "Why are your young hearts sad, O beautiful children of morning?
> Why do your young eyes gaze timidly over the sea?"

"Where *did* you crib that quotation from, Flip," asked Power, laughing; "your mind's like a shallow brook, and the colour of it always shows the stratum through which you have been flowing last."

"Shallow brook, quotha?" said Henderson; "a deep and mighty river, sir, you mean; irresistible by any Power."

"Oh, *do* shut up. Why was I born with a name that could be punned on? No more puns, Flip, if you love me," said Power; and they all three walked under the noble Norman archway that formed the entrance to the school.

"By the powers," said Henderson to Walter, as the other left them, "you *have* got a new friend worth having, Walter. *He* doesn't make himself at home with every one, I can tell you; and if he and Dubbs cultivate you, I should think it's about time for any one else to be ashamed of cutting you, my boy."

"I'm quite happy now," said Walter; "with you and Kenrick and him for friends. I don't care so much for the rest. I wonder why he likes me?"

"Well, because he thinks the fellows a great deal too hard on you for one thing. How very good and patient you've been, Walter, under it all."

"It is hard sometimes, Flip, but I deserve it. Only now and then I'm afraid that you and Ken will get quite tired of me, I've so few to speak to. Harpour and that lot would be glad enough that I should join them, I know, and but for you and Ken I should have been driven to do it."

"Never mind, Walter, my boy; the fellows'll come round in time."

St. Winifred's, or The World of School

So, step by step, with the countenance of some true and worthy friends, and by the help of a stout and uncorrupted heart, by penitence and by kindliness, did our brave little Walter win his way. He was helped, too, greatly, by his achievements in the games. At football he played with a vigour and earnestness which carried everything before it. He got several bases, and was the youngest boy in the school who ever succeeded in doing this. Gradually but surely his temporary unpopularity gave way; and even before he began to be generally recognised again, he bade fair *ultimately* to gain a high position in the estimation of all his schoolfellows.

There was one scene which he long remembered, and which was very trying to go through. One fine afternoon the boys' prize for the highest jump was to be awarded, and as the school were all greatly interested in the competition, they were assembled in a dense circle in the green playground, leaving space for the jumpers in the middle. The fine weather had also tempted nearly all the inhabitants of St Winifred's to be spectators of the contest, and numbers of ladies were present, for whom the boys had politely left a space within the circle. When the chief jumping prize had been won by an active fellow in the sixth-form, another prize was proposed for all boys under fifteen.

Bliss, Franklin, and two other boys at once stepped into the circle as competitors, and threw off their jackets.

"You must go in for this, Walter," said Henderson. "You're sure to get it."

"Not I. I won't go in, Flip," said Walter, who was naturally in a desponding mood, as he looked round on those four hundred faces, and saw among them all scarcely one sympathising glance. "*You* go in and win. And never mind talking to me up here, Henderson; it can't be pleasant for you, I know, when all the other fellows are cutting me."

"Pooh! Walter. *They're* in the wrong box; not you and I. `Athanasius contra mundum,' as Power says. Do go in for the prize."

Walter shook his head gloomily. "I don't like to, before all these fellows. They'd hiss me or something."

"Well, if *you* won't, *I* won't; that's flat."

St. Winifred's, or The World of School

"Oh, do, Henderson. I'm sure you'd get it. Don't ask me to go in, that's a good fellow."

"None but these four going in for the little jump? What, only four?" said one of the young athletes, who carried little blue flags, and arranged the preliminaries. "Come in some more of you."

"Here are two more," said Henderson; "stick down our names— Henderson and Evson;" and pulling Walter forward with him inside the circle, he sat down and began to take off his shoes, that he might run and jump more easily on the turf.

Thus prominently mentioned, Walter could hardly draw back, so putting the best face on it he could, he, too, flung off his jacket and shoes.

The movable spar of wood over which the boys jumped was first put at a height of three feet, which they could all easily manage, and the six, one after another, cleared it lightly. Even then, however, it was pretty easy to judge by their action which was the best jumper, and the connoisseurs on the field at once decided that the chance lay between Henderson and Walter; Walter was by far the most active and graceful jumper, but Henderson had the advantage of being a little the taller of the two.

The spar was raised half an inch each time, and when it had attained the height of three feet and a half, two of the candidates failed to clear it after three trials.

Bliss was the next to break down. His awkward jumps had excited a great deal of laughter, and when he finally failed, Henderson found time even then to begin a line or two of his monody on Blissidas, which was a standing joke against poor Bliss, who always met it by the same invariable observation of, "I'll lick you afterwards, Flip."

Only three competitors were now left—Franklin, Henderson, and Walter—and they jumped on steadily till they had reached the height of four feet and one inch, and then Franklin broke down, but recovered himself in the second chance.

The struggle now became very exciting, and as Franklin and Henderson again cleared the bar at the height of four feet four, each of them were loudly clapped. But Walter—who jumped last always, because he had been the last candidate to come forward— although he cleared it with an easy bound, received no sign of encouragement from any of the boys. He cleared it in perfect silence, only broken by Mr Paton, who was looking on with a group of other masters, and who said encouragingly—"Very well done, Evson; capital!"

The bar was raised an inch, and again the three boys cleared it, and again the first two were greeted with applause, and Walter was left unnoticed except by Power and Kenrick, who applauded him heartily, and patted him on the back. But indeed their clapping only served to throw into stronger relief the loud applause which the others received. Walter almost wished that they would desist. He was greatly agitated; and his friends saw that he was trembling with emotion. He had been much mortified the first time to be thus pointedly scorned in so large a crowd of strangers, and made a marked object of reprobation before them all; but that this open shame should be thus *steadily* and *continuously* put upon him, made his heart swell with sorrow and indignation at the ungenerous and unforgiving spirit of his schoolfellows.

Once more the bar was raised an inch. The other two got over it amid a burst of applause, and this time Walter, who was unnerved by the painful circumstances in which he found himself, brushed against it as he came over, and knocked it off. The bar was replaced, and at his second trial, (for three were allowed), he jumped so well that he flew easily over it. Always before, a boy who had recovered himself after a failure had been saluted with double cheering, but again Walter's proceedings were observed by that large crowd in dead silence, while he could not help overhearing the whispered queues which asked an explanation of so unusual a circumstance.

"Why don't they cheer him as well as the others?" asked a fair young girl of her brother. "He looks such a nice boy."

"Because he did a very shabby thing not long ago," was the reply.

He could stand it no longer. He glanced round at the speakers more in sorrow than in anger, and then, instead of returning to the starting-point, he turned hastily aside, and, declining the contest, plunged into the thickest of the crowd.

"Evson's giving it up. What a pity!" said several boys.

St. Winifred's, or The World of School

"No wonder he's giving it up," said Power indignantly, "after the way you fellows treat him. Never mind them, Walter," he said, taking him by the arm; "they will be ashamed of themselves by and by."

"You're not going to withdraw, Evson?" asked one of the chief athletes, in a kind tone.

"Yes," said Walter, retiring still farther to hide himself amid the crowd.

"Nonsense!" said Henderson, who had heard the answer; "come, Walter, it'll spoil all the fun if you don't go on."

"I can't, Flip," said Walter, turning aside, and hastily brushing away the tears which *would* come into his eyes.

"Do, Walter, they all wish it," whispered Henderson; "be brave, and get the prize in spite of all; here's Paton coming round; I'm sure it's to cheer you up."

"Very well, Flip, I will, if it pleases you; but it's rather hard," he said, fairly bursting into tears. "Remember, it's only for your sake I do it, Flip."

"Go on, Walter; don't give way," said Mr Paton aloud, in his gentlest and most encouraging voice, as the boy hastily re-entered the arena, and took his place.

This time Franklin finally broke down, Henderson barely scrambled over, and Walter, nerved by excitement and indignation, cleared the bar by a brilliant flying leap. There was no mistake about the applause this time. The boys had seen how their coolness had told on him. They were touched by the pluck he showed in spite of his dejected look, and as though to make up for their former deficiency, they clapped him as loud as either of the others.

And now a spirited contest began between Henderson and Walter. Four feet six and a half they both accomplished—Walter the first time, and Henderson the third. When Henderson, at his last trial, barely succeeded, a loud shout rose from the field, quite enthusiastic enough to show that the wishes of the school were on his side. This decided Walter, for he was too anxious that Henderson, who had set his heart upon the prize, and was now quite eager with emulation, should be the successful competitor. At four feet

St. Winifred's, or The World of School

seven, therefore, he meant to break down, but, at the same time, to clear the bar so nearly each time of trial, that it might not be *obvious* to any one that he was not putting forth his best strength. The first time, however, he jumped so carelessly that Henderson suspected his purpose, and, therefore, the second time he exerted himself a little more, and, to his own astonishment, accomplished the leap without having intended to do so. Henderson also just succeeded in managing it, and as Walter refused to try another half-inch, the prize was declared, amid loud cheers, to be equally divided between them, after the best competition that ever had been known.

The boys and the spectators now moved off to the pavilion, where the prizes were to be distributed by Mrs Lane. But when Walter's name was called out with Henderson's, the latter only stepped forward. Walter had disappeared; and the boys were again made to feel, by his voluntary absence, what bitterness of heart their unkind conduct caused him.

Henderson took the prize for his friend, when he received his own. The prizes were a silver-mounted riding-whip, and a belt with a silver clasp, and Mrs Lane told Henderson that she was sorry for the other victor's absence, and that either of them might choose whichever prize he liked best. When the crowd had dispersed, Henderson, knowing Walter's haunts, strolled with Kenrick to a little fir-grove on the slope of Bardlyn Hill, not far above the sea. Here, as they expected, they found Walter. He was sitting in a listless attitude, with his back towards them, and he started as he heard their footsteps.

"You let yourself be beaten, Evson Walter,
And afterwards you proved a base defaulter,"

said Henderson, who was in high spirits, as he clapped his hands on Walter's shoulders, and continued:

"Behold I bring you now the silver prizes,
Meant to reward your *feets* and exercises."

Even Walter could not help smiling at this sally, but he said at once, "You must keep both prizes, Flip; I don't mean to take either—indeed I won't; I shouldn't have gone in at all but for you."

"Oh, do take one," said Kenrick; "the fellows will think you too proud if you don't."

St. Winifred's, or The World of School

"I don't care what they think of me, Ken; you saw how they treated me. Flip, I'd take the prize in a minute to please you, but, indeed, it would only remind me constantly of this odious jumping, and I'd much rather not."

"I can't take *both* prizes, Walter," said Henderson.

"Well, I'll tell you what—give one to Franklin; he jumped very well, and he's not half a bad fellow. Don't press me, Flip; I can't refuse you anything if you do, because you've been so very, very kind; but you don't know how wretched I feel."

Henderson, who had looked annoyed, cleared up in a moment.

"All right, Walter; it shall be as you like. Franklin shall have it. You've had quite enough to bear already. So, cheer up, and come along."

It was soon known in the school how Walter had yielded the prize to Franklin, and it was known, too, that next day he had gone to jump with Henderson, Franklin, and some others, and had cleared the bar at four feet eight, which none of them had been able to do. The boys admired his conduct throughout; and from that day forward many were as anxious to renew an acquaintance with him, as they had previously been to break it off.

And there was an early opportunity of testing this; for a few days after the scene just described the champion race for boys under fifteen was tried for, and when Walter won it by accomplishing the distance in the shortest time that had yet been known, and by distancing the other runners, he was received with a cheer, which was all the more hearty because the boys were anxious to do him a tardy justice. If Walter had not been too noble to be merely patronised, and too reserved to be "hail-fellow-well-met" with every one, he would have fallen more easily and speedily into the position which he now slowly but honourably recovered.

It need hardly be said that, in his school-work, Walter struggled with all his might to give satisfaction to Mr Paton, and to spare him from all pain. There was something really admirable in the way he worked, and taxed himself even beyond his strength, to prove his regret for Mr Paton's loss, by doing all that was required of him. Naturally quick and lively as he was, he sat as quiet and attentive in school, as if he had been gifted with a disposition as unmercurial as that of Daubeny himself. In order to make sure of his lessons, he went over them with Henderson, (who entered eagerly into his wishes), with such care, that they, both of them, astonished themselves with their own improving progress. If they came to any insuperable difficulties, Kenrick or Power gladly helped them, and explained everything to them with that sympathetic clearness of instruction which makes one boy the best teacher to another. The main difficulty still continued to be the repetition and grammar rules; but in order to know them, at least by rote, Walter would get up with the earliest gleam of daylight, and would put on his trousers and waistcoat after bedtime, and go and sit, book in hand, under the gaslight in the passage. This was hard work, doubtless; but it brought its own reward in successful endeavour and an approving conscience. Under this discipline his memory rapidly grew retentive; no difficulty can stand the assaults of such batteries as these, and Walter was soon free from all punishments, and as happy as the day was long.

One little cloud alone remained—the continued and obvious displeasure of his tutor, and one or two of Mr Paton's chief friends among the masters. One of these was Mr Edwards, who, among other duties, had the management of the chapel choir. But at length Mr Edwards gave him a distinguished proof of his returning respect. He sat near Walter in chapel, and the hymn happened to be one which came closely home to Walter's heart after his recent troubles. This made him join with great feeling in the singing, and the choir–master was struck with the strength and rare sweetness of his voice. As he left the chapel, Mr Edwards said to him, "Evson, there is a vacancy for a treble in the choir; I heard you sing in chapel to–day, and I think that you would supply the place very well. Should you like to join?"

Walter very gladly accepted the offer; partly because he hailed the opportunity of learning a little about music, and because the choir–boys were allowed several highly–valued and exceptional privileges; but chiefly because they were always chosen by the masters with express reference to character, and therefore the invitation to join their number was the clearest proof that could be given him that the past was condoned.

The last to offer him the right hand of forgiveness, but the best and warmest friend to him when once he had done so, was Mr Percival. He still passed him with only the coldest and most distant recognition, for he not only felt Mr Paton's loss with peculiar sorrow, but was also vexed and disappointed that a boy whose character he had openly defended should have proved so unworthy of his encomium. It happened that the *only* time that Walter was ever again sent to detention, was for a failure in a long lesson, including much which had been learnt on the morning that he was out of school, which, in consequence, he found it impossible, with all his efforts, to master. Mr Paton saw how mortified and pained he was to fail, and when he sent him to detention, most kindly called him up, and told him that he saw the cause of his unsuccess, and was not *in the least* displeased at it, although, as he had similarly punished other boys, he could not make any exception to the usual rule of punishment. On this occasion, it was again Mr Percival's turn to sit with the *detenus*, and seeing Walter among them, he too hastily concluded that he was still continuing a career of disgrace.

"What! you here again?" he said with chilling scorn, as he passed the seat where Walter sat writing. "After what has happened, I should have been ashamed to be sent here, if I were you."

After his days and nights of toil, after his long, manly, noble struggle to show his penitence, after his heavy and disproportionate punishment, it was hard to be so addressed by one whom he respected, in the presence of all the idlest in the school, and in consequence of a purely accidental and isolated failure. Walter looked up with an appealing look in his dark blue eyes; but Mr Percival had passed on, and he bent his head over his paper with the old sense that the past could *never* be forgotten, the recollection of his disgrace *never* obliterated. No one was observing him; and as the feeling of despair grew in him, a large tear dropped down upon his paper; he wiped it quietly away, and continued writing, but another and another fell, and he could not help it. For Mr Percival was almost the only master whose goodwill he very strongly coveted, and whose approval he was most anxious to attain.

When next Mr Percival stopped and looked at Walter, he saw that his words had wounded him to the heart, and knew well why the boy's lines were blurred and blotted, when he showed them up with a timid hand and downcast look.

He was touched. "I have been too hard on you, Evson," he said. "I see it now. Come to tea with me after chapel this evening; I want to speak with you."

CHAPTER ELEVEN. HAPPIER HOURS.

Sir, you are one of those that will not serve God if the

St. Winifred's, or The World of School

devil bid you.—*Othello, Act 1, Scene 1.*

When chapel was over, Walter, having brushed his hair, and made himself rather neater and more spruce than a schoolboy usually is at the middle of a long half, went to Mr Percival's room. Mr Percival, having been detained, had not yet come in; but Henderson, Kenrick, and Power, who had also been asked to tea, were there waiting for him when Walter arrived, and Henderson was, as usual, amusing the others and himself with a flood of mimicry and nonsense.

"You know that mischievous little Penkridge," said Kenrick; "he nearly had an accident this morning. We were in the classroom, and Edwards was complaining of the bad smell of the room—"

"Bad smell!" interrupted Henderson, "I'll bet you what you like Edwards didn't say bad smell. *He's* not the man to call a spade a spade; he calls it an agricultural implement for the trituration of the soil."

"Why, what *should* he say?" asked Kenrick, "if he didn't say `bad smell'?"

"Why, `What a malodorous effluvium!'" said Henderson, imitating exactly the master's somewhat drawling tone; "`what a con–cen– trra–ted malarious miasma; what an unendurable—' I say, Power, give us the Greek, or Hebrew, or Kamschatkan for `smell'."

"*odoedee*," suggested Power.

"That's it to a T," said Henderson; "I bet you he observed, `What an un–en–duu–rrable *odoedee.*' Now, didn't he? Confess the truth."

"Well, I believe he did say something of the kind," said Kenrick, laughing; "at least I know he called it Stygian and Tartarean. But, as I was saying, he set Penkridge, (who happened to be going round with the lists), to examine the cupboards, and see if by chance some inopportune rat had died there; and Penkridge, opening one of them where the floor was very rotten, and poking about with his foot, knocked a great piece of plaster off the great schoolroom ceiling, and was as nearly as possible putting his foot through it."

St. Winifred's, or The World of School

"Fancy if he had," said Walter, "how astonished we should have been down below. I say, Henderson, what *would* Paton have said?"

"Oh! Paton," said Henderson, delighted with any opportunity for mimicry, "he'd have whispered quietly, in an emotionless voice, `Penkridge, Penkridge, come here—come here, Penkridge. This is a very unusual method, Penkridge, of entering a room—highly irregular. If you haven't broken your leg or your arm, Penkridge, you must write me two hundred lines.'"

"And Robertson?" asked Kenrick.

"Oh! Robertson—he'd have put up his eyeglass," said Henderson, again exactly hitting off the master's attitude, "and he'd have observed, `Ah! Penkridge has fallen through the floor; probably fractured some bones. Slippery fellow, he won't be able to go to the Fighting Cocks *this* afternoon, at any rate.' Whereupon Stevens would have gone up to him with the utmost tenderness, and asked him if he was hurt; and Penkridge, getting up, would, by way of gratitude, have grinned in his face."

"Well, you'd better finish the scene," said Power; "what would Percival have said?"

"Thunder–and–lightning? Oh! that's easy to decide; he'd have made two or three quotations; he'd have immediately called the attention of the form to the fact that Penkridge had been:—

"`Flung by angry Jove sheer o'er
The crystal battlements; from morn
Till noon he fell, from noon till dewy eve
A winter's day, and as the tea–bell rang,
Shot from the ceiling like a falling star
On the great schoolroom floor.'"

"Would he, indeed?" said Mr Percival, pinching Henderson's ear, as he came in just in time to join in the laugh which this parody occasioned.

Tea at St Winifred's is a regular and recognised institution. There are few nights on which some of the boys do not adjourn after chapel to tea at the masters' houses, when they have

St. Winifred's, or The World of School

the privilege of sitting up an hour and a half later. The masters generally adopt this method of seeing their pupils, and the boys in whom they are interested. The institution works admirably; the first and immediate result of it is, that there boys and masters are more intimately acquainted, and being so, are on warmer and friendlier terms with each other than perhaps at any other school —certainly on warmer terms than if they never met except in the still and punishment-pervaded atmosphere of the schoolrooms; and the second and remoter result is, that not only in the matter of work already alluded to, but also in other and equally important particulars, the tone and character of St Winifred's boys is higher and purer than it would otherwise be. There is a simplicity and manliness there which cannot fail to bring forth its rich fruits of diligence, truthfulness, and honour. Many are the boys who have come from thence, who, in the sweet yet sober dignity of their life and demeanour, go far to realise the beautiful ideal of Christian boyhood. Many are the boys there who are walking, through the gates of humility and diligence, to certain, and merited, and conspicuous honour.

I know that there are many who believe in none of these things, and care not for them; who repudiate the necessity and duty of early godliness; who set up no ideal at all, because to do so would expose them to the charge of sentiment or enthusiasm, a charge which they dread more than that of villainy itself. These men regard the heart as a muscle consisting of four cavities, called respectively the auricles and the ventricles, and useful for no other purpose but to aerate the blood; all other meanings of the word they despise or ignore. They regard the world not as a scene of probation, not as a passage to a newer and higher life, but as a "convenient feeding-trough" for every low passion and unworthy impulse; as a place where they can build on the foundation of universal scepticism a reputation for superior ability. This degradation of spirit, this premature cynicism, this angry sneering at a tone superior to their own, this addiction to a low and lying satire, which is the misbegotten child of envy and disbelief, has infected our literature to a deplorable and almost hopeless extent. It might be sufficient to leave it, in all its rottenness and inflation, to every good man's silent scorn, if it had not also so largely tainted the intellect of the young. If, in popular papers or magazines, boys are to read that, in a boy, lying is natural and venial; that courtesy to, and love for, a master, is impossible or hypocritical; that swearing and corrupt communication are peccadilloes which none but preachers and pedagogues regard as discreditable; how can we expect success to the labours of those who toil all their lives, amid neglect and ingratitude, to elevate the boys of England to a higher and holier view? I have seen this taint of *atheistic disregard for sin* poison article after article, and infuse its bitter principle into many a young man's heart; and worse than this—adopted as it is by writers whom some consider to be mighty in intellect and leaders of opinion, I have seen it corrode the consciences and degrade the philosophy of far better and far worthier men.

It is a solemn duty to protect, with all the force of heart and conscience, against this DANGEROUS GOSPEL OF SIN, this "giving to manhood's vices the privilege of boyhood." It was *not* the gospel taught at St Winifred's; there we were taught that we were baptized Christian boys, that the seal of God's covenant was on our foreheads, that the oath of His service was on our consciences, that we were His children, and the members of His Son, and the inheritors of His kingdom; that His laws were our safeguard, and that our bodies were the temples of His Spirit. We were not taught—that was left for the mighty intellects of this age to discover—that as we were boys, a Christian principle and a Christian standard were above our comprehension, and alien from our possible attainments; we did not believe then, nor will I now, that a clear river is likely to flow from a polluted stream, or a good tree grow from bitter fibres and cankered roots.

Walter and the others spent a very happy evening with Mr Percival. When tea was over they talked as freely with him, and with each other in his presence, as they would have done among themselves; and the occasional society of their elders and superiors was in every way good for them. It enlarged their sympathies, widened their knowledge, and raised their moral tone.

Among many other subjects that evening they talked over one which never fails to interest deeply every right-minded boy—I mean their homes. It was no wonder that, as Walter talked of the glories of Semlyn lake and its surrounding hills, his face lighted up, and his eyes shone with pleasant memories. Mr Percival, as he looked at him, felt more puzzled than ever at his having gone wrong, and more confirmed than ever in the opinion that he had been hard and unjust to him of late, and that his original estimate of him was the right one after all.

Power's home was a statelier one than Walter's. His father, Sir Lawrence Power, was a baronet, the owner of broad acres, whose large and beautiful mansion stood on one of the undulations in a park shadowed by ancestral trees, under whose boughs the deer fed with their graceful fawns around them. Through the park flowed a famous river, of which the windings were haunted by herons and kingfishers, and the pleasant waters abounded in trout and salmon. And to this estate and title Power was heir though of course he did not tell them this while he spoke of the lovely scenery around the home where his fathers had so long lived.

Henderson, again, was the son of a rich merchant, who had two houses—one city and one suburban. He was a regular little man of the world. After the holidays he had always seen the last feats of Saltori, and heard the most recent strains of Tiralirini. He always went to a round of entertainments, and would make you laugh by the hour while he sang the songs or imitated the style of the last comic actor or Ethiopian minstrel.

While they were chatting over their holiday amusements and occupations, Kenrick said little; and, wondering at his silence, Mr Percival asked him in what part of the world he lived.

"I, sir?" he said, as though awaked from a reverie; "oh, I live at Fuzby, a village on the border of the fens, and in the very middle of the heavy clays." And Kenrick turned away his head.

"Don't abuse the clay," said Walter, to cheer him up. "I'm very fond of the clay; it produces good roses and good strawberries— and those are the two best things going, in any soil."

"Half-past ten, youngsters," said Mr Percival, holding up his watch; "off with you to bed. Let yourselves in through the grounds; here's the key. Good-night to you. Walter," he said, calling him back as he was about to leave, "one word with you alone; you three wait for him a moment outside. I wanted to tell you that, although I have seemed harsh to you, I dare say, of late, yet now I hear that you are making the most honourable efforts, and I have quite forgotten the past. My good opinion of you, Walter, is quite restored; and whenever you want to be quiet to learn your lessons, you may always come and sit in my room."

Mr Percival was not the only St Winifred's master who thus generously abridged his own leisure and privacy, to assist the boys in what he felt an interest. Walter thanked him with real gratitude, and rejoined the other three. "He's let me sit in his room," said Walter.

"Has he?" said Henderson; "so he has me. How jolly! we shall get on twice as well."

St. Winifred's, or The World of School

"What's that?" said Power, pointing upwards, as they walked through the garden to their house door.

Glancing in the direction, Walter saw a light suddenly go out in his dormitory, and a great bundle, (apparently), disappear inside the window, which was then shut down.

"I'll go and see," he said. "Good–night, you fellows."

All was quiet when he reached his room, but one of the candles, ineffectually extinguished, was still smoking, and when he looked to Eden's bed he saw, by the gaslight that shone through the open door, that the child was awake, and crying bitterly.

"What's the matter, Eden?" he said kindly, sitting down upon his bed.

"If you peach," said Harpour and Jones together, "you know what you'll get."

"Have you fellows been bullying poor little Eden?" asked Walter indignantly.

"I've not," and, "I've not," said Anthony and Franklin, who were better than the rest in every way; and, "I haven't touched the fellow, Evson," said Cradock, who meant no harm, and at Walter's earnest request had never again annoyed Eden since the first night.

"Poor little Eden—poor little fiddlestick," said Jones; "it does the young cub good."

"Send him home to his grandmamma, and let him have his bib and his nightcap," growled Harpour; "is he made of butter, and are you afraid of his melting you, Evson, that you make such a fuss with him? You want your lickings yourself, and shall have them if you don't look out."

"I don't care what you do to *me*, Harpour," rejoined Walter, "and I don't think you'll do very much. But I do tell you that it's a blackguard shame for a great big fellow like you to torment a little delicate chap like Eden; and what's more, you shan't do it."

"Shan't! my patience, I like that! why, who is to prevent me?"

"I suppose he'll turn sneak, and peach," said Jones; "he'd do anything that's mean, we all know."

Walter was always liable to that taunt now. It was a part of his punishment, and the one which lasted longest. From any other boy he might have winced under it; but really, coming from Jones, it was too contemptible to notice.

"You shut up, Jones," he said angrily; "you shan't touch Eden again, I can tell you, whatever Harpour does, and he'd better look out what he does."

"Look out yourself," said Harpour, flinging a football boot at Walter's head.

"You'll find your boot on the grass outside to-morrow morning," said Walter, opening the window, and dropping it down. He wasn't a bit afraid, because he always went on the instinctive and never- mistaken assumption, that a bully must be a coward in his inmost nature. Cruelty to the weaker is incompatible with the generosity of all true courage.

"By Jove, I'll thrash you for that to-morrow," shouted Harpour.

"*To-morrow!*" said Walter, with great contempt.

"Oh, don't make him angry, Walter," whispered Eden; "you know what a strong fellow he is," (Eden shuddered, as though *he* had reason to know); "and you can't fight him; and you mustn't get a thrashing for my sake. I'm not worth that. I'd rather bear it myself, Walter;—indeed I would."

"Good-night, poor little Eden," said Walter; "you're safe to- night at any rate. Why, how cold you are! What *have* they been doing to you?"

"I daren't tell you to-night, Walter; I will to-morrow," he answered in a low tone, shivering all over.

"Well, then, go to sleep now, my little man; and don't you be afraid of Harpour or any one else. I won't let them bully you if I can help it."

Eden squeezed Walter's hand tight, and sobbed his thanks, while Walter gently smoothed the child's pillow and dried his tears.

Poor Eden! as I said before, he was too weak, too delicate, too tenderly nurtured, and far, far too young for the battle of life in a public school. For even at St Winifred's, as there are and must be at all great schools, there were some black sheep in the flock undiscovered, and therefore unseparated from the rest.

CHAPTER TWELVE. MY BROTHER'S KEEPER.

> 'Tis in ourselves that we are thus or thus. Our bodies are
> gardens to the which our wills are gardeners.—*Othello,
> Act 1, Scene 3.*

As Walter lay awake for a few quiet moments before he sent his thoughts to rest, he glanced critically, like an Indian gymnosophist, over the occurrences of the day. He could not but rejoice that the last person for whom he felt real regard had forgiven him his rash act, and that his offence had thus finally been absolved on earth as in heaven. He rejoiced, too, that Mr Percival's kind permission to learn his lessons in his room would give him far greater advantages and opportunities than he had hitherto enjoyed. Yet Walter's conscience was not quite at ease. The last scene had disturbed him. The sobs and shiverings of little Eden had fallen very reproachfully into his heart. Walter felt that he might have done far more for him than he had done. He had, indeed, even throughout his own absorbing troubles, extended to the child a general protection, but not a special care. It never occurred to him to excuse himself with the thought that he was "not his brother's keeper." The truth was that he had found Eden uninteresting, because he had not taken the pains to be interested in him, and while one voice within his heart reproved him of neglect and selfishness, another voice seemed to say to him, in a firm yet kindlier tone, "Now that thou art converted, strengthen thy brethren."

For indeed as yet Eden's had been a very unhappy lot. Bullied, teased, and persecuted by the few among whom accident had first thrown him, and judged to belong to their set by others who on that account considered him a boy of a bad sort, he was almost friendless at St Winifred's. And the loneliness, the despair of this feeling, weighing upon his heart, robbed him of all courage to face the difficulties of work, so that in school as well as out

St. Winifred's, or The World of School

of it, he was always in trouble. He was for ever clumsily scrawling in his now illegible hand the crooked and blotted lines of punishment which his seeming ignorance or sluggishness brought upon him; and although he was always to be seen at detention, he almost hailed this disgrace as affording him at least some miserable shadow of occupation, and a refuge, however undesirable, from the torments of those degraded few to whom his childish tears, his weak entreaties, his bursts of impotent passion, caused nothing but low amusement. Out of school his great object always was to hide himself; anywhere, so as to be beyond the reach of Jones, Harpour, and other bullies of the same calibre. For this purpose he would conceal himself for a whole afternoon at a time up in the fir-groves, listlessly gathering into heaps the red sheddings of their umbrage, and pulling to pieces their dry and fragrant cones; or, when he feared that these resorts would be disturbed by some little gang of lounging smokers, he would choose some lonely place, under the shadow of the mountain cliffs, and sit for hours together, aimlessly rolling white lumps of quartz over the shingly banks. Under continued trials like these he became quite changed. The childish innocence and beauty of countenance, the childish frankness and gaiety of heart, the childish quickness and intelligence of understanding, were exchanged for vacant looks, stupid indifference, and that half-cunning expression which is always induced by craven fear. Accustomed, too, to be waited upon and helped continually in the home where his mother, a gay young widow, had petted and spoiled him, he became slovenly and untidy in dress and habits. He rarely found time or heart to write home, and even when he did, he so well knew that his mother was incapable of sympathy or comprehension of his suffering, that the dirty and ill-spelt scrawl rarely alluded to the one dim consciousness that brooded over him night and day—that he couldn't understand life, and only knew that he was a very friendless, unhappy, unpitied little boy. If he could have found even one to whom to unfold and communicate his griefs, even one to love him unreservedly, all the inner beauty and brightness of his character would have blown and expanded in that genial warmth. He once thought that in Walter he had found such an one, but when he saw that his dulness bored Walter, and that his listless manners and untidy habits made him cross, he shrank back within himself. He was thankful to Walter as a protector, but did not look upon him as a friend in whom he could implicitly confide. The flower without sunshine will lose its colour and its perfume. Six weeks after Arthur Eden, a merry, bright-eyed child, alighted from his mother's carriage at the old gate of St. Winifred's School, no casual stranger would have recognised him again in the pale and moping little fellow who seemed to be afraid of every one whom he met.

St. Winifred's, or The World of School

Oh, if we knew how rare, how sweet, how deep human love can be, how easily, yet how seldom it is gained, how inexpressible the treasure is when once it *has* been gained, we should not trample on human hearts as lightly as most men do! Any one who in that hard time had spoken a few kindly words to Eden—any one who would have taken him gently for a short while by the hand, and helped him over the stony places that hurt his unaccustomed feet —any one who would have suffered, or who would have invited him, to pour his sorrows into their ears and assist him to sustain them—might have won, even at that slight cost, the deepest and most passionate love of that trembling young heart. He might have saved him from hours of numbing pain, and won the rich reward of a gratitude well-deserved and generously repaid. There were many boys at St Winifred's gentle-hearted, right-minded, of kindly and manly impulses; but all of them, except Walter, lost this golden opportunity of conferring pure happiness by disinterested good deeds. They did not buy up the occasion, which goes away and burns the priceless books she offers, if they are not purchased unquestioningly and at once.

And Walter regretfully felt that he was very nearly too late; so nearly, that perhaps in a week or two more Eden might have lost hopelessly, and for ever, all trace of self-respect;—might have been benumbed into mental imbecility by the torpedo-like influence of helpless grief. Walter felt as if he had been selfishly looking on while a fellow-creature was fast sinking in the water, and as if it were only at the last possible moment that he had held out a saving hand. But, by God's grace, he *did* hold out the saving hand at last, and it was grasped firmly, and a dear life was saved. Years after when Arthur Eden had grown into, but stop, I must not so far anticipate my story. Suffice it to say, that Walter's kindness to Eden helped to bring about long afterwards one of the chief happinesses of his own life.

"Come a stroll, Eden, before third school, and let's have a talk," he said, as they came out from dinner in Hall the next day.

Eden looked up happily, and he was proud to be seen by Walter's side in the throng of boys, as they passed out, and across the court, and under the shadow of the arch towards Walter's favourite haunt, the seashore. Walter never felt weak or unhappy for long together, when the sweetness of the sea wind was on his forehead, and the song of the waves in his ear. A run upon the shore in all weathers, if only for five minutes, was his daily pleasure and resource.

St. Winifred's, or The World of School

They sat down; the sea flashed before them a mirror of molten gold, except where the summits of the great mountain of Appenfell threw their deep broad shadows, which seemed purple by contrast with the brightness over which they fell. Walter sat, full of healthy enjoyment as he breathed the pure atmosphere, and felt the delicious wind upon his glowing cheeks; and Eden was happy to be with him, and to sit quietly by his side.

"Eden," said Walter, after a few moments, "I'm afraid you've not been happy lately."

The poor child shook his head, and answered, "No one cares for me here; every one looks down on me, and is unkind; I've no friends."

"What, don't you count me as a friend, then?"

"Yes, Walter, you're very kind; I'm sure I *couldn't* have lived here if it hadn't been for you; but you're so much above me, and—"

Walter would not press him to fill up the omission, he could understand the rest of the sentence for himself.

"You mustn't think I don't feel how good you've been to me, Walter," said the boy, drawing near to him, and taking his hand; "but—"

"Yes, yes," said Walter; "I understand it all. Well, never mind, I *will* be a friend to you now."

A tear trembled on Eden's long eyelashes as he looked up quickly into Walter's face. "Will you, Walter? thank you, I have no other friend here; and please—"

"Well, what is it?"

"Will you call me Arthur, as they do at home?"

Walter smiled. "Well now," he said, "tell me what they were doing to you last night."

"You won't tell them I told you, Walter," he answered, looking round, with the old look of decrepit fear usurping his face, which had brightened for the moment.

St. Winifred's, or The World of School

"No, no," said Walter impatiently; "why, what a little coward you are, Eden."

The boy shrank back into himself as if he had received a blow, and relaxed his grasp of Walter's hand; but Walter, struck with the sensitive timidity which unkindness had caused, and sorry to have given him pain in all his troubles, said kindly:

"There, Arty, never mind; I didn't mean it; don't be afraid; tell me what they did to you. I saw a light in our dormitory as I was coming back from Percival's, and I saw something dragged through the window. What was it?"

"That was me," said Eden naively.

"You?"

"Yes; poor me. They let me down by a sheet which they tied round my waist."

"What, from that high window? I hope they tied you tight."

"Only one knot; I ever so nearly slipped out of it last night, and that's what frightened me so, Walter."

"How horribly dangerous," said Walter indignantly.

"I know it is horribly dangerous," said Eden, standing up, and gesticulating violently, in one of those bursts of passion which flashed out of him now and then, and were the chief amusement of his persecutors; "and I dream about it all night," he said, bursting into tears, "and I know, I know that some day I shall slip, or the knot will come undone, and I shall fall and be smashed to atoms. But what do they care for that? and I sometimes wish I were dead myself, to have it all over."

"Hush, Arty, don't talk like that," said Walter, as he felt the little soiled hand trembling with passion and emotion in his own. "But what on earth do they let you down for?"

"To go to—but you won't tell?" he said, looking round again. "Oh, I forgot, you didn't like my saying that.—But it's they who have made me a coward, Walter; indeed it is."

St. Winifred's, or The World of School

"And no wonder," thought Walter to himself. "But you needn't be afraid any more," he said aloud; "I promise you that no one shall do anything to you which they'd be afraid to do to me."

"Then I'm safe," said Eden joyfully. "Well, they made me go to— to Dan's."

"Dan's? what, the fisherman's just near the shore."

"Yes; ugh!"

"But don't you know, Arty, that Dan's a brute, and a regular smuggler, and that if you were caught going there, you'd be sent away?"

"Yes; you can't think, Walter, how I *hate*, and how frightened I am to go there. There's Dan, and there's that great lout of a wicked son of his, and they're always drunk, and the hut—ugh! it's so nasty; and last night Dan seized hold of me with his horrid red hand, and wanted me to drink some gin, and I shrieked." The very remembrance seemed to make him shudder.

"Well then, after that I was nearly caught. I think, Walter, that even you would be a coward if you had such long long frights. You know that to get to Dan's, after the gates are locked, the only way is to go over the railing, and through Dr Lane's garden, and I'm always frightened to death lest his great dog should be loose, and should catch hold of me. He did growl last night. And then as I was hurrying back—you know it was rather moonlight last night, and not very cold—and who should I see but the Doctor himself walking up and down the garden. I crouched in a minute behind a thick holly tree, and I suppose I made a rustle, though I held my breath, for the Doctor stopped and shook the tree, and said, `shoo,' as though he thought a cat were hidden there. I was half dead with fright, though I did hope, after all, that he would catch me, and that I might be sent away from this horrid place. But when he turned round, I crept away, and made the signal, and they let down the sheet, and then, as they were hauling me up, I heard voices—I suppose they must have been yours and Kenrick's; but they thought it was some master, and doused the glim, and oh so nearly let me fall; so Walter, please don't despise me, or be angry with me because you found me crying and shivering in bed. The cold made me shiver, and I couldn't help crying; indeed I couldn't."

St. Winifred's, or The World of School

"Poor Arty, poor Arty," said Walter soothingly. "But have they ever done this before?"

"Yes, once, when you were at the choir-supper one night."

"They never shall again, I swear," said Walter, frowning, as he thought how detestably cruel they had been. "But what did they send you for?"

"For no good," said Eden.

"No; I knew it would be for no good, if it was to Dan's that they sent you."

"Well, Walter, the first time it was for some drink; and the second time for some more drink," he said after a little hesitation.

Walter looked serious. "But don't you know, Arty," he said, "that it's very wrong to get such things for them? If they want to have any dealings with that beast Dan, who's not fit to speak to, let them go themselves. Arty, it's very wrong; you mustn't do it."

"But how can I help it?" said the boy, looking frightened and ashamed. "Oh, must I always be blamed by every one," he said, putting his hands to his eyes. "It isn't *my* sin, Walter, it's theirs. They made me."

"Nobody can ever make any one else do what's wrong, Arty."

"Oh yes; it's all very easy for *you* to say that, Walter, who can fight anybody, and who are so strong and good, and whom no one dares bully, and who are not laughed at, and made a butt of, as I am."

"Look at Power," said Walter, "or look at Dubbs. They came as young as you, Arty, and as weak as you, but no one ever made *them* do wrong. Power somehow looks too noble to be bullied by any one; they're afraid of him, I don't know why. But what had Dubbs to protect him? Yet not all the Harpours in the world would ever make him go to such a place as Dan's."

Poor Eden felt it hard to be blamed for this; he was not yet strong enough to learn that the path of duty, however hard and thorny, however hedged in with difficulties and antagonisms, is always the easiest and the pleasantest in the end.

"But they'd half kill me, Walter," he said plaintively.

"They'll have much more chance of doing that as it is," said Walter. "They'd thrash you a little, no doubt, but respect you more for it. And surely it would be better to bear one thrashing, and not do what's wrong, than to do it and to go two such journeys out of the window, and get the thrashings into the bargain? So even on *that* ground you ought to refuse. Eh, Arty?"

"Yes, Walter," he said, casting down his eyes.

"Well; next time either Harpour, or any one else, tries to make you do what's wrong, remember they *can't* make you, if you don't choose; and say flatly *No*! and stick to it in spite of everything, like a brave little man, will you?"

"I did say No! at first, Walter; but they threatened to frighten me," he said. "They knew I daren't hold out."

Yes; there was the secret of it all. Walter saw that they had played on this child's natural terrors with such refinement of cruelty, that fear had become the master principle in his mind; they had only to touch that spring and he obeyed them mechanically like a puppet, and because of his very fear was driven to do things that might well cause genuine fear, till he lived in such a region of increasing fear and dread, that Walter's only surprise was that he had not been made an idiot already. Poor child; it was no wonder that he was becoming more stupid, cunning, untidy, and uninteresting, every day. And all this was going on under the very eyes of many thoroughly noble boys, and conscientious masters, and yet they never saw or noticed it, and looked on Eden as an idle and unprincipled little sloven. O our harsh human judgments! The Priest and the Levite still pass the wounded man, and the good Samaritans are rare on this world's highways.

What was Walter to do? He did not know the very name of psychology, but he did know the unhinging desolating power of an overmastering spirit of fear. He knew that fear hath torment, but he had no conception by what means that demon can be exorcised. Yet he thought, as he raised his eyes for one instant to Heaven in silent supplication, that there were few devils who would not go out by prayer, and he made a strong resolve that he would use every endeavour to make up for his past neglectfulness, and to save this poor unhappy child.

"I'm not blaming you, Arthur," he said, "but I like you, and don't want to see you go wrong, and be a tool in bad boys' hands. I hope you ask God to help you, Arthur?"

Eden looked at him, but said nothing. He had been taught but little, and by example he had been taught *nothing* of the Awful Far-off Friend who is yet so near to every humble spirit, and who even now had sent His angel to save this lamb who knew not of His fold.

"Listen to me, Arthur—ah there I hear the third school-bell, and we must go in—but listen; I'll be your friend; I want to be your friend. I'll try and save you from all this persecution. Will you always trust me?"

Eden's look of gratitude more than repaid him, and Walter added, "And, Arty, you must not give up your prayers. Ask God to help you, and to keep you from going wrong, and to make you brave. Won't you, Arty?"

The little boy's heart was full even to breaking with its weight of happy tears; it was too full to speak. He pressed Walter's hand for one moment, and walked in by his side, without a word.

CHAPTER THIRTEEN. DAUBENY.

La Genie c'est la Patience.—*Buffon*.

I suppose that no days of life are so happy, as those in which some great sorrow has been removed. Certainly Walter's days as his heart grew lighter and lighter with the consciousness that Mr Paton had forgiven him, that all those who once looked on him coldly had come round, that his difficulties were vanishing before steady diligence, and that, young as he was, he was winning for himself a name and a position in the school, were very full of peace. O pleasant days of boyhood! how mercifully they are granted to prepare us, to cheer us, to make us wise for the struggles of future life. To Walter at this time life itself was an exhilarating enjoyment. To get up in the morning bright, cheerful, and refreshed with thoughts

St. Winifred's, or The World of School

Pleasant as roses in the thickets blown.
And pure as dew bathing their crimson leaves;

to get over his lessons easily and successfully, and receive Mr Paton's quiet word of praise; to shake with laughing over the flood of nonsense with which Henderson always deluged every one who sat near him at breakfast-time; to help little Eden in his morning's work, and to see with what intense affection and almost adoration the child looked up to him; to stroll with Kenrick under the pine woods, or have a pleasant chat in Power's pretty little study, or read a book in the luxurious retirement of Mr Percival's room, or, if it were a half-holiday, to join in the skating, hare and hounds, football, or whatever game might be on hand; all these things were to Walter Evson one long unbroken pleasure. At this time he was the brightest, and pleasantest, and happiest of all light-hearted and happy English boys.

The permission to go, whenever he liked, to Mr Percival's room was his most valued privilege. There he could always secure such immunity from disturbance as enabled him to learn his lessons in half the time he would otherwise have been obliged to devote to them; and there too he could always ask the master's assistance when he came to any insuperable difficulty, and always enjoy the society of Henderson and the one or two other boys who were allowed by Mr Percival's kindness to use the same retreat. From the bottom of his form he rapidly rose to the top, and at last was actually placed first. A murmur of pleasure ran through the form on the first Sunday when his name was read out in this honourable position, and it gave Walter nearly as much satisfaction to hear Henderson's name read out *sixth* on the same day; for before Walter came, Henderson was too volatile ever to care where he stood in form, and usually spent his time in school in drawing caricatures of the masters, and writing parodies of the lesson or epigrams on other boys; up till this time Daubeny had always been first in the form, and he deserved the place if any boy did. He was not a clever boy, but nothing could exceed his well-intentioned industry. Like Sir Walter Raleigh he "toiled terribly." It was an almost pathetic sight to see Dubbs set about learning his repetitions; it was a noble sight too. There was a heroism about it which was all the greater from its being unnoticed and unrecorded. Poor Dubbs had no privacy except such as the great schoolroom could afford, and there is not much privacy in a room, however large, which is the common habitation of fifty boys. Nevertheless the undaunted Daubeny would choose out the quietest and loneliest corner of the room, and with elbows on knees and hands over his ears to shut out the chaotic noises which surrounded him, would stay repeating the lines

St. Winifred's, or The World of School

to himself with attention wholly concentrated and absorbed, until, after perhaps an hour's work, he knew enough of them to enable him to finish mastering them the next morning. Next morning he would be up with the earliest dawn, and would again set himself to the task with grand determination, content if at the end of the week he gained the distinguished reward of being head in his form, and could allow himself the keen pleasure of writing home to tell his mother of his success.

When Daubeny had first come to St Winifred's, he had been forced to go through very great persecution. As he sat down to do his work he would be pelted with orange peel, kicked, tilted off the form on which he sat, ridiculed, and sometimes chased out of the room. All this he had endured with admirable patience and good humour; in short, so patiently and good-humouredly that all boys who had in them a spark of sense or honour very soon abandoned this system of torment, and made up for it as far as they could by respect and kindness, which always, however, took more or less the form of banter. It is not to be expected that boys will ever be made to see that steady strenuous industry, even when it fails, is a greater and a better thing than idle cleverness, but those few who were so far in advance of their years as to have some intuition of this fact, felt for the character of Daubeny, a value which gave him an influence of a rare and important kind. For nothing could daunt this young martyr—not even failure itself. If he were too much bullied and annoyed to get up his lesson overnight, he would be up by five in the morning working at it with unremitting assiduity. Very often he *overdid* it, and knew his lesson all the worse in proportion as he had spent upon it too great an amount of time. Without being positively stupid, his intellect was somewhat dull, and as his manner was shy and awkward he had not been quite understood at first, and no master had taken him specially in hand to lighten his burdens. His bitterest trial, therefore, was to fail completely every now and then, and be reproached for it by some master who little knew the hours of weary work which he had devoted to the unsuccessful attempt. This was particularly the case during his first half-year, during which he had been in Mr Robertson's form. It happened that, from the very weariness of brain induced by his working too hard, he had failed in several successive lessons, and Mr Robertson, who was a man of quick temper and stinging speech, had made some very cutting remarks upon him, and sent him moreover to detention—a punishment which caused to his sensitive mind a pain hardly less acute than the master's pungent and undeserved sarcasm. This mishap, joined to his low weekly placing, very nearly filled him with despair, and this day might have turned the scale, and fixed him in the position of a heavy and disheartened boy, but for Power, who had come to St. Winifred's at the same time with Daubeny, and who, although in his unusually rapid progress he had long left Daubeny behind, was then in the same form and the same dormitory with him, and knew how he worked. Power used always to say to his friends that Dubbs was the worthiest, the bravest, the most upright and conscientious boy in all St Winifred's School. Daubeny, on the other hand, had for Power the kind of adoration of the savage for the sun; he was the boy's beau–ideal of a perfect scholar and a perfect being. It was a curious sight to see the two boys together—Power with his fine and thoughtful face beaming with intelligence, Dubbs with large heavy features and awkward gait; Power sitting down with his book and perfectly mastering the lesson in a quarter of an hour, and then turning round to say, with a bright arch look, "Well, Dubbs, I've learnt the lesson; how far are you?"

"Learnt the lesson? O lucky fellow;—I only know one stanza and that not perfectly; let me see—`Nam quid Typhoeus et validus Mimas nam quid'—no; I don't know even that, I see."

"Here, let me hear you."

Whereupon Dubbs would begin again, and flounder hopelessly at the end of the third line, and then Power would continue it all through with him, fix the sense of it in his memory, read it over, suggest little mnemonic dodges and associations of particular words and lines, and not leave him until he knew it by heart, and was ready with gratitude enough to pluck out his right eye and give it to Power, if needed, there and then.

The early failures we have been speaking of took place when Power had been staying out of school with a severe cold, and being in the sick–room had not seen Daubeny at all. He had come out again on the morning when, after Daubeny's failure, Mr Robertson had called him incorrigibly slothful and incapable, and after muttering some more invectives had said something about his being hopeless. As he listened to the master's remarks, although he knew that they only arose from misconception, Power's cheeks flushed up with painful surprise, and his eyes sparkled with indignation for his friend. He wanted Daubeny to tell Mr Robertson how many hours he had spent in being "incorrigibly slothful" over that particular lesson, but this at the time he could not get him to do.

"Besides," said Daubeny, "if he knows me to be quite hopeless,"— and here the poor boy grew scarlet as he recalled the undeserved insult—"it's no disgrace to me to fail."

St. Winifred's, or The World of School

When detention was over, Power sought out his friend, and found him sitting on the top of a little hill by the side of the river alone, and with a most forlornly disconsolate air. Power saw that he had been crying bitterly, but had too much good taste to take any notice of the fact.

"Well, Power, you see what credit I get, and yet you know how I try. I'm a `bad, idle boy,' it seems, and `incorrigibly slothful,' and `hardly fit for the school,' and `I must be put down to a lower form if I don't make more effort;'—oh! I forgot though, you heard it all yourself. So you know my character," he said, with a melancholy smile.

"Never mind, old fellow. You've done your best, and none of us can do more. You know the soldier's epitaph—`Here lies one who tried to do his duty;'—a prince could not have better, and you deserve that if any one ever did."

"I wish I were you, Power," said Daubeny; "you are so clever, you can learn the lessons in no time; every one likes you, and you get no end of credit, while I'm a mere butt, and when I've worked hard it's a case of *kathedeitai onos*, as the lesson-book says."

"Pooh, Dubbs," said Power, kindly putting his arm on his shoulder; "you're just as happy as I am. A fellow with a clear conscience *can't* be in low spirits very long. Don't you remember the pretty verse I read to you the other day, and which made me think of you while I read it—

"`Days that, in spite
Of darkness, by the light
Of a clear mind are day all night'?"

"Don't think I *envy* you, Power—you won't think that, will you?" said Dubbs, with the tears glistening in his eyes.

"No, no, my dear old boy. Such a nature as yours can't envy, I know; I'm sure you're as happy when I succeed as when you succeed yourself. I think I've got the secret of it, Dubbs. You work *too* much; you must take more exercise—play games more—give less time to the work. I'm sure you'll do better then, for half is better than the whole sometimes. And, Dubbs, I may say to you what I wouldn't say to any other boy in the whole school—but I've found it *so* true, and I'm sure you will too, and that is, Bene orasse est bene studuisse."

Dubbs pressed his hand in silence. The hard thoughts which had been gathering were dissipated in a moment, and as he walked back to the school and to new heroic efforts, by Power's side, he felt that he had learnt a secret full of strength. He did better and better. He broke the neck of his difficulties one by one, and had soon surpassed boys who were far more brilliant, but less industrious, than himself. Thus it was that he fought his way up to the position of one of the steadiest and most influential boys among those of his own standing, because all knew him to be sterling in his virtues, unswerving in his rectitude, most humble, and most sincere. During all his school career he was never once overtaken in a serious fault. It may be that he had fewer temptations than boys more gifted and more mercurial; he was never exposed to the singularly powerful trials which compensated for the superiority of others to him in good looks, and popular manners, and quick passions; but yet his blamelessness had something in it very beautiful, and his noble upward struggles were remembered with fond pleasure in after days.

Walter, like all other sensible boys, felt for Daubeny a very sincere admiration and regard. Daubeny's fearless rectitude, on the night when his own indulged temper led him into such suffering, had left a deep impression on his mind, and, since then, Dubbs had always been among the number of his more intimate friends. Hence, when Walter wrested from him the head place, he was half sorry that he should cause the boy to lose his well-merited success, and almost wished that he had come out second, and left Daubeny first. He knew that there was not in his rival's nature a particle of envy, but still he feared that he might suffer some disappointment. But in this he was mistaken; Daubeny was a firm believer in the principle of *La carriere ouverte aux talens*; he was, under the circumstances, quite as happy to be second as to be first; and among the many who congratulated Walter, none did so with a heartier sincerity than this generous and single-minded boy.

People still retain the notion that boyish emulation is the almost certain cause of hatreds and jealousies. Usually, the fact is the very reverse. An *ungenerous* rivalry is most unusual, and those schoolfellows who dispute with a boy the prizes of a form are commonly his most intimate associates and his best friends. Certainly Daubeny liked Walter none the less for his having wrested away from him with so much ease a distinction which had caused himself such strenuous efforts to win.

St. Winifred's, or The World of School

The pleasant excitement of contending for a weekly position made Daubeny work harder than ever. Indeed, the whole form seemed to have received a new stimulus lately. Henderson was astonishing everybody by a fit of diligence, and even Howard Tracy seemed less totally indifferent to his place than usual. So willingly did the boys work, that Mr Paton had not half the number of punishments to set, and perhaps his late misfortune had infused a little more tenderness and consideration into a character always somewhat stern and unbending. But, instead of rising, Daubeny only lost places by his increased work; he was making himself ill with work. At the end of the next week, instead of being first or second, he was only fifth; and when Mr Percival, who always had been his friend rallied him on this descent, he sighed deeply, and complained that he had been suffering lately from headaches, and supposed that they had prevented him from doing so well as usual.

This remark rather alarmed the master, and on the Sunday afternoon he asked the boy to come a walk with him, for the express purpose of endeavouring to persuade him to relax efforts which were obviously being made to the injury of his health.

When they had once fairly reached the meadows by the riverside, Mr Percival said to him:

"You are overdoing it, Daubeny. I can see myself that your mind is in a tense, excited, nervous condition from work; you must lie fallow, my dear boy."

"Oh! I'm very strong, sir," said Daubeny; "I've a cast–iron constitution, as that amusing plague of mine, Henderson, always tells me."

"Never mind, you must really work less. I won't have that getting up at five in the morning. If you don't take care, I shall *forbid* you to be higher than twentieth in your form under heavy penalties, or I shall get Dr Keith to send you home altogether, and not let you go in to the examination."

"Oh no, sir, you really mustn't do that. I assure you that I enjoy work. An illness I had when I was a child hindered and threw me back very much, and you can't think how eager I am to make up for that lost time."

"The time is not lost, my dear Daubeny, if God demanded it in illness for His own good purposes. Be persuaded, my boy; abandon, for the present, all struggle to take a high place until you feel quite well again, and then you shall work as hard as you like. Remember knowledge itself is valueless in comparison with health."

Daubeny felt the master's kind intention; but he could not restrain his unconquerable eagerness to get on. He would have succumbed far sooner, if Walter and Power had not constantly dragged him out with them almost by force, and made him take exercise against his will. But, though he was naturally strong and healthy, he began to look very pale, and his best friends urged him to go home and take a holiday.

Would that he had taken that good and kind advice!

CHAPTER FOURTEEN. APPENFELL.

> To breathe the difficult air
> Of the iced mountain top.—*Manfred*.

> Fetzo auf den Schroffen Zinken
> Hangt sie, auf dem hochsten Grat,
> Wo die Felsen jah versinken,
> Und verschwunden ist der Pfad.—*Schiller*.

It was some weeks before the examination, and the close of the half-year, when one day Walter, full of glee, burst out of the schoolroom at twelve, when the lesson was over, to tell Kenrick an announcement just made to the forms, that the next day was to be a whole holiday.

"Hurrah!" said Kenrick, "what's it for?"

"Oh! Somers has got no end of a scholarship at Cambridge—an awfully swell thing—and Dr Lane gave a holiday directly he got the telegram announcing the news."

"Well done, old Somers!" said Kenrick. "What shall we do?"

"Oh! I've had a scheme for a long time in my head, Ken; I want you to come with me to the top of Appenfell."

"Whew–w–w! but it's a tremendous long walk, and no one goes up in winter."

"Never mind, all the more fun and glory, and we shall have the whole day before us. I've been longing to beat that proud old Appenfell for a long time. I'm certain we can do it."

"But do you mean that we two should go alone?"

"Oh no; we'll ask Flip, to amuse us on the way."

"And may I ask Power?"

"If you like," said Kenrick, who was, I am sorry to say, not a little jealous of the friendship which had sprung up between Power and Walter.

"And would you mind Daubeny joining us?"

"Not at all; and he's clearly overworking himself. It'll do him good. Let me see—you, Power, Flip, Dubbs, and me; that'll be enough, won't it?"

"Well, I should like to ask Eden."

"Eden!" said Kenrick, with the least little touch of contempt in his tone of voice.

"Poor little fellow," said Walter, smiling sadly; "so you too despise him. No wonder he doesn't get on."

"Oh! let him come by all means, if you like," said Kenrick.

"Thanks, Ken—but now I come to think of it, it's too far for him. Never mind; let's go before dinner, and order some sandwiches for to-morrow, and forage generally, at Cole's."

St. Winifred's, or The World of School

Power and Daubeny gladly consented to join the excursion. At tea, Walter asked Henderson if he'd come with them, and he, being just then in a phase of nonsense which made him speak of everything in a manner intended to be Homeric, answered with oracular gravity:

"Him addressed in reply the laughter–loving son of Hender:
Thou askest me, O Evides, like to the immortals,
Whether thee I will accompany, and the much–enduring Dubbs,
And the counsellor Power, and the revered ox–eyed Kenrick,
To the tops of thousand–crested many–fountained Appenfell."

"Grotesque idiot," said Kenrick, laughing; "cease this weak washy everlasting flood of twaddle, and tell us whether you'll come or no."

"Him sternly eyeing, addressed in reply the mighty Henderides,
Heavy with tea, with the eyes of a dog, and the heart of a reindeer:
What word has escaped thee, the barrier of thy teeth?
Contrary to right, not according to right, hast thou spoken."

"For goodness' sake shut up before you've driven us stark raving mad," said Walter, putting his hand over Henderson's lips. "Now, yes or no; will you come?"

"Thee will I accompany," said Henderson, struggling to get clear of Walter, "to many–fountained Appenfell—"

"Hurrah! that'll do. We have got an answer out of you at last; and now go on spouting the whole *Iliad* if you like."

Full of spirits they started after breakfast the next morning, and as they climbed higher and higher up the steep mountainside the keen air exhilarated them, and showed, as through a crystal glass, the exceeding glory of the hills flung on every side around them, and the broad living sparkle of the sea caught here and there in glimpses between the nearer peaks. Walter, Henderson, and Kenrick were in front, while at some distance behind them Power helped on Daubeny, who soon showed signs of fatigue.

St. Winifred's, or The World of School

"Look at that happy fellow Evson," said Daubeny, sighing; "how he is bounding along in front. How active he is."

"You seem out of spirits," said Power kindly; "what's the matter?"

"Oh, nothing. A little tired, that's all."

"You're surely not fretting about having lost the head place."

"Oh no. `Palmam qui meruit ferat.' As Robertson said the other day in his odd, fantastic way of expressing his thoughts—`In the amber of duty you must not always expect to find the curious grub success.'"

"Depend upon it, you'd be higher if you worked less, my dear fellow. Let me persuade you—don't work for examination any more."

"You all mistake me. It's not for the *place* that I work, but because I want to *know*, to *learn*; not to grow up quite stupid and empty-headed as I otherwise should do."

"What a love for work you have, Daubeny."

"Yes, I have now; but do you know, it really wasn't natural to me. As a child, I used to be idle and get on very badly, and it used to vex my poor father, who was then living, very much. Well, one day, not long before he died, I had been very obstinate, and would learn nothing. He didn't say much, but in the afternoon, when we were taking a walk, we passed an old barn, and on the thatched roof was a lot of grass and stonecrop. He plucked a handful, and showed me how rank and useless it was, and then, resting his hand upon my head, he told me that it was the type of an idle, useless man—`grass upon the house-tops, withered before it groweth up, wherewith the mower filleth not his hand, nor he that gathereth the sheaves his bosom.' Somehow the circumstance took hold of my imagination; it was the last scene with my poor father which I vividly remember. I have never been idle since then."

Power mused a little, and then said, "But, dear Dubbs, you'll make your brain heavy by the time examination begins; you won't be able to do yourself justice."

He did not answer; but a weary look, which Power had often observed with anxiety, came over his face.

"I'm afraid I must turn back, Power," he said; "I'm quite tired— done up."

"I've been thinking so, too. Let me turn back with you."

"No, no! I won't spoil your day's excursion. Let me go alone."

"Hi! you fellows," said Power, shouting to the three in front. They were too far in advance to hear him, so he told Daubeny to sit down while he overtook them, and asked if any of them would prefer to turn back.

"Dubbs is too tired to go any farther," he said, when he reached them, breathless with his run. "I don't think he's very well, and so I'll just go back with him."

"Oh no; you really mustn't, *I* will," said each of the other three almost in a breath. Every one of the four was most anxious to get on, and reach the top of Appenfell, which was considered a very great feat among the boys even in summer, as the climb was dangerous and severe; and yet each generously wished to undergo the self-denial of turning back. As their wills were about equally strong, it would have ended in *all* of them accompanying Daubeny, had he not, when they reached him, positively refused to turn on such conditions, and suggested that they should decide it by drawing lots.

Power wrote the names on slips of paper, and Walter drew one at hazard. The lot fell on Henderson, so he at once took Daubeny's arm, relieving his disappointment by turning round, shaking his fist at the top of Appenfell, and saying, "You be hanged! I wish you were rolled out *quite flat* and planted with potatoes!"

"There," said Power, laughing, "I should think that was about the grossest indignity the Genius of Appenfell ever had offered to him; so now you've had your revenge, take care of Dubbs. Good-bye."

"How very kind it is of you to come with me, Flip," said Daubeny; "I don't think I could manage to get home without your help; but I'm quite vexed to drag you back. Good-bye, you fellows."

St. Winifred's, or The World of School

Walter, Power, and Kenrick found that to reach the cairn on the top of Appenfell taxed all their strength. The mountain seemed to heave before them a succession of huge shoulders, and each one that they surmounted showed them only fresh steeps to climb. At last they reached the piled confusion of rocks, painted with every gorgeous and brilliant colour by emerald moss and golden lichen, which marked the approach to the summit; and Walter, who was a long way the first to get to the top, shouted to encourage the other two, and, after resting a few minutes, clambered down to assist their progress. Being accustomed to the hills, he was far less tired than they were, and could give them very efficient help.

At the top they rested for some time, eating their scanty lunch, chatting, and enjoying the matchless splendour of the prospect which stretched in a cloudless expanse before them on every side.

"Power," said Walter in a pause of their talk, "I've long been meaning to ask you a favour."

"It's granted then," said Power, "if *you* ask it, Walter."

"I'm not so sure; it's a very serious favour, and it isn't for myself; moreover, it's very cool."

"The greater it is, the more I shall know that you trust my friendship, Walter; and, if it's cool, it suits the time and place."

"Yet, I bet you that you'll hesitate when I propose it."

"Well, out with it; you make me curious."

"It is that you'd give little Eden the run of your study."

"Little Eden the run of my study! Oh yes, if you wish it," said Power, not likely to object after what he had said, but flushing up a little, involuntarily. It was indeed a great favour to ask. Power's study was a perfect sanctum; he had furnished it with such rare good taste, that, when you entered, your eye was attracted by some pretty print or neat contrivance wherever you looked. It was Power's peculiar pride and pleasure to beautify his little room, and to sit there with any one whom he liked; but to give up his privacy, and let a little scapegrace like Eden have the free run of it, was a proposition which took him by surprise. Yet it was a good deal for Power's own sake that Walter had ventured to ask it. Power's great fault was his over-refinement; the fastidiousness which marred his proper influence, made him unpopular with many boys, and shut him up in a reserved and introspective habit of mind. By a kind of instinct, Walter felt that it would be good to disturb this epicurean indifference to the general interests of the school, and the kind of intellectualism which weakened the character of this attractive and affectionate, yet shy and self-involved boy.

"Ah, I see," said Walter archly; "you're as bad as Kenrick; you Priests and Levites won't touch my poor little wounded traveller."

"But I don't see what I could do for him," said Power; "I shouldn't know what to talk to him about."

"Oh yes, you would; you don't know how his gratitude would pay you for the least interest shown in him. He's been so shamefully bullied, poor little chap, I hardly like to tell you even the things that that big brute Harpour has made him do. He came here bright and neat, and merry and innocent; and now—" He would not finish the sentence, and his voice faltered; but checking himself, he added more calmly, "This, remember, has been done to the poor little fellow *here*, at St Winifred's; and when I remember what I might have been myself by this time, but for— but for one or two friends, my heart quite bleeds for him. Anyhow, I think one ought to do what one can for him. I wish I'd a study, I know, and he shouldn't be the only little fellow who should share it. I've got so much good from being able to learn my own lessons in Percival's room, that I'd give anything to be able to do as much for some one else."

"He shall come, Walter," said Power, "with all my heart. I'll ask him directly we get back to St Winifred's."

"Will you? I thank you. That is good of you; I'm sure you won't be sorry in the long run."

Power and Kenrick were both thinking that this new friend of theirs, though he had been so short a time at St Winifred's, was teaching them some valuable lessons. Neither of them had previously recognised the truth which Walter seemed to feel so strongly, that they were to some extent directly responsible for the opportunities which they lost of helping and strengthening the boys around them. Neither of them had ever done anything worth speaking of to lighten the heavy burden laid on some of the little boys at St Winifred's; and now they heard Walter talking with something like remorse about a child, who had no special claim whatever on his kindness, but whom he felt that he might more efficiently have rescued from evil associates, evil words, evil ways, and all the heart-misery they cannot fail to bring. The sense of a new mission, a neglected duty, dawned upon them both.

They sat for a time silent, and then Kenrick, shaking off his reverie, pointed down the hill and said:

"Do look at those magnificent clouds; how they come surging up the hill in huge curving masses."

"Yes," said Power; "doesn't it look like a grand charge of giant cavalry? Why, Walter, my dear fellow, how frightened you look."

"Well, no," said Walter, "not frightened. But I say, you two, supposing those clouds which have gathered so suddenly don't clear away, do you think that you could find your way down the hill?"

"I don't know; I almost think so," said Kenrick dubiously.

"Ah, Ken, I suspect you haven't had as much experience of mountain mists as I have. We *may* find our way somehow; but—"

"You mean," said Power, with strange calmness, "that there are lots of precipices about, and that shepherds have several times been lost on these hills?"

"Let's hope that the mist will clear away, then," said Walter; "anyhow, let's get on the grass, and off these awkward boulders, before we are surrounded."

"By all means," said Kenrick; "charges of cloud-cavalry are all very well in their way; but—"

St. Winifred's, or The World of School

CHAPTER FIFTEEN. IN THE CLOUDS.

Aenaoi nephelai
arthoomen phanerai droseran physin euageeton
patros ap' Ookeanou baryacheos
ypseeloon areoon koryphas epi.
Aristophanes. The Clouds 275.

The three boys scrambled with all their speed, Walter helping the other two down the vast primeval heap of many-tinted rock- fragments which form the huge summit of Appenfell, and found themselves again on the short slippery grass, hardened with recent frosts, that barely covered the wave-like sweep of the hillside. Meanwhile the vast dense masses of white cloud gathered below them, resting here and there in the hollows of the mountains like gigantic walls and bastions, and leaning against the abrupter face of the precipice in one great unbroken barrier of opaque, immaculate, impenetrable pearl. As you looked upon it the chief impression it gave you was one of immense thickness and crushing weight. It seemed so compressed and impermeable that one could not fancy how even a thunderbolt could shatter it, or the wildest blast of any hurricane dissipate its enormous depth. But as yet it had not enveloped the peaks themselves. On them the sun yet shone, and where the boys stood they were still bathed in the keen yet blue and sunny air, islanded far up above the noiseless billows of surging cloud.

This was not for long. Gradually, almost imperceptibly, the clouds stole upon them—reached out white arms and enfolded them in sudden whirls of thin and smoke-like mist; eddied over their heads and round their feet swathed them at last as in a funeral pall, blotting from their sight every object save wreaths of dank vapour, rendering wholly uncertain the direction in which they were moving, and giving a sense of doubt and danger to every step they took. Kenrick had only told the master who had given them leave of absence from dinner that they meant to go a long walk. He had not mentioned Appenfell, not from any want of straightforwardness, but because they thought that it might sound like a vainglorious attempt, and they did not want to talk about it until they had really accomplished it. But in truth if they had mentioned this as their destination, no wise master would have given them permission to go, unless they promised to be accompanied by a guide; for the ascent of Appenfell, dangerous even in summer to all but those who well knew the features of the mountain, became in winter a perilous and

St. Winifred's, or The World of School

foolhardy attempt. The boys themselves, when they started on their excursion, had no conception of the amount or extent of the risk they ran. Seeing that the morning gave promise of a bright and clear day, they had never thought of taking into account the possibility of mists and storms.

The position in which they now found themselves was enough to make a stout heart quail. By this time they were hopelessly enveloped in palpable clouds, and could not see the largest objects a yard before them. In fact, even to see each other they had to keep closely side by side; for once, when Kenrick had separated from them for a little distance, it was only by the sound of his shouts that they found him again. After this they crept on in perfect silence, each trying to conceal from the other the terror which lay like frost on his own spirits; unsuccessfully, for the tremulous sound which the quick palpitation of their hearts gave to their breathing showed plainly enough that all three of them recognised the frightfulness of their danger.

Appenfell was one of those mountains, not unfrequent, which is on one side abrupt and bounded by a wall of almost fathomless precipice, and on the other descends to the plain in a cataract of billowy undulations. It had one feature which, although peculiar, is by no means unprecedented. At one point, where the huge rock wall towers up from the ghastly depth of a broad ravine, there is a lateral ridge—not unlike the Mickledore of Scawfell Pikes—running right across the valley, and connecting Appenfell with Bardlyn, another hill of much lower elevation, towards which this ridge runs down with a long but gradual slope. This edge was significantly called the Razor, and it was so narrow that it would barely admit the passage of a single person along its summit. It was occasionally passed by a few shepherds, accustomed from earliest childhood to the hills, but no ordinary traveller ever dreamed of braving its real dangers, for, even had the path been broader, the horrible depth of fall on either side was quite sufficient to render dizzy the steadiest head, and if a false step were taken, the result, to an absolute certainty, was frightful death. For so nearly perpendicular were the sides of this curious partition, that the narrow valley below, offering no temptation to any one to visit it, had not, within the memory of man, been trodden by any human foot. To add to the horror inspired by the Razor, a shepherd had recently fallen from it in a summer storm; his body had been abandoned as unrecoverable, and the ravens and wild cats had fed upon him. Something—a dim gleam of uncertain white among the rank grass—was yet visible from one point of the ledge, and the bravest mountaineer shuddered when, looking down the gloomy chasm, he recognised in that glimpse the mortal remains of a fellow-man.

St. Winifred's, or The World of School

"Are you sure that we are on the right path, Walter?" asked Power, trying to speak as cheerfully and indifferently as he could.

"Certain," said Walter, pulling out of his pocket the little brass pocket-compass which had been his invariable companion in his rambles at home, and which he had fortunately brought with him as likely to be useful in the lonely tracts which surrounded St Winifred's. "The bay lies due west from here, and I'm sure of the *general* direction."

"But I think we're keeping too much to the right, Walter," said Kenrick.

"Look here," said Walter, stopping; "the truth is—and we may just as well be ready for it—that we're between two dangers. On the right is Bardlyn rift; on the left we have the sides of Appenfell, and no precipices, but—"

"I know what you're thinking of—the old mines."

"Yes; that's why I've been keeping to the right. I think even in this mist we could hardly go over the rift, for I fancy that we could at least discover when we were getting close to it; but there are three or four old mines we don't know in the least where they lie exactly, and one might stumble over one of the shafts in a minute."

"What in the world shall we do?" said Power, stopping, as he realised the full intensity of peril. "As it is we can't see where we're going, and very soon we shall have darkness as well as mist. Besides it's so frightfully cold, now that we are obliged to go slowly."

"Let's stop and consider what we'd best do," said Kenrick. "Walter, what do *you* say?"

"We can only do one of two things. Either go on, and trust to God's mercy to keep us safe, or sit still here and hope that the mist may clear away."

"That last'll never do," answered Kenrick; "I've seen the mist rest on Appenfell for days and days."

"Besides," said Power, "unless we move on, at all hazards, night will be on us. A December night on Appenfell, without food or extra coverings, and the chance of being kept indefinitely longer—" The sentence ended in a shudder.

St. Winifred's, or The World of School

"Yes; I don't know what we should look like in the morning," said Kenrick. "Let's move on at all events; better that than the chance of being frozen and starved to death."

They moved on again a little way through the clouds with uncertain and hesitating steps, when suddenly Walter cried out in an agitated voice, "Stop! God only knows where we are. I feel by a kind of instinct that we're somewhere near the rift. I don't know what else should make me tremble all over as I am doing; I seem to *hear* the rift somehow. For God's sake stop. Just let's sit down a minute till I try something."

"But it's now nearly four o'clock," said Kenrick in a querulous tone, as he halted and pulled out his watch, holding it close to his face to make out the time. "An hour more and all daylight will be gone, and with it all chance of being saved. Surely we'd better press on. That's *uncertain* danger, but to stop is certain—"

"Certain death," whispered Power.

"Just listen then, one second," said Walter, and, disembedding a huge piece of stone, he rolled it with all his force to their right, listening with senses acutely sharpened by danger and excitement. The stone bounded once, then they heard in their ears a rush, a shuffling of loose stones and sliding earth, the whirring sound of a heavy falling body, and then for several seconds a succession of distant crashes, startling with fright the rebounding mountain echoes, as the bit of rock whirled over the rift and was shattered into fragments by being dashed against the sides of the precipice.

"Good God!" cried Walter, clutching both the boys and dragging them hurriedly backwards, "we are standing at this moment on the very verge of the chasm. It won't do to go on; every step may be death."

A pause of almost unspeakable horror followed his words; after the fall of the rock had revealed to them how frightful was the peril which they had escaped, all three of them for a moment felt paralysed in every limb, and after looking close into each other's faces, blanched white by a deadly fear, Kenrick and Power sat down in an agony of despair.

"Don't give way, you fellows," said Walter, to whom they both seemed to look for help; "our only chance is to keep up our hope and spirits. I think that, after all, we must just stay here till the mist clears up. Don't be frightened, Ken," he said, taking the boy's hand;

"nothing can happen to us but what God intends."

"But the night," whispered Kenrick, who was most overpowered of the three; "fancy a night spent here. Mist and cold, hunger and dark. Oh, this horrible uncertainty and suspense. Oh, for some light," he cried in an agony; "I could almost die if we had but light."

"O God, give us light," murmured Walter, echoing the words, and uttering aloud unconsciously his intense prayer; and then he fell on his knees, and the others, too, hid their faces in their hands as they stood upon the bleak mountainside, and prayed to Him whom they knew to be near them, though they were there alone, and saw nothing save the ground they knelt upon, and the thick clammy fog moving slowly around and above them in aimless and monotonous change. To their excited imagination that fog seemed like a living thing; it seemed as though it were actuated with a cold and deathful determination, and as though it were peopled by a thousand silent spirits, leaning over them and chilling their hearts as they shrouded them in the gigantic foldings of their ghostly robes.

And soon, as though their passionate prayer had been heard, and an angel had been sent to rend the mist, the wind, rushing up from the ravine, tore for itself a narrow passage,—and a gleam of wavering light broke in upon them through the white folds of that deathful curtain, showing them the wall of sunken precipice, and the dark outline of Bardlyn Hill. If this had been a moment in which they could have admired one of Nature's most awfully majestic sights, they would have gazed with enthusiastic joy on the diorama of valley and mountain revealed through this mighty rent in the side of their misty pavilion, filled up by the blue far-off sky; but at this moment of dominant terror they had no room for any other thoughts but how to save their lives from the danger that surrounded them.

"Light," cried Walter, springing up eagerly; "thank God! Perhaps the mist is going to clear away." But the hope was fallacious, for in the direction where their path lay all was still dark, and the chilly mist soon closed again, though not so densely, over the wound which the breeze from the chasm below them had momentarily made.

"Did you see that we are *close to the Razor*?" said Walter, who alone of the three maintained his usual courage, because custom had made him more familiar with the danger of the hills. "Now a thought strikes me, Ken and Power. If you like we'll make an attempt to cross the Razor. The only thing will be not to lose one's footing; one can't *miss* the way at any rate, and when once we get to Bardlyn it's as easy to get down to the road which runs round it to St Winifred's as it is to walk across the school court."

"Cross the Razor?" said Kenrick; "why, none but some few shepherds ever dare to do that."

"True, but what man has done, man can do. I'm certain it's our best chance."

"Not for me;" "Or for me," said the other two.

"Well, look here," said Walter; "it would be very dangerous of course, but while we talk our chance of safety lessens. You two stay here. I'll try the Razor; if I get safe across I shall reach Bardlyn village in no time, and there I could get some men to come and help you over. Do you mind? I won't leave you if you'd rather not."

"Oh, Walter, Walter, don't run the risk," said Power; "it's too awful."

"It's lighter than ever on that side," said Walter; "I'm not a bit afraid. I'm certain we could not get safe down the other way, and we should die of exposure if we spent the night here. Remember, we've only had one or two sandwiches apiece. It's the last chance."

"Oh no, you really shan't, dear Walter. You don't know how terrific the Razor is. I've often heard men say that they wouldn't cross it for a bag of gold," said Power.

"Don't hinder me, Power; I've made up my mind. Good–bye, Power; good–bye, Ken," he said, wringing their hands hard. "If I get safe across the Razor, I shan't be more than an hour and a half at the very latest before I stand here with you again, bringing help. Good–bye; God bless you both. Pray for me, but don't fear."

So saying, Walter tore himself away from them, and with an awful sinking at heart they saw him pass through the spot where the mist was thinnest, and plant a steady step on the commencement of the Razor path.

St. Winifred's, or The World of School

CHAPTER SIXTEEN. ON THE RAZOR.

Nun gar dee pantessin epi xyrou histatai akmees,
Hee mala lygros alethros ... eee bioonai.
Iliad, 10, 173 to 174.

The brave boy knew well that the fate of the others, as well as his own, hung on his coolness and steadiness, and stopping for one moment to see that he would have light enough to make sure of his footing all along the path, he turned round, shouted a few cheery words to his two friends, and stepped boldly on the ledge.

He was accustomed to giddy heights, and his head had never turned as he looked down the cliffs at St Winifred's, or the valleys at home. But his heart began to beat very fast with the painful sense that every step which he accomplished was dangerous, and that the nerve which would readily have borne him through a brief effort, would here have to be sustained for fully twenty minutes, which would be the least possible time in which he could make the transit. The loneliness, too, was frightful; in three minutes he was out of sight of his friends; and to be there without a companion, in the very heart of the mighty mountains, traversing this haunted and terrible path, with not an eye to see him if he should slip and be dashed to atoms on the unconscious rocks;— this thought almost overmastered him, unmanned him, filled him with a weird sense of indescribable horror. He battled against it with all his might, but it came on him like a foul harpy again and again, sickening his whole soul, making his forehead glisten with the damp dews of anticipated death. At last he came to a stunted willow which had twisted its dry roots into the thin soil, and, clinging to the stem of it with both arms, he was forced to stop and close his eyes, and praying for God's help, he summoned together all the faculties of his soul, and buffeted this ghastly intruder away so thoroughly that it did not again return. As a man might shoot a vulture, and look at it lying dead at his feet, so with the arrow of a heartfelt supplication Walter slew the hideous imagination that had been flapping its wings over him; nor did he stir again till he was sure that it had lost its power. And then, opening his eyes, he bore steadily and cautiously on, till all of a sudden, in the fast fading sunlight, something glinted white in the valley beneath his feet. In a moment it flashed upon him that this was the unreached skeleton a thousand feet below, the sight of which imparted a superstitious horror to the Devil's Way, as the peasants called the narrow path along the Razor. Nor was this all; for some rags of the man's dress, torn off by his headlong fall, still fluttered on a stump of blackthorn not thirty feet below. And now, again, the poor boy's heart quailed with an uncontrollable emotion of physical and mental fear. For a moment he tottered, every nerve was loosened, his legs bent under him, and, dropping down on his knees, he clutched the ground with both hands. It was just one of those swift spasms of emotion, on which, in moments of peril, the crisis usually depends. Had Walter's will been weak, or his conscience a guilty one, or his strength feeble, or his body unstrung by ill-health, he would have succumbed to the sudden terror, and, fainting first, would the next instant have rolled over the edge to sudden and inevitable death.

All these results were written before him as with fire, as he shut his eyes and clung with tenacious grasp to the earth. But happily his mind was strong, his conscience stainless, his powers vigorous, his body in pure health, and in a few moments, which seemed to him an age, he had recovered his presence of mind by one of those noble efforts which the will is ever ready to make for those who train it right. Before he opened his eyes he had braced himself into a thorough strength, and once more commending himself to God, he rose firm and cool to continue his journey, averting his glance from the spectacle of death which gleamed below.

He found that his best plan was to fix his eyes rigidly on the path, and not suffer them to swerve for a moment to either side. Whenever he did so, the wavering sensation came over him again, but so long as he trod carefully and never let his eyes wander off the place of his footsteps, he found that he got along securely and even swiftly. He had only one more difficulty with which to contend. In one place the sort of path which the Razor presented was broken and crumbled away, and here Walter's heart again sank despairingly within him, as his attention was suddenly arrested by the additional and unexpected peril. But to turn back was now out of the question, and as it seemed impossible to walk for these few feet, he again knelt down, and crawled steadily along on hands and knees, about the length of two strides, until the path was hard and firm enough for him to proceed as before. The end was now accomplished; in five minutes more he sprang on the broad firm side of Bardlyn Hill, and shouting aloud to relieve his spirits from their tumult of joy and thankfulness, he raced down Bardlyn, gained very quickly the mountain road, and ran at the top of his speed till, just as the sun was setting, he reached the group of cottages, which took their name from the hill on which they stood.

Knocking at the first cottage, he inquired for some guide or shepherd who was thoroughly acquainted with all the mountain paths, and was directed to the house of a man named Giles, who had been occupied for years among the neighbouring sheep-walks.

Giles listened to his story with open eyes. "Thee bi'st coom over t' Razor along Devil's Way," said he in amazement; "then thee bi'st just the plookiest young chap I've seen for many a day."

"We must get back over it, too, to reach them," said Walter.

"Oh ay; *I* be'ant afeared of t' Razor; I've crossed him many a time, and I'll take a bit rope over and help they other chaps. We'll take a lantern, too. Don't you be afeared, sir, we'll get 'em all right," he said, observing how anxious and excited Walter seemed to be.

"Come, then," said Walter, "quick, quick. I promised to come back to them at once. You shall be well paid for your trouble."

"Tut, tut," said the man, "the pay's naught. Why I'd come if it were only a dumb sheep in danger, let alone a brace of lads like you."

They set off with a lantern, a rope, and some food, and Giles was delighted at the quick and elastic step of the young mountaineer. The lantern they soon extinguished. It was not needed; for though the sun had now set, a glorious full moon had begun to pour her broad flood of silver radiance over the gloomy hills by the time they had reached Bardlyn rift.

"There ain't no call for *you* to cross again, sir," said the man; "I'll just go over by myself, and look after the young gentlemen."

"Oh, let me come, I must come," said Walter; "the mist's quite off it now, so that it's just as easy under this moonlight as when I came; and, besides, if you take a coil of the rope in your hand I'll take hold of the other end."

"Well, you're the right sort, and no mistake," said the man. "God bless you for a brave young heart. And, truth to tell, I'll be very glad to have ye with me, for they do say as how poor old Waul's ghost haunts about here, and it 'ud be fearsome at night. I know that there's One as keeps them as has a good conscience, but yet I'll be glad to have ye all the same."

St. Winifred's, or The World of School

The moonlight flung on every side the mysterious and gigantic shadows of rocks and hills, seeming to glimmer with a ghastly hue as it fell and struggled into the black depths of the untrodden rift; but habit made the Devil's Way seem nothing to the mountain shepherd, and he protected Walter, (who twined round his wrist one end of the rope), from the danger of stumbling, as effectually as Walter protected him from all ghostly fears. When they reached the broken piece, the only difference he made was to walk with great caution, and plant his feet deeply into the earth, bidding Walter follow in the traces he made, and supporting him firmly with his hand. They got across in much less time than Walter had occupied in his first passage, and as they reached Appenfell they saw the two boys standing dimly on the verge of the moonlit mist, while all below them the rest of Appenfell was still wrapt, as in some great cerecloth, by the snowy folds of seething cloud.

"Good heavens! but who are those?" said Walter, pointing to two shadowy and gigantic figures which also faced them. "Oh, *who* are those?" he asked wildly, and in such alarm that if the shepherd had not seized him firmly he must have fallen.

"There, there—don't be frighted," said Giles; "those be'ant no ghosts, but they be just our own shadows on the mist. It's a queer thing, but I've seen it often and often on these hills, and some scholars have told me as how that kind of thing be'ant uncommon on mountains."

"What a goose I was to be so horribly frightened," said Walter; "but I didn't know that there were any spectres of that sort on Appenfell. All right, Giles; go on."

Till Walter and the shepherd had taken their last step from the Devil's Way on to the side of Appenfell, the boys stood watching them in intense silence; but no sooner were they safe, than Power and Kenrick ran up to Walter, poured out their eager thanks, and pressed his hands in all the fervour of affectionate gratitude. They felt that his courage and readiness had, at the risk of his own life, saved them from such a danger as they had never in their lives experienced before. Already they were suffering with hunger and shuddering with the December air, their limbs felt quite benumbed, their teeth were chattering lugubriously, and their faces were blue and pinched with cold. They eagerly devoured the brown bread and potato-cake which the man had brought, and let him and Walter chafe a little life into their shivering bodies. By this time fear was sufficiently removed to enable them to feel some sort of appreciation of the wild beauty of the scene, as the moonlight pierced on their left the flitting scuds of restless mist, and on their right fell softly over Bardlyn Hill, making a weird contrast between the tender brightness of the places where it fell, and the pitchy gloom that hid the depths of the rift, and brooded in those undefined hollows over which the precipices leaned.

To return down Appenfell was, (the experienced shepherd informed them), quite hopeless. In such a mist as that, which might last for an indefinite time, even *he* would be totally unable to find his way. But now that they were warm and satisfied with food, and confident of safety, they even enjoyed the feeling of adventure when Giles tied them together for their return across the Devil's Way. First he tied the rope round his own waist, then round Power's and Kenrick's, and finally, as there was not enough left to go round Walter's waist, he tied the end round his right arm. Thus fastened, all danger was tenfold diminished, if not wholly removed, and the two unaccustomed boys felt a happy reliance on the nerve and experience of Giles and Walter, who were in front and rear. It was a scene which they never forgot, as the four went step by step through the moonlight along the horrible ledge, safe only in each other's help, and awestruck at their position, not daring to glance aside or to watch the colossal grandeur of their own shadows as they were flung here and there against some protruding rock. Power was next to Walter, and when they reached the spot beneath which the whiteness glinted and the rags fluttered in the wind, Walter, in spite of himself, could not help glancing down, and whispering, "Look," in a voice of awe. Power unhappily did look, and as all the boys at St Winifred's were familiar with the story of the shepherd's fate, and had even known the man himself, Power at once was seized with the same nervous horror which had agitated Walter—grew dizzy, stumbled, and slipped down, jerking Kenrick to his knees by the sudden strain of the rope. Happily the rope checked Power's fall, and Kenrick's scream of horror startled Giles, who, without losing his presence of mind, instantly seized Kenrick with an arm that seemed as strong and inflexible as if it had been hammered out of iron, while at the same moment Walter, conscious of his rashness, clutched hold of Power's hand and raised him up. No word was spoken, but after this the boys kept close to their guides, who were ready to grasp them tight at the first indication of an uneven footstep, and who almost lifted them bodily over every more difficult or slippery part. The time seemed very long to them, but at last they had all reached Bardlyn Hill in safety, and placed the last step they ever meant to place on the narrow and dizzy passage of the Razor's edge.

And stopping there they looked back at the dangers they had passed—at Appenfell piled up to heaven with white clouds; at Bardlyn rift looming in black abysses beneath them; at the thin broken line of the Devil's Way. They looked

> as a man with difficult short breath,
> Forespent with toiling, 'scaped from sea to shore,
> Turns to the perilous wide waste, and stands
> At gaze.

They stood silent till Power said, in ejaculations of intense emphasis, "Thank God!"—and then pointing downwards with a shudder. "Oh, Walter!" and then once again, "Thank God!"—which Walter and Kenrick echoed; and then they passed on without another word. But those two words, so uttered, were enough.

The man, who was more than repaid by the sense that he had rendered them a most important aid, and who had been greatly fascinated by their manly bearing, entirely refused to take any money in payment for what he had done.

"Nay, nay," he said; "we poor folks are proud too, and I won't have none of your money, young gentlemen. But let me tell you that you've had a very narrow escape of your lives out there, and I don't doubt you'll thank the good God for it with all your hearts this night; and if you'll just say a prayer for old Giles too, he'll vally it more than all your moneys. So now, good-night to you, young gentlemen, for you know your way now easy enough. And if ever you come this way again, maybe you'll come in and have a chat for remembrance' sake."

"Thank you, Giles, that we will," said the boys.

"And since you won't take any money, you'll let me give you this," said Walter. "You *must* let me give you this; it's not worth much, but it'll show you that Walter Evson didn't forget the good turn you did us." And he forced on the old shepherd's acceptance a handsome knife, with several strong blades, which he happened to have in his pocket; while Power and Kenrick, after a rapid whispered consultation, promised to bring him in a few days a first-rate plaid to serve him as a slight reminder of their gratitude for his ready kindness. Then they all shook hands with many thanks, and the three boys, eager to find sympathy in their perils and deliverance, hastened to St Winifred's, which they reached at eight o'clock, just when their absence was beginning to cause the most serious anxiety.

St. Winifred's, or The World of School

They arrived at the arched gateway as the boys were pouring out of evening chapel, and as every one was doubtfully wondering what had become of them, and whether they had encountered any serious mishap. When the Famulus admitted them, the fellows thronged round them in crowds, pouring into their ears a succession of eager questions. The tale of Walter's daring act flew like wildfire through the school, and if any one still retained against him a particle of ill–feeling, or looked on his character with suspicion, it was this evening replaced by the conviction that there was no more noble or gallant boy than Walter among them, and that if any equalled him in merit, it was one of those whose intimate friendship for him had on this day been deepened by the grateful knowledge that to him, in all human probability, they owed their preservation from an imminent and overpowering peril. Even Somers, in honour of whose academic laurel the whole holiday had been given, and who that evening returned from Cambridge, was less of a hero than either of the three who had thus climbed the peak of Appenfell and braved so serious an adventure; far less crowned with schoolboy admiration than the young boy who had thrice crossed and recrossed the Devil's Way, and who had crossed it first unaided and with full knowledge of its horrors, while the light of winter evening was dying away, and the hills around him reeked like a witch's caldron with wintry mists.

Walter, grateful as he was for each pat on the back and warm pressure of the hand, which told him how thoroughly and joyously his doings were appreciated, was not intoxicated by the enthusiasm of this boyish ovation. It was indeed a proud thing to stand among those four hundred schoolfellows, the observed of all observers, greeted on every side by happy, smiling, admiring faces, with every one pressing forward to give him a friendly grasp, every one anxious to claim or to form his acquaintance, and many addressing him with the kindliest greetings whose very faces he hardly knew;—but the deeper and more silent gratitude of his chosen friends, and the manly sense of something bravely and rightly done, was more to him than this. Yet this was something very sweet. When the admiration of boys is fairly kindled it is the brightest, the most genial, the most generously hearty in the world. Few succeed in winning it; but he who has been a hero to others in manhood only, has had but a partial taste of the rich triumph experienced by him who has had the happiness in boyhood of being a hero among boys.

Here let me say how one or two people noticed Walter when first they saw him that evening.

St. Winifred's, or The World of School

While numbers of boys were shaking hands with him, whom he hardly saw or recognised in the crowd by the mingled moonlight and lamplight that streamed over the court where they stood, Walter felt one squeeze that he recognised and valued. Looking among the numerous faces, he saw that it was Henderson who was greeting him without a word. No nonsense or joke this time, and Walter noticed that the boy's lips were trembling with emotion, and that there was a light as of tears in his laughter-loving eyes.

"Ah, Henderson!" said Walter, in that tone of real regard and pleasure which is the truest sign and pledge of friendship, and which no art can counterfeit, "I'm so glad to see you again: how did you and Dubbs get on?"

"All right, Walter," said Henderson; "but he's gone to bed with a bad headache. Come in and see him before you go to bed. I know he'd like to say good-night."

"Well done, Evson—well done indeed," was the remark of Somers, as he noticed Walter for the first time since the scene of the Private Room.

"Excellent, my gallant little Walter," said Mr Percival, as he passed by. Mr Paton, who was with him, *said* nothing, but Walter knew all that he would have expressed when he caught his quiet approving smile, and felt his hand rest for a moment, as with the touch of Christian blessing, on his head.

It is happiness at all times to be loved, and to deserve the love; but happiest of all to enjoy it after sorrow and sin. But we must escape from this ordeal of prosperity, of flattering words and intoxicating fumes of praise, as soon as we can. Who would not soon be enervated in that tropical and luxurious atmosphere? If it be dangerous, happily it is not often that he or we shall breathe its heavy sweetness, but far other are the dangers we shall mostly undergo.

"Dr Lane wants you," said the Famulus, just in time to save the tired boys from their remorseless questioners. They went at once to the head-master's house. He received them with a stately yet sincere kindness; questioned them on the occurrences of the day; warned them for the future against excursions so liable to accident as the winter ascent of Appenfell; and then spoke a few friendly words to each of them. For both Kenrick and Power he had a strong personal regard, and for the latter especially a feeling closely akin to friendship and affection. After they were gone he kept Walter behind, and said, "I am indeed most sincerely rejoiced, Evson, to meet you again under circumstances so widely different, from those in which I saw you last. I have heard for some time past how greatly you have improved, and how admirably you are now doing. I am glad to have the opportunity of assuring you myself how entirely you have succeeded in winning back my approbation and esteem." Walter attended with a glistening eye, and the master shook hands with him as he bowed and silently withdrew.

"Tea has been ordered for you in Master Power's study," said the footman, as they left the master's house.

CHAPTER SEVENTEEN. THE GOOD RESOLVE.

Am I my brother's keeper?—Genesis 3, 10.

"Let's come and see Dubbs before tea." said Walter, on rejoining the other two; "Henderson told me he was ill in bed, poor fellow."

They went at once to the cottage, detached from the rest of the school buildings, to which all invalids were removed, and they were allowed to go to Daubeny's room; but although he was expecting their visit he had fallen asleep. They noticed a worn and weary expression upon his countenance, but it was pleasant to look at him; for although he was a very ordinary-looking boy, with somewhat heavy features, yet whatever beauty can be infused into any face by honesty of purpose and innocence of heart, was to be found in his; and you could not speak to Daubeny for five minutes without being attracted by the sense that you were talking to one whose character was singularly free from falsehood or vanity, and singularly unstained by evil thoughts.

"There lies one of the best and worthiest fellows in the school," whispered Power, as he raised the candle to look at him.

Low as he had spoken, the sound awoke the sleeper. He opened his eyes dreamily at first, but with full recognition afterwards, and said, "Oh, you fellows, I'm so delighted to see you; when I saw Henderson last, he told me that you hadn't come back, and that people were beginning to fear some accident; and I suppose that's the reason why I've been dreaming so uneasily, and fancying that I saw you tumbling down the rift, and all kinds of things."

"Well, we were very near it, Dubbs; but thanks to Walter, we escaped all right," said Power.

Daubeny looked up inquiringly. "We must tell you all about it to-morrow," said Power. "How are you feeling?"

"Oh, I don't know; not very well; but it's no matter; I dare say I shall be all right soon."

"Hush, you young gentlemen," said the nurse; "this'll never do; you oughtn't to have awoke Master Daubeny just as he was sleeping so nice."

"Very sorry, nurse; good-night, Dubbs; hope you'll be all right to-morrow," said they, and then adjourned to Power's study.

The gas was lighted in the pretty little room, and the matron, regarding them as heroes, had sent them a very tempting tea. They ate it almost in silence, for they were quite tired out. It seemed an age since they had started in the morning with Henderson and Daubeny. Directly tea was finished, Kenrick, exhausted with fatigue and excitement, fell asleep in his chair, with his head thrown back and his lips parted.

"There, I think that's a sign that we ought to be going to bed," said Walter, laughing as he pointed at him.

"Oh no," said Power, "not yet; it's so jolly sitting here; don't wake him, but come and draw your chair next to mine by the fire and have a chat."

Walter obeyed the invitation, and for a few minutes they both sat gazing into the fire, reading faces in the embers, and pursuing their own thoughts. Each of them was happy in the other's presence; and Walter, though more than a year Power's junior, and far below him in the school, was delighted with the sense of fully possessing, in the friendship of this most promising and gifted boy, a treasure which any one in the world might well have envied him.

St. Winifred's, or The World of School

"It's been a strange day, hasn't it, Walter?" said Power at last, laying his hand on Walter's, and looking at him. "I shall never forget it; you have thrown a new light on one's time here."

"Have I, Power? How? I didn't know it."

"Why, on the top of Appenfell there, you opened my eyes to the fact that I've been living here a very selfish life. I know that I get the credit of being very conceited and exclusive, and all that sort of thing; but being naturally shy, I thought it better to keep rather aloof from all but the very few towards whom I felt at all drawn. I see now," he said sadly, "that at the bottom this was mainly selfishness. Why, Walter, all the time I've been here, I haven't done as much for any single boy as you, a new fellow, have done for little Eden this one half-year. But there's time to do better yet; and by God's help I'll try. I'll give Eden the run of my study to-morrow; and as there's plenty of room, I'll look out for some other little chap who requires a refuge for the destitute."

"Thank you, for Eden's sake," said Walter; "I'm sure you'll soon begin to like him, if he gets at home with you."

"But that's the worst of it," continued Power; "so few ever do get at home with me. I suppose my manner's awkward—or something; but I'd give anything to make fellows friendly in five minutes as you do. How do you manage it?"

"I really don't know; I never think about my own manner, or anything else. I suppose if one feels the least interest in any fellow, that he will probably feel some interest in me; and so, somehow, I'm on the best terms with all I care to know."

"Well, Ken and I had a long talk after you left us to cross the Devil's Way; and I hope that the memory of that may make us three friends firm and fast, tender and true, as long as we live. We were in a horrible fright about you; and I suppose that, joined to our own danger, gave a solemn cast to our conversation; but we agreed that if we three, as friends, were united in the silent resolution to help others, and especially new fellows and young, as much as ever we can, we might do a great deal. Tell me, Walter, didn't you find it a very hard thing when you first came to keep right among all sorts of temptations?"

St. Winifred's, or The World of School

"Yes, I did, Power, very hard; and I confess, too, that I sometimes wondered that not one boy, though there are, as I see now, lots of thoroughly good and right fellows here, ever said one word, or did one thing to help me."

"It's all wrong, all wrong," said Power; "but it was you first who made me see it. Walter, I shall pray to-night that God, who has kept us safe, may teach and help us here to live less for ourselves. Who knows what we might not do for the school?"

They both sat for a short time in thoughtful silence. Boys do not often talk openly together about prayer or religion, though perhaps they do so even more than men do in common life. It is right and well that it should be so; it would be unnatural and certainly harmful were it otherwise. And these boys would probably never have talked to each other thus, if a common danger had not broken down completely the barriers of conventional reserve. Never again from this day did they allude to this sacred resolution; but they acted up to it, or strove to do so, not indeed unwaveringly, yet with manful courage, in the strength of that pure, strong, beautiful unity of heart and purpose which this day had cemented between them for the rest of their school life.

"But you seem to aim higher than I do, Power," said Walter; "I certainly found lots of wickedness going on here, but I never hoped to change that. All I hoped to do was to save one or two fellows from being cruelly bullied and spoiled. We can't alter the wrong tone which nearly all the fellows have on some matters."

"Yet," said Power, "there was once a man, a single man, in a great corrupted host, who stood between the living and the dead, and the plague was stayed."

"Then rose up Phinees and prayed, and so the plague ceased," whispered Walter to himself.

All further conversation was broken by Kenrick, who at this moment awoke with a great yawn, and looking at his watch, declared that they ought to have been in bed long ago.

"Good-night, Ken; I hope we shall sleep as sound as you," said Power.

"Walter here will dream of skeletons and moonlit precipices, I bet," said Kenrick.

"Not I, Ken; I'm far too tired. Good-night, both."

Sleepy as they were, *two* of those boys did not fall asleep that night till they had poured out with all the passion of full hearts, words of earnest supplication for the future, of trembling gratitude for the past. Two of them;—for Kenrick, with all the fine points of his character, was entirely destitute of any sense of religion, and had in many points the standard of a schoolboy rather than that of a Christian.

When Walter reached his room, the rest were asleep, but not Eden. He sat up in his bed directly Walter entered, and his eyes were sparkling with animation and pleasure.

"Oh, Walter," he said, "I couldn't go to sleep for joy. Every one's praising you to the skies. I am so proud of you, and it is so very good of you to be friends with me."

"Tush, Arty," said Walter, smiling, "one would think I'd done something great to hear you talk, whereas really it was nothing out of the way. I meant to have taken you with us, but I thought it would be too far for you."

"Taking me with you, and Kenrick, and Power!" said Eden, opening his large eyes; "how kind of you, Walter! but only fancy Power or Kenrick walking with me!"

"Why not, Arty? Power's going to ask you to-morrow to sit in his study, and learn your lessons there whenever you like."

"Power ask *me*!"

"You! Why not?"

"Why, he's *such* a swell."

"Well, then, you must try and be a swell too."

"No, no, Walter; I'm doing ten times as well as I did, but I shall never be a swell like Power," said the child simply. "And I know it's all your doing, not his. Oh, how shall I ever learn to thank and pay you for all you do for me?"

"By being a good and brave little boy, Arty. Good-night, and God bless you."

"Good-night, Walter."

CHAPTER EIGHTEEN. THE MARTYR-STUDENT.

> Impositique rogis juvenes ante ora parentum.—*Georgic 4,
> 1, 71.*

The days that followed, as the boys resumed the regular routine of school-work, passed by very rapidly and pleasantly—rapidly, because the long-expected Christmas holidays were approaching; pleasantly, because the boys were thoroughly occupied in working up the subjects for the final examination. For Walter especially, those days were lighted up with the warm glow of popularity and success. He was aiming with boyish eagerness to win one more laurel by gaining the first place in his form, and whenever he was not taking exercise, either in some school-game or by a ramble along his favourite cliffs and sands, he was generally to be found hard at work in Mr Percival's rooms, learning the voluntary repetitions, or going over the trial subjects with Henderson, who had now quite passed the boundary line which separated the idle from the industrious boys.

One morning Henderson came in chuckling and laughing to himself, "So Power's taking a leaf out of your book, Walter. I declare he's becoming a regular sociable grosbeak."

"Sociable grosbeak? what *do* you mean?"

"Oh, don't you know that I'm writing a drama called the `Sociable Grosbeaks,' in which you and Ken and I are introduced; I didn't mean to introduce Power, he wasn't gregarious enough; but I *shall* now, and he shall prologise."

"But why is he more sociable now?"

"Why, he's actually let one of the—oh, I forgot, I mustn't call names—well, he's given Eden the run of his study."

"Oh yes; I knew that," said Walter, smiling. "At first, it was the funniest thing to see them together, they were both so shy; but after a day or two they were quite friends, and now you may find Eden perched any day in Power's window-seat, grinding away at his Greek verbs, and as happy as a king. Power helps him in his work, too. It'll be the making of the little fellow. Already he's coming out strong in form."

"Hurrah for the grosbeaks," said Henderson. "I *did* mean to chaff Power about it, but I won't, for it really is very kind of him."

"Yes; and so it is of Percival to let us sit here; but I wish that dear old Dubbs could be doing trial-work here with us."

"He's very ill," said Henderson, looking serious; "*very* ill, I'm afraid. I saw him to-day for a minute, but he seemed too weak to talk."

"Is he? poor fellow! I knew that he was staying out, but I'd no notion that it was anything dangerous."

"I don't know about *dangerous*, but he's quite ill. Poor Daubeny; you know how very, very patient and good he is, yet even he can't help being sad at falling ill just now. You know he was to have been confirmed to-morrow week, and he's afraid that now he won't be well enough, and will have to put it off."

"Yes; he's mentioned his confirmation to me several times. Lots of fellows are going to be confirmed this time—about a hundred, I believe—but I don't suppose one of them thinks of it so solemnly as dear old Dubbs—unless, indeed, it's Power, who also is to be confirmed."

The confirmation was to take place on a Sunday, and the candidates had long been engaged in a course of preparation. The intellectual preparation was carefully undertaken by Dr Lane and the tutors of the boys; but this answer of the lips was of comparatively little value, except in so far as it tended to guide, and solemnise, and concentrate the preparation of the heart. In too many this approaching responsibility produced no visible effect in the tenor of outward life—they talked and thought as lightly as before, and did not elevate the low standard of schoolboy morality; but there were *some* hearts in which the dreary and formless chaos of passion and neglect then first felt the divine stirring of the brooding wings, and some spiritual temples were from that time filled more brightly than before with the Shechinah of the Presence, and bore, as in golden letters on a new entablature, the inscription, "Holiness to the Lord."

To this confirmation some of the best boys, like Power and Daubeny, were looking forward, not with any exaggerated or romantic sentimentality, but with a deep humility, a manly exultation, an earnest hope. They were ready and even anxious to confirm their baptismal vow, and to be confirmed in the sacred strength which should enable them for the future more unswervingly to fulfil it. Of these young hearts the grace of God took early hold, and in them reason and religion ran together like warp and woof to frame the wed of a sweet and exemplary life. Bound by the most solemn and public recognition of, and adhesion to, their Christian duty, it would be easier for them henceforth to confess Christ before men—easier to do justice, and to love mercy, and to walk humbly with their God.

"Do you think it would be possible to see Dubbs? I should so like to see him," said Walter.

"Let's ask Percival, he's in the next room; and if Dubbs is well enough I know he'd give anything to see you."

"Please, sir," said Walter, after knocking for admission at the door of the inner room, "do you think that Henderson and I might go to the cottage and see Daubeny?"

"I don't know, Walter. But I want very much to see him myself, if Dr Keith will let me, so I'll come with you and inquire."

Mr Percival walked with the two boys to the cottage, and, after an injunction not to stay too long, they were admitted to the sick boy's bedside. At first, in the darkened room, they saw nothing; but Daubeny's voice—weak and low, but very cheerful— at once greeted them.

"Oh, thank you, sir, for coming to see me. Hallo! Walter, and Flip too; I'm so glad to see you—you in a sick-room again, Flip!"

"We would have come before if we had known that we might see you," said the master. "How are you feeling, my dear boy?"

St. Winifred's, or The World of School

"Not very well, sir; my head aches sadly sometimes, and I get so confused."

"Ah, Daubeny, it's the overwork. Didn't I entreat you, my child, to slacken the bent bow a little? you'll be wiser in future, will you not?"

"In future—oh yes, sir; if ever I get well I'm afraid," he said, with a faint smile, "that you'll find me stupider than ever."

"Stupid, my boy; none of us ever thought you that. It is not the stupid boys that get head removes as you have done the last term or two. I should very much enjoy a talk with you, Daubeny, but I mustn't stay now, the doctor says, so I'll leave these two fellows with you, and give them ten minutes—no longer—to tell you all the school news."

"In future wiser—in future," repeated Daubeny in a low voice to himself once or twice; "ah, yes, too late now. I don't think he knows how ill I am, Walter. My mother's been sent for; I expect her this evening. I shall at least live to see her again."

"Oh, don't," said Henderson, whose quick and sensitive nature was easily excited; "don't talk like that, Daubeny, we can't spare you; you must stay for our sake."

"Dear old fellow," said Daubeny, "you'll have nobody left to chaff; but you can spare me easily enough;" and he laid his fevered hand kindly on Henderson's, who immediately turned his head and brushed away a tear. "Oh, don't cry," he added in a pained tone of voice, "I never meant to make you cry. I'm quite happy, Flip."

"Oh, Daubeny! we can't get on without you!" said Henderson.

"Daubeny! I hardly know the name," said the sick boy, smiling; "no, Flip, let it be Dubbs as of old—a nice heavy name to suit its owner; and you gave it me, you know, so it's your property, Flip, and I hardly know myself by any other now."

"Oh, Dubbs, I've plagued you so," said Henderson, sobbing as if his heart would break; "I've never done anything but tease you, and laugh at you, and you've always been so good and so patient to me. Do forgive me."

St. Winifred's, or The World of School

"Pooh!" said Daubeny, trying to rally him. "Listen to him, Walter; who'd think that Flip was talking? Teased me, Flip?" he continued, as Henderson still sobbed at intervals, "not you! I always enjoyed your chaff, and I knew that you liked me at heart. You've all been very kind to me. Walter, I'm so glad I got to know you before! It's so pleasant to see you here. Give me your hand; no, Flip, let me keep yours too; it's getting *dark*. I like to have you here. I feel so happy. I wish Power and Ken would come too, that I might see all my friends."

"Good−night, Daubeny; I can't stay, I mustn't stay," said Henderson; and, pressing his friend's hand, he hurried out of the room to indulge in a burst of grief which he could not contain; for, under his trifling and nonsensical manner, Henderson had a very warm and susceptible and feeling heart, and though he had always made Daubeny a subject of ridicule, he never did it with a particle of ill−nature, and felt for him—dissimilar as their characters were—a most fervent and deep regard.

"Look after him when I am gone, Walter," said Daubeny sadly, when he had left the room. "He is a dear good fellow, but so easily led. Poor Flip; he's immensely changed for the better since you came, Walter."

"I have been very fond of him all along," said Walter; "he is so full of laughter and fun, and he's very good with it all. But, Dubbs, you are too desponding; we shall have you here yet for many pleasant days."

"I don't know; perhaps so, if God wills. I am very young. I should like to stay a little longer in the sunshine. Walter, I should like to stay with *you*. I love you more, I think, than any one except Power;" and as he spoke, a quiet tear rolled slowly down Daubeny's face.

Walter only pressed his hand. "You can't think how I pitied you, Walter, in that accident about Paton's manuscript. When all the fellows were cutting you, and abusing you, my heart used to bleed for you; you used to go about looking so miserable, so much as if all your chances of life were over. I'm afraid I did very little for you then, but I *would* have done anything. I felt as if I could have given you my right hand."

"But, Dubbs, you were the first who spoke to me after that happened, the first who wasn't ashamed to walk with me. You can't think how grateful I felt to you for it; it rolled a cold weight from me. It was like stretching a saving hand to one who was drowning; for every one knew how good a fellow *you* were, and your countenance was worth everything to me just then."

"You really felt so?" said Daubeny, brightening tip, while a faint flush rested for a moment on his pale face. "Oh, Walter, it makes me happy to hear you say so." There was a silence, and, with Walter's hand still in his, he fell into a sweet sleep, with a smile upon his face. When he was quite asleep, Walter gently removed his hand, smoothed his pillow, looked affectionately at him for a moment, and stole silently from the room.

"How did you leave him?" asked Henderson eagerly, when Walter rejoined him in Mr Percival's room.

"Sleeping soundly. I hope it will do him good. I did not know how much you cared for him, Flip."

"That's because I always made him a butt," said Henderson remorsefully; "but I didn't really think he minded it, or I wouldn't have done so. I hardly knew myself that I liked him so. It was a confounded shame of me to worry him as I was always doing. Conceited donkey that I was, I was always trying to make him seem stupid; yet all the while I could have stood by him cap in hand. Oh, Walter, I hope he is not going to die!"

"Oh no, I hope not; and don't be miserable at the thought of teasing him, Flip; it was all in fun, and he was never wounded by any word of yours. Remember how he used to tell you that he was all the time laughing at you, not you at him. Come a turn on the shore, and let's take Power or Ken with us."

"Sociable grosbeaks again," said Henderson, laughing in the midst of his sorrow.

"Yes," said Walter; "never mind. There are but few birds of the sort after all."

They found Eden with his feet up, and his hands round his knees, on the window-seat, perfectly at his ease, and chattering to Power like a young jackdaw. A thrill of pleasure passed through Walter's heart, as a glance showed him how well his proposal had succeeded. Power evidently had had no reason to repent of his kindness, and Eden looked more like the bright and happy child which he had once been, than ever was the case since he had come to St Winifred's. He was now clean and neat in dress, and the shadows of fear and guilt which had begun to darken his young face were chased away.

Power readily joined them in their stroll along the shore, and listened with affectionate sympathy to their account of Daubeny.

"What is it that has made him ill?" he asked.

"There's no doubt about that," answered Walter; "it's overwork which has brought on a tendency to brain-fever."

"I was afraid so, Walter;" and then Power repeated half to himself the fine lines of Byron on Kirke White.

> "So the struck eagle stretched upon the plain,
> No more through rolling clouds to soar again,
> Viewed his own feather on the fatal dart,
> And winged the barb that quivered in his heart;
> Keen were his pangs, but keener far to feel,
> He nursed the pinion that impelled the steel;
> While the same plumage that had warmed his nest,
> Drank the last life blood of his bleeding breast."

"What grand verses!" said Walter. "Poor, poor Daubeny!"

"I've never had but one feeling about him myself," said Power, "and that was a feeling almost like reverence. I hope and trust that he'll be well enough for to-morrow week. I always looked forward to kneeling next to him when we were confirmed."

"Ah, you loved him, Power," said Henderson, "because your tastes were like his. But I owe a great deal to him;—more than I can ever tell you. I don't feel as if I could tell you now, while he lies there so ill, poor fellow. He has saved me more than once from vigorous efforts to throw myself away. But for him I should have gone to the devil long, long ago. I was *very* near it once." He sighed, and as they walked by the violet margent of the evening waves, he offered up in silence an earnest prayer that Daubeny might live.

The blind old poet would have said that the winds carried the prayer away and scattered it. But no winds can scatter, no waves can drown, the immortal spirit of one true prayer. Unanswered it *may* be—but scattered and fruitless, *not*!

CHAPTER NINETEEN. THE SCHOOL-BELL.

> To me the thought of death is terrible,
> Having such hold of life; to you it is not
> More than the sudden lifting of a latch;
> Nought but a step into the open air,
> Out of a tent already luminous
> With light that shines through its transparent folds.
> *Longfellow's Golden Legend.*

"I've got a good piece of news for you, Master Daubeny," said the kind old school-nurse.

"What is it? is my mother here?" he said eagerly; "oh! let her come and see me."

She was at the door, and the next moment his arms were round her neck in a long embrace. "Darling, darling mother," he exclaimed, "now I shall be happy, now that you have come. Nay, you mustn't cry, mother," he said, as he felt one of her fast flowing tears upon his forehead; "you've come to help me in bearing up."

"Dearest Johnny," she said, "I trust yet that God will spare the widow's only son; He who raised the son of the widow of Nain will pity us."

"His ways are not ours, mother dear; I do not think that I shall recover. My past life hangs before me like a far-off picture already; I lie and look at it almost as if it were not mine, and my mind is quite at peace; only sometimes my head is all confused."

"God's will be done, Johnny," sobbed the poor lady. "But I do not think I can live, if you be taken from me."

"Taken—but not for ever, mother," he said, looking up into her face.

St. Winifred's, or The World of School

"Oh, Johnny, *why, why* did you not spare yourself, and work less? It is the work which has killed you."

"Only because it fell heavier on me than on other boys. They got through it quickly, but I was not so clever, and it cost me more to do my duty. I tried to do it, mother dear, and God helped me. All is well as it is. Oh, my head, my head!"

"You must rest, darling. My visit and talk has excited you. Try to go to sleep."

"Then sit there, mother, opposite me, so that I may see you when I wake."

She kissed his aching brow, and sat down, while he composed himself to rest. She was a lady of about fifty, with bands of silver hair smoothed over her calm forehead, and in appearance not unlike her son. But there was something very sweet and matronly about her look, and it was impossible to see her without feeling the respect and honour which was her due.

And she sat there, by the bedside, looking upon her only son, the boy who had been the light of her life; and she knew that he was dying—she knew that he was fading away before her eyes. Yet there was a sweet and noble resignation in her anguish; there was a deep and genuine spirit of submission to the will of Heaven, and a perfect faith in God's love, whatever might be the issue, in every prayer she breathed, as with clasped hands, and streaming eyes, and moving lips, she gazed upon his face. He might appear dull and heavy to others, but to her he was dear beyond all thought; and now she was to lose him. In her inmost heart she knew that she *must* suffer that great pang; that God was taking to Himself the son who had been so good and true to her, so affectionate, so sweet-tempered, so unselfish, that even from his gentle and quiet infancy he had never by his conduct caused her a moment's pain. She had long been looking forward to the strong and upright manhood which should follow this pure boyhood; but that dear boy was not destined to be the staff of her declining years; *her* hands were to close his eyes in the last long sleep, and she was to pass alone under the overshadowing rocks that close around the valley of human life. God help the mother's heart who must pass through scenes like this!

Poor Daubeny could not sleep. Brain-fever is usually accompanied by delirium, and as he turned restlessly upon his pillow, his mind began to wander away to other days and

St. Winifred's, or The World of School

scenes.

"Stupid, sir? yes, I know I am, but I can't help it; I've really done my best. I was up at five o'clock this morning, trying, trying so hard to learn this repetition. Indeed, indeed, I'm not idle, sir. I'll try to do my duty if I can. Oh, Power, I wish I were like you; you learn so quickly, and you never get abused as I do after it all."

And then the poor boy fancied himself sitting under the gas-lamp in the passage as he had so often done, and trying to master one of his repetition lessons, repeating the lines fast to himself as he used to do—

"Hac arte Pollux et vagus Hercules,
Enisus—enisus arces—enisus arces attigit igneas,
Quos inter Augustus—

"How *does* it go on?—

"Hac arte Pollux et vagus Hercules,
Enisus arces attigit igneas, attigit igneas,
Quos inter Augustus recumbens—

"Oh, what *does* come next?" and he stopped with an expression of pain on his face, pressing his hands tight over his brow.

"Don't go on with the repetition, Johnny, dear," said the poor mother. "I'm sure you know it enough now."

"Oh no! not yet, mother; I shall be turned, I know I shall to-morrow, and it makes him so angry; he'll call me idle and incorrigible, and all kinds of things." And then he began again—

"Sed quid Typhoeus aut validus Mimas,
Aut quid minaci Porphyrion statu,
Quid Rhoetus—Rhoetus—quid Rhoetus—

St. Winifred's, or The World of School

"Oh, I shall break down there, I know I shall;" and he burst into tears. "It's no good trying to help me, Power, I *can't* learn it."

"Leave off for to-night at least, Johnny," said his mother in a tone of anguish; "you can learn the rest to-morrow. Oh, what shall I do?" she asked, turning to the nurse; "I cannot bear to hear him go on like this."

"Be comforted, ma'am," said the nurse, wiping away her own tears. "He's a dear good lamb, and he'll come to hisself soon afore he goes off."

"*Must* he die then?" she asked, trembling in every limb.

"Hush, good lady; we never know what God may please to do in His mercy. We must bow to His gracious will, ma'am, as you knows well, I don't doubt. He's fitter to die than many a grown man is, poor child, and that's a blessing. I wish though he wasn't a-repeating of that there heathenish Latin."

But Daubeny's voice was still humming fragments of Horace lines, sometimes with eager concentration, and then with pauses at parts where his memory failed, at which he would grow distressed and anxious—

"Quid Rhoetus ... quid Rhoetus evulsisque truncis,
Enceladus.

"Oh, I *cannot* learn this; I think I'm getting more stupid every day. Enceladus—"

"If you love me, Johnny, give it up for to-night, that's a darling boy," said his mother.

"But, mother, it's my *duty* to know it; you wouldn't have me fail in duty, mother dear, would you? why, it was you who told me to persevere, and do all things with my might. Well, I will leave it for to-night." Then, still unconscious of what he was doing, the boy got up and prayed, as it was evident that he *had* done many a time, that God would strengthen his memory and quicken his powers, and enable him to do his duty like a man. It was inexpressibly touching to see him as he knelt there—thin, pale, emaciated, the shadow of his former self, kneeling in his delirium to offer up his old accustomed prayer.

St. Winifred's, or The World of School

And when he got into bed again, although his mind still wandered, he was much calmer, and a new direction seemed to have been given to his thoughts. The prayer had fallen like dew on his aching soul. He fancied himself in Power's study, where for many a Sunday the two boys had been used to sit, and where they had often learnt or read to each other their favourite hymns. Fragments of these hymns he was now repeating, dwelling on the words with an evident sense of pleasure and belief—

"A noble army—men and boys,
   The matron and the maid,
Around the Saviour's throne rejoice,
   In robes of light arrayed.

"*They* climbed the steep ascent of heaven,
   Mid peril, toil, and pain;
O God, to_us may strength be given,
   To follow in their train.

"Isn't that beautiful, Power?

"And when on upward wing,
   Cleaving the sky,
Sun, moon, and stars forgot,
   Upwards I fly;
Still all my song shall be,
   Nearer, my God, to Thee,
     Nearer to Thee."

And as he murmured to himself in a soothed tone of voice these verses, and lines of "Jerusalem the Golden," and "O for a closer walk with God," and "Rock of Ages," the wearied brain at last found repose, and Daubeny fell asleep.

He lingered on till the end of the week. On the Saturday he ceased to be delirious, and the lucid interval began which precedes death. It was then that he earnestly entreated to be allowed to see those school–friends whose names had been so often on his lips—Power, Walter, and Henderson. The boys, who had daily and eagerly inquired for him, entered with a feeling of trembling solemnity the room of sickness. The near presence of death filled them with an indescribable awe, and they felt desolate at the approaching loss of a friend whom they loved so well.

"I sent to say good-bye," he said, smiling sweetly. "You must not cry and grieve for me. I am happier than I ever felt before. Good- bye, Walter. It's for a long, long, long time; but not for ever. Good-bye, my dear old Flip—naughty fellow to cry so, when I am happy; and when I am gone, Flip, think of me sometimes, and of talks we've had together, and take your side manfully for God and Christ. Good-bye, Power, my best friend; we meant to get confirmed together, you know, but God has ordered it otherwise." And then he whispered low—

"Lord, shall we come? come yet again?
Thy children ask one blessing more?
To come not now alone, but then
When life, and death, and time are o'er;
Then, then, to come, O Lord, and be
Confirmed in heaven—confirmed by Thee.

"Oh, Power, that line fills me with hope and joy; think of it for me when I am dead;" and his voice trembled with emotion as he again murmured, "Confirmed in heaven—confirmed by Thee. I'm afraid I'm too weak to talk any more. Oh, what a long, long good- bye it will be, for years, and years, and years; to think that when you have gone out of the room we shall never meet in life again, and I shall never hear your pleasant voices. Oh, Flip, you make me cry against my will by crying so. It's hard to say, but it must be said at last, Good-bye, God bless you, with all my heart." He laid his hand on their heads as they bent over him, and once more whispering the last "Good-bye," turned away his face, and made the pillow wet with his warm tears.

The sound of his mother's sobs attracted him. "Ah, mother darling, we are alone now; you will stay with me till I die. I am tired."

"I feared that their visit would excite you too much, my child."

"Oh, no, mother; I couldn't bear to die without seeing them, I loved them so much. Mother, will you sing to me a little—sing me my favourite hymn."

St. Winifred's, or The World of School

She began in a low, sweet voice—

> "My God, my Father, while I stray,
> Far from my home in life's rough way,
> O teach me from my heart to say,
>   Thy will be done,
>   Thy will be—"

She stopped, for sobs choked her voice. "I am sorry I cannot, Johnny. But I cannot bear to think how soon we must part."

"Only for a short time, mother, a short time. I said a long time just now, but *now* it looks to me quite short, and I shall be with God. I see it all now so clearly. Do you remember those lines—

> "The soul's dark cottage, battered and decayed,
> Lets in new light through chinks that time has made.

"How true they are! Oh, darling mother, how very, very good you have always been to me, and I pay you with all my heart's whole love." He pressed upon her lips a long, long kiss, and said, "Good-night, darling mother. I am falling asleep, I think."

His arms relaxed their loving embrace, and glided down from her shoulder; his head fell back; the light faded from his soft and gentle eyes, and he was asleep.

Rightly he said "asleep,"—the long sleep that is the sweetest and happiest in that it knows no waking here; the long sweet sleep that no evil dreams disturb; the sleep after which the eyes open upon the light of immortality, and the weary heart rests upon the bosom of its God. Yes, Daubeny had fallen asleep.

God help thee, widowed mother; the daily endearments, the looks of living affection, the light of the boy's presence, are for thee and for thy home no more. There lies the human body of thy son; his soul is with the white-robed, redeemed, innumerable multitude in the Paradise of God.

St. Winifred's, or The World of School

For hours, till the light faded into darkness, as this young life had faded into death, she sat fixed in that deep grief which finds no utterance, and knows of no alleviation, with little consciousness save of the dead presence, and of the pang that benumbed her aching heart. And outside rang the sound of games and health, and the murmur of boy-voices came to her forlorn ear. There the stream of life was flashing joyously and gloriously in the sunshine, while here, in this darkened room, it had sunk into the sands, and lost itself under the shadow of the dark boughs. But she was a Christian; and as the sweet voices of memory, and conscience, and hope, and promise whispered to her in her loneliness their angel messages, her heart melted and the tears came, and she knelt down and took the dead hand of her son in hers, and said, between her sobs, while her tear-stained eyes were turned to heaven, "O God, teach me to understand Thy will."

And through the night the great bell of the church of St. Winifred's tolled the sound of death; and, mingled with it stroke for stroke, in long, tremulous, thrilling notes that echoed through the silent buildings, rang out the thin clear bell of St. Winifred's School. The tones of that school-bell were usually only heard as they summoned the boys to lessons with quick and hurried beatings. How different now were the slow occasional notes,—each note trembling itself out with undisturbed vibrations which quivered long upon the air,—with which it told that for one at least whom it had been wont to warn, hurry was possible no longer, and there was boundless leisure now! There was a strange pulse of emotion in the hearts of the listening boys, when the sound of those two passing bells struck upon their ears as they sat at evening work, and told them that the soul of their schoolfellow had passed away, and that God's voice had summoned His young servant to His side.

"You hear it, Henderson?" said Walter, who sat next to him.

"Yes," answered Henderson in an awestruck voice, "Daubeny is dead."

The rest of that evening the two boys sat silent and motionless, full of the solemn thoughts which can never be forgotten. And for the rest of that evening the deep church-bell tolled, and the shrill school-bell tolling after it, shivered out into the wintry night air its tremulous message that the soul of Daubeny had passed away.

St. Winifred's, or The World of School

CHAPTER TWENTY. FAREWELL.

> Be the day weary or be the day long,
> At last it ringeth to evensong.

There was a very serious look on the faces of all the boys as they thronged into chapel the next morning for the confirmation service. It was a beautiful sight to see the subdued yet noble air, full at once of humility and hope, wherewith many of the youthful candidates passed along the aisle, and knelt before the altar, and with clasped hands and bowed heads awaited the touch of the hands that blessed. As those young soldiers of Christ knelt meekly in their places, resolving with pure and earnest hearts to fight manfully in His service, and praying with childlike faith for the aid of which they felt their need, it was indeed a spectacle to recall the ideal of virtuous and Christian boyhood, and to force upon the minds of many the contrast it presented with the other too familiar spectacle of a boyhood coarse, defiant, brutal, ignorant yet conceited, young in years but old in disobedience, in insolence, in sin.

When the good bishop, in the course of his address, alluded to Daubeny's death, there was throughout the chapel instantly that silence that can be felt—that deep unbroken hush of expectation and emotion which always produces so indescribable an effect.

"There was one," he said, "who should have been confirmed to-day, who is not here. He has passed away from us; he will never be present at an earthly confirmation; he is `confirmed in heaven— confirmed by God.' I hear, and I rejoice to hear, that for that confirmation he was indeed prepared, and that he looked forward to it with some of his latest thoughts. I hear that he was pre- eminent among you for the piety, the purity, the amiability of his life and character, and his very death was caused by the intense earnestness of his desire to use aright the talents which God had entrusted to him. Oh! such a death of one so young yet so fit to die is far happier than the longest and most prosperous of sinful lives. Be sobered but not saddened by it. It is a proof of God's merciful and tender love that this one of your schoolfellows was taken in the clear and quiet dawn of a noble and holy life, and not some other in the scarlet blossom of precocious and deadly sin. Be not saddened therefore at the loss, but sobered by the warning. The fair, sweet, purple flower of youth falls and fades, my young brethren, under the sweeping scythe of death, no less surely than the withered grass of age. Oh! be ready—be ready with the girded loins and the lighted lamp—to obey the summons of your God. Who knows for which of us next, or how soon, the bell of death may toll? Be ye therefore ready, for you know not at what day or at what hour the voice may call to you!"

The loss of a well-known companion whom all respected and many loved—the crowding memories of school life—the still small voice of every conscience, gave strange meaning and force to the bishop's simple words. As they listened, many wept in silence, while down the cheeks of Walter, of Power, and of Henderson, the tears fell like summer rain.

In the evening Walter was seated thoughtfully by the fire in Power's study, while Power was writing at the table, stopping occasionally to wipe his glistening eyes.

"He was my earliest friend here," he said to Walter, almost apologetically, as he hastily brushed off the drop which had fallen and blurred the paper before him. "But I know it is selfish to be sorry," he added, as he pushed the paper towards Walter.

"May I read this, Power?" asked Walter.

"Yes; if you like;" and he drew his chair by his, while Walter read in Power's small clear handwriting—

    A FAREWELL.

      Never more!
Like a dream when one awaketh
    Vanishing away;
Like a billow when it breaketh
    Scattered into spray;
Like a meteor's paling ray,
Such is man, do all he can;
Nothing that is fair can stay.
Sorrow staineth, man complaineth,
Sin remaineth ever more;
Like a wave upon the shore

St. Winifred's, or The World of School

Soundeth ever from the chorus
Of the spirits gone before us,
"Ye shall meet us, ye shall greet us
In the sweet homes of earth, in the places of our birth,
Never more again, never more!"
So they sing, and sweetly dying
Faints the message of their voices,
Dying like the distant murmur, when a mighty host rejoices,
But the echoes are replying with a melancholy sighing,
   Never more again! never more!

   Far away,
Far, far away are the homes wherein they dwell,
We have lost them, and it cost them
Many a tear, and many a fear
When God forbade their stay;
But their sorrow, on the morrow
Ceased in the dawning of a lighter, brighter day;
And *our* bliss shall be certain, when death's awful curtain,
Drawn from the darkness of mortal life away,
To happy souls revealeth what it darkly now concealeth,
Yielding to the glory of heaven's eternal ray.
Far, far away are the homes wherein they dwell,
But we know that they are blest, and ever more at rest,
And we utter from our hearts, "It is well."

"May I keep them, Power?" he asked, looking up.

"Do, Walter, as a remembrance of to-day."

"And may I make one change, which the bishop's sermon suggested?"

"By all means," said Power; and Walter, taking a pencil, added after the line "Nothing that is fair can stay," these words— which Power afterwards copied, writing at the top, "In Memoriam, J.D."

St. Winifred's, or The World of School

Nothing that is fair can stay;
   But while Death's sharp scythe is sweeping,
   We remember 'mid our weeping,
   That a Father–hand is keeping
Every vernal bloom that falleth underneath its chilly sway.
   And though earthly flowers may perish,
   There are buds His hand will cherish,
And the things unseen Eternal—these can never pass away;
   Where the angels shout Hosanna,
   Where the ground is dewed with manna,
These remain and these await us in the homes of heaven for aye!

The lines are in Walter's desk; and he values them all the more for the tears which have fallen on them, and blurred the neatness of the fine clear handwriting.

On the following Tuesday our boys saw the dead body of their friend. The face of poor Daubeny looked singularly beautiful with the placid lines of death, as all innocent faces do. It was the first time they had seen a corpse; and as Walter touched the cold cheek, and placed a spray of evergreen in the rigid hand, he was almost overpowered with an awful sense of the sad sweet mystery of death.

"It is God who has taken him to Himself." said Mrs Daubeny, as she watched their emotion. "I shall not be parted from him long. He has left you each a remembrance of himself, dear boys, and you will value them, I know, for my poor child's sake, and for his widowed mother's thanks to those who loved him."

For each of them he had chosen, before he died, one of his most prized possessions. To Power he left his desk; to Henderson, his microscope; to Kenrick, a little gold pencil–case; and to Walter, a treasure which he deeply valued, a richly–bound Bible, in which he had left many memorials, of the manner in which his days were spent; and in which he had marked many of the rules which were the standard of his life, and the words of hope which sustained his gentle and noble mind.

The next day he was buried; only the boys in his own house, and those who had known him best, followed him to the grave. They were standing in two lines along the court, and the plumed hearse stood at the cottage door. Just at that moment the rest of the boys began to flock out of the school, for lessons were over. Each as he came out caught sight of the hearse, the plumes waving and whispering in the sea-wind, and the double line of mourners; and each, on seeing it, stood where he was, in perfect silence. Their numbers increased each moment, till boys and masters alike were there; and all by the same sudden impulse stopped where they were standing when first they saw the hearse, and stood still without a word. The scene was the more strangely impressive because it was accidental and spontaneous. Meanwhile, the coffin was carried downstairs, and placed in the hearse, which moved off slowly across the court between the line of bareheaded and motionless mourners. It was thus that Daubeny left St. Winifred's, and passed under the Norman arch; and till he had passed through, the boys stood fixed to their places, like a group of statues in the usually noisy court.

He was buried in the churchyard under the tower of the grand old church. It was a lovely spot; the torrent murmured near it; the shadows of the great mountains fell upon it; and as you stood there in the sacred silence of that memory-haunted field, you heard far-off the solemn monotone of the everlasting sea. There they laid him, and the stream of life, checked for a moment, flashed on again with turbulent and sparkling waves. Ah me!—yet why should we sigh at the merciful provision, which causes that the very best of us, when we die, leaves but a slight and transient ripple on the waters, which a moment after flow on as smoothly as before?

Mrs Daubeny left St Winifred's that evening; her carriage looked strange with her son's boxes and other possessions piled up in it. Who would ever use that cricket-bat or those skates again? Power and Walter shook hands with her at the door as she was about to start; and just at the last moment, Henderson came running up with something, which he put on the carriage seat without a word. It was a bird-cage, containing a little favourite canary, which he and Daubeny had often fed.

CHAPTER TWENTY ONE. KENRICK'S HOME.

> Yonder there lies the village and looks how quiet and small,
> And yet bubbles o'er like a city with gossip and scandal and spite.
> *Tennyson, Maud.*

It was the last evening. The boys were all assembled in the great schoolroom to hear the result of the examination. The masters in their caps and gowns were seated round Dr Lane on a dais in the centre of the room; and every one was eager to know what places the boys had taken, and who would win the various form prizes. Dr Lane began from the bottom of the school, and at the *last* boy in each form, so that the interest of the proceedings kept on culminating to the grand climax. The first name that will interest us was Eden's, and both Walter and Power were watching anxiously to see where he would come out in his form. Power had been so kindly coaching him in his work that they expected him to be high; but it was as much to *his* surprise as to their gratification, that his name was read out *third*. Jones and Harpour were, as was natural, last in their respective forms.

At length Dr Lane got to Walter's form. Last but one came Howard Tracy, who was listening with a fine superiority to the whole announcement. Anthony and Franklin were not far from him. Henderson expected himself to be about tenth; but the tenth name, the ninth, and the eighth, all were read, and he had not been mentioned; his heart was beating fast, and he almost fancied that there must have been some mistake; but no; Dr Lane read on.

"Seventh, Gray.

"Sixth, Mackworth.

"Fifth; Whalley.

"*Fourth*, Henderson," and Walter had hardly done patting him on the back, and congratulating him, when Dr Lane had read:

"Third, Manners.

"Second, Carlton.

"*First*"—the Doctor always read the word first with peculiar emphasis, and then brought out the name of the boy who had attained that distinction with great empressement—"*First, Evson.*"

St. Winifred's, or The World of School

Whereupon it was Henderson's turn to pat him on the back, which he did very vigorously; and not only so, but in his enthusiasm began to clap—a demonstration which ran like wildfire through all the ranks of the boys, and before Dr Lane could raise his voice to secure silence—for approbation on those occasions in the great schoolroom was not at all *selon regle*—our young hero had received a regular ovation. For since the day on Appenfell, Walter had been the favourite of the school, and they were only too glad to follow Henderson in his irregular applause. There was an intoxicating sweetness in this popularity. Could Walter help keenly enjoying the general regard which thus, defiant of rules, broke out in his honour into spontaneous acclamations?

Dr Lane's stern "Silence!" heard above the uproar, soon reduced the boys to order, and he proceeded with the list. Kenrick was read out first in his form, and Power, as a matter of course, again first in the second fifth, although in that form he was the youngest boy. Somers came out head of the school, by examination as well as by seniority of standing; and in his case, too, the impulse to cheer was too strong to be resisted. The head of the school was, however, tacitly excepted from the general rule, and Dr Lane only smiled while he listened to the clapping, which showed that Somers was regarded with esteem and honour by the boys, in spite of his cold manners and stern regime.

"Hurrah for the Sociable Grosbeaks!" said Henderson, as the boys streamed out of the room. "Why, we carry all before us! And only fancy me fourth! Why, I'm a magnificent swell, without ever having known it. You look out, Master Walter, or I shall have a scrimmage with you for laurels."

"Good," said Walter. "Meanwhile, come and help me to pack up my laurels in my box. And then for home! Hurrah!"

And he began to sing the exquisite air of:

Domum, domum, dulce domum,
Dulce, dulce, dulce domum.

In which Power and Henderson joined heartily; while Kenrick walked on in silence.

Next day the boys were scattered in every direction to their various homes. It need not be said that Walter passed very happy holidays that Christmas time. Power came and spent a

St. Winifred's, or The World of School

fortnight with him; and let every boy who has a cheerful and affectionate home imagine for himself how blithely their days passed by. Power made himself a universal favourite, always unselfish, always merry, and throwing himself heartily into every amusement which the Evsons proposed. He and they were mutually sorry when the time came for them to part.

From Semlyn Lake, Walter's home, to Fuzby, Kenrick's home, the change is great indeed; yet I must take the reader there for a short time, before we return to the noisy and often troubled precincts of St Winifred's School.

Before Power came to stay with the Evsons, Walter, with his father's full permission, had written to ask Kenrick to join them at the same time, and this is the answer he got in reply.

"My Dear Walter,—

"I can't tell you how much your letter tempted me. I should so like to come; I would give *anything* to come and see you. To be with you and Power at such a place as Semlyn must be—oh, Walter, it almost makes me envious to think of you there. But I can't come, and I'll tell you frankly the reason. I can't afford, or rather I mean that my mother cannot afford, the necessary travelling expenses. I look on you, Walter, as my best school friend, so I may as well say at once that we are *very, very* poor. If I could even get to you by walking some of the way, and going third-class the rest, I would jump at the chance, but lucky fellow, *you* know nothing of the *res angusta domi*.

"You must be amused at the name of this place, Fuzby-le-Mud. What charming prospects the name opens, does it not? I assure you the name fits the place exactly. My goodness! how I do hate the place. You'll ask why then we live here? Simply because we *must*. Some misanthropic relation left us the house we live in, which saves rent.

"Yet, if you were with me, I think I could be happy even here. I don't venture to ask you. First of all, we couldn't make you one-tenth part as comfortable as you are at home; secondly, there isn't the ghost of an amusement here, and if you came, you'd go back to St Winifred's with a fit of blue devils, as I always do; thirdly, the change from Semlyn to Fuzby-le-Mud would be like walking from the Elysian fields and the asphodel meadows, into mere *borboros*, as old Edwards would say. So I *don't* ask you; and yet if you could come—why, the day would be marked with white in the dull calendar of—Your ever affectionate—

"Harry Kenrick."

As Fuzby lay nearly in the route to St Winifred's, Walter, grieved that his friend should be doomed to such dull holidays, determined, with Mr Evson's leave, to pay him a three days' visit on his way to school. Accordingly, towards the close of the holidays, after a hopeful, a joyous, and an affectionate farewell to all at home, he started for Fuzby, from which he was to accompany Kenrick back to school; a visit fraught, as it turned out, with evil consequences, and one which he never afterwards ceased to look back upon with regret.

The railroad, after leaving far behind the glorious hills of Semlyn, passes through country flatter and more uninteresting at every mile, until it finds itself fairly committed to the fens. Nothing but dreary dykes, muddy and straight, guarded by the ghosts of suicidal pollards, and by rows of dreary and desolate mills, occur to break the blank grey monotony of the landscape. Walter was looking out of the window with curious eyes, and he was wondering what life in such conditions could be like, when the train uttered a despairing scream, and reached a station which the porter announced as Fuzby-le-Mud. Walter jumped down, and his hand was instantly seized by Kenrick with a warm and affectionate grasp.

"So you're really here, Walter. I can hardly believe it. I half repent having brought you to such a place; but I was *so* dull."

"I shall enjoy it exceedingly, Ken, with you. Shall I give my portmanteau to some man to take up to the village?"

"Oh no; here's a—well, I may as well call it a *cart* at once— to take it up in. The curate lent it me, and he calls it a pony-carriage; but it is, you see, nothing more or less than a cart. I hope you won't be ashamed to ride in it."

"I should think not," said Walter gaily, mounting into the curious little oblong wooden vehicle.

St. Winifred's, or The World of School

"It isn't very far," said Kenrick, "and I dare say you don't know any one about here; so it won't matter."

"Pooh, Ken; as if I minded such nonsense." Indeed Walter would not have thought twice about the conveyance, if Kenrick had not harped upon it so much, and seemed so much ashamed of it, and mortified at being obliged to use it.

"Shall I drive?" asked Walter.

"Drive? Why, the pony is stone blind, and as scraggy as a scarecrow, so there's not much driving to be had out of him. Fancy if the aristocratic Power, or some other St Winifred's fellow saw us! Why it would supply Henderson with jokes for six weeks," said Kenrick, getting up, and touching the old pony with his whip. Both he and Walter were wholly unconscious that their equipage *had* been seen, and contemptuously scrutinised by one of their schoolfellows. Unknown to Walter, Jones was in the train; and, after a long stare at the pony-chaise, had flung himself back in his seat to indulge in a long guffaw, and in anticipating the malicious amusement he should feel in retailing at St Winifred's the description of Kenrick's horse and carriage. Petty malignity was a main feature of Jones's mind.

"That is Fuzby," said Kenrick laconically, pointing to a straggling village from which a few lights were beginning to glimmer; "and I wish it were buried twenty thousand fathoms under the sea."

Ungracious as the speech may seem, it cannot be wondered at. A single muddy road runs through Fuzby. Except along this road— muddy and rutty in winter, dusty and rutty in summer—no walk is to be had. The fields are all more or less impassable with ditches and bogs. Kenrick had christened it "The Dreary Swamp." Nothing in the shape of a view is to be found anywhere, and barely a single flower will design to grow. The air is unhealthy with moisture, and the only element to be had there in perfection is earth.

All this, Kenrick's father—who had been curate of the village— had fancied would be at least endurable to any man upheld by a strong sense of duty. So when he had married, and had received the gift of a house in the village, he took thither his young and beautiful bride, intending there to live and work until something better could be obtained. He was right. Over the mere disadvantages of situation he might easily have triumphed, and he might have secured there, under different circumstances, a fair share of happiness, which lies in ourselves and not in the localities in which we live. But in making his calculation he had always assumed that it would be easy to get on with the inhabitants of Fuzby; and here lay his mistake.

The Vicar of Fuzby, a non-resident pluralist, only appeared at rare intervals to receive the adoration which his flock never refused to any one who was wealthy. His curate, having a very slender income, came in for no share at all of this respect. On the contrary, the whole population assumed a right to patronise him, to interfere with him, to annoy and to thwart him. There was at Fuzby one squire—a rich farmer, coarse, ignorant, and brutal. This man, being the richest person in the parish, generally carried everything in his own way, and among other attempts to imitate the absurdities of his superiors, had ordered the sexton never to cease ringing the church-bell, however late, until he and his family had taken their seats. A very few Sundays after Mr Kenrick's arrival the bell was still ringing eight minutes after the time for morning service, and sending to desire the sexton to leave off, he received the message that—"Mr Hugginson hadn't come yet."

"I will not have the congregation kept waiting for Mr Hugginson or any one else," said the curate.

"Oh, zurr, the zervus hain't begun afore Muster Hugginson has come in this ten year."

"Then the sooner Mr Hugginson is made to understand that the hours of service are not to be altered at his convenience the better. Let the bell cease immediately."

But the sexton, a dogged, bovine, bullet-headed labourer, took no notice whatever of this injunction, and although Mr Kenrick went into the reading-desk, continued lustily to ring the bell until the whole Hugginson family, furious that their dignity should thus be insulted, sailed into church at the beginning of the psalms.

Next morning Mr Kenrick turned the sexton out of his place, and received a most wrathful visit from Mr Hugginson, who, after pouring on him a torrent of the most disgusting abuse, got scarlet in the forehead, shook his stick in Mr Kenrick's face, flung his poverty in his teeth, and left the cottage, vowing eternal vengeance.

St. Winifred's, or The World of School

With him went all the Fuzby population. It would be long to tell the various little causes which led to Mr Kenrick's unpopularity among them. Every clergyman similarly circumstanced may conjecture these for himself; they resolved themselves mainly into the fact that Mr Kenrick was abler, wiser, purer, better, more Christian, than they. His thoughts were not theirs, nor his ways their ways.

> He had a daily beauty in his life
>   That made them ugly.

And so, to pass briefly and lightly over an unpleasant subject, Fuzby was brimming over with the concentrated meanness of petty malignant natures, united in the one sole object of snubbing and worrying the unhappy curate. To live among them was like living in a cloud of poisonous flies. If Dante had known Fuzby-le-Mud, he could have found for a really generous and noble spirit no more detestable or unendurable inferno than this muddy English village.

The chief characteristic of Fuzby was a pestilential spirit of gossip. There was no lying scandal, there was no malicious whisper, that did not thrive with rank luxuriance in that mean atmosphere, which, at the same time, starved up every great and high-minded wish. There was no circumstance so minute that calumny could not insert into it a venomous claw. Mr Kenrick was one of the most exemplary, generous, and pure-minded of men; his only fault was quickness of temper. His noble character, his conciliatory manners, his cultivated mind, his Christian forbearance, were all in vain. He was poor, and he could not be a toady: these were two unpardonable sins; and he, a true man, moved like an angel among a set of inferior beings. For a time he struggled on. He tried not to mind the lies they told of him. What was it to him, for instance, if they took advantage of his hasty language to declare that he was in the constant habit of swearing, when he knew that even from boyhood no oath had ever crossed his lips? What was it to him that these uneducated boors, in their feeble ignorance, tried constantly to entrap him into something which they called unorthodox, and to twist his words into the semblance of fancied heresy? It was more painful to him that they opposed and vilified every one whom he helped, and whose interests, in pity, he endeavoured to forward. But still he bore on, he struggled on, till the *denouement* came. It is not worth while entering into the various schemes invented for his annoyance, but at last an unfortunate, although purely accidental, discrepancy was detected in the accounts of one of the parish charities which Mr Kenrick officially managed. Mr Hugginson seized his long-looked-for opportunity:

he went round the parish, and got a large number of his creatures among the congregation to affirm by their signatures that Mr Kenrick had behaved dishonestly. This memorial he sent to the bishop, and disseminated among all the clergy with malicious assiduity. At the next clerical meeting Mr Kenrick found himself most coldly received. Compelled in self-defence to take legal proceedings against the squire, he found himself involved in heavy expenses. He won his cause, and his character was cleared; but the jury, attending only to the technicalities of the case, and conceiving that there was enough *prima facie* evidence to justify Mr Hugginson's proceedings, left each side to pay their own costs. These costs swallowed up the whole of the poor curate's private resources, and also involved him in debt. The agony, the suspense, the shame, the cruel sense of oppression and injustice, bore with a crushing weight on his weakened health. He could not tolerate that the merest breath of suspicion, however false, should pass over his fair and honourable name. He pined away under the atrocious calumny; it poisoned for him the very life- springs of happiness, and destroyed his peace of mind for ever. This young man, in the flower of youth—a man who might have been a leader and teacher of men—a man of gracious presence and high power—died of a broken heart. He died of a broken heart, and all Fuzby built his conspicuous tomb, and shed crocodile tears over his pious memory. Truly, as some one has said, very black stains lie here and there athwart the white conventionalities of common life!

This had happened when our little Kenrick was eight years old; he never forgot the spectacle of his poor father's heart-breaking misery during the last year of his life. He never forgot how, during that year, sorrow and anxiety had aged his father's face, and silvered his hair, young as he was, with premature white, and so quenched his spirits, that often he would take his little boy on his knee, and look upon him so long in silence, that the child cried at the intensity of that long, mournful, hopeless gaze, and at the tears which he saw slowly coursing each other down his father's careworn and furrowed cheeks. Ever since then the boy had walked among the Fuzby people with open scorn and defiance, as among those whose slanders had done to death the father whom he so proudly loved. In spite of his mother's wishes, he would not stoop to pay them even the semblance of courtesy. No wonder that he hated Fuzby with a perfect hatred, and that his home there was a miserable home.

Yet if any one *could* have made happy a home in such a place, it would have been Mrs Kenrick. Never, I think, did a purer, a fairer, a sweeter soul live on earth, or one more like the angels of heaven. The winning grace of her manners, the simple sweetness of her address, the pathetic beauty and sadness of her face, would have won for her, and *had* won for her, in any other place but Fuzby, the love and admiration which were her due.

She had a mind that envy could not but call fair.

But at Fuzby, from the dominant faction of Hugginson, and the small vulgar-minded sets who always tried to browbeat those who were poor, particularly if their birth and breeding were gentle, she found nothing but insulting coldness, or still more insulting patronage. When first she heard the marriage-bells clang out from the old church tower of her home, and had walked by the side of her young husband, a glad and lovely bride, she had looked forward to many happy years. With *him*, at any rate, it seemed that no place could be very miserable. Poor lady! her life had been one long martyrdom, all the more hard to bear because it was made up for the most part of small annoyances, petty mortifications, little recurring incessant bitternesses. And now, during the seven years of her widowhood, she had gained a calmer and serener atmosphere, in which she was raised above the *possibility* of humiliation from the dwarfed natures and malicious hearts, in the midst of which she lived. They could hurt her feelings, they could embitter her days no longer. To the hopes and pleasures of earth she had bidden farewell. Still young, still beautiful, she had reached the full maturity of Christian life, meekly bearing the load of scorn, and disappointment, and poverty, looking only for that rest which remaineth to the people of God. In her lonely home, with no friend at Fuzby to whom she could turn for counsel or for consolation, shut up with the sorrows of her own lonely heart, she often mused at the slight sources, the *little sins* of others, from which her misery had sprung; she marvelled at the mystery that man should be to man "the sorest, surest ill." Truly, it *is* a strange thought! Oh! it is pitiable that, as though death, and want, and sin were not enough, we too must add to the sum of human miseries by despising, by neglecting, by injuring others. We wound by our harsh words, we dishonour by our coarse judgments, we grieve by our untender pride, the souls for whom Christ died; and we wound most deeply, and grieve most irreparably, the noblest and the best.

The one tie that bound her to earth was her orphan son—her hope, her pride; all her affections were centred in that beautiful boy. Now, if I were writing a romance, I should of course represent that yearning mother's affection as reciprocated with all the warmth and passion of the boy's heart. But it was not so. Harry Kenrick did indeed love his mother; he would have borne anything rather than see her suffer any great pain; but his manners were too often cold, his conduct wilful or thoughtless. He did not love her—perhaps no child can love his parents— with all the *abandon* and intensity wherewith she loved him. The fact is, a blight lay upon Kenrick whenever he was at home—the Fuzby blight he called it. He hated the place so much, he hated the people in it so much, he felt the annoyances of their situation with so keen and fretful a sensibility, that at Fuzby, even though with his mother, he was never happy. Even her society could not make up to him, for the detestation with which he not unnaturally regarded the village and its inhabitants. At school he was bright, warm-hearted, and full of life; at home he seemed to draw himself into a shell of reserve and coldness; and it was a deep unspoken trial to that gentle mother's heart that she could not make home happy to the boy whom she so fondly loved, and that even to her he seemed indifferent; for his manners— since he had been to school and learned how very differently other boys were circumstanced, and what untold pleasures centred for them in that word "home"—were to her always shy and silent, appeared sometimes almost harsh.

I wish I could represent it otherwise; but things are not often truly represented in books; and is not this a very common, as well as a very tragic case? Not even in her son could Mrs Kenrick look for happiness; even his society brought with it trials almost as hard to bear as those which his absence caused. Yet no mother could have brought up her child more wisely, more tenderly, with more undivided and devoted care. Harry's *heart* was true could she have looked into it; but at Fuzby a cold, repellant manner fell on him like a mildew. And Mrs Kenrick wept in silence, as she thought—though it was not true—that even her own son did not love her, or at least did not love her as she had hoped he would. It was the last bitter drop in that overflowing cup which it had pleased God that she should be called upon to drink.

The boys drove up to the door of the little cottage. It stood in a garden, but as the garden was overlooked by Fuzbeians on all sides, it offered few attractions, and was otherwise very small and plain. They were greeted by Mrs Kenrick's soft and pleasant voice.

"Well, dear Harry, I am delighted that you have brought back your friend."

Harry's mind was preoccupied with the poverty-stricken aspect which he thought the house must present to his friend, and he did not answer her, but said to Walter:

"Well, Walter, here is the hut we inhabit. We have only one girl as a servant. I'll carry up the box. I do pretty nearly everything but clean the shoes."

St. Winifred's, or The World of School

Mrs Kenrick's eyes filled with sad tears at the bitter words; but she checked them to greet Walter, who advanced and shook her by the hand so cordially, and with a manner so respectfully affectionate, that he won her heart at once.

"Harry has not yet learned," she said playfully, "that poverty is not a thing to be ashamed of; but I am sure, Walter—forgive my using the name which my boy has made so familiar to me—that you will not mind any little inconveniences during your short stay with us."

"Oh no, Mrs Kenrick," said Walter; "to be with you and him will be the greatest possible enjoyment."

"I wish you wouldn't flap our poverty in every one's face, mother," said Kenrick almost angrily, when Walter had barely left the room.

"Oh, Harry, Harry," said Mrs Kenrick, speaking sadly, "you surely forget, dear boy, that it is your mother to whom you are speaking. And was it I who mentioned our poverty first? Oh, Harry, when will you learn to be contented with the dispensations of God? Believe me, dearest, we might make our poverty as happy as any wealth, if we would but have eyes to see the blessings it involves."

The boy turned away impatiently, and as he ran upstairs to rejoin his friend, the lady sat down with a deep sigh to her work. It was long ere Kenrick learnt how much his conduct was to blame; but long after, when his mother was dead, he was reminded painfully of this scene, when he accidentally found in her handwriting this extract from one of her favourite authors:—

"It has been reserved for this age to perceive the blessedness of another kind of poverty; not voluntary nor proud, but accepted and submissive; not clear-sighted nor triumphant, but subdued and patient; partly patient in tenderness—of God's will; partly patient in blindness—of man's oppression; too laborious to be thoughtful, too innocent to be conscious; too much experienced in sorrow to be hopeful—waiting in its peaceful darkness for the unconceived dawn; yet not without its sweet, complete, untainted happiness, like intermittent notes of birds before the daybreak, or the first gleams of heaven's amber on the eastern grey. Such poverty as this it has been reserved for this age of ours to honour while it afflicted; it is reserved for the age to come to honour it and to spare."

CHAPTER TWENTY TWO. BIRDS OF A FEATHER.

> What, man I know them, yea,
> And what they weigh even to the utmost scruple;
> Scrambling, out-facing, fashion-monging boys,
> That lie, and cog, and flout, deprave, and slander.
> *Much Ado about Nothing*, Act 5, Scene 1.

Walter could not help hearing a part of this conversation, and he was pained and surprised that Kenrick, whom he had regarded as so fine a character, should show his worst side at home, and should speak and act thus unkindly to one whom he was so deeply bound to love and reverence. And he was even more surprised when he went downstairs again and looked on the calm face of his friend's mother, so lovely, so gentle, so resigned, and felt the charm of manners which, in their natural grace and sweetness, might have shed lustre on a court. All that he could himself do was to show by his own manner to Mrs Kenrick, the affection and respect with which he regarded her. When he hinted to Kenrick, as delicately and distantly as he could, that he thought his manner to his mother rather brusque, Kenrick reddened rather angrily, but only replied, "Ah, it's all very well for you to talk; but you don't live at Fuzby."

"Yet I've enjoyed my visit very much, Ken; you can't think how much I love your mother."

"Thank you, Walter, for saying so. But how would you like to *live always* at such a place?"

"If I did I should do my best to make it happy."

"Make it *happy!*" said Kenrick; and as he turned away he muttered something about making a silk purse out of a sow's ear. Soon after he told Walter some of those circumstances about his father's life which we have recently related.

When the three days were over the boys started for St. Winifred's. They drove to the

St. Winifred's, or The World of School

station in the pony-chaise before described, accompanied, against Kenrick's will, by his mother. She bore up bravely as she bade them good-bye, knowing the undemonstrative character of boys, and seeing that they were both in the merriest mood. She knew, too, that their gaiety was natural: the world lay before *them*, bright and seductive as yet, with no shadow across its light; nor was she all in all to Harry as he was to her. He had other hopes, and another home, and other ties; and remembering this she tried not to grieve that he should leave her with so light a heart. But as she turned away from the platform when the train had started, taking with it all that she held dearest in the world, and as she walked back to the lonely home which had nothing but faith—for there was not even hope—to brighten it, the quiet tears flowed fast over the fair face beneath her veil. Yet as she crossed over her lonely threshold her thoughts were not even then for herself, but they carried her on the wings of prayer to the throne of mercy, for the beloved boy from whom she was again to be separated for nearly five long months.

The widowed mother wept; but the boy's spirits rose as he drew closer to the hills and to the sea, which told him that St. Winifred's was near. He talked happily with Walter about the coming half—eager with ambition, with hope, with high spirits, and fine resolutions. He clapped his hands with pleasure when they reached the top of Bardlyn Hill and caught sight of the school buildings.

Having had a long distance to travel they were among the late arrivals, and at the great gate stood Henderson and Power ready to greet them and the other boys who came with them in the same coach. Among these were Eden and Bliss.

"Ah, Eden," said Henderson, "I've been writing a poem about you—

"I'm a shrimp, I'm a shrimp of diminutive size,
Inspect my antenna and look at my eyes;
Quick, quick, feel me quick, for cannot you see
I'm a shrimp, I'm a shrimp, to be eaten with tea!

"And who's this?—why," he said, clasping his hands and throwing up his eyes in mock rapture, "this indeed is Bliss!"

"I'll lick you, Flip," said Bliss, only in a more good-humoured tone than usual, as he hit at him.

"I think I've heard that observation before," said Henderson, dodging away. "Ah, Walter, how do you do, my dear old fellow? I hope you're sitting on the throne of health, and reclining under the canopy of a well-organised brain."

"More than you are, Flip," said Walter, laughing. "You seem madder than ever."

"That he is," said Power; "since his return he's made on an average fifteen thousand bad puns. You ought to be grateful though, for he and I have got some coffee going for you in my study. Come along; the Familiar will see that your luggage is all right."

"Yes; and I shall make bold to bring in a shrimp to tea," said Henderson, seizing hold of Eden.

"All right. I meant to ask you, Eden," said Power, shaking the little boy affectionately by the hand, "have you enjoyed the holidays?"

"Not very much," said Eden.

"You're not looking as bright as I should like," said Power; "never mind; if you didn't enjoy the holidays you must enjoy the half."

"That I shall. I hope, Walter, you'll be in the same dormitory still. What shall I do if you're not?"

"Oh, how's that to be, Flip?" asked Walter; "you said you'd try to get some of us put together in one dormitory. That would be awfully jolly. I don't want to leave you, Eden, and would like you to be moved too; but I can't bear Harpour and that lot."

"I've partly managed it and partly failed," said Henderson. "You and the shrimp still stay with the rest of the set in Number 10, but as there was a vacant bed I got myself put there too."

"Hurrah!" said Walter and Eden both at once; "that's capital."

"Let me see," said Walter; "there are Jones and Harpour—brutes certainly both of them; and Cradock—well, he's rather a bargee, but he's not altogether bad; and Anthony and

St. Winifred's, or The World of School

Franklin, who are both far jollier than they used to be; indeed I liked old Franklin very much; so with you and Eden we shall get on famously."

The first few days of term passed very pleasantly. The masters met the boys in the kindliest spirit, and the boys, fresh from home and with the sweet influences of home still playing over them, did not begin at once to reweave the ravelled threads of evil school tradition. They were all on good terms with each other and with themselves, full of good resolutions, cheerful, and happy.

All our boys had got their removes. Walter had won a double remove, and was now under his friend Mr Percival. Kenrick was in the second fifth, and Power, young as he was, had now attained the upper fifth, which stands next to the dignity of the monitors and the sixth.

The first Sunday of term was a glorious day of early autumn, and the boys, according to their custom, scattered themselves in various groups in the grounds about St Winifred's School. The favourite place of resort was a broad green field at the back of the buildings, shaded by noble trees and half encircled by a bend of the river. Here, on a fine Sunday, between dinner and afternoon school, you were sure to find the great majority of the boys walking arm in arm by twos and threes, or sitting with books on the willow trunks that overhung the stream, or stretched out at full length upon the grass, and lazily learning their Scripture repetition.

It was a sweet spot and a pleasant time; but Walter generally preferred his beloved seashore; and on this afternoon he was sitting there talking to Power, while Eden, perched on the top of a piece of rock close by, kept murmuring to himself his afternoon lesson. The conversation of the two boys turned chiefly on the holidays which were just over, and Power was asking Walter about his visit to Kenrick's house.

"How did you enjoy the visit, Walter?"

"Very much for some things. Mrs Kenrick is the sweetest lady you ever saw."

"But Ken is always abusing Fuzby—isn't that the name?"

"Yes; it isn't a particularly jolly place, certainly, but he doesn't make the best of it; he makes up his mind to detest it."

"Why?"

"Oh, I don't know. They didn't treat his father well. His father was curate of the place."

"As far as I've seen, Fuzby isn't singular in that respect. It's no easy thing in most places for a poor clergyman to keep on good terms with his people."

"Yes; but Ken's father does seem to have been abominably treated." And Walter proceeded to tell Power the parts of Mr Kenrick's history which Kenrick had told him.

When he had finished the story he observed that Eden had shut up his book and was listening intently.

"Hallo, Arty," said Walter, "I didn't mean you to hear."

"Didn't you? I'm so sorry. I really didn't know you meant to be talking secrets, for you weren't talking particularly low."

"The noise of the waves prevents that. But never mind; I don't suppose it's any secret. Ken never told me not to mention it. Only of course you mustn't tell any one, you know, as it clearly isn't a thing to be talked about."

"No," said Eden; "I won't mention it, of course. So other people have unhappy homes as well as me," he added in a low tone.

"What, isn't your home happy, Arty?" asked Power.

Eden shook his head. "It used to be, but this holidays mamma married again. She married Colonel Braemar—and I *can't bear* him." The words were said so energetically as to leave no doubt that he had some grounds for the dislike; but Power said:

"Hush, Arty, you must try to like him. Are you sure you know your Repetition perfectly?"

St. Winifred's, or The World of School

"Yes."

"Then let's take a turn till the bell rings."

While this conversation was going on by the shore, a very different scene was being enacted in the Croft, as the field was called which I above described.

It happened that Jones, and one of his set, named Mackworth, were walking up and down the Croft in one direction, while Kenrick and Whalley, one of his friends, were pacing up and down the same avenue in the opposite direction, so that the four boys passed each other every five minutes. The first time they met, Kenrick could not help noticing that Jones and Mackworth nudged each other derisively as he passed, and looked at him with a glance unmistakably impudent. This rather surprised him, though he was on bad terms with them both. Kenrick had not forgotten how grossly Jones had bullied him when he was a new boy, and before he had risen out of the sphere in which Jones could dare to bully him with impunity. He was now so high in the school as to be well aware that Jones would be nearly as much afraid to touch him as he always was to annoy any one of his own size and strength; and Kenrick had never hesitated to show Jones the quiet but quite measureless contempt which he felt for his malice and meanness. Mackworth was a bully of another stamp; he was rather a clever fellow, set himself up for an aristocrat on the strength of being second cousin to a baronet, studied Debrett's *Peerage*, dressed as faultlessly as Tracy himself, and affected at all times a studious politeness of manner. He had been a good deal abroad, and as he constantly adopted the airs and the graces of a fashionable person, the boys had felicitously named him French Varnish. But Mackworth was a dangerous enemy, for he had one of the most biting tongues in the whole school, and there were few things which he enjoyed more than making a young boy wince under his cutting words. When Kenrick came to school, his wardrobe, the work of Fuzbeian artists, was not only well worn—for his mother was too poor to give him new clothes—but also of a somewhat odd cut; and accordingly the very first words Mackworth had ever addressed to Kenrick were:

"You new fellow, what's your father?"

"My father is dead," said Kenrick in a low tone.

"Then what *was* he?"

St. Winifred's, or The World of School

"He was curate of Fuzby."

"Curate was he; a slashing trade that," was the brutal reply. "Curate of Fuzby? are you sure it isn't Fusty?"

Kenrick looked at him with a strange glowing of the eyes, which, so far from disconcerting Mackworth, only made him chuckle at the success of his taunt. He determined to exercise the lancet of his tongue again, and let fresh blood if possible.

"Well, glare–eyes! so you didn't like my remark?"

Kenrick made no answer, and Mackworth continued:

"What charity boy has left you his cast–off clothes? May I ask if your jacket was intended to serve also as a looking–glass? and is it the custom in your part of the country not to wear breeches below the knees?"

There was a corrosive malice in this speech so intense that Kenrick never saw Mackworth without recalling the shame and anguish it had caused. Fresh from home, full of quick sensibility, feeling ridicule with great keenness, Kenrick was too much pained by these words even for anger. He had hung his head and slunk away. For days after, until, at his most earnest entreaty, his mother had incurred much privation to afford him a new and better suit, he had hardly dared to lift up his face. He had fancied himself a mark for ridicule, and the sense of shabbiness and poverty had gone far to crush his spirit. After a time he recovered, but never since that day had he deigned to speak to Mackworth a single word.

He was surprised, therefore, at the obtrusive impertinence of these two fellows, and when next he passed them, he surveyed them from head to foot with a haughty and indignant stare. The moment after he heard them burst into a laugh, and begin talking very loud.

"It was the rummiest vehicle you ever saw," he heard Jones say; "a cart, I assure you—nothing more or less, and drawn by the very scraggiest scarecrow of a blind horse."

He caught no more as the distance between them lessened, but he heard Jones bubbling over with a stupid giggle at some remark of Mackworth's about *glare–eyes* being drawn

St. Winifred's, or The World of School

by a *blind* horse.

"How rude those fellows are, Ken," said Whalley; "what do they mean by it?"

"Dogs!" said Kenrick, stamping angrily, while his face was scarlet with rage.

"If they're trying to annoy you, Ken," said Whalley, who was a very gentle, popular boy, "don't give them the triumph of seeing that they succeed. They're only Varnish and Whitefeather;—we all know what *they're* like."

"Dogs!" said Kenrick again; "I should like to pitch into them."

"Let's leave them, and go and sit by the river, Ken."

"No, Whalley. I'm sure they mean to insult me, and I want to hear how, and why."

There was no difficulty in doing this, for Jones and his ally were again approaching, and Jones was talking purposely loud.

"I never could bear the fellow; gives himself such airs."

"Yes; only fancy going to meet his friends in a hay-wagon! what a start! Ho! ho! ho!"

"It's such impudence in a low fellow like that," ... and here Kenrick lost some words, for, as they passed, Jones lowered his voice; but he heard, only too plainly, the words "father" and "dishonest parson";—the rest he could supply with fatal facility.

For half an instant he stood paralysed, his eyes burning with fury, but his face pale as ashes. The next second he sprang upon Jones, seized with both hands the collar of his coat, shook him, flung him violently to the ground, and kicked his hat, which had fallen off in the struggle, straight into the river.

"What the deuce go you mean by that?" asked Jones, picking himself up. "I'll just give you—fifth-form, or no fifth-form— the best licking you ever had."

St. Winifred's, or The World of School

"You'll just not presume to lay upon him the tip of your finger," said Whalley, who was quite as big as Jones, and was very fond of Kenrick.

"Not for flinging me down, and kicking my hat into the water?"

"No, Jones," said Whalley quietly. "I don't know what you were talking about, but you clearly meant to insult him, from your manner."

"What's the row? what's up?" said a number of boys, who began to throng round.

"Only a plebeian splutter of rage from our well-bred friend there," said Mackworth, pointing contemptuously at Kenrick, who stood with dilated nostrils, still heaving with rage.

"But what about?"

"Heaven only knows;—*apropos* of just nothing."

"You're a liar," said Kenrick impetuously. "You know that you told lies and insulted me; and if you say it again, I'll do the same again."

"Only try!" said Jones in a surly tone.

"Insulted you?" said Mackworth in bland accents. "We were talking about a dishonest parson, as far as I remember. Pray, are you a dishonest parson?"

"You'd better take care," said Kenrick, with fierce energy.

"Take care of what? We didn't ask *you* to listen to our conversation; listeners hear no—"

"Bosh!" interposed Whalley; "you know you were talking at the top of your voices, and we couldn't help hearing you."

"And what then? Mayn't we talk as loud as we like?—I assure you, on my word of honour," he said, turning to the group around them, "we didn't even mention Kenrick's name. We were merely talking about a certain dishonest parson who rode in hay-carts, when the fellow sprung on Jones like a tiger-cat. I'm sure, if he's any objection to our talking of such unpleasant people we won't do so in his hearing," paid Mackworth, in an excess of venomous politeness.

"French Varnish," said Whalley, with honest contempt, moved beyond his wont with indignation, though he did not understand the cause of Kenrick's anger. "I wonder why Kenrick should even condescend to notice what such fellows as you and Jones say.— Come along, Ken; you know what we all think about those two;" and, putting his arm in Kenrick's, he almost dragged him from the scene, while Jones and Mackworth, (conscious that there was not a single other boy who would not condemn their conduct as infamous when they understood it), were not sorry to move off in another direction.

But when Whalley had taken Kenrick to a quiet place by the riverside, and asked him, "what had made him so furious?" he returned no answer, only hiding his face in his hands. He had indeed been cruelly insulted, wounded in his tenderest sensibilities; he felt that his best affections had been wantonly and violently lacerated. It made him more miserable than he had ever felt before, and he could not tolerate the wretched thought that his father's sad history, probably in some distorted form, had been, by some means or other, bruited about among unsympathising hearers, and made the common property of the school. He knew well indeed the natural delicacy of feeling which would prevent any other boy, except Jones or Mackworth, from ever alluding to it even in the remotest way. But that they should know at all the shameful charge which had broken his father's heart, and brought temporary suspicion and dishonour on his name, was gall and wormwood to him.

Yet, what possible means could this have become known to them? Kenrick knew of one way only. He thought over what Jones had said. "A cart and blind horse—ah! I see; there is *only one person* who could have told him about that. So, *Walter Evson*, you amuse yourself and Jones by making fun of our being poor, and by ridiculing what you saw in our house; a very good laugh you've all had over it in the dormitory, I've no doubt."

Kenrick did not know that Jones had seen them from the window of the railway carriage, and that as he had been visiting an aunt at no great distance, he had heard there the particulars of Mr Kenrick's history. He clutched angrily at the conclusion, that *Walter* had betrayed him, and turned him into derision. Naturally passionate, growing up during the wilful years of opening boyhood without a father's wise control, he did not stop to inquire, but leapt at once to a false and obstinate inference. "It must be so; it clearly *is* so," he thought; "yet I could not have believed it of him;" and he burst into a flood of bitter and angry tears.

The fact was that Kenrick, though he would hardly have admitted it even to himself, was in a particularly ready mood to take offence. He had observed that Walter disapproved of his manner towards his mother, and his sensitive pride had already been ruffled by the fact that Walter had exercised the moral courage of pointing out, though in the most delicate and modest way, the brusquerie which he reprobated. At the time he had said little, but in reality this had made him very, very angry; and the more so because he was jealous enough to fancy that he now stood second only, or even third, in Walter's estimation, and that Power and Henderson had deposed him from the place which he once held as his chief friend; and that Walter had also usurped *his* old place in *their* affections. This displeased him greatly, for he was not one who could contentedly take the second place. He could not have had a more excellent companion than the manly and upright Whalley; but in his close intimacy with him he had rather hoped to pique Walter, and show him that his society was not indispensable to his happiness. But Walter's open and generous mind was quite incapable of understanding this unworthy motive, and with feelings far better trained than those of Kenrick, he never felt the slightest qualm of this small jealousy.

"Never mind, my dear fellow," said Whalley, patting him on the back; "why should you care so much because two *such* fellows as Whitefeather and Varnish try to be impudent. I shouldn't care the snap of a finger for anything they could say."

"It isn't that, Whalley, it isn't that," said Kenrick proudly, drying his tears. "But how did those fellows know the things they were hinting at? Only one person ever heard them, and he must have betrayed them to laugh at me behind my back. It's *that* that makes me miserable."

"But whom do you mean?"

"The excellent Evson," said Kenrick bitterly. "And mark me, Whalley, I'll never speak to him again."

"*Evson?*" said Whalley, "I don't believe he's at all the fellow to do it. Are you certain?"

"Quite. No one else could know the things."

"But surely you'll ask him first?"

"It's no use," answered Kenrick gloomily; "but I *will*, in order that he may understand that I have found him out."

CHAPTER TWENTY THREE. A BROKEN FRIENDSHIP.

> Everard, Everard, which was the truest,
>   God in the future, and Time will show;
> Ne'er will I stoop to defence or excuses—
> If you despise me—be it so!
> But, my Everard, still (for I love you)
>   This to the end my prayer shall be—
> Ne'er may you be so sternly treated,
>   Never be judged as you judge me.—*F.*

Kenrick did not happen to meet Walter during the remainder of that Sunday, because Walter was chiefly sitting in Mr Percival's room, but the next day, still nursing the smouldering fire of his anger, he determined to get the first opportunity he could of meeting him, in order that he might tax him with his supposed false friendship and breach of confidence.

Accordingly, when school was over next day, he went with Whalley to look for him in the playground. Walter was walking with Henderson, never dreaming that anything unpleasant was likely to happen. Henderson was the first to catch sight of them, and as he never saw Whalley without chaffing him in some ridiculous way or other—for Whalley's charming good humour made him a capital subject for a joke—he at once began, as might have been expected, to sing—

> "O Whalley, Whalley up the bank,
> And Whalley, Whalley down the brae,
> And Whalley, Whalley by yon burnside—"

St. Winifred's, or The World of School

Whereupon his song was interrupted by Whalley's giving chase to him, which did not end till he had been led a dance half round the school buildings, while the ground was left clear for Kenrick's expostulations.

Walter came up to him as cordially as usual, but stopped short in surprise, when he caught the scornful lowering expression of his friend's face; but as Kenrick did not speak at once, he took him by the hand, and said, "Why, Ken, what's the matter?"

Kenrick very coldly withdrew his hand.

"Evson, I came to ask you if—whether—if you've been telling to any of the fellows all about me;—all I told you about my father?"

As Walter instantly remembered that he had mentioned the story to Power, he could not at once say, "No," but was about to explain.

"Telling any of the fellows all about you and your father?" he repeated; "I didn't know—"

"Please, I don't want any excuses. If you haven't, it's easy to say No; if you *have*, I only want you to say Yes."

"But you never told me that I wasn't to—"

"Yes or no?" said Kenrick, with an impatient gesture.

"Well, I suppose I must say Yes then; but hear me explain. I only mentioned it to—"

"That's enough, thank you. I don't want to hear any more. I don't want to know whom you mentioned it to;" and Kenrick turned short on his heel, and began to walk off.

"But hear me, Ken," said Walter eagerly, walking after him, and laying his hand on his shoulder.

"My name's Kenrick," said he, shaking off Walter's hand. "You may apologise if you like; but even then I shan't speak to you again."

St. Winifred's, or The World of School

"I have nothing to apologise for. I only told—"

"I tell you I don't care whom you `only' told. It's `only' all over the school. And it's not the `only' time you've behaved dishonourably."

"I don't understand you," said Walter, who was rapidly getting into as great a passion as Kenrick.

"Betraying confidence is *almost* as bad as breaking open desks, and burning—" Such a taunt, coming from Kenrick, was base and cruel, and he knew it to be so.

"Thank you for the allusion," said Walter; "I deserve it, I own, but I'm surprised, Kenrick, that *you*, of all others, should make it. *That*, I admit, was an act of sin and strange folly for which I must always feel humiliated, and implore to be forgiven. And every generous person *has* long ago forgiven me and forgotten it. But in *this* case, if you weren't in such a silly rage, I could show you that I've done nothing wrong. Only I know you wouldn't listen *now*, and I shan't condescend—"

"*Condescend*! I like that," said Kenrick, interrupting him with a scornful laugh, which made Walter's blood tingle. "*You* condescend to *me*, forsooth." Higher words might have ensued, but at this moment Henderson, still pursued by Whalley, came running up, and seeing that something had gone wrong, he said to Kenrick:

"Hallo, Damon! what has Pythias been saying to you?"

Kenrick vouchsafed no answer, but turning his back on them, went off abruptly.

"He's very angry with you, Evson," said Whalley, "because he thinks you've been telling Jones and that lot his family secrets."

"I've done nothing whatever of the kind," said Walter indignantly. "I admit that I did thoughtlessly mention it to Power; and one other overheard me. It never occurred to me for a moment that Kenrick would mind. You know I wouldn't dream of speaking about it ill-naturedly, and if that fellow wasn't blind with rage I could have explained it to him in five minutes."

"If you merely mentioned it to Power I'm sure Kenrick would not so much mind. I'll tell him about it when he's cooler," said Whalley.

"As you like, Whalley; Kenrick has no business to suspect me in that shameful way, and to abuse me, and treat me as if I was quite beneath his notice, and cast old faults in my teeth," answered Walter with deep vexation. "Let him find out the truth for himself. He can, if he takes the trouble."

Both the friends were thoroughly angry with each other; each of them imagined himself deeply wronged by the other, and each of them, in his irritation, used strong and unguarded expressions which lost nothing by repetition. Thus the "rift of difference" was cleft deeper and deeper between them; and, chiefly through Kenrick's pride and precipitancy, a disagreement which might at first have been easily adjusted, became a serious, and threatened to become a permanent, quarrel.

"Power, did you repeat what I told you about Kenrick to any one?" asked Walter, next time he met him.

"Repeat it?" said Power; "why, Walter, do you suppose I would? What do you take me for?"

"All right, Power; I knew that you couldn't do such a thing; but Kenrick declares I've spread it all over the school, and has just been abusing me like a pickpocket." Walter told him the circumstances of the case, and Power, displeased for Walter's sake, and sorry that two real friends should be separated by what he could not but regard as a venial error on Walter's part, advised him to write a note to Kenrick, and explain the true facts of the case again.

"But what's the use, Power?" said Walter; "he would not listen to my explanation, and said as many hard things of me as he could."

"Yes, in a passion. He'll be sorry for them directly he's calm; for you know what a generous fellow he is. You can forgive them, I'm sure, Walter, and win the pleasure of being the first to make an advance."

St. Winifred's, or The World of School

Walter, after a little struggle with his resentment, wrote a note, and gave it to Whalley to give to Kenrick next time he saw him. It ran as follows:

"My Dear Kenrick,—

"I think you are a little hard upon me. Who can have told Jones anything about you and your home secrets I don't know. He *could* not have learnt them through me. It's true I did mention something about your father to Power when I was talking in the most affectionate way about you. I'm very sorry for this, but I never dreamt it would make you so angry. Power is the last person to repeat such a thing. Pray forgive me, and believe me always to be—Your affectionate friend,

"Walter Evson."

Kenrick's first impulse on receiving this note was to seek Walter on the earliest occasion, and "make it up" with him in the sincerest and heartiest way he could. But suddenly the sight of Jones and Mackworth vividly reminded his proud and sensitive nature of the scene that had caused him such acute pain. He did not see how Jones *could* have learnt about the vehicle, at any rate, without Walter having laughed over it to some one. Instead of seeking further explanation, or thinking no evil and hoping all things, he again gave reins to his anger and suspicion, and wrote:

"I am bound to believe your explanation as far as it goes. But I have reason to *know* that *something* more must have passed than what you admit yourself to have said. I am astonished that you should have treated me so unworthily. I would not have done so to you. I will try to forget this unpleasant business; but it is only in a sense that I can sign myself again—Your affectionate friend,

"H. Kenrick."

St. Winifred's, or The World of School

Walter had not expected this cold, ungracious reply. When Whalley gave him Kenrick's note he tore it open eagerly, anticipating a frank renewal of their former friendship; but a red spot rose to his cheeks as he saw the insinuation that he had not told the whole truth, and as he tore up the note, he indignantly determined to take no further step towards a reconciliation.

Yet as he thought how many pleasant hours they had spent together, and how firmly on the whole Kenrick had stood by him in his troubles, and how lovable a boy he really was, Walter could not but grieve over this difference. He found himself often yearning to be on the old terms with Kenrick; he felt that at heart he still loved him well, and after a few days he again stifled all pride, and wrote:

"Dear Ken,—

"Is it possible that you will not believe my word?

"If you still feel any doubt about what I have said, do
come and see me in Power's study. I am sure that I would
convince you in five minutes that you must be under some
mistake; and if I have done you any wrong, or if you
think that I have done you any wrong, Ken, I'll
apologise sincerely without any pride or reserve. I miss
your society very much, and I still am and shall be,
whatever you may think and whatever you may say of me—
Yours affectionately,

"W.E."

As he naturally did not wish any third person to know what was passing between them he did not entrust this note to any one, but himself placed it between the leaves of an Herodotus which he knew that Kenrick would use at the next school. He had barely put it there when a boy who wanted an Herodotus happened to come into the classroom, and seeing Kenrick's lying on the table, coolly walked off with it, after the manner of boys, regardless of the inconvenience to which the owner might be put. As this boy was reading a different part of Herodotus from that which Kenrick was reading, Walter's note lay between the leaves where it had been placed, unnoticed. When the book was done with, the boy forgot it, and left it in school, where, after kicking about for some days unowned, it was consigned with other stray volumes to a miscellaneous cupboard, where it lay undisturbed for years. Kenrick supposed that it was lost, or that some one had "bagged" it; and, unknown to Walter, his note never reached the hands for which it had been destined. In vain he waited for a reply; in vain he looked for some word or sign to show that Kenrick had received his letter. But Kenrick still met him in perfect silence, and with averted looks; and Walter, surprised at his obstinate unkindness, thought that he *could* do nothing more to disabuse him of his false impression, and was the more ready to forego a friendship which by every honourable means he had endeavoured to retain.

Poor Kenrick! he felt as much as Walter did that he had lost one of his truest and most pleasant friends, and he, too, often yearned for the old intercourse between them. Even his best friends, Power, Henderson, and Whalley, all thought him wrong; and in consequence a coolness rose between them and him. He felt thoroughly miserable, and did not know where to turn; yet none the less he ostentatiously abstained from making the slightest overture to Walter; and whereas the two boys might have enjoyed together many happy hours, they felt a continual embarrassment at being obliged to meet each other very frequently in awkward silence, and apparent unconsciousness of each other's presence. This silent annoyance recurred continually at all hours of the day. They threw away the golden opportunity of smoothing and brightening for each other their schoolboy years. It is sad that since true friends are so few, such slight differences, such trivial misunderstandings, should separate them for years. If a man's penitence for past follies be humble and sincere, his crimes and failings may well be buried in a generous oblivion; but, alas! his own friends, and they of his own household, are too often *the last* to forgive and to forget. Too often they do not condone the fault till years of unhappiness and disappointment have intervened; till the wounds which they have inflicted are cicatrised; till the sinner's loneliness has taught him to look for other than human sympathy; till he is too old, too sorrowful, too heart-broken, too near the Great White Throne, to expect any joy from human friendship, or any consolation in human love.

Twice did chance throw the friends into situations in which a reconciliation would have been easy. Once, when the school was assembled to hear the result of some composition prizes, they found themselves accidentally seated, one on each side of Power. The mottos on the envelopes which were sent in with the successful exercises were always read out before the envelope was opened, and in one of the prizes for which there had been many competitors, the punning motto, *Ezouiazoo*, told them at once that Power had again achieved a brilliant success. The Great Hall was always a scene for the triumphs of this happy boy. Both Walter and Kenrick turned at the same moment to congratulate him, Walter seizing his right hand and Kenrick his left. Power, after thanking them for their warm congratulations, grasped both their hands, and drew them towards each other. Kenrick was aware of what he meant, and his heart fluttered as he now hoped to regain a lost friend; but just at that moment Walter's attention happened to be attracted by Eden, who, though sitting some benches off, wished to telegraph his congratulations to Power. Unfortunately, therefore, Walter turned his head away, before he knew that Kenrick's hand was actually touching his. He did not perceive Power's kind intention until the opportunity was lost; and Kenrick, misinterpreting his conduct, had flushed with sudden pride, and hastily withdrawn his hand.

On the second occasion Walter had gone up the hill to the churchyard, by the side of which was a pleasant stile, overshadowed by aged elms, on which he often sat reading or enjoying the breeze and the view. It suddenly occurred to him that he would look at Daubeny's grave, to see if the stone had yet been put up. He found that it had just been raised, and he was sorrowfully reading the inscription, when a footstep roused him from his mournful recollections. A glance showed him that Kenrick was approaching, evidently with the same purpose. He came slowly to the grave and read the epitaph. Their eyes met in a friendly gaze. A sudden impulse to reconciliation seized them both, and they were on the verge of shaking hands, when three boys came sauntering through the churchyard;—one of them was the ill-omened Jones. The association jarred on both their minds, and turning away without a word they walked home in different directions.

CHAPTER TWENTY FOUR. EDEN'S TROUBLES.

Et tibi quae Samios diduxit littera ramos,
Surgenten dextro monstravit limite callem.
    Persae, 3, 56.

There has the Samian V's instructive make,
Pointed the road thy doubtful foot should take;
There warned thy raw and yet unpractised youth,
To tread the rising right-hand path of truth.
    Brewster.

St. Winifred's, or The World of School

They went home in different directions, and morally too their paths henceforth were widely diverse. The Pythagoreans chose the letter V as their symbol for a good and evil life. The broad, sloping, almost perpendicular left-hand stroke is an apt emblem for the facile downward descent into Avernus; the precipitous and narrow right-hand stroke aptly presents the slippery, uphillward struggle of a virtuous course. I remember to have seen, as a child, another and a similar emblem which impressed me much. On the one side of the picture a snail was slowly creeping up a steep path; on the other a stag rushed and bounded unrestrained down the sheer proclivities of a wide and darkening hill. Improvement is ever slow and difficult; degeneracy is too often startlingly rapid. From henceforth, as we shall have occasion to see hereafter, Walter was progressing from strength to strength, adding to faith virtue, and to virtue temperance, and to temperance knowledge, and to knowledge brotherly kindness, and to brotherly kindness charity—

Springing from crystal step to crystal step
Of the bright air;

—while our poor Kenrick was gradually descending deeper and deeper into darkness and despair.

Yet he loved Walter, and sighed for the old intimacy, while he was daily abusing his character and affecting to scorn his conduct. In short, a change came over Kenrick. There had always been a little worm at the root of his admiration of and affection for Walter. It was jealousy. He did not like to hear him praised so loudly by his friends and schoolfellows; and besides this, he was vexed that Walter, Henderson, and Power, were more closely allied to each other than to him. He had struggled successfully against these unworthy feelings so long as Walter was his friend, but now that he had allowed himself to seek a quarrel with him they grew up with tremendous luxuriance. And he was so thoroughly in the wrong, and so obstinate in persisting to misunderstand and misrepresent his former friend, that gradually, by his pertinacity and injustice, he alienated the regards of all those who had once been his chosen companions. Even Whalley grew cool towards him. He had to look elsewhere for associates, and unhappily he looked in the wrong direction.

Meanwhile Walter, although he constantly grieved at the loss of a friend, was otherwise very happy. The boys at St Winifred's were not overworked; there was enough work to stimulate but not to oppress them, and Walter's work grew more promising every day. He was fond of praise, and Mr Percival, while he always took care so to praise him as to obviate the danger of conceit, was not so scant of his approbation as most men are. His warm and generous appreciation encouraged and rewarded Walter's exertions, so that he was quite the "star" of his form. Many other boys did well under Mr Percival. There was a bright and cheerful emulation among them all, and they took especial pains with their exercises, which Mr Percival varied in every possible way, so as to call out the imagination and the fancy, to exercise both the reason and the understanding, and to test the powers of attention and research. His method was so successful that it was often a real pleasure to look over the exercises of his form, and he had adopted one plan for keeping up the boys' interest in them, which was eminently useful. All the *best* exercises, if they attained to any positive excellence, were sent to Dr Lane; and at the end of the half-year, a number, printed opposite to the boy's name, showed how often he had thus been "sent up for good." If in one fortnight *four* separate exercises were so sent up, the form obtained, by this proof of industry, the remission of an hour's work, and as this honour could never be cheaply won it was highly prized. Now two or three times Walter's unusually brilliant exercises had been the chief contribution towards winning those remitted hours, and this success caused him double happiness, because it necessarily made him a general favourite with the form. Henderson (who had only got a single remove at the beginning of the term, but had worked so hard in his new form that he had succeeded in his purpose of winning a remove *during* the term, and so being again in the same division with Walter) did his best to earn the same distinction, but he only succeeded when the exercise happened to be an English one, and on a subject which gave some opportunity for his sense of the ludicrous. He generally contrived to introduce some purely fictitious "Eastern Apologue" as he called it; and as he rarely managed to keep the correct Oriental colouring, his combinations of Sultans, Tchokadars, Odaliques, and white bears were sometimes so inexpressibly absurd that Mr Percival, to avoid fits of laughter, was obliged to look over his exercises alone. Nor were his eccentricities always confined to his English themes; his Latin verses were occasionally no less extraordinary, and in one set, on the suicide of Ajax, the last few lines consisted of fragmentary words interspersed here and there with numerous stars —a phenomenon which he explained to Mr Percival in the gravest manner possible, by saying that here the voice of Ajax was interrupted by sobs!

Happy in his work, Walter was no less happy in his play. The glorious midday bathes on the hard sparkling yellow sands when the sea was smooth as the blue of heaven, and clear as transparent glass—the long afternoons on the green and sunny cricket-field—the strolls over the mountains, and lazy readings under a tree in the fragrant fir-groves—all invigorated him, and gave to his face the health, and to his heart the mirth, which told of an innocent life and a vigorous frame.

But it must not be supposed that he escaped troubles of his own, and his first trouble arose out of the kind boyish protectorate which he had established over little Eden's interests.

His rescue of Eden from the clutches of a bad lot was one of Walter's proudest and gladdest reminiscences. Instead of moping about miserable and lonely, and rapidly developing into a rank harvest the evil seeds which his tormentors had tried to plant in his young heart, Eden was now the gayest of the gay. Secure from most annoyances by possessing the refuge of Power's study, and the certainty of Walter's help, he soon began to assert his own position among all the boys of his own age and standing. No longer crushed and intimidated by bullying and bad companions, he was lively, happy, and universally liked, but never happier than when Walter and Power admitted him, as they constantly did, into their own society.

Harpour and Jones, in their hatred against Walter, had an especial reason to keep Eden as far as they could under subjection, in addition to their general propensity to bully and domineer. They did not care to torment him when Walter was present, because with him, in spite of their hostility, they felt it wise to maintain an armed neutrality. But whenever Walter was absent, they felt themselves safe. None of the other boys in their dormitory interfered except Henderson, and his interposition, though always generous, was both morally and physically weaker than Walter's. He would not, indeed, allow any positive cruelty, but he was not thoughtful or stable enough to see the duty of interfering to prevent other and hardly less tolerable persecutions.

It so happened that at a game of cricket Walter by accident had received a blow on the knee from the cricket-ball bowled by Franklin, who was a tremendously hard and swift bowler. The hurt which this had caused was so severe that he was ordered by Dr Keith to sleep on the ground floor in the cottage for a fortnight, in order to save him the exertion of running up and down so many stairs. The opportunity of this prolonged absence was maliciously seized by the tyrants of Number 10; but Eden bore up far more manfully than he had done in the old days. He was quite a different, and a far braver little fellow, thanks to Walter, than he had been the term before; and, looking forward to his friend's speedy return, he determined to bear his troubles without saying a word about them. He was far more bullied during this period than Henderson knew of, for some of the threats and commands by which he was coerced were given in Henderson's absence, as he was allowed to sit up half an hour later than those in the form below. For instance, Eden was ordered never to look at a book or to finish learning his lessons in the bedroom; and he was strictly forbidden to get up until the second bell rang in the morning. If he disobeyed these orders, he was soused with water, pelted with shoes, and beaten with slippers, and on the whole he found it better to be content to lose place in form, and to get impositions for missing chapel, than to attempt to brave these hindrances. When, however, he had been late two mornings running, Henderson got the secret out of him, and at once entreated Harpour and Jones to abandon this cruelty, throwing out hints that if they refused, he would take some measures to get it stopped by one of the monitors. If Eden had been plucky enough to embrace his natural right of obtaining protection from one of his own schoolfellows in the sixth, he would have been efficiently defended. Appealing to a monitor in order to secure immunity from disgraceful, and wholly intolerable bullying, is a very different thing from telling a master; and although the worst boys tried to get it traditionally regarded as an unmitigated form of sneaking, yet the public opinion of the best part of the school would have been found to justify it. But the two bullies knew that Eden would never have the heart to venture on this appeal; and although they desisted from this particular practice at Henderson's request, they knew that he was too wavering a character, and too fond of popularity, to be *easily* induced to make them his open enemies. If Eden had only told Walter, he knew that Walter would have sheltered him from unkindness at all hazards; but he was a thoroughly grateful child, and did not wish to get Walter into any difficulties on his account. So, in schoolboy phrase, there was nothing left for him but to "grin and bear it"; which he heroically did, earnestly longing for Walter's return to the dormitory as for some golden age. But his trials were not over yet.

Is there in human nature an instinctive cruelty? That there is in it—*when ill-trained*—an absorbing selfishness, a total absence of all tenderness and delicate consideration, is abundantly obvious. But besides this, there is often an astonishing and almost incredible tendency to take positive pleasure in the infliction of pain. Now it so happens that Jones and Harpour were bad boys, as I have shown already, in the worst sense of the word, and yet the real *enjoyment* which they felt in making little Eden's life miserable is an inexplicable phenomenon. One would have thought that the mere sight of the little boy, his tender age, his delicate look, his extreme gentleness and courtesy of manner, and the mute appealing glance in his blue eyes, would have sufficed to protect him from wanton outrage. It *did* suffice with most boys; but if anything, it added zest and piquancy to the persecutions of those two big bullies.

Reader, have you ever been "taken prisoner"? that is to say, have you ever been awaked from a sweet sleep by feeling an intolerable agony in your right toe, and finding that it is caused by somebody having tied a string tight round it without waking you, and then pulling the said string with all his force? If not, congratulate yourself thereupon, and accept the assurance of one who has undergone it, that the pain caused by this process is absolutely excruciating. It was this pain which made Eden start up with a scream during one of the nights I speak of, and the cry rose in intensity as he grew fully awake to the sensation.

"Hallo! what's the row, Eden?" said Henderson, starting up in bed; but the child could only continue his screams, and Henderson, springing out of bed, stumbled against the string, and instantly (for the trick was a familiar one) knew what was being done. As quick as thought he seized the string with his right hand and, by pulling it *towards* Eden, slackened the horrible tension of it, while with his left hand he rapidly took out a knife from his coat pocket and cut the cord in two.

Jones and Harpour, tittering at the success of their machination, were standing with the string in their hands just outside the door in the passage, and the sudden jerk showed them that the string was severed.

"I'll tell you what it is," said Henderson to them, with the most deliberate emphasis, "I don't care if you do lick me for telling you the truth, but you two are just a couple of the greatest brutes in the school."

"What's the matter, Flip?" asked Franklin, from his bed, in a drowsy tone.

"Matter! why, those two *brutes*," said Henderson with strong indignation, "have been taking poor little Eden prisoner, and hurting him awfully."

"What a confounded shame!" said Franklin and Anthony in one voice; for they, too, though they were sturdy fellows, had had some experience of the bullies in their earlier schooldays; and of late, following Walter's example, they had always energetically opposed this maltreatment of Eden.

"Draw it mild, you three, or we'll kick you," said Harpour.

"But we won't draw it mild," said Franklin; "it's quite true; you and Jones *are* brutes to bully that poor little fellow so. He never hurt you."

"What an uppish lot you nips are," said Harpour; "it's all that fellow Evson's doing. Hang me, if I don't take it out of you;" and he advanced with a slipper in his hand towards Franklin.

"Touch him if you dare," said Henderson; "if you do, Anthony and I will stick by him; and Cradock, you'll see fair-play, won't you?"

"Pooh!" said Cradock. "I'm asleep. Fight it out by yourselves."

"Never mind these little fools, Harpour," said Jones; "they're beneath your notice. Besides, it's time to turn off to sleep." For Jones had earned his soubriquet by always showing a particularly large white feather when there was any chance of a fray.

"Phew, Jones; none of us would give much for *you*," said Henderson contemptuously. "*Little* fools, indeed! You know very well that *you* daren't lay a finger on the least of us, whether we're beneath your notice or no. An ostrich is a big bird, but its white feathers are chiefly of use in helping it to run away." He went to Eden's bedside, for the child was still sobbing with pain, and was evidently in a great state of nervous agitation.

"Never mind, Eden," he said in a kind and soothing voice; "think no more of it; we won't let them take you prisoner again." And as he spoke he took his place by Eden's side, and looked with angry defiance at the two bullies.

"Those fellows hurt me so," said Eden in an apologetic tone, bravely trying to check his tears. "Oh, I wish Evson would come back."

"He is coming back in a night or two; his knee is nearly well. I haven't helped you enough, poor little fellow. I'm so sorry. I say, you *brutes*," he continued, raising his voice, "next time you bully Eden, I'll tell Somers, as sure as fate."

St. Winifred's, or The World of School

"Tell away then," jeered Harpour; "better go and tell him before your shoes wear out."

"Ah, you'll change your tone, Master Harpour, when you've been well whopped," answered Henderson.

"I should like to see Somers or any one else whop me," said Harpour in an extremely "Ercles vein": "by Jove! Lane himself shouldn't do it."

"Oh, indeed!"

"I'll `oh, indeed' you!" said Harpour, getting out of bed; but here Cradock interfered, seized Harpour with his brawny arm, and said:

"There, that's badgering enough for one night. Do let a fellow go to sleep."

Harpour got into bed again, and Henderson, once more reassuring Eden that he should not be again molested, followed his example. But, half with fright and half with pain, the poor boy lay awake most of the night, and when he *did* fall asleep he constantly started up again with troubled dreams.

Next morning, the two parties in the dormitory would hardly speak to each other. They rose at daggers drawn, and in the highest dudgeon. Henderson was glad Anthony and Franklin had openly espoused the right side, and was pleased at *anything* which drew them out of the pernicious influence of the other two. This wasn't by any means a pleasant state of things for Jones and Harpour, and it made them hate Eden, the innocent cause of it, more than ever. Moreover, Harpour, who was not accustomed to be openly bearded, did not choose to let the reins of despotism slip so easily out of his hands, and determined to avenge himself yet, and to show that neither entreaties nor threats should prevent him from being as great a bully as he chose.

"Understand *you*, Henderson," he said, while they were dressing, "that I shall do exactly what I like to that little muff there."

Eden reddened and said nothing; but Henderson, looking up from his washhand basin, replied, "And understand *you*, Harpour, that if you bully him any more, I'll tell the head of the school."

Harpour made a spring at Henderson to thrash him for these words, but again the burly Cradock interposed, saying good-humouredly, as he put himself in Harpour's way, "There, stop squabbling, for goodness' sake, you two, and let's have a little peace. Flip, you shut up."

CHAPTER TWENTY FIVE. EDEN'S TROUBLES.

>Alas! how easily things go wrong!
>* * * * * * * *
>And there follows a mist and a weeping rain,
>And life is *never* the same again!
>George Macdonald, *Phantastes*.

Eden felt an immeasurable delight when Walter was allowed to come back to the dormitory, and now he thought himself happy in a perfect security from further torment.

But the two tyrants had other views. Harpour, at once passionate and dogged, was not likely to forget that he had been thwarted and defied; and if he had been so inclined, Jones would not have allowed him to do so, but kept egging him on to show his contempt for the younger and weaker boys who had tried to check his bullying propensities. On the last occasion when he had ordered Eden to go to Dan's, Eden had taken Walter's advice, and firmly refused to go. Harpour did not think it safe to compel him, but he threw out some significant threats which filled the little boy with vague alarm and weighed heavily on his spirits. He did not tell any one of these threats, hoping that they would end in nothing, and, in case of any emergency, trusting implicitly on Walter for a generous and efficient protection.

But the threats did *not* end in nothing.

One night, after the others had fallen asleep, Eden, feeling quite free from all anxiety, was sleeping more soundly and sweetly than he had done for a fortnight, when a blaze of light, flashing suddenly upon his eyes, made him start up in his bed. Harpour and Jones were taking this opportunity to fulfil their threats of frightening him. At the foot of his bed stood a figure in white, with a hideous, deformed head, blotched with scarlet; bending over him was another white figure, with an enormous black face, holding over its head a shining hand.

In an instant the boy fell back, pale as death, uttering a shriek so shrill and terrible, so full of wildness and horror, that every other boy in the dormitory sprang up, alarmed and wide awake.

Walter and Henderson leaped out of bed immediately; and to Walter, who was unprepared, the start of surprise at what he saw was so sudden, that for a moment he stood absolutely paralysed and bewildered, because the shock on the nerves had preceded the recognition, though by an infinitesimally short time. But Henderson, who knew how Jones and Harpour had been going on, and what their threats had been, instantly, and before the abrupt and unusual spectacle had power to unnerve him, saw the true state of the case, and, springing out upon the figure which stood at the end of Eden's bed, tore the mask away, stripped off the sheet, and displayed Jones's face before he had time to hide it, administering, as he did so, a hearty blow on Jones's chest, which made that hero stagger several paces back.

Although Walter saw almost at once the trick that was being played with masks, sheets, and phosphorus, yet the sudden shock upon his nerves not being *absolutely co-instantaneous* with the discovery, produced on him the effect of utter dizziness and horror. Henderson's prompt and vigorous onslaught aroused him to a sense of the position, and with a fierce expression of disgust and anger, he bounded upon Harpour, who, being thus suddenly attacked, dropped upon the floor the dark lantern which he held, and hastily retreated, flinging the sheet over Walter's head.

Walter had barely disentangled himself from the folds of the sheet, when an exclamation from Henderson attracted the notice of all the boys in the room, and brought them flocking round Eden's bed. Henderson had picked up the dark lantern, and was kneeling with it over the unconscious boy, whose face was so ashy white, and who, after several sharp screams, had sunk into so deep a swoon, that Henderson, unused to such sights, naturally exclaimed:

"Good God! you've killed him."

"Killed him?" repeated the others, standing aghast.

St. Winifred's, or The World of School

"Pooh! he's only fainted, you little fools," said Jones, who hurried up to look in Eden's face. "Here, we'll soon bring him to; Harpour, just get us some water."

"You shan't touch him, you shan't come near him," said Walter furiously; "stand back, you hateful bullies. Henderson and I will attend to him; and, depend upon it, you shall give account for this soon. What! you *will* come?" he continued, shaking Jones's arm violently, and then flinging him back as easily as though he had been a child; "if either you or Harpour come near the bed, I'll fetch Robertson instantly. Eden would go off again in a swoon if he saw such brutes as you when he recovered."

In such a mood Walter was not to be resisted. The two plotters, picking up their masks, retired somewhat crestfallen, and sat down on their beds, while the rest, with the utmost tenderness, adopted every means they knew to recall Eden's fluttered and agitated senses.

But his swoon was deeper than they could manage, and, growing too violently alarmed to trust themselves any longer, Henderson and Walter proposed to carry him to the sick-room, and put him at once under the care of Dr Keith. It was in vain that Jones and Harpour entreated, threatened, implored them to delay a little longer, lest by taking Eden to the sick-room their doings should be discovered. Wholly disregarding all they said, the two boys uplifted their still fainting friend, and when Harpour attempted to interfere between them and the door, Cradock and Franklin, now *thoroughly* sickened by their proceedings, pulled him aside and let them pass.

Dr Keith instantly administered to Eden a restorative, and after receiving from Walter a hurried explanation of the circumstances, gently told the boys that they would be only in the way there, that Eden was evidently in a critical position, and that they had better return at once to their dormitories.

Walter and Henderson, when they returned, were assailed by the others with eager inquiries, to which they could only give gloomy and uncertain answers. They would not vouchsafe to take the slightest notice of Jones or Harpour, but met all their remarks with resolute silence. But before he went to sleep, Walter said, "I may as well let you fellows know that I intend to report you to Somers to-morrow."

"Then you'll be a sneak," observed Harpour.

St. Winifred's, or The World of School

"It is not sneaking to prevent brutal bullying like yours, by giving others the chance of stopping it, and preventing little chaps like poor Eden, whom you've nearly frightened to death, from being so shamefully treated. Anyhow, sneaking or not, I'll do it."

"If you *do* tell Somers, look out for yourself—that's all."

"I'm not afraid," was the brief retort.

Harpour knew that he meant what he said, and, being now desperate, he got up half an hour earlier next morning to try and extort from him, by main force, a promise to hold his tongue about the affair of the night before. If he had at all understood Walter's character, he might have saved himself this very superfluous trouble.

Walter was awoken by a shake from Harpour, who, with Jones, was standing by his bed. He saw what was coming, for Harpour, who had a pair of braces tightly knotted in his hand, briefly opened the proceedings by saying, "Are you going to sneak about me, or not?"

"To sneak—no; to tell the head of the school—yes."

"Then, by Jove, you shall have something worth telling; I'll take my revenge out of you beforehand. I shall be sent away—think of that."

"So much the better. One bully the less."

"Oh, that's your tune? Take that." The buckle of the brace descended sharply on Walter's back, drawing blood; the next instant he had wrested it out of Harpour's hand, and returned the blow.

The scuffle had awoken the rest. Walter jumped out of bed, and was hurrying on his trousers and slippers, when Harpour knocked him down.

"Fair-play, Harpour," said Henderson and Franklin angrily, seizing Harpour's arms; "you're surely not going to fight him, Walter?"

St. Winifred's, or The World of School

"Yes; see fair-play, you fellows; Cradock, you will, won't you? Fair-play is all I want. Flip, you see that Jones tries no mean dodge. Now, Harpour, are you ready? Then take that."

Walter hit him a steady blow in the face, and the fight between these unequally-matched combatants—a boy not fifteen against a much stronger boy of seventeen—began. The result could not be dubious. Walter fought with indomitable pluck; it was splendid to see the sturdiness with which he bore up under the blows of Harpour's strong fist, which he could only return at intervals. He was tremendously punished, while Harpour was barely touched, except by one well-directed blow which flashed the fire out of his eyes. At last he dealt Walter a heavy blow full on the forehead; the boy reeled, caught hold of the washhand-stand to stay his fall, and dragged it after him on the floor with a thundering crash, dashing the jug and basin all to shivers.

The smash brought in Mr Robertson, whose rooms were nearest to Number 10. He opened his eyes in amazement as he came in. On one of the beds lay the two masks and dark lantern which had been used to frighten Eden; on the floor, supported by Franklin and Henderson, sat poor Walter, his nose streaming with blood, and his face horribly bruised and disfigured; Harpour sheepishly surveyed his handiwork; and Jones, on the first alarm, had rushed back to bed, covered himself with blankets, and lay to all appearance fast asleep.

"Evson! what's all this?" asked the master in astonishment.

Walter, sick and giddy, was in no condition to answer; but the position of affairs was tolerably obvious.

"Is this *your* doing?" asked Mr Robertson of Harpour very sternly, pointing to Walter.

"He hit me first."

"Liar," said Henderson, glaring up at him.

"Hush, sir; no such language in my presence," said Mr Robertson. "Cradock, do you mean to say that a big fellow like you could stand by, and see Harpour thus cruelly misuse a boy not nearly his size?"

St. Winifred's, or The World of School

"It was a fight, sir."

"Fight!" said Mr Robertson; "look at those two boys, and don't talk nonsense to me."

"I oughtn't to have let them fight, I know," said Cradock; "and I wish, sir, you'd put Harpour and Jones into another room, they're always bullying Eden, and it was for him that Evson fought."

"Harpour," said Mr Robertson, "you are absolutely despicable; a viler figure than you present at this moment could not be conceived. I shall move you to another dormitory, where some monitor can restrain your brutality; and, meanwhile, I confine you to gates for a month, and you will bring me up one hundred lines every day till further notice."

He was leaving the room, but catching sight of Walter, he returned, and said kindly, "Evson, my poor boy, I'm afraid you're sadly hurt; I'm truly sorry for you; you seem to have been behaving in a very noble way, and I honour you. Henderson, I think you'd better go with him to Dr Keith," he continued; for Walter, though he heard what was said, was too much hurt and shaken to speak a word.

"Come, Walter," said Henderson, gently helping him to rise; "I hope you're not very much hurt, old fellow. That brute Harpour won't trouble you again, anyhow; nor his parasite Jones. Lean on my arm. Franklin, you come and give Walter your arm, too."

They helped him to the sick-room, for he could barely trail his legs after him. Dr Keith laid him down quietly on a sofa, put some arnica to the bruises on his face, and told him to lie still and go quietly to sleep. "He is not very much hurt," he said, in answer to the inquiries of the boys; "but the fall he has had is quite sufficiently serious in its consequences to render absolute rest necessary to him for some days. You may come and see him sometimes."

"And now, you fellow, Harpour," said Henderson, re-entering the dormitory; "as you've knocked up Evson, and half killed Eden, *I'll* tell Somers. Do you hear? and I hope he'll thrash you till you can't stand."

"He daren't; Robertson's punished me already."

"He dare, and will; you won't get off so lightly as all that."

"You're a set of sneaks; and I'll be even with you yet," growled Harpour, too much cowed to resent Henderson's defiance.

Henderson laughed scornfully; and Cradock said, "And *I'll* tell the whole school what bullies you've been, Harpour and Jones."

"And *I*," said Franklin; "I don't envy you two."

"The school doesn't consist altogether of such softs as your lot, luckily," answered Harpour.

"Softs or not, we've put a spoke in *your* wheel for the present," answered Franklin; "I congratulate you on the rich black eye which one of the softs, half your size, has given you."

"They're not worth snarling with, Franklin," said Henderson; "we shall be rid of him and Jones from Number 10 henceforth; that's one blessing."

CHAPTER TWENTY SIX. A TURBULENT SCHOOL MEETING.

> I hate when vice can bolt her arguments,
> And virtue have no tongue to check her pride.
> Milton's *Comus*.

Next morning, after second school, Power went to see how Eden and Walter were getting on. He opened the door softly, and they did not observe his entrance.

Eden, very pale, and with an expression of pain and terror still reflected in his face, lay in a broken and restless sleep. Walter was sitting as still as death by the head of the bed. A book lay on his knees, but he had not been reading. He was in a "brown study," and the dreamy far-off look with which his eyes were fixed upon vacancy showed how his thoughts had wandered. It was the same look which attracted Power's attention when he first saw Walter in chapel, and which had shown him that he was no common boy. It often made him watch Walter, and wonder what *could* be occupying his thoughts.

It was looking at poor little Eden that had suggested to Walter's mind the train of thought into which he had fallen. As he saw the child tossing uneasily about, waking every now and then to half-consciousness with a violent start, occasionally delirious, and to all appearance seriously ill—as he thought over Dr Keith's remark, that even when he was quite well again, his nervous system would be probably found to have received a shock, of which the effects would *never* be obliterated during life, he could not help fretting very bitterly over the injury and suffering of his friend. And his own spirits were greatly shaken. It was of little matter that every time he raised his hand to cool his forehead, or ease the throbbing of his head, he felt how much he was bruised, cut, and swollen, or that the looking-glass showed him a face so hideously disfigured; he knew that this would grow right in a day or two, and he cared nothing for it. But when Harpour's blow knocked him down, he had dashed his head with some violence on the floor, and this had hurt him so much and made him feel so ill, that Dr Keith was not without secret fears about the possibility of a concussion of the brain. Yet all the sorrow which Walter now felt was for Eden, and he was not thinking of himself.

He was mentally staring face to face at the mystery of human cruelty and malice. The little boy, whose fine qualities so few besides himself had discovered, was lying before him in pain and nervous prostration, solely because malignant unkindness seemed to give pleasure to two bad, brutal fellows. Walter had himself rescued Eden by his consistent kindness from being bullied, corrupted, tormented—yet apparently to little purpose. That the poor boy's powers would be decidedly injured by this last prank was certain. Dr Keith had dropped mysterious hints, and Walter had himself heard how wild and incoherent were Eden's murmurs. If he should become an idiot? O God! that men and boys should have *such* hearts!

And then and there Walter, while yet a boy, solemnly and consciously recorded an unspoken vow that *he* at least, till death, would do all that lay in his own power to lighten, not to increase, the sum of human misery; that he would study all things that were kind, and gentle, and tender-hearted, in his dealings with others; that he would ever be on the watch against wounding thoughts, and uncharitable judgments, and unkind deeds; above all, that he would strive with all his power against the temptation to cutting and sarcastic words, against calumny, and misrepresentation, against envy, hatred, malice, and all uncharitableness. These were the noble thoughts and high resolves which were passing through the boy's mind when Power's quiet footstep entered the room.

Power stopped for a minute to look at the somewhat saddening picture in the darkened room;—Walter still as death, deep in thought, his chin leaning on his hand, and his face presenting an uncouth mixture of shapes and colours as he sat by Eden's bedside; and Eden turning and moaning in an unrefreshing sleep.

Walter started from his reverie and smiled, as Power noiselessly approached.

"My poor Walter, how marked you are!"

"Oh, never mind, it's nothing. I had a good cause, and it's done good."

"Poor fellow! But how's Arty? He looks wretchedly ill."

"He's in a sad way I'm afraid, Power," said Walter, shaking his head.

"I hope he'll be all right soon."

"Yes, I hope so; but we shall have to take great care of him."

"Poor child, poor child!" said Power, bending over him compassionately.

"Has Flip told Somers of Harpour?" asked Walter.

"I don't know whether you are quite up to hearing school news yet?"

"Oh yes! tell me all about it," said Walter eagerly.

"Well, I've no good news to tell. It's a case of *ponos ponooi ponon pherei*, as Percival said when I told him about you and Eden. By the bye, he sent all sorts of kind messages, and will come and see you."

"Thanks;—but about Harpour?"

St. Winifred's, or The World of School

"Well, Flip meant to tell Somers, but the whole thing spread over the school at once, before morning chapel was well over; so, Dimock being head of Robertson's house, thought it was *his* place to take it up. He sent for Harpour in the classroom, and told him he meant to cane him for his abominable, ruffianly conduct; but before he'd begun, Harpour seized hold of the cane, and wouldn't let it go. Luckily Dimock didn't fly into a rage, nor did he let himself down by a fight which Harpour wanted to bring on. He simply let go of the cane quite coolly, and said, `Very well, Harpour, it would have been a good deal the best for you to have taken quietly the caning you so thoroughly deserve; as you don't choose to do that, I shall put the matter in Somers' hands. I'm glad to be rid of the responsibility.'"

"Did it end there?"

"Not a bit of it; the school are in a ferment. You know the present monitors, and particularly Somers, aren't popular; now Harpour *is* popular, although he's such a brute, because he's a great swell at cricket and the games. I'm afraid we shall have a regular monitorial row. The monitors have convened a meeting this morning to decide about Harpour; and, to tell you the truth, I shouldn't wonder if the school got up a counter-meeting."

"Don't any of the masters know about Eden?"

"Not officially, though I should think some rumours must have got to them."

"But surely it's very odd that the school should side with Jones and Harpour, after the shameful mischief they've done?"

"Odd, *a priori*; but lots of things always combine to make up a school opinion, you know; the fellows just catch up what they hear first. But who do you think is foremost champion on the school side—stirring them up to resist, abusing you, abusing Flip, abusing the monitors and making light of Harpour's doings?"

Walter asked, "Who?" but he knew beforehand that Power's answer would be—"Kenrick!"

St. Winifred's, or The World of School

After this he said nothing, but put his hand wearily to his head, which, in his weak state, was aching violently with the excitement of the news which Power had told him.

"Ah. I see, Walter, you're not quite well enough yet to be bothered. I'll leave you quiet. Good–bye."

"Good–bye. Do come again soon, and tell me how things go on."

Strolling out from the sad sick–room into the court, Power was attracted into the great schoolroom by the sound of angry voices. Entering, he found half the school, and all the lower forms, collected round the large desk at which the head–master usually sat. A great many were talking at once, and every tongue was engaged in discussing the propriety, in this instance, of any monitorial interference.

"Order, order," shouted one or two of the few fifth–form fellows present; "let's have the thing managed properly. Who'll take the chair?"

There was a general call for Kenrick, and as he was one of the highest fellows in the room, he got into the chair, and amid a general silence delivered his views of the present affair.

"You all know," he said, "that Dimock meant to cane Harpour because he played off a joke against one of the fellows last night. Harpour refused to take the caning, and the monitors are holding a meeting this morning to decide what to do about Harpour. Now *I* maintain that they've no right to do anything; and it's very important that we shouldn't let them have just their own way. The thing was merely a joke. Who thinks anything of just putting on a mask in fun, to startle another fellow? one constantly hears of its being done merely to raise a laugh, and we must all have often seen pictures of it. Of course, in this case, every one is extremely sorry for the consequences, but it was impossible to foresee *them*, and nobody has an right to judge of the act because it has turned out so unluckily. I vote that we put the question—`Have the monitors any right to interfere?'"

Loud applause greeted the end of Kenrick's speech, and the little bit at the end about separating an act from its consequences told wonderfully among the boys. They raised an almost unanimous cry of, "Well done, Ken," "quite right," "Harpour shan't be caned."

St. Winifred's, or The World of School

Henderson had been watching Kenrick with an expression of intense anger and disdain. At the end of his remarks, he sprang, rather than rose up, and immediately began to pour out an impetuous answer. His first words, before the fellows had observed that he meant to speak, were drowned in the general uproar; and when they had all caught sight of him, an expression of decided disapprobation ran round the throng of listeners. It did not make him swerve in the slightest degree. Looking round scornfully and steadily, he said:

"I know why some of you hiss. You think I told Dimock of Harpour. As it happens, I *didn't*; but I'm neither afraid nor ashamed to tell you all, as I told Harpour to his face, that I had fully intended to do it,—or rather I meant to tell, not Dimock, but Somers. *Will* you let me speak?" he asked angrily, as his last sentence was interrupted by a burst of groans, commenced by a few of those whose interests were most at stake, and taken up by the mass of ignorant boys.

Power plucked Henderson by the sleeve, and whispered, "Hush, Flip; go on, but keep your temper."

"I've as much right to speak—if this is meant for a school meeting—as Kenrick or any one else; and what I have to say is this:—Kenrick has been merely throwing dust in your eyes, misleading you altogether about the true state of the case. It's all very fine, and very easy for him to talk so lightly of its being `a joke,' and `a bit of fun,' and so on; but I should like to ask him whether he believes that? and whether he's not just hunting for popularity, and mixing up with it a few private spites? and whether he's not thoroughly ashamed of himself at this moment? There! you may see that he is," continued Henderson, pointing at him; "see how he is blushing scarlet, and looking the very picture of degradation."

Here Kenrick started up, and most irascibly informed Henderson that he wasn't going to sit there and be slanged by him, and that as he was in the chair, he would not let Henderson go on any more unless he cut short his abuse; and while Kenrick was saying this, in which he entirely carried the meeting with him, Power again whispered, "You're getting too personal, Flip;—but go on; only say no more about Kenrick—though I'm afraid it's all true."

"Well, at any rate, I will say this," continued Henderson, whose flow of words was rather stopped by his having been pulled up so often;—"and I ought to know, for I was in the room at the time, and I appeal to Anthony and Franklin, and all the rest of the dormitory, to say if it isn't true. It *wasn't* a joke. It wasn't *meant* for a joke. It was a piece of deliberate, diabolical—"

"Oh! oh! oh!" began a few of Harpour's claqueurs, and the chorus was again swelled by a score of others.

"I repeat it—of deliberate, diabolical cruelty, chosen just because there was nothing more cruel they dared to do. And," he said, speaking at the top of his voice, to make himself heard over the clamour, "the fellows who did it are a disgrace to St. Winifred's, and they deserve to be caned by the monitors, if any fellows ever did."

He sat down amid a storm of disapprobation, but his look never quailed for an instant, as he glanced steadily round, and noticed how Kenrick, though in favour with the multitude, and so much higher in the school, did not venture to meet his eye. And he was more than compensated for the general disfavour, by feeling Power's hand rest on his shoulder, and hearing him whisper, "That's *famous*, Flip; you're a dear plucky fellow. Walter himself couldn't have done it more firmly."

Then Belial–like, rose Mackworth, perfectly at his ease, intending as much general mischief as lay in his power, and bent on saying as many unpleasant things as he could. In this, however, his benevolent views were materially frustrated by Henderson, who made his contemptuous comments in a tone sufficiently loud to be heard by many, and quite distinctly enough to disconcert Mackworth's oratory.

"As the gentleman who has just sat down has poured so many bottles of wrath—"

"Bottles of French varnish," suggested Henderson.

"On our heads generally, I must be allowed to make a few remarks in reply. His speech consisted of nothing but rabid abuse, without a shred of argument."

"Rabid fact without a shred of fudge," interpolated Henderson.

"If for every trifling freak fellows were to be telling the monitors, we had better inaugurate at once the era of sneaks and cowards."

St. Winifred's, or The World of School

"Era of sham polish and fiddlestick ends," echoed Henderson; and Mackworth, who had every intention of making a very flourishing speech, was so disconcerted by this unwonted pruning of his periods, that he somewhat abruptly sat down, muttering anathemas on Henderson, and flustered quite out of his usual bland manner.

"Something has been said about cowardice and sneaking," said Whalley, getting up. "I should like to know whether you think it more cowardly to fight a fellow twice one's size, and to mark him pretty considerably too," (a remark which Whalley unceremoniously emphasised by pointing at Harpour's black eye), "or to lay a plot to frighten in the dark a mere child, very nervous and very timid, who has never harmed any one in his life?"

Next, Howard Tracy, addressing the meeting, running his hand occasionally through his hair, "would put the question on a different footing altogether. As to what had been done to Eden, he stood on neutral ground, and gave no opinion. But who, he asked, were these monitors that they should thrash *any one at all*? He had never heard that they were of particularly good families, or that they had anything whatever which gave them a claim to interfere with other fellows. The question was, whether a parcel of monitors were to domineer over the school?"

"The question was nothing of the kind," said Franklin very bluntly; "it was, whether big bullies, like Harpour, were to be at perfect liberty to frighten fellows into idiots, or beat them into mummies, at their own will and pleasure? That was the only question. Harpour or Somers—bullies or monitors—which will you have, boys?"

And after this arose a perfect hubbub of voices. Some got up and ridiculed the monitors; others extolled Harpour, and tried to make out that he was misused for being called to account for a mere frolic; others taunted Evson and Henderson with a conspiracy against their private enemies. On the whole, they were nearly unanimous in agreeing that the school should prevent the monitors from any exercise of their authority.

And then, in the midst of the hubbub, Power rose, "in act more graceful," and there was an immediate and general call for silence. To the great majority of the boys, Power was hardly known except by name and by sight; but his school successes, his rare ability, his stainless character, and many personal advantages, commanded for him the highest admiration. His numerous slight acquaintances in the school all liked his pleasant and playful courtesy, and were proud to know him; his few friends entertained for him an almost extravagant affection. His ancient name, his good family, and the respect due to his high position in the school, would alone have been sufficient to gain him a favourable hearing; but, besides this, he had hitherto come forward so little, that there was a strong curiosity to see what line he would take, and how he would be able to speak. There were indeed a few who were most anxious to silence him as quickly as possible, knowing what effect his words would be likely to produce; and when he began, they raised several noisy interruptions; but Kenrick, for very shame, was obliged at first to demand for him the attention which, after the first sentence or two, his quiet, conciliatory, and persuasive manner effectually secured.

Reviewing the whole tumultuary discussion, he began by answering Kenrick. After alluding to the long course of bullying which had been ended in this manner, he appealed to the common sense of the meeting whether the thing could be regarded as a mere joke, when they remembered Eden's tender age, and highly susceptible nature? Was it not certain, and must it not have been obvious to the bullies, that serious, if not desperately dangerous results *must* follow? What those results had been was well-known, and in describing what he had seen of them in the sick-room only half an hour before, Power made a warm appeal to their feelings of pity and indignation—an appeal which every one felt to be manly, and which could not fail of being deeply touching, because it was both simple and natural.

"Then," said Power, "the next speaker talked about sneaking and cowardice. Well, those charges had been sufficiently answered by Whalley, and, indeed, on behalf of his friends Evson and Henderson, he perhaps need hardly condescend to answer them at all. His friend Henderson had been long enough among them to need no defence, and if he *did*, it would be sufficiently supplied by the high courage, of which they had just seen a specimen. As for Evson, any boy who had given as many proofs of honour and manliness as *he* had done during his two terms at St. Winifred's, certainly required no one's shield to be thrown over *him*. Would any of them show their courage by walking across the Razor on some dark foggy winter's night? and would they find in the school any other fellow of Evson's age who would not shrink from standing up in a regular fair fight with another of twice his own strength and size? Those charges he thought he might throw to the winds; he was sure that no one believed them; but there was, he admitted, one cowardice of which his two friends had often been guilty, and it was a cowardice for which they need not blush; he meant the cowardice, the arrant, the noble cowardice of being afraid *not* to do what they thought right, and of being afraid to do what they *knew* to be base and

St. Winifred's, or The World of School

wrong."

In these remarks Power quite carried his audience away with him; the strain was of a higher mood than boys had often heard from boys, and it was delivered with an eloquence and earnestness that raised a continuous applause. This, however, Power checked by going on speaking until he was obliged to stop and take breath; but *then* it burst out in the most unmistakable and enthusiastic manner, and entirely drowned the few and timid counter- demonstrations of the Jones and Mackworth school.

"Now I have detained you too long," said Power, "and I apologise for it," (go on! go on! shouted the boys); "but as so *many* have spoken on the other side, and so few on this, perhaps you will excuse me," (yes, yes!) "Well, then, Tracy has asked, `Who are the monitors? and what right have they to interfere?' I answer, that the monitors are our schoolfellows, and are simply representatives of the most mature form of public school opinion. They have all been lower boys; they have all worked their way up to the foremost place; they are, in short, the oldest, the cleverest, the strongest, and the wisest among us. And their right depends on an authority voluntarily delegated to them by the masters, by our parents, and by ourselves—a right originally founded on justice and common sense, and venerable by very many years of prestige and of success. At any rate, a fellow who behaves as Harpour has done, has the *least* right to complain of this exercise of a higher authority. If he had a right—and he has no right except brute strength, if that be a right—to bully, beat, torment, and perhaps injure for life a poor little inoffensive child, and by doing so to render the name of the school infamous, I maintain that the monitors, who have the interest of the school most at heart, who are ranged *ex officio* on the side of truth, of justice, and of honour, have infinitely more right to thrash him for it. Supposing that there were no monitors, what would the state of the school be? above all, what would be the condition of the younger and weaker boys? they would be the absolutely defenceless prey of a most odious tyranny. Let me say then, that I most distinctly and emphatically approve of the manner, in which my friends have acted; that I envy and admire the moral courage which helped them to behave as they did; and that if the school attempts on this occasion to resist the legitimate and most wholesome exercise of the monitors' power, it will suffer a deep disgrace and serious loss. I oppose Kenrick's motion with every feeling of my heart, and with every sentiment of my mind. I think it dangerous, I think it useless, and I think it *most unjust*."

St. Winifred's, or The World of School

A second burst of applause followed Power's energetic words, and continued for several minutes. He had utterly changed the opinions of many who were present, and Kenrick felt his entire sympathy and admiration enlisted on behalf of his former friend. He would at the moment have given anything to get up and retract his previous remarks, and beg pardon for them. But his pride and passion were too strong for him, and coldly rising, he put it to the meeting, "whether they decided that the monitors had the right to interfere or not."

Jones, Mackworth, Harpour, and others, were eagerly canvassing for votes, and when Kenrick demanded a show of hands, a good many were raised on their side. When the opposite question was put, at first only Power, Henderson, Whalley, and Franklin held up their hands; but they were soon followed by Bliss, then by Anthony and Cradock, and then by a great many more who took courage when they saw what champions were on their side. The hands were counted, and there was found to be an equal number on both sides. The announcement was received with dead silence.

"The chairman of course has a casting–vote," said Mackworth.

Kenrick sat still for a moment, not without an inward conflict; and then, afraid to risk his popularity with those whom he had now adopted as his own set, he said, rising:

"And I give it *against* the right of the monitors."

A scene of eager partisanship and loud triumph ensued, during which Power once more stood forward, and observed:

"You must allow me to remind you that the present meeting in no way represents the sense of the school. I do not see a dozen boys present who are above the lowest fifth–form; and I do earnestly entreat those who have gained this vote not to disturb the peace and comfort of the school by attempting a collision between themselves and the monitors, who will certainly be supported by the nearly unanimous opinion of the upper fifth forms."

"We shall see about that," answered Kenrick in a confident tone. "At any rate, the vote is carried." He left the chair, and the boys broke up into various groups, still eagerly discussing the rights and wrongs of the question which had been stirred.

"*So*, Power," said Kenrick with a sneer, which he assumed to hide his real feelings, "all your fine eloquence is thrown away, you see. We've carried the day after all, in spite of you."

"Yes, Ken," said Power gently; "you've carried it *quocunque modo*. How comes Kenrick to be on the same side as Jones, Mackworth, and Harpour?"

CHAPTER TWENTY SEVEN. THE MONITORS.

In the teeth of clenched antagonisms.—Tennyson.

The meeting over, Henderson, who had not seen Walter since the morning, flew up to the sick-room to tell him the news, which he was sure would specially interest him. As he entered, the same spectacle was before him which Power had already seen—little Eden restless, and sometimes wandering—Walter seated silently by the bed watching him, his legs crossed, and his hands clasped over one knee. The curtains were drawn to exclude the glare. Walter could read but little, for his eyes were weak after the fight; but his thoughts and his nursing of his little friend kept him occupied. Henderson, fresh from the hot excitement of the meeting, was struck with the deep contrast presented by this painfully quiet scene.

He was advancing eagerly, but Walter rose with his finger on his lip, and spoke to him in a whisper, for Eden had just dropped off to sleep.

Henderson shook him warmly by the hand, and whispered—"I've such lots to tell you;" and, sitting down by Walter, he gave him an account of what had just taken place. "You should have heard Power, Walter; upon my word he spoke like an orator, and regularly bowled the Harpour lot off their legs. It's splendid to see him coming out so in the school—isn't it?"

"It is indeed; and thanks to you, too, Flip, for sticking up for me."

"Oh, what I did was just nothing. But only fancy that fellow Kenrick fighting against us like this, and giving his casting-vote against Harpour's being thrashed! You've no idea, Walter, how that fellow's changed."

St. Winifred's, or The World of School

He was interrupted, for Eden woke with a short scream, and, starting up in bed, looked round with a scared expression, shuddering and moaning as he fell back again on his pillow.

"Oh, don't, don't, don't frighten me," he said appealingly, while the perspiration burst out over his pale face; "please, Harpour, *please* don't. Oh, Walter, Walter, *do* help me."

"Hush, my poor little fellow, I'm here," said Walter tenderly, as he smoothed his pillow; "don't be afraid, Arty, you're quite safe, and I'm staying with you. They only put on masks to frighten you; it was nothing but that."

Bending over the bed, he talked to him in a gentle, soothing voice, and tried to make him feel at ease, while the child flung both his arms round his neck, sobbing, and still clung tight to his hand when Walter had succeeded in allaying the sudden paroxysm of terror.

Henderson, deeply touched, had looked on with glistening eyes. "How kind you are, Walter," he said, taking his other hand, and affectionately pressing it. "I should just like to have Kenrick here, and show him what his new friends have done."

"Don't be indignant against him, Flip. I wish, indeed, he would but come into this room, and make it up with us, and be what he once was. But he did not even take the slightest notice of the letter I wrote him, entreating him to overlook any fault I had been guilty of, however unconsciously. I never meant to wrong him, and I love him as much as ever."

"Love him!" said Henderson, "*I* don't; his new line isn't half to my fancy. He must be jolly miserable, that's one comfort."

"Hush! he was our friend, Flip, remember; indeed, *I* feel as a friend to him still, whatever his feelings are for *me*. But why do you think he must be miserable?"

"Because you can see in his face and manner, that all the while he knows he's in the wrong, and is thoroughly ashamed at bottom."

"Well, let's hope he'll come round again all the sooner. Have you broken with him, then?"

"Well, nearly. We are barely civil to each other, that's all, and I don't suppose we shall be even that now; for I pitched into him to-day at the meeting."

Walter only sighed, and just then Power stole into the room.

"Hallo!" he said, "Flip, I believe you and I shall kill the invalids between us. I just met Dr Keith on the stairs, and he only gave me leave to come for five minutes, for he says they both need quiet. You, I suspect, Master Flip, took French leave."

"I like that," said Henderson, laughing, "considering that this is your *second* visit, and only my first. I've been telling Walter about the meeting."

"The credit—if there be any—is yours, Flip; you broke the ice, and showed the Harpourites that they weren't going to carry it all their own way, as they fancied."

"I'm so glad you came out strong, Power," said Walter; "Flip says you took them all by storm."

"That's Flip's humbug," said Power; "but," he whispered, "if I did any good, it's all through you, Walter."

"How do you mean?"

"Why, first of all, I wasn't going to hear animals like Mackworth abuse you; and next, but for you I should have continued my old selfish way of keeping aloof from all school concerns. It cost me an effort to conquer my shyness, but I remembered our old talk on Appenfell, Walter."

Walter smiled gratefully, and Power continued, "But I've come to tell you both a bit of news."

"What's that?" they asked eagerly.

"Why, there's a notice on the board, signed by Somers, to say that `All the school are requested to stay in their places after the master has left the room at two o'clock calling–over.'"

St. Winifred's, or The World of School

"Whew! what a row we shall have!" said Henderson.

"How I wish I were well enough to be out now," said Walter. "I hate to be shut up while all this is going on."

"Poor fellow, with *that* face?" said Power. "No; you must be content to wait and get well."

"It isn't the face that keeps me in, Power; it's the bang on the head, Keith says."

"Yes; and Keith says that he doesn't know when you *will* be well if these young chatterboxes stay with you," said the good-humoured doctor, entering at the moment. "Vanish, both of you!"

The boys smiled and bade Walter good-bye, as they wished him speedy relief from Dr Keith's prison. "And when do you think poor little Eden may come and sit in my study again?" asked Power. "I miss him very much."

"You mustn't think of that for a long time," answered the doctor.

"How about this two o'clock affair?" said Henderson, as they left the room.

"Upon my word, I don't know. Sit next to me, Flip, in case of a row."

"Are the monitors strong enough, do you think?"

"We shall see."

The school was in a fever of excitement and curiosity. At dinner-time nothing else was talked of by the lower boys, but the upper forms kept a dignified silence.

Two o'clock came. The names of all the school were called over, and amid perfect silence the master of the week left the hall. Then Somers stood up in the dais and said:

"Is Harpour here?—the rest please to keep their places."

St. Winifred's, or The World of School

"I'm here—what do you want of *me*?" said Harpour sulkily, as he stood up in his place.

"First of all, I want to tell you before the whole school that you have been behaving in a most shamefully cruel and blackguard way, and in a way that has produced disastrous consequences to one of the little fellows. A big fellow like you ought to be *thoroughly* ashamed of such conduct. If you were capable of a blush you ought to blush for it. It is our duty as monitors, and my duty as Head of the school, to punish you for this conduct, as Dr Lane has left it in our hands; and I am going to cane you for it. Stand out."

"I won't. I'll see you d——d first."

A sensation ran through the school at this open defiance; but Somers, quite unmoved, repeated:

"I take no notice of your words further than to tell you that if you swear again you shall have an additional punishment; but once again I tell you to stand out."

Harpour quailed a little at his firm tone, and at the total absence of all support from his followers; but he again flatly refused to stand out.

"Very well," said Somers; "you have already defied the authority of one monitor, and that is an aggravation of your original offence. I should have been glad to have avoided a scene, but if your common sense doesn't make you bear the punishment coolly, you shall bear it by force. Will you stand out?—no?—then you shall be made. Fetch him here, some one," he said, turning to the sixth-form.

The second monitor, Danvers, quietly seized Harpour's right arm, and Macon, one of the biggest fellows in the fifth-form, of his own accord got up and seized the other. Harpour's heart sank at this, for Danvers and the other were with him in the cricket eleven, and he was not as strong as either of them singly.

"Now mark," said Somers; "caned you *shall* be, to redeem the character of the school; but unless you take it without being *made* to take it, your name shall also be immediately struck off the school list, and you shall leave St Winifred's this evening. You'll be no great loss, I take it. So much I may tell you as a proof that the Head-master has left *us* to vindicate the name of St Winifred's."

St. Winifred's, or The World of School

Seeing that resistance was useless, Harpour accordingly stood out in the centre of the room, but not until he had cast an inquiring look among those who embraced his side; and these, who, as we have seen, were tolerably numerous, all looked at Kenrick that he might give some hint as to what they should do. Thus appealed to, Kenrick rose and said:

"I protest against this caning."

"You!" said Somers, turning contemptuously in that direction; "who are you?"

The general titter which these words caused made Kenrick furious, and he cried out angrily:

"It is against the opinion of the majority of the school."

"We shall see," said Somers, with stinging *sang froid*; "meanwhile, you may sit down, and let the majority of the school speak for themselves, otherwise you may be requested to occupy a still more prominent position. I shall have something to say to *you* presently."

"Let's rescue him," said Kenrick, springing forward, and several fellows stirred in answer to the appeal; but Macon, seizing hold of Tracy with one arm, and Mackworth with the other, thrust them both down on the floor, and Danvers, catching hold of Kenrick, swung him over the form, and pinned him there. The general laugh with which this proceeding was received showed that only a small handful of the school were really opposed to the monitors, and that most boys thoroughly concurred with them, and held them to be in the right. So Macon quietly boxed Jones's ears, since Jones was making a noise, and then told him and the others that they might return to their places.

Crimsoned all over with shame and anger, Kenrick sat down, and Somers proceeded to administer to Harpour a most severe caning. That worthy quite meant to stretch to the utmost his powers of endurance, and made several scornful remarks after each of the first blows. But Somers had no intention to let him off too easily; each sneer was followed by a harder cut, and the remarks were very soon followed by a silent but significant wince. It was not until a writhe had been succeeded by a sob, and a sob by a howl, that Somers said to him:

"Now you may go."

St. Winifred's, or The World of School

And Harpour did go to his seat, in an agony of mingled pain and shame. He had boasted repeatedly that he would never take a thrashing from any one; but he *had* taken it, and succumbed to it, and that too in the presence of the whole school. He was tremendously ashamed; he never forgot the scene, and determined never to lose an opportunity of revenging it.

The school felt it to be an act of simple justice, and that the punishment was richly deserved. They looked on in stern silence, and those lower boys who had in the morning determined to interfere, gazed with some discomfiture upon their champion's fall.

"And now, Master Kenrick, *you* stand here;—what, no!—Stand here, sir."

Kenrick only glared defiance.

"Danvers, hand him here;" but Danvers stepped up to Somers and whispered, "Don't be too sharp on him, Somers, or you'll drive him to despair. Remember he's high in the fifth, and has been a distinguished fellow. Don't make too much of this one escapade."

"All right. Thanks, Danvers," said Somers; and added aloud, in a less sarcastic tone—"Come here, Kenrick; I merely wish to speak a word with you;" and then Danvers kindly but firmly took the boy's hand, and led him forward.

"You said the majority of the school denied our right to interfere?"

No answer.

"Do you consider yourself in person to be the majority of the school, pray?"

No answer.

"We are all perfectly aware, sir, of your meeting, and of your precious casting-vote. But you must be informed that a rabble of shell and fourth-form boys do not constitute the school in any sense of the word. And understand too that, even if the majority of the school *had* been against us, we monitors are not quite so ignorant of our solemn duty as to make that any reason for letting a brutal and cowardly act of bullying go unpunished. You have been very silly, Kenrick, and have been just misled by conceit. Yes, you may look angry; but you know me of old; you've never received anything but kindness at my hands since the day you were my fag, and I tell you again that you've just been misled by conceit. Think rather less of yourself, my good fellow. You ought to have known better. Your friend Power has shown you an infinitely more sensible example. *You* may sit down, sir, with this warning; and, in the name of the monitors, I beg to thank the other fellows, especially Evson and Henderson, who did their best to protect little Eden. They behaved like thorough gentlemen, and it would be well if more of you younger boys were equally alive to the true honour of the school."

"I wish he'd be more conciliatory," whispered Dimock to Danvers; "he's plucky and firm, but so very dictatorial and unpersuasive. Besides, he's forgotten to thank Power."

"Yes," said Danvers, "his tone spoils all. Somers," he said, "you've omitted to mention Power, and the fellows will be gone in a minute."

"I've been talking so much, you say it."

"Not I; I'm no speaker.—Here, Dimock will."

"Ay, that'll do. One minute more, please," called Somers, raising his hand to the boys, who, during this rapidly whispered conversation, were beginning to leave their places.

"Somers wishes me to add," said Dimock, "that all the monitors and many of the sixth and fifth forms wish to express our best thanks to Power for the exceedingly honourable and fearless way, in which he this morning maintained the rights and duties which belong to us. You younger fellows know very well that we monitors extremely dislike to interfere, that we do so only on the rarest occasions, and that we are always most anxious to avoid caning. You know that we never resort to it unless we are obliged to do so by the most flagrant offences, which would otherwise sap the honour and character of the school. Let us all be united and work together for the good of St Winifred's. Don't let any interested parties lead you to believe that we either do or wish to tyrannise. Our authority is for your high and direct advantage;— I appeal to you whether you do not know it."

"Yes, yes, Dimock," answered many voices; and before they streamed out of the hall, they gave "three cheers for the monitors," which were so heartily responded to, that the hissing of Harpour, Kenrick, and others, only raised a laugh, which filled to the very brim the bitter cup of hate and indignation which Kenrick had been forced that day to drink. To be addressed like that before the whole school—snubbed, reproved, threatened —it was intolerable; that he, Kenrick, high in the school, brilliant, promising, successful, accustomed only to flattery and praise, should be publicly set down among a rabble of lower boys —it made him mad to think of it.

"A nice tell-tale mess you've made of this business, Power," he said savagely, the red spot still lingering on his cheek, as he confronted his former friend; "I hope you're ashamed of yourself."

"I, Ken? no."

"Then you ought to be."

"Honestly, Ken, who ought to be most ashamed—you, the advocate of Harpour and his set, or I, who merely defended my best friend for behaving most honourably—as he always does?"

"*Always!*" sneered Kenrick.

Power turned on him his clear bright eye, and said nothing for a moment; but then he laid his arm across his shoulder in the old familiar manner, and said, "You are not happy now, Ken, as you used to be."

"Why the devil not?"

Power shook his head. "Because your heart is nobler than your acts; your nature truer than your conduct; and *that* is and will be your punishment. Why do you nurse this bad feeling till it has so mastered you?"

Kenrick stood still, his cheeks flushed, his eyes downcast; and Power, as he turned away, sadly repeated, half to himself, the wonderful verse—

Virtutem *videant, intabescantque relicta.*

Kenrick understood it; it came to his heart like an arrow, and rankled there; it made a wound, the faithful wound of a friend, better than the kisses of an enemy;—but the time of healing was far-off yet.

CHAPTER TWENTY EIGHT. FALLING AWAY.

> Oh deeper dole!
> That so august a spirit, sphered so fair,
> Should from the starry sessions of his peers,
> Decline to quench so bright a brilliancy
> In hell's sick spume. Ay me, the deeper dole!
> *Tannhauser.*

It was generally on Sundays that boys walked in the Croft with those who were, and whom they wished to be considered as, their most intimate and confidential friends. To one who knew anything of the boys' characters, it was most curious and suggestive to observe the groups into which they spontaneously formed themselves. The sets at St Winifred's were not very exclusive or very accurately defined; and one boy might, by virtue of different sympathies or accomplishments, belong to two or three sets at once. Still there were some sets whose outermost circles barely touched each other; and hitherto the friends among whom Kenrick had chiefly moved would never have associated intimately with the fellows among whom Harpour was considered as the leading spirit.

It was therefore with no little surprise that Mr Percival, who with Mr Paton passed through the Croft on his Sunday stroll, observed Kenrick—not with his usual companions, Power or Walter or Whalley—but arm in arm with Harpour and Tracy, and accompanied by one or two other boys of similar character. It immediately explained to him much that had taken place. He had heard vague rumours of the part Kenrick had taken at the meeting; he had heard both from him and from Walter that they were no longer on good terms with each other; but now it was further plain to him that Kenrick was breaking loose from all his old moorings, and sailing into the open sea of wilfulness and pride.

"What are you so much interested about?" asked Mr Paton, as his colleague followed the boys with his glance.

"I am wondering how and why this change has come over Kenrick."

"What change?"

"Don't you see with whom he is walking? Oh, I forgot that you never notice that kind of outer life among the boys; on the other hand, I always do; it helps me to understand these fellows, and do more for them than I otherwise could."

"You observe them to some purpose, Percival, at any rate, for your influence among them is wonderful—as I have occasion to discover every now and then."

"But Kenrick puzzles me. `_Nemo repente fuit turpissimus,' one used to think; yet that boy has dropped from the society of such a noble fellow as Power, with his exquisite mind and manners, plumb into the abyss of intimacy with Harpour! There must be something all wrong."

A very little observation showed Mr Percival that his conjectures about Kenrick were correct. Clever as he was, his work deteriorated rapidly; the whole expression of his countenance changed for the worse; he was implicated more than once in very questionable transactions; he lost caste among the best and most honourable fellows, and proportionately gained influence among the worst and lowest lot in the school, whose idol and hero he gradually became. His descent was sudden, because his character had always been unstable. The pride and passion which were mollified and restrained as long as he had moved with wise and upright companions, broke forth with violence when once he fancied himself slighted, and had committed himself to a course which he well knew to be wrong. There was one who conjectured much of this at a very early period. It was Kenrick's mother; his letters always indicated the exact state of his thoughts and feelings; and Mrs Kenrick knew that the coldness and recklessness which had lately marked them were proofs that her boy was going wrong. The violence, too, with which he spoke of Evson, and the indications that he had dropped his old friends and taken up with new and worse companions, filled her mind with anxiety and distress; yet what could she do, poor lady, in her lonely home? There was one thing only that she could do for him in her weakness; and those outpourings of sorrowful and earnest prayer were not in vain.

St. Winifred's, or The World of School

Mr Percival tried to make some effort to save Kenrick from the wrong courses which he had adopted; he asked him quietly to come and take a glass of wine after dinner; but the interview only made matters worse. Kenrick, not unelated by his popularity among the lower forms as a champion of the supposed "rights" of the school, chose to adopt an independent and almost patronising tone towards his tutor; he entered in a jaunty manner, and glancing carelessly over the table, declined to take any of the fruit to which the master invited him to help himself. He determined to be as uncommunicative as possible; avoided all conversation, and answered Mr Percival's questions on all subjects by monosyllables, uttered in a disrespectful and nonchalant tone. Yet all the while he despised himself, and was ill at ease. He knew the deep kindness of the master's intentions, and felt that he ought to be grateful for the interest shown towards him; but it required a stronger power and a different method from his own, to exorcise from his heart the devil of self-will; and besides this, it cannot be denied that in the first bloom and novelty of sin, in the free exercise of an insolent liberty, there is a sense of pleasure for many hearts; it is the honey on the rim of the poison-cup, the bloom on the Dead-sea apple, the mirage on the scorching waste.

Mr Percival understood him thoroughly, and saw that he must be left to the bitter teachings of experience. Always fond of Kenrick, he had never been blind to his many faults of character, and was particularly displeased with his present manner, which he knew to be only adopted on purpose to baffle any approach to advice or warning.

"Good-morning, Kenrick," he said, rising rather abruptly, while a slight smile of pity rested on his lips.

"Good-morning, sir," said Kenrick; and as he rose in an airy manner to leave the room, Mr Percival put a hand on each of the boy's shoulders, and looked him steadily in the face. Kenrick tried to meet the look, not with the old open gaze of frank and innocent confidence, but with an expression half shrinking, half defiant. His eyes fell immediately, and satisfied by this perusal of his features that Kenrick was going wrong, Mr Percival said only this:

"Your face, my boy, is as a book where men
May read strange matters."

St. Winifred's, or The World of School

Kenrick had tried to be off-hand and patronising in manner, but the attempt had failed egregiously, and he felt very uncomfortable as he left the room where he had so often met with kindness, and which he *never* entered on the same terms again.

Meanwhile our two invalids, Walter and Eden, recovered but slowly. But for the kindness of every one about them their hours would have passed very wearily in the sick-room. Their tedium was enlivened by constant visits from Henderson and Power, who never failed to interest Walter by their school news, and especially by telling of those numerous little incidents which tended to show that although after the late excitements there was a certain detumescence, still the general effect had been to arouse a spirit of opposition to all constituted authority. Kenrick's name was sometimes on their lips, but as they could not speak of him favourably, and as the subject was a painful one, they rarely talked much about him.

Among other visitors was Dr Lane, who, as well as Mrs Lane, showed great solicitude about them. The Doctor, who had been told by Dr Keith that, but for Walter's tender nursing, Eden's case might have assumed a far more dangerous complexion, lent them interesting books and pictures, and often came for a few minutes to exchange some kind words with them. Mrs Lane asked them to the Lodge, read to them, sang to them, played chess and draughts with them, and often gave them drives in her carriage. These little gracious acts of simple kindness won the hearts of both the boys, and hastened their convalescence.

Sometimes Walter was allowed to take Eden for a stroll on the shore during school hours, when there was no danger of their being excited or interrupted by the boisterous society of other boys. There was one favourite spot where the two often sat reading and talking. It was by the mouth of the little river—a green knoll sheltered under the rising hills, to the very feet of which the little waves came rippling musically as the summer tide flowed in. And here Eden would lie down at full length on the soft grass, and doze quietly, while the gentle breeze lifted his fair hair from his forehead with refreshful coolness; or he would listen while Walter read to him some stirring ballad or pleasant tale.

And thus in the course of a fortnight Walter was himself again, and Eden, not long after, was so far recovered as to be allowed to join his schoolfellows in the usual routine. He was, however, removed with Walter and Henderson and Power to another dormitory, which they had to themselves; and the promise of this, relieving his mind from a constant source of dread, helped him to recover. The boys, too, conscious how great a wrong had been done to him, received him back among them with unusual consideration and delicate kindness. They pitied him heartily. It was impossible not to do so when they looked at his wan sad face, so changed in expression; and when they observed his timid shrinking manner, and the tremor which came over him at any sudden sight or sound. So every voice was softened when they spoke to him, and the manner of even the roughest boys became to him affectionate and even caressing. If any had felt inclined to side with Harpour against the monitors before, the sight of Eden went very far to alter their convictions.

Yet the poor child was never happy except when he was in Walter's society, and in Power's study. Even there he was changed. The bright merry laugh which once rang out incessantly was rarely or never heard now; and a somewhat sad smile was all that could be elicited from him. He seemed, too, to have lost for a time all his old interest in work. The form competition had no further attraction for him; the work seemed irksome, and he had no spirits to join in any game. Once Power kindly rallied him on his general listlessness, but Eden only looked up at him appealingly, and said, while the weak tears overflowed his eyes, "Don't be angry with me, Power, I can't help it; I don't feel quite right yet. Oh, Power, I'm afraid you'll never like me again as you did."

"Why, Arty, your illness is all the more reason why I should."

"But, Power, I shall never be the same as I once was. It seems as if some light had gone out and left me in the dark."

"Nonsense, Arty; the summer holidays will bring you round again."

But Eden only shook his head, and muttered something about Colonel Braemar not being kind to him and his little sister.

"Do you think they would let you come and stay part of the holidays with us?"

Eden brightened up in a moment, and promised to write and ask.

CHAPTER TWENTY NINE. WALTER'S HOLIDAYS.

> Such delights
> As float to earth, permitted visitants,
> When in some hour of solemn jubilee
> The massy gates of Paradise are thrown
> Wide open.
> Coleridge, *Religious Musings*.

In scenes like these, part sunshine and part storm, the half-year rolled round, and brought the long-desired summer holidays. Once more the end of the half-year saw Power as usual brilliantly successful, and Walter again at the head of his form.

Henderson too, although he could not proceed with Walter, *pari passu*, was among the first six, and had gained more than one school distinction. But Kenrick this time had failed as he had never done before; he was but fourth in his form, and although this was the natural fruit of his recent idleness, it caused him cruel mortification.

The end of term did not pass off quite so smoothly and pleasantly as it generally did. The opposition to monitorial authority which Harpour had commenced, and Kenrick abetted, did not pass away at once; it left a large amount of angry feeling in the minds of numerous boys who had, each of them, influence in their several ways. Kenrick himself always went to the verge of impertinence whenever he could possibly do so in dealing with any of the sixth, and to Somers his manner was always intentionally rude, although he just managed to steer clear of any overt insubordination. He could of course act thus without risk of incurring any punishment, and without coming to any positive collision. Many boys were unfortunately but too ready to imitate his example.

These dissensions did not positively break out on the prize day, but they made the proceedings far less pleasant and unanimous than they would have been. The cheers usually given to the head of the school were purposely omitted, from the fear of provoking any counter-demonstration, and there remained an uneasy feeling in many minds. The success of the concert which was yearly given by the school choir after the distribution of prizes was also marred by traces of the same dissension. In this concert Walter had a solo to sing, and although he sang it remarkably well in his sweet ringing voice, he was vexed to hear a few decided hisses among the plaudits which greeted him. Altogether the prize day—a great day at St Winifred's—was less successful than it had ever been known to be.

It brought, however, one pleasure to Walter, in the acquaintance of Sir Lawrence and Lady Power, who had heard of him so often in their son's letters, that they begged to be introduced to him as soon as they arrived. He was a great deal with them during the day, and he helped Power to show them all that was interesting about the school and its environs. They saw Eden too, and Lady Power kindly pressed her invitation on Mrs Braemar, who was also present, and who was not sorry that Arty could stay with a family so well connected, and of such high position. When Walter left them, Power earnestly asked his mother what she thought of his friend?

"He is the most charming boy I ever saw," said Lady Power, "and I rejoice that you have chosen him as a friend. But you don't tell me anything about Kenrick, of whom you were once so fond; how is that?"

"I am still fond of him, mother, but he has changed a good deal lately." At that moment Kenrick passed by arm in arm with Harpour, as though to confirm Power's words, and recognised him with an ostentatiously careless nod.

It was thus that Walter's first year at St Winifred's ended; and in spite of all drawbacks he felt that it had been a distinguished and happy year. He was now yearning for home, and he felt that he could meet his dear ones with honest pride. He made arrangements to correspond with Henderson and Eden in the holidays, and Power promised again to visit him at Semlyn, on condition that he would come back with him and spend a week at Severn Park, that so there might be a double bond of union between them.

Very early the next morning the boys were swarming into coaches, carriages, brakes, and every conceivable vehicle which could by any possibility convey them to the nearest station. A hearty cheer accompanied each coach as it rolled off with its heavy and excited freight; by nine o'clock not a boy was left behind. The great buildings of St Winifred's were still as death; the foot– fall of the chance passer–by echoed desolately among them. A strange, mournful, conscious silence hung about the old monastic pile. The young life which usually played like the sunshine over it was pouring unwonted brightness into many happy English homes.

St. Winifred's, or The World of School

It was late in the afternoon when Walter found himself on the top of the hill which looks down over Semlyn Lake. The water lay beneath him a sheet of placid silver; the flowers were scattered on every side in their beds of emerald and sunlit moss; the air, just stirred by the light breeze, was rich and balmy with the ambrosial scent of the summer groves; and high overhead the old familiar hills reared their magnificent summits into the deep unclouded blue. But Walter's bright eye was fixed on one spot only of the enchanting scene—the spot where the gables of his father's house rose picturesquely on the slope above the lake, and where a little bay in the sea of dark green firs gave him a glimpse of their garden, in which he could discover the figures of his brothers and sisters at their play. A sense of unspoken, unspeakable happiness flowed into the boy's warm heart, and if at the same moment his eyes were suffused with tears, they were the tears that always spring up when the fountain of the heart is stirred by any strong emotion to its inmost depths—the tears that come even in laughter to show that our very pleasures have their own alloy.

The coach was still behind him toiling slowly up the ascent. Leaving it to convey his luggage to the house, he plunged down a green winding path, ankle-deep in soft grasses and innumerable flowers, which led to his home by a short cut down the valley, along the burnside, and under the waving woods. That sweet woodland path, cool and fragrant on the most burning summer day, where he had often gathered the little red ripe wild strawberries that peeped out here and there from between the scented spikes of golden agrimony, and under the white graceful flowers of the circoea, was familiar and dear to him from the earliest childhood. He plunged into it with delight, and springing along with joyous steps, reached in ten minutes the wicket-gate which led into his father's grounds. The first thing to see and recognise him was a graceful pet fawn of his sister's, which at his whistle came trotting to him with delight, jingling the little silver bell which was tied by a blue riband round its neck. Barely stopping to caress the beautiful little creature's head, he bounded through the orchard into the garden, and the next instant the delighted shout of his brothers and sisters welcomed him back, as they ran up, with all the glee of innocent and happy childhood, to greet him with their repeated kisses.

"Ah, there are papa and mamma," he cried, breaking away from the laughing group, as his mother advanced with open arms to meet him, and pressed him to her heart in a long embrace.

"I'm first in my form, papa," he said, looking joyously up into his father's face. "Head remove again."

"Are you, Walter? I am so happy to hear it. Few things could give me more pleasure."

"But that's nothing to being at *home*," he said, shouting aloud in the uncontrolled exuberance of his spirits, and hardly knowing which way to turn in the multiplicity of objects which seemed to claim his instant attention.

"Do come the rounds with me, Charlie," he said to his favourite brother, "and let me see all the dear old places again. We shall be back in a few minutes."

"And then, I dare say, you'll be glad of some tea," said his mother.

"*Rather!*" said Walter; "let's have it out here on the lawn, mother."

The proposal was carried by acclamation, and very soon the table was laid under the witch–elm before the house, while Walter's little sisters had heaped up several dishes with freshly plucked fruit, laid in the midst of flowers and vine leaves, and Walter, his face beaming and his eyes dancing with happiness, was asking and answering a thousand incessant questions, while yet he managed to enjoy very thoroughly a large bunch of grapes and an immense plate of strawberries and cream.

And when tea was over they still sat out in the lovely garden until the witch–elm had ceased to chequer their faces with its rain of flickering light; and until the lake had paled from pure gold to rose–colour, and from rose–colour to dull crimson, and from dull crimson to silver–grey, and rippled again from silver– grey into a deep black blue, relieved by a thousand flashing edges of molten silver and quivering gold, under the crescent moon and the innumerable stars. And the bats had almost ceased to wheel, and in the moist air of early night the flowers were diffusing their luscious sweetness, and the nightingale was flooding the grove with her unimaginable rapture, and the eager talk had hushed itself into a delicious calm of happy silence, before they moved. It was a beautiful picture;—the father and mother still youthful enough to enjoy life to the full, happy at heart, and proud of their eldest boy; his two young brothers looking up to him with such eager hope and love; the little sisters with their arms twined round his neck, and their fair hair falling over his shoulders; the noble, mirthful, fearless, thrice happy boy himself;—a family circle unseparated by distance, unshadowed by sorrow, unbroken by death, seated in this exquisite scene on the lawn of their own happy English home.

Thrice happy! yes, in spite of sin and sorrow, and retribution and remorse, there *are* hours when the cup sparkles in our hands, filled to the brim; not, (as often), with earthly waters; not with the intoxicating wine that flames in the magic bowl of pleasure; not with the red and ragged lees of wrath and satiety; but with the crystal rivers of the water of life itself. There *are* such hours; at any rate for some. Whether they come to all mankind I know not; whether the squalid Andaman or the hideous Fuegian ever feel them I know not; nay, I know not whether they ever come, whether they ever can come, to the wretched outcasts of earth's abject poverty and fathomless degradation; whether they ever come, whether they ever can come, to the cruel and the proud, to the malicious and the mean, to the cynical and discontented; yet, if they come not to these, God help them! for they are the surest pledges of our immortality; and to the young and innocent—ay, and even to the young and guilty—they do sometimes come;—these hours of absorbing limitless enjoyment; these glimpses of dimly remembered paradise; these odours snatched from a primal Eden, from a golden age when justice still lived upon the earth, and crime was as yet unknown. There are such hours, and for this English family this hour was one of them.

Thrice happy Walter! and almost like a dream of happiness these holidays at home—and at *such* a home—flew by. Every day and hour was a change from pleasure to pleasure; among the hills, in the boat on the sunlit lake, plunging for his cool morning swim in the fresh waters, cricketing, riding, fishing, walking with his father and mother and brothers, sitting and talking at the cool nightfall in the moonlit garden, Walter was as happy as the day was long. And when Power came to spend a week with them, again charming every one whom he saw with his cheerful unselfishness and engaging manners, and himself charmed beyond expression with all he saw at Walter's home, they agreed that nothing was wanting to make their happiness "an entire and perfect chrysolite."

Power, we have seen, was something of a young poet, and on the day he left Semlyn with Walter, who was to accompany him home, he sat a long time silent in the train, and then tore out a leaf of his pocket-book, on which he had scribbled the following lines on:—

SEMLYN LAKE.

St. Winifred's, or The World of School

If earthly homes can shine so fair
   With sky and wave so purely blue,
Beneath the balmy purple air,
   If hills can don so rich a hue;

If fancy fails to paint a scene
   In Eden's soft and floral glades,
Where azure clear and golden green
   More sweetly blend with silver shades;

If marked and flecked with sinful stains,
   Earth hath not lost her power to bless,
But still, beneath the cloud, remains
   So steeped in perfect loveliness;

Merged, as we are, in doubt and fear,
   Yet, when we yearn for realms of bliss,
We scarce can dream, while lingering here,
   Of any fairer heaven than this.

Poor verses, and showing too delicate a sensibility to be healthy in any boy; yet dear to me and dear to Walter for Power's sake, and because they show the strange charm which Semlyn has for those who have the gift of appreciating those natural treasures with which earth plentifully fills her lap.

PART TWO

CHAPTER THIRTY. OLD AND NEW FACES.

Pudorem, amicitiam, pudicitiam, divina atque, humana
promiscua, nihil pensi neque moderati habere.—*Sallust.*

And now, gentle or ungentle reader, we must imagine that two whole years have passed since the conclusion of those summer holidays, before we again meet our young friends of St. Winifred's.

St. Winifred's, or The World of School

The two years—as what years are not?—have been full of change. Walk across the court with me, and let us discover what we can about the present state of things.

The first we meet are Walter and Power—taller and manlier looking than they were, but otherwise little changed in appearance. Walter, with his dark hair and blue eyes, his graceful figure and open face, is still the handsome, attractive- looking boy we used to see. Power, too, has the same refined, thoughtful look, the same delicate yet noble features, the same eyes, which we recognise at once as the clear and bright index of a beautiful and unstained soul.

And neither of these boys has failed in the promise of their earlier days, and the warm friendship with which they regarded each other has done much to bring about this result. Each in his own way has rejoiced in his youth, has passed an innocent and happy boyhood, stored with pleasant reminiscences for after days, filled with high hopes and manly principles, with habits well regulated, and that fine self-control which had taught them—

> Rapt in reverential awe,
> To sit, self-governed in the fiery prime
> Of youth, obedient at the feet of law.

They have enjoyed the gifts of early years without squandering them in wasteful profusion; they have felt and known that the purest pleasures were also the sweetest and the most permanent. Their minds are well cultivated, their bodies are in vigorous health, their hearts are glowing with generous impulse and warm enthusiasm; and if sorrow should ever darken their after years, it can never drive them to despair, for they have wandered in the pleasant paths of wisdom, they have drunk the pure cup of innocence, they will carry out of the torrid zone of youth clear consciences, unremorseful memories, and unpolluted minds.

Who is this who saunters across the playground, talking in loud, self-confident tones with two or three fellows round him, his hands in his pockets, his air haughty and nonchalant, and his cap a little on one side? He is still pleasant looking, his face still shows the capabilities for good and great things, but we are obliged to say of him:

St. Winifred's, or The World of School

Quantum mutatus ab illo
Hectore!

Yes, Kenrick—for it is he—is altered for the worse. Something or other has left, in its traces upon his face, the history of two degenerate years. His cheek does not look as if it were capable any longer of an ingenuous blush, and there is a curl about his lip and nostril which speaks of perpetual unhealthy scorn, that child of mortified vanity and conceit, which brazens out the reproaches of self-distrust and self-reproach. See with what a careless, almost patronising air he barely notices the master, who is passing by him. He has just flung a slight nod to Power, studiously taking care not to notice Walter at all. Look, too, at the boys who are with him; they are not boys with whom we like to see him; they are an idle lot, precocious only in folly and in vice. And that little fellow, who seems to be his especial favourite, is not at all to our taste; he seems the coolest of them all. For during the last two years Kenrick has entirely lost his balance; he has deserted his best friends for the adulation of younger boys, who fed his vanity, and the society of elder boys, who perverted his thoughts, and vitiated his habits. He has slackened in the career of honourable industry, he has deflected from the straight paths of integrity and virtue. Already the fresh eagerness of youth has palled into satiety, already some of its sparkling wine for him is bitter as vinegar; with him already pleasure has become a hectic fever instead of a healthy glow. Alas! he is not happy. Within these two years he has lost—and his countenance betrays the fact in its ruined beauty—he has lost the true joys of youth, and known instead of them the troubles of the envious, the fears of the cowardly, the heaviness of the slothful, the shame of the unclean. He has lost something of the instinctive shrinking, even in thought, from all that is vile and base, the loathing of falsehood, the kindness that will not willingly give pain, the humility which has lowly thoughts of its own worth;—he has lost his joy in things lovely, and excellent, and of good report; he has changed them for the mirth of fools, which is like crackling thorns—changed them for the feet that go down to death, for the steps that lay hold of hell. It is a mean price for which he has sold his peace of conscience —"the sweetness of the cup that is charged with poison, the beauty of the serpent whose bite is death."

Eden, who is seated reading on one of the benches by the wall, has recovered from his illness, but he is not, and never will be, what, but for Harpour's brutality, he might have been. He is a nervous, timid, intellectual boy. No game, unfortunately, has any attraction for him. The large liquid eyes, swimming sometimes with strange lustre, and often varying in colour, the delicate flush which any pulse of emotion drives glowing into the somewhat pale face, give to him an almost girlish aspect, and tell the tale of a weakened constitution. Eden's development has been quite altered by his fright; most of the vivacity and playfulness of his character has vanished; and although it flashes out with pleasant mirth when he is alone with his few closest friends, such as Walter and Power, his manner is, for the most part, very quiet and reserved. Yet Eden has a position of his own in the school; and unobtrusive as he is, his opinion is always listened to with kindness and respect. When he came into school again after his recovery he was received, as I have said already, with almost brotherly affection by all the boys, who felt how much he had been wronged. He became the child and protege of the school, and any cruelty to *him* would, after this, have been violently resented. Devoting himself wholly to work and reading, he became very successful in his progress, and is now in the second fifth. But what chiefly marks him is his extreme gentleness, and the eager way in which he strives to help all the younger and most helpless boys. Experience of suffering has given him a keen sympathy with the oppressed, and young as he is he is still doing a useful work.

There is Harpour playing rackets, and he is playing remarkably well. He is now nineteen, and a personage of immense importance in the school, for he is head of the cricket eleven, Walter being head of the football. Harpour is quite unchanged, and if he was doing mischief when we knew him two years ago, he is doing twice as much mischief now. His influence is unmitigatedly pernicious. With just enough cunning skill to escape detection, he yet signalises himself by complicity in every form of wrong which goes on in the school, and some new wrongs he introduces and invents. But nothing delights him so much as to instigate other boys to resist the authority of the masters. They know him to be a nucleus of disorder and wickedness, but he has acted with such consummate ingenuity as to avoid even laying himself open to any distinct proof of his many offences.

He is just now stopping for a minute in his game to talk to those three boys, who have been strutting up and down the court arm in arm, and whom we easily recognise. The one with the red puffy face, with an enormous gold pin in his cravat, a bunch of charms hanging to his chain, and a ring on his hand, which he loses no opportunity of displaying, is our friend Jones, with vulgarity as usual stamped on every feature, and displayed in every movement which he makes; the tall slim fellow, with an air of feeble fastness, an indecisive mouth, a habit of running his hand through his light-coloured hair, and a gaze which usually settles in fixed admiration on his faultless boots, can be no one but Howard Tracy; the third, a fellow with far more meaning and strength in his face, betrays himself to be Mackworth, by the insinuating plausibility and Belial-like grace of his manner and aspect. A dangerous serpent this; one never sees him, or hears him speak, or observes the dark glitter of his eye, without being reminded of a cerastes lythely rustling through the dry grass towards its victim.

And there at last—I thought we should never see him—is our dear young joker of jokes, the same unaltered Flip whom we know, running down the school steps. His face is overflowing with mirth and fun, and now he is stopping and holding both his sides for laughter, while, with little touches of his own, he retails some of the strange blunders which Bliss has made in the *viva voce* examination that morning; to which his friend Whalley listens with the same good-humoured smile which he had of old. Henderson is a perfect mimic, but never uses his powers of mimicry in an ill-natured spirit; and his imitation of Bliss's stolid perplexity and Dr Lane's comments are very ludicrous. While he is in the middle of this narrative, Bliss himself appears on the scene and relieves his feelings by delivering the only pun he ever made in his life, and observing, in a solemn tone of voice:

"Flip, don't be flippant;" a remark which he has substituted for the "I'll lick you, Flip," of old days.

"You dear old Blissidas, I *think* I've heard that pun once or twice before," observes Henderson, calmly pulling undone the bow of Bliss's necktie, and running off to escape retaliation, followed at his leisure by Whalley, who knows Bliss to be much too lazy to pursue the chase very far.

Let us come and hear—for we have put on our cap of darkness and are invisible, coming and going where we like, unobserved—what our four fast friends at the racket-court are talking about.

"We shall have lots of lark this half," observes Harpour, leaning on his racket.

"Yes; such fun, old boy," answers Jones.

"I declare this dull old place was getting quite lively before last holidays," says Mackworth; "we shall soon get things all right here."

St. Winifred's, or The World of School

"Fancy that fellow Power head of the school," said Harpour, bursting into a roar of scornful laughter, echoed in faint sniggerings by Jones and Tracy.

"Might as well have a jug of milk and water head of the school," sneered Mackworth.

"Or a bottle of French polish, I should think," casually suggests Henderson, who, *en passant*, has heard the last remark.

"D—–that fellow," says Mackworth, stamping; "by Jove, I'll be even with him some day."

"Is he one of the new monitors?" asks Jones.

"Yes," says Tracy, "and Evson's another;" and at Walter's name the faces of all four grew darker; "and Kenrick's a third."

"Oh, Kenrick is, is he? that's all right. Jolly fellow is Ken," observes Harpour approvingly.

"Yes, quite up to snuff," adds Jones; "and a thorough gentlemanly chap," assents Mackworth; for, amazing to relate, Kenrick is on good terms with these fellows now, though he has never spoken to Walter yet.

"Of good family, too, on the mother's side," drawls Tracy, with his hand lifting his locks.

"I say, old fellows," says Harpour, with many knowing looks and winks, and pokings of his friends in the ribs, "I say, stunning tap at Dan's, you know, eh? I say;" whereupon the others laugh, and Belial Mackworth observes, "And let those monitors try to peach if they dare. We'll soon have *them* under our thumb."

After which, as their conversation is supremely repulsive, let us go and take a breath of delicious pure sea air, and seat ourselves by Walter and Power on the shore. Walter is in good, and even gay spirits, being fresh from Semlyn, but Power seems a little grave and depressed.

"Look, Walter," he says, shying a round stone at a bit of embedded rock about twenty yards before them, but missing it; "I believe it was that identical rock—"

"*That* identical rock," said Walter, taking a better shot, and hitting it;—"well, what about it?"

"On which you were standing one autumn evening three years ago, when the tide was coming in—"

"And to save me wet trousers you took off your shoes and stockings, and carried me in on your back," said Walter. "I remember it well, Rex; it was a happy day for me. I recollect I'd been very miserable; it was after the Paton affair, you know, and every one was cutting me. Your coming to speak to me was about the last thing in the world I expected, and the best thing I could have hoped. I'd often wanted to know you, longed to have you as a friend; but I used to look up to you as such a young swell in those days that I never thought we should meet each other."

"Pooh!" said Power; "but wasn't it good now of me to break the ice and speak first? I declare, I think I've never done it with any one else. *You'd* never have done it—now confess? Only fancy, we mightn't have known each other till this day."

"I shouldn't have done it at *that* time," said Walter, "because I was in Coventry; but—well, never mind, Rex, we understand each other. I was looking at some porpoises, I remember."

"Yes; happy days they were after that. I wish the time was back again! Fancy you a monitor, and me head of the school!"

"Fancy! we've got up the school so much faster than we used to expect."

"Yes; but I wish we could change places, and you be head, and I sixth monitor as you are. You'll help me, Walter, won't you?"

"You don't doubt that, Rex, I'm sure; *all* the help *I* can give is yours."

"If it weren't for that I think I would have left, Walter. I don't think somehow I've influence enough for head. I'm not swell enough at the games."

"You play though now, and enjoy them; and I don't half believe you, Rex, when you talk of having wished to leave. That would have been cowardice, you know, and you're not the boy to leave your post."

"Here I am then in my place, armour on, visor down, determined not to fly, like the Roman soldier whose skeleton was found in the sentry-box at Pompeii," said Power, playfully getting up and assuming a military attitude.

"And here am I," said Walter, laughing, as he stood beside him with one foot advanced—"I, your sixth Hyperaspistes."

"The sixth!—the *first* you mean," said Power. "The four monitors, between you and me, won't, I fear, help us much. Browne is very short-sighted, and always shutting up with a headache; Smythe is a mere book-worm, and a regular butt even among the little fellows—worse that useless—no dignity or anything else; Kenrick," (for Kenrick had so far kept the advantage of his original start that, much as he had fallen off in work, Walter had not yet got above him)—"well, you know what Ken is!"

"Yes, I know what Ken is now—*Hesperos en phthimenois*—he's our chief danger—a doubtful general in the camp. Hallo, Flip, *you* here?" said he, as Henderson came up and joined them.

"Myself, O Evides; who's the doubtful general in the camp?—not I, I hope."

"You, Flip? no; but Kenrick. We're talking about the monitors."

"A doubtful general!—a traitor, you mean, an enemy, a spy," said Henderson hotly. "There, now, don't stop me, Power; abuse is a good safety-valve; the scream of the steam-engine letting off superfluous vapour. I should dislike him far worse if I bottled up against him a silent spite, hated him in the dark, and didn't openly abuse him sometimes."

Power's large and gentle mind, and Walter's generous temper, prevented them from joining in Henderson's strong language; but they felt no less than he did that, if they were to work for the good of the school, Kenrick would be their most dangerous, though not their declared, opponent. A monitor who seemed to recognise none of a monitor's duties, who openly broke rules and defied discipline, who smoked and went to public-houses, and habitually associated with inferiors, and those the least creditable set in the school, did more to damage the authority of the upper boys than *any* number of external assaults on them if they were consistent and united among themselves.

"I foresee storms ahead," said Power, with a sigh. "Flip, you must stand by me as well as Walter."

"Never fear," said Henderson; "but remember I'm only the junior monitor of the lot, and I'm so quick-tempered, I'm always afraid of stirring up a commotion some day with the Harpoons,"—as Henderson had christened the Harpour lot.

"You must be like the lightning-kite then," said Power. "and turn the flash away from us."

> "And dash the beauteous terror to the ground,
> Smiling majestic—"

observed Henderson, parodying the gesture, and making the others laugh.

"Do you remember Somers, and Dimock, and Danvers? what big fellows the monitors used to be then!" said Power.

"And do you remember certain boys whom Somers, and Dimock, and Danvers praised on a certain occasion?" said Walter. "Come, Rex, don't despond. We weren't afraid then, why should we be now?"

"But then they had Macon, and fellows like that, to uphold them in the school."

"So have *we*," said Henderson; "first and foremost Whalley, who's now got his remove into the upper sixth; then there's dear old Blissidas, who has arms if he hasn't got brains, and who is as staunch as a rock; and best of all perhaps there's Franklin, second in both elevens, brave as a lion, strong as a bull. By the bye, *he'll* have a lightning-kite ready made for you no doubt; he's accustomed to the experiment."

St. Winifred's, or The World of School

"Why, Flip, you talk as if we were going to have a pitched battle," said Power, ignoring his joke about Franklin.

"So we are—practically and morally. Look out for skirmishes from the Harpour lot; especially the world, the flesh, and the devil, whom I just saw arm in arm."

"What *do* you mean, Flip?" asked Walter, laughing.

"Mean! nothing at all—only Tracy, Jones, and Mackworth. Tracy's the world, Jones is the flesh—raw flesh; and Mackworth's the other thing."

"I'll tell you of two more who won't let the school override us if they can help it," said Walter; "Cradock and Eden."

"Briareus and Paradise," said Henderson; "poor Eden, he can't do much for us except look on with large troubled eyes."

"Can't he though, Flip? he's got a good deal of power."

"He's got a great deal of good from Power, I know, but—"

"But don't be a donkey, Flip."

"Do shut up. Why should you two expect such a dead assault on the monitors this half?" said Power.

"Why, the fifth has in it a more turbulent lot just now than I ever knew before; big, impudent fellows, with no good in them, and quite at the beck of the Harpour set," said Walter.

"Yes, and with that fellow Kenrick for a protagonist," said Henderson; "he and Harpour have always been at mischief about the monitors since they caught it so tremendously from Somers. Well, never mind; *aide toi et ciel t'aidera*. Why, look, there's Paradise, taking charge as usual of a little new fellow; who is it?"

"Look and see," said Walter, as a little fellow came up, with an unmistakable family resemblance—a pretty boy, with fresh round cheeks, and light hair, which shone like gold when the sunshine fell upon it.

"Why, Walter—why, this must be your brother. Well, I declare! an Evides secundus, Evides redivivus. Just what you were the day you came, and made Jones look small three years ago. How do you do, young 'un?" He shook him kindly by the hand and said, "You're a lucky little fellow to have a monitor brother, and Eden to look after you from the first. I wish *I'd* been so lucky, I know."

"Oh, Walter, what a *jolly* place this is," said his little brother—"jollier than Semlyn even."

"Wait a bit, Charlie; don't make up your mind too soon," said Walter; while Eden looked at the boy with a somewhat sad smile playing on his lips.

CHAPTER THIRTY ONE. AMONG THE NOELITES.

But, I pray you, who is his companion? Is there no young
squarer now that will make a voyage with him to the devil?
Much Ado about Nothing.

Etiam si quis a culpa vacuus in amicitiam ejus inciderat,
quotidiano usu par similisque caeteris efficiebatur.—
Sallust.

The changes described in the last chapter were not the only ones which seriously affected the prosperity of St Winifred's School, for the staff of masters was also partly altered during the last two years, and the alterations had not been improvements. Mr Paton—who had by this time manfully resumed his old theological labours, and who, to please Walter, had often employed him as a willing amanuensis in attempting to replace the burnt manuscript —had retired from his mastership to a quiet country living, to which he had been presented by Sir Lawrence Power. Strange as it may seem, Mr Paton chiefly, though of course indirectly, owed this living to Walter, who had first talked to Sir Lawrence about Mr Paton, in terms of deep regard. The opportunity, therefore, which Walter had sought so earnestly, of atoning in some way for the mischief which he had done to his old master, was amply granted to him; and Mr Paton never felt more strongly, that even out of the deepest apparent evils God can bring about undoubted blessings. St Winifred's, however, was the loser by his promotion. The benefit of his impartial justice and stern discipline, and the weight of his firm and manly character in the councils of the school, was gone. And St Winifred's had suffered a still greater loss in the departure of Mr Percival, who had accepted, some months before, the offer of a tutorship in his own university. Had he continued where he was, his influence, his well-deserved popularity, his kind, wise, conciliatory manner, the gratitude which rewarded his ready and self-denying sympathy, would, in the troubled period which ensued, have been even more useful than his brilliant scholarship and successful method of teaching a form. These two masters had left amid the universal regret of the boys and of their colleagues, and their places had been filled up by younger, less able, and less experienced men.

And worse than this, Dr Lane, soon after the term began, was taken seriously ill, and was ordered to the German baths for two months, during which his work was done by another master, who had not the same influence. From all which causes, this half-year at St Winifred's was the most turbulent, the most riotous, and the most unhappy ever known in that honourable and ancient school.

So little Charlie Evson soon found reason to revise and modify his opinion, that St Winifred's—as he *then* saw it—was jollier than even Semlyn itself. His name had been entered in the list of Mr Percival's house, before it was known that he was going to leave. Walter liked Mr Percival so much better than he did his own tutor, Mr Robertson, and had experienced from him so much more kindness, that he thought it would be an advantage for Charlie to be placed directly under so wise and kind a friend; and Mr Evson, afraid that his little son would be quite overshadowed by his elder brother, and that Walter's influence, which was very transcendent over Charlie's mind, would make him too dependent on another, and prevent him from developing his own natural character, was by no means averse to the arrangement. But since Mr Percival had left, Charlie, with the other boys in the house, was handed over to the charge of Mr Noel, a new master, who had to win his way and learn his work, neither of which he succeeded in doing until he had committed many mistakes.

In this house were Kenrick and Mackworth—Kenrick, as monitor, was in some measure responsible for the character of the house, and he had Charlie as one of his fags. At this time, as I have already observed with sorrow, Kenrick's influence was not only useless for good, but was even positively bad. There was *no* other monitor who did not try to be of some use to his fags; many of the monitors, by quiet kindnesses and useful hints, by judicious help and unselfish sympathy, were of most real service to the boys who nominally "fagged" for them, but who, in point of fact, were required to do nothing except taking an occasional message, seeing that the study fires did not go out, and carrying up the tea and breakfast for a week each, in order of rotation. Few St Winifred's boys would have hesitated to admit that they would have been less happy, and would have had fewer chances in school life, if they had not been fags as first, and thereby found friends and protectors in the boys for whom they fagged. Kenrick, however, did not follow the good example which had become almost traditional; for, filled as he was with the spirit of wilful pride, and on bad terms with the order to which he belonged, he either spoiled his fags by petting and pampering them, and letting them see his own disregard for duty, or, if they did not take his fancy, he snubbed and disregarded them—at any rate, did nothing whatever to help them.

Kenrick was quite willing to have placed Charlie Evson in the first of these classes, for he was a boy whom it was impossible to see and not to like. His antagonistic position towards most of his own body made him the head of a sort of faction in the school, and he would have been proud beyond measure to have had any boy like Charlie as one of his followers. But Kenrick had better reasons for wishing to attach Charlie to himself. Deeply as he had degenerated, disgraceful as his present conduct was, Kenrick, in the secret depths of his soul, sighed and pined for better things; though vice, and folly, and pride had their attractions for him, he was still sick at heart for the purer atmosphere which he had left. He looked at Charlie with vague hopes, for through him he thought that he might yet perhaps, without lowering his pride by actually seeming to have made any advance, bring about a reconciliation with his best and earliest friends, bring about a return to his former and more upright course.

But this was not to be. When a boy goes wrong he strews every step of his downward career with obstacles against his own return; and he little dreams how difficult of removal some of these obstacles will be. The obstacle in this case was another little fag of Kenrick's named Wilton. I am sorry to write of that boy. Young in years, he was singularly old in vice. A more brazen, a more impudent, a more hardened little scapegrace—in schoolboy language, "a cooler hand"—it would have been impossible to find. He had early gained the nickname of Raven from his artful looks. His manner was a mixture of calm audacity and consummate self-conceit. Though you knew him to be a thorough scamp, the young imp would stare you in the face with the effrontery of a man about town. He was active, sharp, and nice- looking, and there was nothing which he was either afraid or ashamed to do. He had not a particle of that modesty which in every good boy is as natural as it is graceful; he could tell a lie without the slightest hesitation or the faintest blush; nay, while he was telling it, though *he* knew that you *knew* it to be a lie, he would not abash for an instant the cold glance of his wicked dark eyes. Yet this boy, like Charlie, was only thirteen years old. And for all these reasons, Wilton was the idol of all the big bad boys in the school; and in spite of all these reasons—for the boy had in him the fascination of a serpent—he was the declared favourite of Kenrick too.

The three boys who gave the tone to Mr Noel's house were Kenrick, Mackworth, and Wilton. They formed as it were an electric chain of bad influence, and as they were severally prominent in the chief divisions of the school, they had peculiar opportunities for doing harm. Kenrick's evil example told with extraordinary power through the whole house, and especially upon the highest boys, who naturally imitated him. I do not mean to say that Kenrick had sunk so low that wilfully and consciously he lowered the character of the house, which as monitor he ought to have improved and raised; but he *did* so whether with intention or not; he did so negatively by neglecting all his duties, and by giving no direct countenance to what was right; he did so positively by not openly discountenancing, and by actually practising, many things which he knew to be wrong. The bad work was carried on by Mackworth, who was the most prominent fifth- form boy in the house. This boy's ability, and strength of will, and keenness of tongue, gave him immense authority, and enabled him to carry out almost everything he liked. To complete the mischief, among the lower boys Wilton reigned supreme; and as Wilton was prouder of Kenrick's patronage than of anything else, and by flattery and cajolery could win over Kenrick to nearly anything, the worst part of the characters of these boys acting and reacting on each other, leavened the house through and through with all that is least good, or true, or lovely, or of a good report. The mischief began before Mr Percival left, but it never could have proceeded half so far, if Mr Noel's inexperience, and the very kindness which led him to relax the existing discipline, had not tempted the boys to unwonted presumption.

Such was the state of things when Charlie entered Mr Noel's house. Walter knew that Mr Percival's promotion had frustrated the plan he had formed when he advised his father to put Charlie in that house, but the step could not now be recalled, nor, indeed, was Walter or any other monitor aware how bad the state of things had become. For among other dangerous innovations, Mackworth and Wilton had brought about a kind of understanding, that the house should to some extent keep to itself, resent all intrusion into its own precincts, and maintain a profound silence about its own secrets. Besides all this, Walter bitterly and sorrowfully felt that for some reason, which he was unable to fathom, the whole school was just then in an unsatisfactory state, and that Charlie, for whom his whole heart yearned with brotherly love and pity, would be exposed to severe temptations in whatever house he should be placed. He hoped too that, as Charlie would always have the run of his and of Power's study, it would make little difference to him that he was under a different house-master.

To Mackworth and Wilton the arrival of one or two new boys was a matter of some importance, but little anxiety. The new boys were necessarily young, and in the present united state of the house it was tolerably certain that they would catch the prevalent spirit, and be quickly assimilated to the condition of the others. The task of moulding them—if they were at all difficult to manage—fell to Wilton, and he certainly accomplished it with astonishing success. A newcomer's sensibilities were not too quickly shocked. The Noelites, for their own purposes, behaved very kindly to him at first; they were first-rate hands at "destroying a boy by means of his best affections," at "seething a kid in its mother's milk." The bad language, the school trickeries and deceits, the dodges for breaking rules and escaping punishments, the agreed-on lies to avoid detection, the suppers, and brandy, and smoking parties, and false keys to get out after lock-up, and all the other detestable symptoms of a vitiated and depraved set were carefully kept in abeyance at first. The new fellow was treated very kindly, was sounded and fathomed cautiously, was taught to get up a strong house feeling by perpetual endeavours to wake in him the *esprit de corps*, was gently ridiculed if he displayed any good principle, was tremendously bullied if he showed signs of recalcitrance, was according to his temperament led, or coaxed, or initiated, or intimidated into the condition of wickedness required of him before the house could continue to go to the devil as fast as it wished to do, and was doing before. This was Mackworth's work, and Wilton acted as his Azazel, and Kenrick did not interfere, though he knew or guessed all that was going on; he did not interfere, he did not prevent it, he did not even remonstrate at first, and afterwards he began by acquiescing, he ended by—yes, the truth must be told—he ended by joining in it all. Oh, Kenrick, when human beings meet face to face before a certain judgment-seat, there are some young souls who will have a bill of indictment against you; the same who may point to Mackworth or to Wilton, and say, as of old, "The serpent beguiled me, and I

St. Winifred's, or The World of School

did eat."

Five new boys had come this half-year. Four of them had been sounded by the rest of the house; one of them, named Stone, had come from a large private school, and was prepared for whatever he might find in more senses than one. Another, Symes, was a boy ill-trained at home, of no particular principles, and quite ready to flow with the stream. A third, Hanley, had come meaning to be good; he had been shocked when he first heard oaths, and when he was first asked if he would mind telling any of the regular lies —"crams" the boys called them—in the event of any master questioning him; but his wounded sensibilities were very quickly healed, and he had passed with fatal facility from disgust to indifference, from indifference to toleration. The fourth, Elgood, was a timid child, for whom no one cared either way, and whom they took care to frighten into promising to do whatever he was ordered. A terrible state of things—was it not? But, ah me! it was so once upon a time. The fifth new boy in Mr Noel's house was Charles Evson; and with this fifth new boy the devil's agents knew instinctively that they would have a great deal of trouble. But they meant to bait their hook very carefully, and they did not at all despair. Their task was made peculiarly piquant by its very difficulty, and by the fact that Charlie was one in whom their declared enemy, Walter Evson, was so nearly concerned. They were determined by fair means or foul to win him over, and make him their proselyte, until he became as much a child of sin as they were themselves. But they proceeded to their task with the utmost caution, and endeavoured to charm Charlie over to their views by showing him great attention, by trying to make things pleasant for him, by flattering him with notice, and seeming to welcome him cordially as one of themselves. Their dissimulation was profound; at first the new boy found everything quite delightful, and before a week was over had caught, as they meant him to catch, the spirit of party, and always was ready to stick up for the Noelites as the best house in the school. So far so good but this was only the first step of initiation into these Eleusinian mysteries.

So Master Wilton—Belial junior, as Henderson always called him —ingratiated himself into Charlie's favour, and tried, not without success, to make himself peculiarly agreeable. At first sight, indeed, Charlie felt an inward repulsion to him. He did not know *why* he did, for, so far from there being anything obviously repulsive in Wilton's look or manners, there were many who thought him the picture of innocence, and considered his manners quite perfection in their politeness and good-breeding. Charlie therefore instantly conquered his first feeling of dislike as uncharitable and groundless: and as

St. Winifred's, or The World of School

Wilton seemed to lay himself out for his friendship, he was oftener with him during the first fortnight than with any other boy. It was strange to see the two together, so utterly different were they in every respect, and so great was the contrast of Charlie's sweet, bright, modest face with the indescribable dangerous coolness of Wilton's knowing smile.

"Look," said Henderson to Whalley, as he saw them together one day in the playground; "there go Ithuriel and Belial junior, very thick at present."

"Yes; I don't like to see it. I don't hear any good of that fellow Wilton."

"Good! I should rather think not."

"Give young Evson a hint, Flip, will you, that Wilton's not a good friend for him. He looks a nice little fellow, and I don't like to tell him, because I don't know him."

"Never fear; when Charlie touches him with his spear, or sees him light on the top of Niphates—one of which things will happen soon enough—he'll not be slow to discover who he is. If not, I'll tell Walter, and he shall be Charlie's Uriel."

"Touches him with his spear!—what spear?—top of Niphates!— Uriel!" said Whalley, with ludicrous astonishment: "here, Power, you're just in time to help me to put a strait-waistcoat on Flip. He says that when Wilton lights on the top of Niphates, which he will do soon, young Evson will discover that he's a scamp. What *does* it all mean?"

"It only means that Flip and I have been reading the *Paradise Lost*," said Power, laughing, "and at present Flip's mind is a Miltonic conglomerate." And he proceeded to explain to Whalley that Ithuriel was one of the cherubs who guarded Eden. ("Only that in this case Eden guards the cherub," observed Henderson parenthetically.)

"—and who, by touching Satan with his spear, made him bound up in his original shape, when he sat like a toad squat at the ear of Eve; and, moreover, that Uriel had recognised Satan through his mask, when, lighting on Niphates, his looks became

"Alien from heaven, with passions foul obscured."

St. Winifred's, or The World of School

"Seriously though," said Henderson, "Uriel must be asleep, or he wouldn't let his little brother get under Belial's wings."

In fact, Wilton was forced to keep on the mask much longer than he had ever meant to do. He could find no joint in Charlie's armour. The boy was so thoroughly manly, so simple-hearted, so trustful and innocent, that Wilton could make nothing of him. If he tried to indoctrinate Charlie into the state of morality among the Noelites, either Charlie did not understand him, or else quite openly expressed his disapproval and even indignation; and when finally Wilton, quite tired out, did throw off the mask, Charlie shook him away from him, turned with a sickening sensation from the unbared features of vice, and unfeignedly loathed the boy who had pretended to be his friend—loathed him all the more because he had tried to like him, but now saw the snare which was being spread in his sight.

Every now and then during their early intercourse Charlie had felt a certain restraint in talking to Wilton; he could not be at ease with him though he tried. He caught the gleam of the snake through the flowers that only half concealed his folds. And Wilton, too, had got very tired of playing a part. He could not help his real wickedness cropping out now and then, yet whenever it did, Charlie started in such a way that even Wilton was ashamed; and though generally the shafts of conscience glanced off from the panoply of steel and ice which cased this boy's heart, yet during these days they once or twice reached the mark, and made him smart with long-unwonted anguish. He was conscious that he was doing the devil's work, and doing it for very poor wages. He felt now and then Charlie's immense superiority to himself, and, in a mood of pity, when, as they were standing one day in Mr Noel's private room to say a lesson, he caught sight of their two selves reflected in the looking-glass over the mantelpiece, and realised the immense gulf which separated them— a gulf not of void chaos and flaming space, but the deeper gulf of warped affections and sinful thoughts—he had felt a sudden longing to be other than what he was, to have Charlie for a true friend, to give up trying to make him a bad boy, and to fall at his feet and ask his pardon. And when he had doggedly failed in his lesson, and got his customary bad mark, and customary punishment, and received his customary objurgation, that he was getting worse and worse, and that his time was utterly wasted—and when he saw the master's face light up with a pleased expression as Charlie went cheerfully and faultlessly through his work—a sudden paroxysm of penitence seized Wilton, and, once out of the room, he left Charlie and ran up the stairs to Kenrick's study, in which he was allowed to sit whenever he liked. No one was there, and throwing himself into a chair, Wilton covered his face with both hands, and burst into passionate tears. A long train of thoughts and memories passed through his mind—memories of his own headlong fall to what he was, memories of younger and of innocent days, memories of a father, now dead, who had often set him on his knee, and prayed, before all other things, that he might grow up a good and truthful boy, and with no stain upon his name. But while memory whispered of past innocence, conscience told him of present guilt; told him that if his father could have foreseen what he would become, his heart would have broken; told him, and he knew it, that his name was a proverb and a byword in the school. But the prominent and the recurring thought was ever this—"Is it too late to mend? Is the door shut against me?" For Wilton remembered how once before his mind was harrowed by fear and guilt as he had listened to Mr Percival's parting sermon on that sad text—one of the saddest in all the Holy Book—"*And the door was shut.*"

Suddenly he was startled violently from his reverie, for the door *was* shut with a bang, and Kenrick, entering, flung himself in a chair, saying, with a vexed expression of voice, "Too late."

It was but a set of verses which Kenrick had written for a prize exercise, and which he had just sent in too late. He had not lost all ambition, but he had no real friend now to inspirit or stimulate him, so that he often procrastinated, and was seldom successful with anything.

But his accidental words fell with awful meaning and strange emphasis on poor Wilton's ear. Wilton had never heard of the Bath Kol, he knew nothing of the power that wields the tongue amid the chances of destiny; but fear made him superstitious, and, forgetting his usual dissimulation, he looked up at Kenrick aghast, without wiping away the traces which unwonted tears had left upon his face.

"Why, Raven, boy, what's the matter?" asked Kenrick, looking at him with astonishment; "much *you* care for my having a set of iambics too late."

"Oh, is that all?" asked Wilton, still looking frightened.

"All? Yes; and enough, too, for me. But,"—stopping suddenly— "why, Raven, what's the row? You've been crying, by all that's odd! Why, I didn't know you'd ever shed a tear since you'd been in the cradle. Raven crying—what a notion! Crocodile tears, eh?"

St. Winifred's, or The World of School

Wilton was ashamed to have been caught crying, and angry to be laughed at. He was leaving the room silently and in a pet, when Kenrick caught him, and, looking at him, said in a kindlier tone:

"Nonsense, Ra; don't mind a little chaff. What's happened? Nothing serious, I hope."

But Wilton was angry and miserable just then, and struggled to get free. He did not venture to tell Kenrick what had really been passing through his mind. "Let me go," he said, struggling to get free.

"Oh, go, by all means," said Kenrick, with his pride all on fire in a moment; "don't suppose that I want you or care for you:" and he turned his back on Wilton, to whom he had never once spoken harshly before.

The current of Wilton's thoughts was turned; he really loved Kenrick, who was the only person for whom he had any regard at all. Besides, Kenrick's support and favour were everything to him just then, and he stopped irresolutely at the door, unwilling to leave him in anger.

"What do you want? Why don't you go?" asked Kenrick, with his back still turned.

Wilton came back to the window, and humbly took Kenrick's hand, looking up at him as though to ask forgiveness.

"How odd you are to–day, Raven," said Kenrick, relenting. "What were you crying about when I came in?"

"Well, I'll tell you, Ken. I was thinking how much better some fellows are than I am, and whether it was *too late* to begin afresh, and whether the door *was open* to me still, when you came in, and said, `Too late,' and banged the door, which I took for an answer to my thoughts."

They were the first serious words Kenrick had ever heard from Wilton; but he did not choose to heed them, and only said, after a pause:

"Other fellows better than you? Not a bit of it. Less plucky, perhaps; greater hypocrites, certainly; but you are the jolliest of them all, Ra."

And with that silly, silly speech Wilton was reassured; a gratified smile perched itself upon his lips, and his eyes sparkled with delight; nor was he soon revisited by any qualms of conscience.

CHAPTER THIRTY TWO. DISENCHANTMENT.

Ho de karkinos hood' epha
chalai ton ophin laboon,
euthea chree ton etairon emen
ksi mee skolia phronein.
Skolion.

"How do you get on with the young Evson, Ra?" asked Mackworth of Wilton, with a sneer.

"Not at all," said Wilton. "He's awfully particular and strait-laced, just like that brother of his. No more fun while he's in the house."

"Confound him," said Mackworth, frowning darkly; "if be doesn't like what he sees, he must lump it. He's not worth any more trouble."

"So, Mack, *you* too have discovered what he's like."

"Yes, I have," answered Mackworth savagely. For all his polish, his courtesies, and civilities had not succeeded in making Charlie conceal how much he feared and disliked him. The young horse rears the first time it hears the adder's hiss, and the dove's eye trembles instinctively when the hawk is near. Charlie half knew and half guessed the kind of character he had to deal with, and made Mackworth hate him with deadly hatred, by the way in which, without one particle of rudeness or conceit, he managed to keep him at a distance, and check every approach to intimacy.

With Kenrick the case was different. Charlie thought that he looked one of the nicest and best fellows in the house, but he could not get over the fact that Wilton was his favourite. It was Wilton's constant and daily boast that Ken would do anything for him; and Charlie felt that Wilton was not a boy whom Walter or Power at any rate would even have tolerated, much less liked. It was this that made him receive Kenrick's advances with shyness and coldness; and when Kenrick observed this, he at once concluded that Charlie had been set against him by Walter, and that he would report to Walter all he did and said. This belief was galling to him as wormwood. Suddenly, and with most insulting publicity, he turned Charlie off from being one of his fags, and from that time never spoke of him without a sneer, and never spoke *to* him at all.

Meanwhile, as the term advanced, St Winifred's gradually revealed itself to Charlie in a more and more unfavourable light. The discipline of the school was in a most impaired state; the evening work grew more and more disorderly; few of the monitors did their duty with any vigour, and the big idle fellows in the fifth set the example of insolence towards them and rudeness to the masters. All rules were set at defiance with impunity, and in the chaos which ensued, every one did what was right in his own eyes.

One evening, during evening work, Charlie was trying hard to do the verses which had been set to his form. He found it very difficult in the noise that was going on. Not half a dozen fellows in the room were working or attempting to work; they were talking, laughing, rattling the desks, playing tricks on each other, and throwing books about the room. The one bewildered new master, who nominally kept order among the two hundred boys in the room, walked up and down in despair, speaking in vain first to one, then to another, and almost giving up the farce of attempting to maintain silence. But seeing Charlie seriously at work he came up and asked if he could give him any assistance?

Charlie gratefully thanked him, and the master sat down to try and smooth some of his difficulties. His doing so was the sign for an audible titter, which there was no attempt to suppress; and when he had passed on, Wilton, whose conduct had been more impertinent than that of any one else, said to Charlie:

"I say, young Evson, how you are grinding!"

"I have these verses to do," said Charlie simply.

"Ha! ha! ha!" laughed Wilton, as though he had made some good joke. "Here, shall I give you a wrinkle?"

"Yes, if it's allowed."

The answer was greeted with another laugh, and Wilton said, "I'll save you all further trouble, young 'un. Observe the dodge; we're all up to it."

He put up a white handkerchief to his nose, and walking to the master, said, "Please, sir, my nose is bleeding. May I go out for a minute?"

"Your nose bleeding? That's the third time your nose has bled this week, and other boys have also come with their noses bleeding."

"Do you doubt my word, sir?" asked Wilton, his handkerchief still held up, and assuming an injured air.

"I should be sorry to do so until you give me reason," answered the master courteously. "It seems a strange circumstance, but you may go."

It would have been very easy to see whether his nose was bleeding or not, but the master was trying, very unsuccessfully at present, whether implicit confidence would produce a sense of honour among the boys.

Wilton went out hardly concealing his laughter, and in ten minutes returned with the verses, finished and written out.

"There," he said, "Ken did those for me; he knocked them off in five minutes. Ken's an awfully clever fellow, though he never opens a book. Don't bore yourself with verses any more; I'll get them done for you."

Charlie glanced at the paper, and saw at once that the verses were perfectly done.

"Do you mean to show up that copy as your own, Wilton?"

"Of course I do."

St. Winifred's, or The World of School

"But we are marked for them."

"Hear, hear! thanks for the information. So much the better. I shall get a jolly good mark."

"Shut up, young Innocence, and don't be a muff," said another Noelite. "We all do the same thing. Take what Heaven sends you and be glad to get it."

"Thank you," said Charlie, looking round; "*you* may, but I'd rather not. It isn't fair."

"Oh, how good we are! how sweet we are! what an angel we are!" said Wilton, turning up the whites of his eyes, while the rest applauded him. But if they meant their jeers to tell on Charlie's resolution, they were mistaken. He looked quietly round at them all with his clear eves, gravely handed the paper back to Wilton, and quietly resumed his work. They were angry to be so foiled, and determined that, if he would not copy the verses, he should at least do them in no other way. One of them took his paper and tore it, another split up his quill pens by dashing them on the desk, while a third seized his dictionary. The master, observing that something was going on at that desk, came and stood by; and as long as he was there, Charlie managed to write out what he had done, while the others, cunningly inserting an occasional mistake, or altering a few epithets, copied out the verses which Kenrick had done for Wilton. But directly the master turned away again, a boy on the opposite side of the table, with the utmost deliberation, took hold of Charlie's fair copy, and emptied the inkstand over it in three or four separate streams.

Vexed as he was—for until this time he had never known unkindness—he took it quietly and good-humouredly. Next morning, before the rest of the boys in his dormitory, who were mainly in his own form, were aware of what he meant to do, he got up early and went to Walter's study, hoping to write out the verses there from memory. But he found the study in the possession of the housemaid; chapel bell rang, and after chapel he went into morning school with the exercise unfinished. For this, he, the only boy in the form who had attempted to do his duty, received a punishment, while the rest looked on unabashed, and got marks for their stolen work. Wilton received nearly full marks for his. The master, Mr Paton's successor, thought it odd that Wilton could do his verses so much better than any of his other work, but he could not detect the cheating, and Wilton always assured him that the verses were entirely his own composition.

St. Winifred's, or The World of School

It was about time now, Wilton thought, to hoist his true colours; but, as he had abundance of brass, he followed Charlie out of the schoolroom, talked to him familiarly as if nothing had happened, and finally took his arm. But this was too much; for the boy, who was as open as the day in all his dealings, at once withdrew his arm, and standing still, looked him full in the face.

"So!" said Wilton, "now take your choice—friends or enemies— which shall it be?"

"If you want me to cheat, and tell lies, and be mean—not *friends*."

"So! enemies then, mind. Look out for squalls, young Evson. One question, though," said Wilton, as Charlie turned away.

"Well?"

"Are you going to sneak about this to your brother?"

Charlie was silent. Without any intention of procuring Walter's interference, he *had* meant to talk to him about his difficulties, and to ask his advice. But if this was to be stigmatised as sneaking he felt that he had rather not do it, for there is no action a boy fears more, and considers more mean than this.

"Oh, I see," said Wilton; "you *do* mean to peach, blab, tell tales, do you? Well, it don't matter much; you'll find he can do precious little; and it will be all the worse for you in the long run."

"I shan't tell him," said Charlie shortly; and those words sealed his lips, as with a heavy heart he entered the breakfast-room, and meditated on troubles to come.

Which troubles came quite fast enough—very fast indeed. For the house, or rather the leading spirits in it, thought that they had wasted quite enough time, and with quite sufficient success in angling for the new boys, and determined to resume without any further delay their ordinary courses. If Charlie was fool enough to resist them, they said, so much the worse for him. During the day, indeed, he was saved from many of the annoyances which Walter had been obliged to endure, by escaping from the Great Schoolroom to the happy and quiet refuge of Walter's, or Power's, or Eden's study. There he could always be unmolested, and enjoy the kindness with which he was treated, and the cheerful, healthy atmosphere which contrasted so strangely in its moral sweetness with the turbid and polluted air of Noelite society. But in the evening at Preparation, and afterwards in the dormitories, he was wholly at the mercy of that bad confederacy which had tried to mould him to its own will. He was in a large dormitory of ten boys, and as this was the principal room in Mr Noel's house, it formed the regular refuge every night for the idle and the mischievously inclined. When the candles were put out at bedtime it was seldom long before they were relit in this room,—which was somewhat remote from the others at the end of a long corridor, and of which the window opened on a secluded part of Dr Lane's garden. If a scout were placed at the end of the corridor he could give timely warning of any danger, so that the chance of detection was very small. Had the candles been relit only for a game of play, Charlie would have been the first to join in the fun. But the Noelites were far too vitiated in taste to be long content with mere bolstering or harmless games. It seemed to Charlie that the candles were relit chiefly for the purpose of eating and drinking forbidden things, of playing cards, or of bullying and tormenting those boys who were least advanced in general wickedness.

"I say, young Evson," said Wilton to him one night soon after the fracas above narrated, "we're going to have some fun to-night. Stone, like a brick as he is, has stood a couple of bottles of wine, and Hanley some cards. We shall have a smoke too."

All this was said in a tone of braggadocio, meant to be exceedingly telling, but it only made Charlie feel that he loathed this swaggering little boy with his premature *savoir vivre*, more and more. He understood too the hint that two of the new fellows had contributed to the house carousal, and fully expected that he would be asked next. He secretly, however, determined to refuse, because he knew well that a mere harmless feast was not intended, but rather a smoking and drinking bout. He had subscribed liberally to all the legitimate funds—the football, the racquet court, the gymnasium; but he saw no reason why he should be taxed for things which he disliked and disapproved. The result of that evening confirmed him in his resolution. It was a scene of drinking, gluttony, secret fear, endless squabbling, and joyless excitement.

"Of course you'll play, and put into the pool?" said Wilton.

"No, thank you."

St. Winifred's, or The World of School

"No, *thank you*," said Wilton, scornfully mimicking his tone. "Of course not; you'll do nothing except set yourself up for a saint, and make yourself disagreeable."

During the evening Stone brought him some wine, which Charlie again declined, with, "No, thank you, Stone." Wilton again echoed the refusal, which was chorused by a dozen others; and from that time Charlie was duly dubbed with the nickname of No–thank–you. He was forcibly christened by this new name, by being held in bed while half a wineglass of port was thrown in his face. The wine poured down and stained his nightshirt, and then they all began to dread that it would lead to their being discovered, and threatened Charlie with endless penalties if he dared to tell. There was, however, little danger, as the Noelites had bribed the servants who waited on them and cleaned their rooms.

The same scene, with slight variations, was constantly repeated, and every fresh refusal was accompanied by a kick or a cuff from the bigger boys, a sneer or an insult from the younger; for Charlie himself was one of the youngest of them all. One night it was, "I say, you fellow—you, No–thank–you—will you fork out for some wine to–night? No? Well then, take that and that, and be hung to you for a little muff." Another time it would be, "Hi there, No–thank–you, we want sixpence for a pack of cards. Oh, you won't be so sinful as to part with sixpence for cards? Confounded little miser;" "Niggard," said another; "Skinflint," shouted a third. And a general cry of "Saint," which expressed the climax of villainy, ended the verbal portion of the contest. And then some one would slap him on the cheek, with "take that," "and that," from another, "and that," from a third—the last being a boot or a piece of soap shied at his head.

It cannot be more wearisome to the reader than it is to me to linger in these coarse scenes; but for Charlie it was a long martyrdom most heroically borne. He was almost literally alone and single–handed against the rest of the house; yet he would not give way. Walter and Power and Henderson all knew that he was bullied, sorely bullied; this they learnt far more from Eden, and from other sources, than from Charlie himself, for he, poor child, held himself bound by his promise to Wilton, and kept his lips resolutely sealed. But these friends knew that he was suffering for conscience' sake; and Walter helped him with tender, brotherly affection, and Power with brave words and kindly sympathy, as well as by noble example, and Henderson by his cheering and playful manner;—and this caused him much happiness all day long, until he felt that, with that short but heart–uttered prayer which he breathed so earnestly from "the altar of his own bedside," he had strength sufficient to meet and to conquer the trials which night brought.

St. Winifred's, or The World of School

In the house one boy and one only helped him. That boy *ought* to have been Kenrick; his monitorial authority and many responsible privileges were entrusted to him, as he well knew, for the main express purpose of putting down all immorality, and all cruelty, with a strong and remorseless hand. It required very little courage to do this; the sympathies of the majority of boys, unless they be suffered to grow corrupted with an evil leaven, are naturally and strongly on the side of right. In Mr Robertson's house, for instance, where Walter and Henderson were monitors, such wrong-doings could not have gone on with impunity, or rather could not have gone on at all. There, a little boy, treated with gross severity or injustice, would not have hesitated for an instant to invoke the assistance of the monitors, whom he looked upon as his natural guardians, and who would be eager to extend to him a generous and efficient protection. The same was the case in Mr Edwardes' house, of which Power was the head. Power, indeed, had no coadjutor on whom he could at all rely. One of the monitors associated with him was Legrange, who rather followed Kenrick's lead, and the other was Brown, who, though well-intentioned, was a boy of no authority. Yet these two houses were in a better condition than any others in the school, because the heads of them did their duty; and it was no slight credit to Walter and Henderson that their house stood higher in character than any other, although it contained both Harpour and Jones. This could not have been the case had not those two worthies found a powerful counterpoise in two other fifth-form fellows, Franklin and Cradock, whose excellence was almost solely due to Walter's influence. Kenrick, on the other hand, never interfered in the house, and let things go on exactly as they liked, although they were going to rack and ruin.

Charlie's sole friend and helper in the house then was, not Kenrick, but Bliss. Poor Bliss quite belied his name, for his school-work, in which he never could by any effort succeed, kept him in a state of lugubrious disappointment. Bliss lived a dim kind of life, seeing all sorts of young boys get above him and beat him in the race, and vaguely groping in thick mental darkness. Do what he would, the stream of knowledge fled from his tantalised lip whenever he stooped to drink; and the fruits, which others plucked easily, sprang up out of his reach when he tried to touch the bough. He was constantly crushed by a desolating sense of his own stupidity, and yet his good temper was charming under all his trials, and he loved with a grateful humility all who tolerated his shortcomings. For this reason he had a sincere affection for Henderson, who plagued him, indeed, incessantly, but never in an unkind or insulting way; and who more than made up for the teasing by patient and constant help, without which Bliss would not have succeeded even as well as he did. Bliss was a strong active fellow, and good at the games, so that with most of the school he got on very well; but, nevertheless, he was generally set down as nearly half witted—a mere dolt. Dolt or not, he did Charlie inestimable service; and if any boy is in like case with Bliss, let him take courage, for even the merest dolt has immense power for good as well as for harm, and Bliss extended to Charlie a gentle and manly sympathy which many a clever boy might have envied. He knew that Charlie was ill-used. Not being in the same dormitory, and joining very little in the house concerns, he was not able to interfere very directly in his aid; but he never failed to encourage him to resist iniquity of every kind. "Hold out, young Evson," he would often say to him; "you're a good, brave little chap, and don't give in; you're in the right and they in the wrong; and right is might, be sure of that."

It was something in those days to meet with approbation for well-doing among the Noelites; and Charlie, with genuine gratitude, never forgot Bliss's kind support; till Bliss left St Winifred's they continued firm friends and fast.

"Have you made any friends in the house?" asked Mr Noel of Charlie on one occasion; for he often seized an opportunity of talking to his younger boys, for whom he felt a sincere interest, and whom he would gladly have shielded from temptation to the very utmost of his power, had he but known that of which he was unhappily so ignorant—the bad state of things among the boys under his care.

"Not many, sir," said Charlie.

"Haven't you? I'm sorry to hear that. I like to see boys forming friendships for future life; and there are some very nice fellows in the house. Wilton, for instance, don't you like him? he's very idle and volatile, I know, but still he seems to me a pleasant boy."

Charlie could hardly suppress a smile, but said nothing; and Mr Noel continued, "Who is your chief friend, Evson, among my boys?"

"Bliss, sir," said Charlie with alacrity.

"Bliss!" answered Mr Noel in surprise. "What makes you like him so much? Is he not very backward and stupid?"

St. Winifred's, or The World of School

But Charlie would not hear a word against Bliss, and speaking with all the open trustfulness of a new boy, he exclaimed, "Oh, sir, Bliss is an excellent fellow; I wish there were many more like him; he's a capital fellow, sir, I like him very much; he's the best fellow in the house, and the only one who stands by me when I am in trouble."

"Well, I'm glad you've found *one* friend, Evson," said Mr Noel; "no matter who he is."

One way in which Bliss showed his friendship was by going privately to Kenrick, and complaining of the way in which Charlie was bullied. "Why don't you interfere, Kenrick?" he asked.

"Interfere, pooh! It will do the young cub good; he's too conceited, by half."

"I never saw a little fellow *less* conceited, anyhow."

Kenrick stared at him. "What business is it of yours, I should like to know?"

"It *is* business of mine; he is a good little fellow, and he's only kicked because the others can't make him as bad a lot as they are themselves; there's that Wilton—"

"Shut up about Wilton, he's a friend of mine."

"Then more shame for you," said Bliss.

"He's worth fifty such chickens as little Evson, any day."

"Chickens!" said Bliss, with a tone as nearly like contempt as he had ever assumed; "it's clear you don't know much about him; I wish, Kenrick, you'd do your duty more, and then the house would not be so bad as it is."

Kenrick opened his eyes wide; he had never heard Bliss speak like this before. "I don't want the learned, the clever, the profound Bliss to teach *me my* duty," he said, with a proud sneer; "what business have you to abuse the house, because it is not full of young ninnies like Evson? You're no monitor of mine, let me tell you."

"You may sneer, Kenrick, at my being stupid, if you like; but, for all your cleverness, I wouldn't be you for something; and if you won't interfere, as you ought, *I will*, if I can." And as Bliss said this, with clear flaming anger, and fixed on Kenrick his eyes, which were lighted up with honest purpose, Kenrick thought he had never seen him look so handsome, or so fine a fellow. "Yes, even *he* is superior to me now," he thought, with a sigh, as Bliss left the room. Poor Ken—there was no unhappier boy at St Winifred's; as he ate and ate of those ashy fruits of sin, they grew more and more dusty and bitter to his parched taste; as he drank of that napthaline river of wayward pride, it scorched his heart and did *not* quench his thirst.

CHAPTER THIRTY THREE. MARTYRDOM.

> Since thou so deeply dost enquire,
> I will instruct thee briefly why no dread
> Hinders my entrance here. Those things alone
> Are to be feared whence evil may proceed,
> Nought else, for nought is terrible beside.
> Carey's *Dante*.

Gradually the persecutions to which Charlie was subjected mainly turned on one point. His tormentors were so far tired of bullying him, that they would have left him in comparative peace if he would have yielded one point—which was this.

The Noelites were accustomed now and then to have a grand evening "spread", as they called it, and when they had finished this supper, which was usually supplied by Dan, they generally began smoking, an amusement which they could enjoy after the lights were out. The smokers used to sit in the long corridor, which, as I have said, led to their dormitory, and the scout was always posted to warn them of approaching danger; but as they did not begin operations till the master had gone his nightly rounds, and were very quiet about it, there was not much danger of their being disturbed. Yet although the windows of the corridor and dormitory were all left wide open, and every other precaution was taken, it was impossible to get rid of the fumes of tobacco so entirely as to avoid all chance of detection. They had, indeed, bribed the servants to secrecy, but what they feared was being detected by some master. The Noelites, therefore, of that dormitory had been accustomed to agree that if they were questioned by any master about the smell of smoking, they would all deny that any smoking had taken place. The other nine boys in the dormitory, with the doubtful exception of Elgood, had promised that they would stick to this assertion in case of their being asked. The question was, "Would Charlie promise the same thing?" If not, the boys felt doubly insecure—insecure about the stability of their falsehood and the secrecy of their proceedings.

And Charlie Evson, of course, refused to promise this. Single-handed he fought this battle against the other boys in his house, and in spite of solicitation, coaxing, entreaty, threats, and blows, steadily declared that he was no tell-tale, that he had never mentioned anything which had gone on in the house, but that *if he were directly asked* whether a particular act had taken place or not, he would still keep silence, but *could not and would not* tell a lie.

Now some of the house—and especially Mackworth and Wilton—had determined, by the help of the rest, to crush this opposition, to conquer this obstinacy, as they called it; and, since Charlie's reluctance could not be overcome by persuasion or argument, to break it down by sheer force. So, night after night, a number of them gathered round Charlie, and tried every means which ingenuity or malice could suggest to make him yield on this one point; the more so, because they well knew that to gain one concession was practically to gain all, and Charlie's uprightness contrasted so unpleasantly with their own base compliances, that his mere presence among them became, from this circumstance, a constant annoyance. One boy with a high and firm moral standard, steadily and consistently good, can hardly fail to be most unpopular in a large house full of bad and reckless boys.

It was a long and hard struggle; so long that Charlie felt as if it would last for ever, and his strength would give way before he had wearied out his persecutors. For now it seemed to be a positive amusement, a pleasant occupation to them, night after night, to bully him. He dreaded, he shuddered at the return of evening; he knew well that from the time when preparation began, till the rest were all asleep, he could look for little peace. Sometimes he was tempted to yield. He knew that at the bottom the fellows did not really hate him, that he might be very popular if he chose, even without going to nearly the same lengths as the others, and that if he would but promise not to tell, his assent would be hailed with acclamations. Besides, said the tempter, the chances are very strongly in favour of your not being asked at all about the matter, so that there is every probability of your not being called upon to tell the "cram", for by some delicate distinction the

St. Winifred's, or The World of School

falsehood presented itself under the guise of "a cram," and not of a naked lie; *that* was a word the boys carefully avoided applying to it, and were quite angry if Charlie called it by its right name. One evening the poor little fellow was so weary and hopeless and sad at heart, and he had been thrashed so long and so severely, that he was *very* near yielding. A paper had been written, the signing of which was tacitly understood to involve a promise to deny that there had been any smoking at night if they were taxed with it; and all the boys except Elgood and Charlie had signed this paper. But the fellows did not care for Elgood; they knew that he dared not oppose them long, and that they could make him do their bidding whenever the time came. Well, one evening, Charlie, in a weak mood, was on the verge of signing the paper, and thus purchasing a cessation of the long series of injuries and taunts, from which he had been suffering. He was sitting up in bed, and had taken the pencil in hand to sign his name. The boys, in an eager group round him, were calling him a regular brick, encouraging him, patting him on the back, and saying that they had been sure all along that he was a nice little fellow, and would come round at last. Elgood was among them, looking on with anxious eyes. He had immensely admired Charlie's brave firmness, and nothing but reliance on the strength of his stronger will had encouraged him in the shadow of opposition. "If young Evson does it," he whispered, "I will directly." Charlie caught the whisper; and in an agony of shame flung away the pencil. He had very nearly sinned himself, and forgotten the resolution which had been granted him in answer to his many prayers; but he had seen the effects of bad example, and nothing should induce him to lead others with him into sin. "Lead us not into temptation, but deliver us from evil," was the instant supplication which rose from his inmost heart, as he threw down the pencil and pushed the paper aside.

"I *can't* do it," he said; "I must not do it; I never told a lie in my life that I remember. Don't ask me any more." Instantly the tone and temper of the boys changed. A shower of words, which I will not repeat, assailed his ears; he was dragged out of bed and thrashed more unmercifully than he had ever been before. "You shall give way in the end, mind that," was the last admonition he received from one of the bigger fellows, as he dragged himself to his bed sobbing for pain, and aching with disquietude of heart. "The sooner it is the better, for you little muffs and would-be saints don't go down with us."

And then for a few evenings, when the candles were put out, and the fellows had nothing better to do, it used to be the regular thing for some one to suggest, "Come, let's *bait* No-thank-you; it'll be rare fun." Then another would say, "Come, No-thank-you, sign the paper like a good fellow, and spare yourself all the rest." "Do," another insidious friend would add; "I am quite sorry to see you kicked and thrashed so often." "I'll strike a light in one second if you will," suggested a fourth. "No, you won't? oh, then, look out, Master No-thank-you, look out for squalls." But still, however beaten or insulted, holding out like a man, and not letting the tears fall if he could help it, though they swam in his eyes for pain and grief, the brave boy resisted evil, and would not be forced to stain his white soul with the promise of a lie.

There were some who, though they dared not say anything, yet looked on at this struggle with mingled shame and admiration— shame for themselves, admiration for Charlie. It could not be but that there were some hearts among so many which had not seared the tender nerves of pity, and more than once Charlie saw kindly faces looking at him out of the cowardly group of tormentors, and heard timid words of disapprobation spoken to the worst of those who bullied him. More often too, some young Noelite who met him during the day would seem to address him with a changed nature, would speak to him warmly and with friendliness, would show by little kind words and actions that he felt for him and respected him, although he had not courage enough to resist publicly the opposing stream. And others of the baser sort observed this. What if this one little new fellow should beat them after all, and end their domination, and introduce in spite of them a truer and better and more natural state of things? it was not to be tolerated for a moment, and he must be put down with a strong hand at once.

Meanwhile Charlie's heart was fast failing him, dying away within him; for under this persecution his health and spirits were worn out. His face, they noticed, was far paler than when he came, his looks almost haggard, and his manner less sprightly than before. He had honourably abstained hitherto from giving Walter any direct account of his troubles, but now he yearned for some advice and comfort, and went to Walter's study, not to complain, but to ask if Walter thought there was any chance of his father removing him to another school, because he felt that at St. Winifred's he could neither be happy nor in any way succeed.

"Well, Charlie boy, what can I do for you?" said Walter, cheerfully pushing away the Greek Lexicon and Aristophanes over which he was engaged, and wheeling round the arm-chair to the fire, which he poked till there was a bright blaze.

"Am I disturbing you at your work, Walter?" said the little boy, whose dejected air his brother had not noticed.

St. Winifred's, or The World of School

"No, Charlie, not a bit; *you* never disturb me. I was just thinking that it was about time to shut up, for it's almost too dark to read, and we've nearly half an hour before tea–time; so come here and sit on my knee and have a chat. I haven't seen you for an age, Charlie."

Charlie said nothing, but he was in a weary mood, and was glad to sit on his brother's knee and put his arm round his neck; for he was more than four years Walter's junior, and had never left home before, and that night the home–sickness was very strongly upon him.

"Why, what's the matter, Charlie boy?" asked Walter playfully. "What's the meaning of this pale face and red eyes? I'm afraid you haven't found St Winifred's so jolly as you expected; disenchanted already, eh?"

"Oh, Walter, I'm very, very miserable," said Charlie, overcome by his brother's tender manner towards him; and leaning his head on Walter's shoulder he sobbed aloud.

"What is it, Charlie?" said Walter, gently stroking his light hair. "Never be afraid to tell me anything. You've done nothing wrong, I hope."

"Oh no, Walter. It's because I won't do wrong that they bully me."

"Is that it? Then dry your tears, Charlie boy, for you may thank God, and nothing in earth or under the earth can *make* you do wrong if you determine not—determine in the right way, you know, Charlie."

"But it's so hard, Walter; I didn't know it would be so *very* hard. The house is so bad, and no one helps me except Bliss. I don't think you were ever troubled as I am, Walter."

"Never mind, Charlie. Only don't go wrong, whatever they do to you. You don't know how much this will smooth your way all the rest of your school life. It's quite true what you say, Charlie, and the state of the school is far worse than I ever knew it; but that's all the more reason we should do our duty, isn't it?"

"Oh, Walter, but I *know* they'll make me do wrong some day. I wish I were at home. I wish I might leave. I get thrashed and kicked and abused every night, Walter, and almost all night long."

St. Winifred's, or The World of School

"*Do* you?" asked Walter, in angry amazement. "I knew that you were rather bullied—Eden told me that—but I never knew it was so bad as you say. By Jove, Charlie, I should like to catch some one bullying you, and—well, I'll warrant that he shouldn't do it again."

"Oh, I forgot, Walter, I oughtn't to have told you; they made me promise not. Only it *is* so wretched."

"Never mind, my poor little Charlie," said Walter. "Do what's right and shame the devil. I'll see if I can't devise some way of helping you; but anyhow, hold up till the end of term, and then no doubt papa will take you away if you still wish it. But what am I to do without you, Charlie?"

"You're a dear, dear good brother," said Charlie gratefully; "and but for you, Walter, I should have given in long ago."

"No, Charlie, not for me, but for a truer friend than even I can be, though I love you with all my heart. But will you promise me one thing faithfully?"

"Yes, that I will."

"Well, promise me then that, do what they will, they shan't make you tell a lie, or do anything else that you know to be wrong."

"I'll promise you, Walter, if I can," said the little boy humbly; "but I've been doing my best for a long time."

"You *couldn't* tell a lie, Charlie boy, without being found out; *that* I feel sure of," said Walter, smiling, as he held his brother's ingenuous face between his hands, and looked at it. "I don't doubt you for an instant; but I'll have a talk with Power about you. As head of the school he may be able to do something perhaps. It's Kenrick's duty properly, but—"

"Kenrick, Walter? He's of no use; he lets the house do just as it likes, and I think he must have taken a dislike to me, for he turned me off quite roughly from being his fag."

St. Winifred's, or The World of School

"Never mind him or any one else, Charlie. You're a brave little fellow, and I'm proud of you. There's the tea-bell; come in with me."

"Ah, Walter, it's only in the evenings when you're away that I get pitched into. If I were but in the same house with you, how jolly it would be." And he looked wistfully after his brother as they parted at the door of the hall, and Walter walked up to the chief table where the monitors sat, while he went to find a place among the boys in his own form and house. He found that they had poured his tea into his plate over his bread-and-butter, so he got very little to eat or drink that evening.

It was dark as they streamed out after tea to go into the preparation room, and he heard Elgood's tremulous voice saying to him, "Oh, Evson, shall you give way to-night, and sign?"

"Why to-night in particular, Elgood?"

"Because I've heard them say that they're going to have a grand gathering to-night, and to make you, and me too; but I can't hold out as you do, Evson."

"I shall try not to give way; indeed, I *won't* be made to tell a lie," said Charlie, thinking of his interview with Walter, and the hopes it had inspired.

"Then *I* won't either," said Elgood, plucking up courage. "But we shall catch it awfully, both of us."

"They can't do more than lick us," said Charlie, trying to speak cheerily, "and I've been licked so often that I'm getting accustomed to it."

"And I'd rather be licked," said a voice beside them, "and be like you two fellows, than escape being licked, and be like Stone and Symes, or even like myself."

"Who's that?" asked Elgood hastily, for it was not light enough to see.

"Me—Hanley. Don't you fellows give in; it will only make you miserable, as it has done me."

St. Winifred's, or The World of School

They went in to preparation, which was succeeded by chapel, and then to their dormitories. They undressed and got into bed, as usual, although they knew that they should be very soon disturbed, for various signs told them that the rest had some task in hand. Accordingly, the lights were barely put out, when a scout was posted, the candles were relighted, and a number of other Noelites, headed by Mackworth, came crowding into the dormitory.

"Now you, No–thank–you, you've got one last chance—here's this paper for you to sign; fellows have always signed it before, and *you* shall too, whether you like or no. We're not going to alter our rules because of you. We want to have a supper again in a day or two, and we can't have you sneaking about it." Mackworth was the speaker.

"I don't want to sneak," said Charlie firmly; "you've been making me wretched and knocking me about all these weeks, and I've never told of you yet."

"We don't want any orations; only Yes or No—will you sign?"

"Stop," said Wilton, "here's another fellow, Mac, who hasn't signed;" and he dragged Elgood out of bed by one arm.

"Oh, *you* haven't signed, haven't you? Well, we shall make short work of you. Here's the pencil, here's the paper, and here's the place for your name. Now, you poor little fool, sign without giving us any more trouble."

Elgood trembled and hesitated.

"Look here," said Mackworth brutally; "I don't want to break such a butterfly as you upon the wheel, but—how do you like that?" He drew a cane from behind his back, and brought it down sharply on Elgood's knuckles, who, turning very white, sat down and scrawled his name hastily on the paper; but no sooner had he done it than, looking up, he caught Charlie's pitying glance upon him, and running the pencil through his signature, said no more, but pushed the paper hastily away and cowered down, expecting another blow, while Charlie whispered, "Courage."

"You must take the other fellow first, Mac, if you want to get on," suggested Wilton. "Evson, as a friend, I advise you not to refuse."

St. Winifred's, or The World of School

"*As a friend!*" said Charlie, with simple scorn, looking full at Wilton. "You are no friend of mine; and, Wilton, I wouldn't even now change places with you."

"Wouldn't you?—Pitch into him, Mac. And you," he said to Elgood, "you may wait for the present." He administered a backhander to Elgood as he spoke, and the next minute Charlie, roused beyond all bearing, had knocked him down. Twenty times before he would have been tempted to fight Wilton, if he could have reckoned upon fair-play; but what he could stand in his own person was intolerable to him to witness when applied to another.

Wilton sprang up in perfect fury, and a fight began; but Mackworth at once pulled Charlie off, and said, "Fight him another time, if you condescend to do so, Raven; don't you see now that it's a mere dodge of his to get off. Now, No-thank-you, the time has come for deeds; we've had words enough. You stand there." He pushed Charlie in front of him. "Now, will you sign?"

"*Never*," said Charlie, in a low but firm tone.

"Then—"

"*Not with the cane, not with the cane*, Mackworth," cried several voices in agitation, but not in time to prevent the cane descending with heavy hand across the child's back.

Charlie's was one of those fine, nervous, susceptible temperaments, which feel every physical sensation, and every mental emotion, with tenfold severity. During the whole of this scene, so painfully anticipated, in which he had stood alone among a group of boys, whose sole object seemed to be to show their hatred, and who were twice as strong as himself, his feelings had been highly wrought; and though he had had many opportunities of late to train his delicate organisation into manly endurance, yet the sudden anguish of this unexpected blow quite conquered him. A thrilling cry broke from his lips, and the next moment, when the cane again tore his shoulders, a fit of violent hysteria supervened, which alarmed the brutes who were trying to master his noble resolution.

And at this crisis the door burst open with a sudden crash, and Bliss entered in a state of burning indignation, followed more slowly by Kenrick.

St. Winifred's, or The World of School

"Oh, I am too late," he said, stamping his foot; "what *have* you been doing to the little fellow?" and thrusting some of them aside, he took up Charlie in his arms, and gradually soothed and calmed him till his wild sobs and laughter were hushed, while the rest looked on silent. But feeling that Charlie shrank as though a touch were painful to him, Bliss unbared his back, and the two blue weals all across it showed him what had been done.

"Look there, Kenrick," he said, with great sternness, as he pointed to the marks; and then, laying Charlie gently down on his bed, he thundered out, in a voice shaken with passion, "You *dogs*, could you look on and allow this? By heavens, Kenrick, if *you* mean to suffer this, I won't. Out of my way, you." Scattering the rest before him like a flock of sheep, he seized Mackworth with his strong hands, shook him violently by both shoulders, and then tearing the cane out of his grasp, he demanded, "Was it you who did this?"

"What are you about, you, Bliss?" said Mackworth, with very ruffled dignity. "Mind what you're after, and don't make such a row, you ass's head," he continued authoritatively, "or you'll have Noel or some one in here."

"Ho! that's your tone, you cruel, reprobate bully," said Bliss, supplied by indignation with an unusual flow of words; "we've had enough of that, and too much. You can look at poor little Evson there, and not sink into the very earth for shame! By heavens, Belial, you shall receive what you've given. I'll beat you as if you were a dog. Take that." The cut which followed showed that he was in desperate earnest, and that however immovable he might generally be, it was by no means safe to trifle with him in such a mood as this. Mackworth tried in vain to seize the cane; Bliss turned him round and round as if he were a child; and as it was quite clear that he did not mean to have done with him just yet, Mackworth's impudent bravado was changed into abject terror as he received a second weighty stroke, so heartily administered, that the cane bent round him, in the hideous way which canes have, and caught him a blow on the ribs.

Mackworth sprang away, and fled, howling with shame and pain, through the open door, but not until Bliss had given him two more blows on the back, with one of the two cutting open his coat from the collar downwards, with the other leaving a mark at least as black as that which he had inflicted on the defenceless Charlie.

"To your rooms the rest of you wretches," said he, as they dispersed in every direction before him. "Kenrick," he continued, brandishing the cane, "I may be a dolt, as you've called me before now, but since you won't do your duty, henceforth I will do it for you."

Kenrick slunk off, half afraid that Bliss would apply the cane to *him*; and, speaking in a tone of authority, Bliss said to the boys in the dormitory, "If one of you henceforth touch a hair of Evson's head, look out; you know me. You little scamp and scoundrel Wilton, take especial care." He enforced the admonition by making Wilton jump with a little rap of the cane, which he then broke, and flung out of window. And then, his whole manner changing instantly into an almost womanly tenderness, he sat by poor little Charlie, soothing and comforting him till his hysterical sobs had ceased; and, when he felt sure that the fit was over, gently bade him good-night, and went out, leaving the room in dense silence, which no one ventured to break but the warm-hearted little Hanley, who, going to Charlie's bedside, said:

"Oh, Charlie, are you hurt much?"

"No, not very much, thank you, Hanley."

Hanley pressed his hand, and said, "You've conquered, Charlie; you've held out to the end. Oh, I wish I were like you."

CHAPTER THIRTY FOUR. A CONSPIRACY FOILED.

Hooste niphades chionos thameiai
hoos toon amphooteroothe lithoi pootoonto thameiai.
Iliad 12, 278.

As the feathery snows
Fall frequent on some wintry day ...
The stony volleys flew.—*Cowper.*

Yes, Charlie had conquered, thanks to the grace that sustained him, and thanks, secondarily, to a good home-training, and to Walter's strong and excellent influence. And in gaining that one point he had gained all. No one dared directly to molest him further, and he had never again to maintain so hard a struggle. He had resisted the beginnings of evil; he had held out under the stress of persecution; and now he could enjoy the smoother and brighter waters, over which he sailed.

His enemies were for the time discomfited, and even the hardy Wilton was abashed. For a week or two there was considerably less bravado in his face and manner, and his influence over those of his own age was shaken. That little rap of the cane which Bliss had given him had a most salutary effect in diminishing his conceit. Hanley retracted his promise to deny all knowledge of anything wrong that went on, and openly defied Wilton; even Elgood ceased to fear him. Charlie had felt inclined to cut him, but, with generous impulse, he forgave all that was past, and, keeping on civil terms with him, did all he could to draw him to less crooked paths.

Mackworth was so ashamed that he hardly ventured to show his face. He had always made Bliss a laughing-stock, had nicknamed him Ass's Head, and had taught others to jeer at his backwardness. He had presumed on his lazy good humour, and affected to patronise and look down on him. An eruption in a long- extinct volcano could not have surprised him more than the sudden outburst of Bliss's wrath, and if the two blows which he had received as he fled before him in sight of the whole house had been branded on his back with a hot iron, they could hardly have caused him more painful humiliation. For some time he slunk about like a whipped puppy, and imagined, not without some ground, that no one saw him without an inclination to smile.

Kenrick, too, had reason to blush. Every one knew that it was Bliss, and not he, who had rescued the house from attaching to its name another indelible disgrace; and when he heard the monitors and sixth-form talking seriously among themselves of the bad state into which the Noelites had fallen, he felt that the stigma was deserved, and that *he*, as being the chief cause of the mischief, must wear the brand.

All Kenrick's faults and errors had had their root in an overweening pride, a pride which grew fast upon him, and the intensity of which increased in proportion as it grew less and less justifiable. But now he had suffered a salutary rebuke. He had been openly blamed, openly slighted, and openly set aside, and was unable to gainsay the justice of the proceeding. He felt that with every boy in the school, who had any right feeling, Bliss was now regarded as a more upright and honourable, nay, even as a more important and influential person than himself. Among other mortifications, it galled him especially to hear the warm thanks and cordial praise which Power and Walter and Henderson expressed, when first they happened to meet Bliss. He saw Walter wring his hand, and overheard him saying in that genial tone in which he himself had once been addressed so often, "Thank you, Bliss, a thousand times, for saving my dear little brother from the hands of those brutes. Charlie and I will not soon forget how much we owe you." Walter said it with tears in his eyes, and Bliss answered with a happy smile, "Don't thank me, Walter; I only did what any fellow would have done who was worth anything."

"And you'll look after Charlie for me now and then, will you?"

"That I will," said Bliss; "but you needn't fear for him—he's a hero, a regular hero—that's what I call him, and I'd do anything for him."

So Kenrick, vexed and discontented, almost hid himself in those days in his own study, the victim of that most wearing of intolerable and sickening diseases—a sense of shame. Except to play football occasionally, he seldom left his room or took any exercise, and fell into a dispirited, broken way of life, feeling unhappy and alone. He had no associates now except his inferiors, for his conduct had forfeited the regard of his equals, and with many of them he was at open feud. The only pleasure left to him was desperately hard work. Not only was he stimulated by a fiery ambition, a mad desire to excel in the half-year's competition, and show what he was yet capable of, and so to some extent redeem his unhappy position, but also his heart was fixed on getting, if possible, the chief scholarship of St Winifred's—a scholarship sufficiently valuable to pay the main part of those college expenses which it would be otherwise impossible for his mother to bear. He feared, indeed, that he had little or no chance against Power, or even against Walter, who were both competitors, but he would not give up all hope. His abilities were of the most brilliant order, and if he had often been idle at St Winifred's, he had, on the other hand, often worked exceedingly hard during the holidays at Fuzby, where, unlike other boys, he had little or nothing else to amuse him. Mrs Kenrick, sitting beside him silent at her work for long hours, would have been glad indeed to see in him more elasticity, more kindliness, less absorption in his own selfish pursuits; but she rejoiced that at home, at any rate, he did not waste his vacant days in idleness, or spend them in questionable amusements and undesirable society.

Almost the only boy of whom he saw much now was Wilton, and but for him, I do believe, that in those days he would have changed his whole tone of thought and mode of life. But he had a strange liking for this worthless boy, who kept alive in him his jealousy of Walter, his opposition to the other monitors, his partisanship, his recklessness, and his pride. Sometimes Kenrick felt this. He saw that Wilton was bad as well as attractive, and that their friendship, instead of doing Wilton any good, only did himself harm. But he could not make up his mind to throw him off, for there was no one else who seemed to feel for him as a close and intimate friend. Many of Kenrick's failings rose from that. He had offended, and rejected, and alienated his early and true friends, and he felt now that it was easier to lose friends than to make them, or to recover their affection when it once was lost.

But the bad set at St Winifred's, though in one house their influence was weakened, were determined not to see it wane throughout the school. Harpour and his associates organised a regular conspiracy against the monitors. When the first light snow fell they got together a very large number of fellows, and snowballed all the monitors except Kenrick, as they came out of morning school. The exception was very much to Kenrick's discredit, and in his heart he felt it to be so. During the first day or two that this lasted the monitors took it good-humouredly, returning the snowballs, and regarding it as a joke, though an annoying one; but when it became more serious, when some snowballs had been thrown at the masters also, and when some of the worst fellows began to collect snowballs beforehand and harden them into great lumps of ice as hard as stones, and when Brown, who was short-sighted, and was therefore least able to protect himself, had received a serious blow, Power, by the advice of the rest, put up a notice that from that time the snowballing must cease, or the monitors would have to punish the boys who did it. This notice the school tried to resist, but the firmness of Power and his friends put a stop to their rebellion. If the notice was disregarded he determined, by Walter's advice, to seize the ringleaders, and not notice the younger boys whom they incited. Accordingly next morning they found the school gathered as usual, in spite of the notice, for the purpose of pelting them, and, saying nothing, they kept their eyes on the biggest fellows in the group. A shower of snowballs flew among them, hitting several of them, and, to the great amusement of the school, knocking over several hats into the snow.

"Harpour," said Walter very sternly, "I saw you throw a snowball. Aren't you ashamed of yourself that you, a fellow at the head of the eleven, should set such a bad example? Don't suppose that your size or position shall get you off. Come before the monitors directly after breakfast."

"Hanged if I do," answered Harpour, with a sulky laugh.

St. Winifred's, or The World of School

"Well, I dare say you *will* be hanged in the long run," was the contemptuous reply; "but come, or else take the consequences."

"Tracy," said Henderson, "I saw you throw a snowball which knocked off Power's hat. It was a hard one too. You come before the monitors with Harpour."

"I shall be quaite delaighted," drawled out Tracy.

"Glad to hear it; I hope you'll be quaite equally delaighted when you leave us." The mimicry was so perfect that all the boys broke into a roar of laughter, which was all the louder because Tracy immediately began to chafe and "smoke."

"And, Jones," said Power, as the laugh against Tracy subsided, "I think I saw *you* throw a snowball and hit Smythe. I strongly suspect, too, that you were the fellow who hit Brown yesterday. I think every one will know, Jones, why you chose Smythe and Brown to pelt, instead of any other monitors. You too come to the sixth-form room after breakfast."

"I didn't throw one," said Jones.

"You astounding liar," said Henderson, "I saw you with my own eyes."

"Oh ay; of course you'll say so to spite me."

"*Spite* you," said Henderson scornfully; "my dear fellow, you don't enter into my thoughts at all. But mark you, Master Jones, I know moreover that you've been the chief getter-up of this precious demonstration. You told the fellows that you'd lead them. I'm not sure that you didn't quote to them the lines—

"Press where ye see my *white plume* shine amid the ranks of war,
And be your oriflamme to-day the helmet of ——Jones."

Another peal of laughter followed this allusion to Jones's well-known nickname of Whitefeather, a nickname earned by many acts of conspicuous cowardice.

"Hush, Flip," whispered Power, "we mustn't make this quite a joke. Jones," he continued aloud, "do you deny throwing a snowball just now at Smythe?"

St. Winifred's, or The World of School

"I didn't throw one," said Jones, turning pale as he heard the hiss, and the murmur of "white feather again," which followed his denial.

"Why, what a pitiful, wretched, sneaking coward you are," burst out Franklin; "I heard you egging on these fellows to pelt the monitors—they wouldn't have done it but for you and Harpour— and I saw you hit Smythe just now. You took care to pelt no one else, and now you deny it before all of us who saw you. Upon my word, Jones, I feel inclined to kick you, and I will too."

"Stop, Franklin," said Walter, laying his hands on his shoulder, "leave him to us now. Do you still deny throwing, Jones?"

"Well, it was only just a little piece of snow," said Jones, showing in his blotched face every other contemptible passion fused into the one feeling of abject fear.

"Faugh!" said Power, with scorn and disgust curling his lip and burning in his glance; "really, Jones, you're almost too mean and nasty to have any dealings with. I don't think we can do you the honour of convening you. You shall apologise to Smythe here and now, and that shall be enough for *you*."

"What! do you hesitate?" said Franklin; "you don't know when you're well off. Be quick, for we all want our breakfast."

"Never mind making him apologise," said Smythe; "he's sunk quite low enough already."

"It's his own doing," said Walter. "We can't have lies like his told without a blush at St Winifred's. Apologise he must and shall."

"Don't do it," said Mackworth.

"What!" said Henderson, "is that Mackworth speaking? Ah! I thought so—Bliss isn't here!"

Henderson's manner was irresistibly comic; and as Mackworth winced and slunk back to the very outside of the crowd, the loud laugh which followed showed that the complete exposure of the worthlessness of their champions had already turned the current of feeling among the young conspirators, and that they were beginning to regret their unprovoked attack on the upper boys.

"Now, then, Jones, this is what you have to read," said Walter, who had been writing it on a slip of paper—"I humbly beg Smythe's pardon for pelting him, and the pardon of all present for my abominable lies."

Jones began to mumble it out, but there arose a general shout of —"On your knees, Whitefeather; on your knees, and much louder."

Franklin, who was boiling over with anger and contempt, sprang forward, took Jones by the neck, and forced him on his knees in the snow, where he made him read the apology, and then let him loose. A shower of snowballs followed him as he ran to the refuge of the breakfast-hall, for there was not a boy present, no matter to what faction he belonged, who did not feel for Jones a very hearty contempt.

"I hope we shall have no more of this, boys," said Power, before the rest dispersed. "There have been monitors at St Winifred's for a hundred years now, and it's infinitely better for the school that there should be. I suppose you would hardly prefer to be at the mercy of such a fellow as that," he said, pointing in the direction of Jones's flight. "I don't know why we should be unpopular amongst you. You know that not one of us has ever abused his authority, or behaved otherwise than kindly to you all. But I am sorry to see that you are set on—set on by fellows who ought to know better. Don't suppose any of you that they will frighten us from doing what we know to be right, or that *you* can intimidate us when we are acting for the good of the school."

They cheered his few simple words, for they were proud of him as head-monitor. They had never had at St Winifred's a better scholar or a more honourable boy; and though Harpour and his friends affected to sneer at him, Power was a general favourite, and the firm attitude which he now assumed increased the respect and admiration which he had always inspired.

"No more notice will be taken of this, you little fellows," said Walter to the crowd of smaller boys; "we know very well that you have merely been the tools in other hands, and that is why we only singled out three fellows. I am quite sure you won't behave in this way again; but if you do, remember we shan't pass it over so lightly."

St. Winifred's, or The World of School

"Come here you, Wilton," said Henderson, as the rest were dispersing. "You've been particularly busy, I see. So! six good hard snowballs in your jacket pocket, eh? Now, you just employ yourself in collecting every one of these snowballs that are lying ready here, and throw them into the pond. Don't let me see *one* when I come out.—Belial junior will have to curtail his breakfast-time this morning, I guess," he continued to Whalley; "the young villain! shall we ever bring him to a right mind?"

Wilton, in a diabolical frame of mind, began his appointed task, and had just finished it as the boys came out of breakfast. "That will do," said Henderson. "I must trouble you for one minute more. Come with me." Shaking with cold and alarm, Wilton obeyed, muttering threats of vengeance, and driven almost frantic by the laughter with which Henderson received them. He walked across to the sixth-form room, and then seeing that all the monitors were assembled, sent him "to tell his friends, Harpour and Tracy, that their presence was demanded immediately."

"Never mind, Raven," said Kenrick to him; "it's a shame of them to bully you."

"I have made him collect some snowballs which he had a chief hand in making, and with one of which yesterday a monitor was seriously hurt; then I have sent him a message for two worthless fellows, whose counsels he generally follows; both of which things I have done to teach him a mild but salutary lesson. Is that what you call bullying?"

"I believe you spite the boy because you know I like him. It's just the kind of conduct worthy of you."

"If it gives you any comfort to say so, Kenrick, pray do; but let me tell you, that after the way you have allowed young Evson and others to be treated in your house, the charge of bullying comes with singularly ill grace from you."

An angry retort sprang to Kenrick's lips; but at that moment the two offenders came to the door, and Power said, "Hush, you two. We need unity now, if ever, and it will be very harmful if these fellows find a quarrel going on. Kenrick, I wish you would try to—"

"Oh yes, it's always Kenrick, of course," said he angrily. "I'll have nothing to do with your proceedings;" and, rising from his place, he flung out of the room, not sorry to be absent from a scene which he thought might compromise his popularity with some of those who excepted him from the list of the monitors, whom they professed to consider as their natural enemies.

Harpour and Tracy had thought that when convened before the monitors they would have an opportunity for displaying plenty of insolence and indifference; but when they found themselves standing in the presence of those fifteen upper boys, each one of whom was in all respects their superior, all their courage evaporated. But they were let off very easily. The monitors were content with the complete triumph they had gained that morning, and with the disgrace to which these fellows had been compelled to submit. All that they now required from them, was an expression of regret for what they had done, and a promise not to offend in the same way again; and when these had been extorted, they were dismissed by Power with some good advice, and a tolerably stern reprimand. Power did this with an ease and force which moved the admiration of all his brother monitors; no one could have done it as he did it, who was not supported by the authority of a high and stainless character consistently maintained. What he said was not without effect; even the coarse burly Harpour dared not look up, but could only fix his eyes on the floor and kick the matting in sullen wrath while this virtuous and noble boy looked at him and rebuked him; but Tracy was more deeply moved. Tracy, weak, foolish, and feebly fast as he was, had some elements of good and gentlemanly feeling in him, and, with more wisely-chosen associates, would have developed a much less contemptible character. When Power had done speaking, he looked up and said, without one particle of his usual affectation:

"I really am sorry for helping to get up this affair. I see I've been in the wrong, and I beg pardon sincerely. You may depend on my not having anything more to do with a thing of this kind."

"Thank you, Tracy," said Walter; "that was spoken like a man. We've known each other for some time now, and I wish we could get on more unitedly. You might do some good in the school if you chose."

"Not much, I'm afraid now," said Tracy, "but I'll tr–ai–y."

"Well, then, Tracy, well shake hands on that resolve, and bygones shall be bygones," said Henderson. "You'll forgive my making fun of you this morning."

He shook hands with Henderson and with Walter, while Power, holding out his hand, said, smiling, "It's never too late to mend."

"No," said Tracy, looking at one of his boots, which he had a habit of putting out before the other.

"He applied your remark to his boots, Power," said Henderson, laughing. "Did you observe how the hole in one of them distressed him?"

So the monitors separated, not without hopes that things were beginning to look a little brighter than before.

CHAPTER THIRTY FIVE. THE FINAL FRACAS.

Ta gar aischra onomata, ou ta pragmata, eioothasin
anthroopoi, ek tou epi pleistoon aischynesthai—
Procopius, *De Bella Goth*. 4, 15.

Legousi tous ta aischra pragmata onomasi chreestois
epikalyptonpas ... asteioos hypokorizesthai.—*Plutarch*.

Harpour, and all who, like him, had long been endeavouring to undermine the authority which was the only safeguard to the morality of the school, felt themselves distinctly baffled. Mackworth had been put to utter rout by Bliss, and though he was almost bursting with dark spite, would not venture to do much; Jones had become a perfect joke through the whole school, and was constantly having white hen's feathers and goose-feathers enclosed to him in little envelopes until he was half-mad with impotent wrath; Harpour himself had been made very decidedly to swallow the leek of public humiliation; and as for Wilton, he began to feel rather small.

Tracy again had openly deserted them. After the interview with Power, Harpour had abused him roundly as a turncoat, and he had told his former associates that he was sorry to have had anything to do with their machinations, that they were going all wrong, and were ruining the school, and that he at any rate felt that he had done mischief enough already, and meant to do no more. This proof of their failing influence exasperated them greatly. Harpour threatened, and Mackworth said all the pungent and insulting things he could, contemptuously mimicking all Tracy's dandiacal affectations. Tracy winced under this treatment; high words followed, and after a scene of noisy altercation, Tracy broke with his former "party," and after the quarrel spoke to them no more.

Dr Lane, too, had now recovered from his fever, and returned to the school. When the reins were in his strong hands, the difference was soon perceived. The abuses which had crept in during his absence were quietly and firmly rectified, and all tendencies to insubordination were repressed with a stern and just decision which it was impossible to gainsay or to resist. The whole aspect of things altered, and, lonely as he was among the Noelites, even Charlie Evson began to like St Winifred's better, and to feel more at home in its precincts.

Still, those who were rebelliously inclined were determined not to give in at once, and anxiously looked out for some opportunity in which they could have Kenrick on their side. If they could but secure this, they felt tolerably confident of giving the monitors a rebuff, and of carrying with them that numerous body in the school who had been taught under their training to resist authority on every possible occasion.

The opportunity was not long wanting. One fine afternoon a poor old woman had come up to the playground with a basket of trifles, by the sale of which she hoped to support herself during the unexpectedly long absence of a sailor son. Her extreme neatness of person, and her quiet, respectable manners, had interested some of the boys in her appearance; and when she came up to sell the little articles, many of which her own industry had made, she generally found ready purchasers. Walter, who knew her well, had visited her cottage, and had often seen the sailor boy on whose earnings she in a great measure depended. This only son had now been away for some time on a distant voyage, and the poor woman, being pressed for the necessaries of life, took her basket once more to the playground of St Winifred's. Charlie had often heard about her from Walter, and he gladly made from her a few small purchases, in which other boys followed his example. While he was doing this, he distinctly saw one of the Noelites—an ill-conditioned fellow in the shell, named Penn—thrust his hand into the old woman's basket, which was now surrounded by a large group of boys, and secrete a small bottle of scent. Charlie waited a moment, expecting to see him pay for it, but Penn, who fancied that he had been unobserved, dropped it quietly into his pocket, and stood looking on with an innocent and indifferent air.

St. Winifred's, or The World of School

Instantly Charlie's indignation knew no bounds. He could hardly believe his own eyes; he knew that a few of the very worst in the school, and some in his own house in particular, would regard this as a venial offence. They would not call it stealing, but "bagging a thing," or, at the worst, "cribbing it"—concealing the villainy under a new name, a name with no very odious associations attached to it; just as they called lying "cramming," under which title it sounded much less repulsive. In fact, these young Noelites took a most Spartan view of these petty larcenies, confining the criminality to the incurring of detection. But they had never succeeded in making Charlie take this view; he never would adopt the change of language by which they altered the accepted meaning of words in accordance with their own propensities and dispositions, and to him this particular act which Penn committed with perfect nonchalance appeared to be not only a theft, but a theft accompanied by a cruelty and deadness to all sense of pity, which dipped it in the very blackest and most revolting dye. He could not restrain, and did not attempt to restrain, the passionate contempt and horror which he felt for this act.

"Penn," he said in a loud and excited voice, not doubting that the sympathies of the others would be as warm as his own, "Penn, you wicked brute, you have stolen that bottle of scent. Here, Mrs Hart, *you* shan't suffer at any rate if there *is* a fellow so base and wicked;" and he at once pulled out his last half– crown, and insisted on her taking it in payment for the stolen article.

Penn, for the moment, was quite taken aback by the scathing flame of Charlie's righteous anger. If there had been none but Noelites there he would have made very light of the accusation, and probably have laughed it off; but there were others looking on who would, he knew, view the transaction in a very different light, so he thought that his safest course lay in a flat denial. It was not reasonable to expect that he would stick at this; a boy who has no scruples about "bagging" the property of a poverty– stricken old woman is not likely to hesitate about telling a "cram" to escape exposure.

"What's all this about, you little fool? I haven't bagged anything."

Charlie was still more amazed; he positively could not understand a great brazen lie like this, and yet it was impossible to doubt that it *was* a lie, against the evidence of his own senses.

St. Winifred's, or The World of School

"You didn't take that scent-bottle? oh! how *can* you tell such a lie? I saw you with my own eyes."

"What do I care for you or your eyes?" was the only answer which Penn vouchsafed to return.

"You're always flying out at fellows like a young turkey-cock, you No-thank-you," said Wilton. "Why don't you thrash him, Penn, for his confounded impudence?"

"Thrash him yourself if you like, Raven; I don't care the snap of a finger for what he says."

"What do you mean, No-thank-you, by charging him with bagging the thing when he says he didn't?" said Wilton in a threatening tone to Charlie; and as Charlie took no notice, he enforced the question by a slap on the cheek; for Wilton had old grudges against Charlie to pay off.

"I didn't speak to *you*, Wilton; but you shan't hit me for nothing; you force me to fight against my will," said Charlie, returning the blow; "you can't say that I'm doing it to get off anything this time, as you did once before."

A long and desperate fight ensued between Charlie and Wilton; too long and too desperate in the opinion of several of the bystanders; but as there was no one near who had any authority, nobody liked to interfere. So, as they were very equally matched, neither of the combatants showed the least sign of giving in, though their faces and clothes were smeared with blood. At last Henderson and Whalley, who were strolling through the playground, caught sight of the crowd, and came up to see what was the matter.

"It's a fight," said Henderson; "young Evson and Belial junior; I'd much rather see them fight than see them friends."

"Yes, Flip; but they've evidently been fighting quite long enough to be good for them. You're a monitor—couldn't you see if they ought not to be separated, and shake hands?"

"Hallo, stop, you two," said Henderson, pushing his way into the crowd. "What's all this about? let's see that it's all right."

"It's a fair fight," said several; "you've no right to stop it."

"I won't stop it unless there's good reason, though I think it's gone on long enough. What began it?"

"No-thank-you charged Penn with—"

"Who is No-thank-you?" asked Whalley.

"Young Evson, then," said Mackworth sulkily, "charged Penn with bagging a scent-bottle from the old woman's basket, and then he was impudent, so Wilton was going to pitch into him."

"And couldn't manage it, apparently," said Whalley; "come, you two, shake hands now."

Charlie, after a moment's hesitation, frankly held out his hand; but Wilton said, "He'd no right to accuse a Noelite falsely as he did."

"It wasn't falsely," said Charlie; "I saw him take it, and a horrid shame it was."

"Is one of your bottles missing, Mrs Hart?" asked Whalley.

"Yes, sir; but now young Master Evson has paid for it, and I don't want no more fighting about it, sir, please."

"Well, my good woman, there's something for you," said Henderson, giving her a shilling; "and I hope nobody will treat you so badly again; you'd better go now. And now, Penn, if you didn't take the bottle, of course you won't mind being searched?"

"Of course I *shall*," said Penn, edging uneasily away to try if possible to get rid of the unlucky bottle, which now felt as if it burned his pocket.

"Stay, my friend," said Whalley, collaring him; "no shuffling away, if you please."

St. Winifred's, or The World of School

"What the devil is your right to search me?" said Penn, struggling in vain under Whalley's grasp; "don't you fellows let him search me."

The attention of all was now fairly diverted from the fight, which, therefore, remained undecided; while the boys, especially the Noelites, formed an angry group round Henderson and Whalley, to prevent them, if possible, from any attempt to search Penn. Meanwhile, seeing that something was going on, other boys came flocking up until a large number of the school were assembled there, while Whalley still kept tight hold of Penn, and Henderson watched that he should play no tricks; the Noelites meantime exclaiming very loudly against the supposed infringement of their abstract rights.

Kenrick was one of those who had now come up; and as several fellows entreated him to stick up for his own house, and not to let Penn be searched, he worked himself into a passion, and pushing into the circle, said loudly, "You've no right to search him; you shan't do it."

"Here's the head of the school, he shall decide," said Henderson, as Power and Walter approached. "State your own case, Kenrick."

"Well, the case simply is, that a scent-bottle has been taken from Mrs Hart; and Penn doesn't see—nor do I—why he should be searched."

"You haven't mentioned that young Evson says he *saw* him take it."

"Why, Charlie, what *have* you been doing?" said Walter, looking at his brother's bruised and smeared face in surprise.

"Only a fight," said Charlie; "I couldn't help it, Walter; Wilton struck me because I charged Penn with taking the bottle."

"Are you absolutely certain that you saw him, Charlie?"

"Yes; I couldn't possibly be mistaken."

"Well then, clearly Penn must be searched," said Walter.

"But stop," said Power; "aren't we beginning at the wrong end? Penn, no doubt, if we ask him quietly, will empty his pockets for our satisfaction."

"No, I won't," said Penn, who was now dogged and sullen.

"Well, Kenrick has taken your part, will you let him or me search you privately?"

"No!"

"Then search him, Henderson."

Instantly a rapid movement took place among the boys as though to prevent this; but before anything could be done, Henderson had seized Penn by both wrists, and Whalley, diving a hand into his right pocket, drew out and held up a little ornamental scent– bottle.

This decisive proof produced for a moment a dead silence among the loud voices raised in altercation; and then Power said:

"Penn, you are convicted of lying and theft. What is St. Winifred's coming to, when fellows can act like this? How am I to punish him?" he asked, turning to some of the monitors.

"Here and now, red–handed, *flagrante delicto*," said Walter. "Some of these lower fellows need an example."

"I think you are right. Symes, fetch me a cane."

"You shan't touch him," said Kenrick; "you'd no right to search him, in the first place."

"I mean to cane him, Kenrick. Who will prevent me?"

"We will," said several voices; among which Harpour's and Mackworth's were prominent.

"You mean to try and prevent it by force?"

St. Winifred's, or The World of School

"Yes."

"And, Kenrick, you abet this?"

"I do," said Kenrick, who had lost all self-control.

"I shall do it, nevertheless; it is my plain duty."

"And I recommend you all not to interfere," said Walter; "for it must and shall be done."

"Harpour," said Franklin, "remember, if you try force, I for one am against you the moment you stir."

"And I," said Bliss, stepping in front of Power; "and I," said Eden, Cradock, Anthony, and others—among whom was Tracy— taking their places by the monitors, and forming a firm front together.

Symes brought the cane. Power took it, and another monitor held Penn firmly by the wrists. At the first stroke, some of the biggest fifth-form fellows made a rush forward, but they were flung back, and could not break the line, while Harpour measured his full length on the turf from the effects of the buffet which Franklin dealt him. Kenrick was among those who pressed forward; and then, to his surprise and shame, Walter, who was the stronger of the two, grasped him by the shoulder, held him back, and said in a low tone, firm yet kind, "You must excuse my doing this, Kenrick; but otherwise you might suffer for it, and I think you will thank me afterwards."

Kenrick was astonished, and he at once desisted. Those were the first and only words which Walter had spoken to him, the only time Walter had touched him, for nearly three years; and in spite of all the abuse, calumny, and opposition which Walter had encountered at his hands, Kenrick could not but feel that they were wise words, prompted, like the action itself, by the spirit of true kindness. He said nothing, but abruptly turned away and left the ground.

The struggle had not lasted a moment, and it was thoroughly repulsed. There could not be the least doubt of that, or of the fact that those who were on the side of righteous order outnumbered and exceeded in strength the turbulent malcontents. Power inflicted on Penn a severe caning there and then. The attempt to prevent this, audacious and unparalleled as it was, afforded by its complete failure yet another proof that things were coming round, and that these efforts of the monitors to improve the tone of the lower boys would tell with greater and greater force. Even the character of the Noelites was beginning to improve; in that bad house a single little new boy had successfully braved an organised antagonism to all that was good, and by his victorious virtuous courage had brought over others to the side of right, triumphing, by the mere force of good principle, over a banded multitude of boys far older, abler, and stronger than himself.

So that now Harpour, Mackworth, and Jones were confined more and more to their own society, and were forced to keep their misconduct more and more to themselves. They sullenly admitted that they were foiled and thwarted, and from that time forward left the school to recover as fast as it could from their vicious influence. Among their other consolations—for they found themselves shunned on all sides—they proposed to go and have a supper at Dan's. One day, before the events last narrated, Power had seen them go in there. He had sent for them at once, and told them that they must know how strictly this was forbidden, what a wretch Dan was, and how ruinous such visits to his cottage must be. They knew well that if he informed of them they would be instantly expelled, and entreated him with very serious earnestness to pass it over this time, the more so because they had no notion that any monitor would ever tell of them, *because, since he had been a monitor, Kenrick had accompanied them there.* Shocked as he was to hear this, it had determined Power not to report them, on the condition, which he made known to the other monitors, and of which he specially and pointedly gave warning to Kenrick, that they would not so offend again. This promise they wilfully broke, feeling perfectly secure, because Dan's cottage was at a remote and lonely part of the shore, where few boys ever walked, and where they had very little chance of being seen, if they took the precaution of entering by a back gate. But within a week of Penn's thrashing, Walter was strolling near the cottage with Eden and Charlie, and having climbed the cliff a little way to pluck for Eden, (who had taken to botany), a flower of the yellow horned poppy which was waving there, he saw them go into Dan's door, and with them—as he felt sure—little Wilton. The very moment, however, that he caught sight of them, the fourth boy, seeing him on the cliff, had taken vigorously to his heels and scrambled away behind the rocks. Walter had neither the wish nor the power to overtake him, and as he had not so much *seen* Wilton as inferred with tolerable certainty that it was he, he only reported Harpour, Mackworth, and Jones to Dr Lane; at the same time sending for Wilton to tell him of his suspicion, and to give him a severe and earnest warning.

St. Winifred's, or The World of School

Dr Lane, on the best possible grounds, had repeatedly announced that he would expel any boy who had any dealings with the scoundrel Dan. He was not likely to swerve from that declaration in any case, still less for the sake of boys whose school career had been so dishonourable and reprobate as that of these three offenders. They were all three publicly expelled without mercy and without delay; and they departed, carrying with them, as they well deserved to do, the contempt and almost the execration of the great majority of the school.

In the course of their examination before the head-master, Jones, with a meanness and malice thoroughly characteristic, had said, "that he did not know there was any harm in going to Dan's, because Kenrick, one of the monitors, had done the same thing." At the time, Dr Lane had contemptuously silenced him, with the remark, "that he would gain nothing by turning informer;" but as Dr Lane was always kept pretty well informed of all that went on by the Famulus, he had reason to suspect, and even to know, that what Jones said was in this instance true. He knew, too, from other quarters, how unsatisfactorily Kenrick had been going on, and the part he had taken in several acts of insubordination and disobedience. Accordingly, no sooner had Harpour, Jones, and Mackworth been banished from St Winifred's, than he sent for Kenrick, and administered to him a reprimand so uncompromising and stern, that Kenrick never forgot it to the end of his life. After upbraiding him for those many inconsistencies and follies, which had forfeited the strong esteem and regard which he once felt for him, he pointed out finally how he was wasting his school life, and how little his knowledge and ability could redeem his neglect of duty and betrayal of trust; and he ended by saying, "All these reasons, Kenrick, have made me seriously doubt whether I should not degrade you altogether from your position of monitor and head of a house. It would be a strong step, but not stronger than you deserve. I am alone prevented by a deep and sincere wish that you should yet recover from your fall; and that, by knowing that some slight trust is still reposed in you, you may do something to prove yourself worthy of that trust, and to regain our confidence. I content myself, therefore, with putting you from your present place to the *lowest* on the list of monitors—a public mark of my displeasure, which I am sure you will feel to be just; and I must also remove you from the headship of your house—a post which I grieve to know that you have very grievously misused. I shall put Whalley in your place, as it happens that no monitor can be conveniently spared. He, therefore, is now the head of Mr Noel's house; and, so far, you will be amenable to his authority which, I hope, you will not attempt to resist."

St. Winifred's, or The World of School

Kenrick, very full of bitter thoughts, hung his head, and said nothing. To know Dr Lane was to love and to respect him; and this poor fatherless boy *did* feel very great pain to have incurred his anger.

"I am unwilling, Kenrick," continued the Doctor, "to dismiss you without adding one word of kindness. You know, my dear boy, that I have your welfare very closely at heart, and that I once felt for you a warm and personal regard; I trust that I may yet be able to bestow it upon you again. Go and use your time better; remember that you are a monitor; remember that the well-being of many others depends in no slight measure on your conscientious discharge of your duties; check yourself in a career which only leads fast to ruin; and thank God, Kenrick, that you are not actually expelled as those three boys have been, but that you have still time and opportunity to amend, and to win again the character you once had."

Turned out of his headship to give way to a fifth-form boy, turned down to the bottom of the monitors, poor Kenrick felt unspeakably degraded; but he was forced to endure a yet more bitter mortification. Before going to Dr Lane he had received a message that he was wanted in the sixth-form room, and, with a touch of his old pride, had answered, "Tell them I won't come." Hardly had he reached his own study after leaving the Doctor, when Henderson entered with a grave face, and saying, "I am sorry, Kenrick, to be the bearer of this," handed to him a folded sheet of paper. Opening it, he found that, at the monitors' meeting, to which he had been summoned, a unanimous vote of censure had been passed upon him in his absence, for the opposition which he had always displayed against his colleagues, and for the disgraceful part which he had taken in attempting to coerce them by force in the case of Penn. The document concluded, "We are therefore obliged, though with great and real reluctance, to take the unusual step of recording in the monitors' book this vote of censure against Kenrick, fourth monitor, for the bad example he has set and the great harm he has done, in at once betraying our interests, and violating the first conditions on which he received his own authority: and we do this, not in a spirit of anger, but solely in the earnest and affectionate hope that this unanimous condemnation of his conduct by all his coadjutors may serve to recall him to a sense of his duty."

Appended were the names of all the monitors;—but, no; as he glanced over the names he saw that one was absent, the name of Walter Evson. Evidently, it was not because Walter *disapproved* of the measure, for, had this been the case, Kenrick knew that his name would have appeared at the end as a formal dissentient; —no, the omission of his name was due, Kenrick saw, to that same high reserve, and delicate, courteous consideration which had marked the whole of Walter's behaviour to him since the day of their disastrous quarrel.

Kenrick appreciated this delicacy, and his eyes were suffused with tears. Wilton, somewhat cowed by recent occurrences, was the only boy in his study at the time, and though Kenrick would have been glad to have some one near him, to whom he could talk of the disgraces which had fallen so heavily upon him, and to whom he could look for a little sympathy and counsel, yet to Wilton he felt no inclination to be at all communicative. There was, indeed, something about Wilton which he could not help liking, but there was and could be no sort of equality between them.

"Ken," said Wilton, "do you remember telling me the other day that I was shedding crocodile tears?—what are crocodile tears? I've always been wanting to ask you."

"It's just a phrase, Ra, for sham tears; and it was very rude of me, wasn't it? Herodotus says something about crocodiles; perhaps he'll explain it for us. I'd look and see if I had my Herodotus here, but I lost it nearly three years ago."

By one of those curious coincidences, which look strange in books, but which happen daily in common life, Tracy at this moment entered with the lost Herodotus in his hand, saying:

"Kenrick, I happened to be hunting out the classroom cupboard just now for a book I'd mislaid, when I found a book with your name in it—an Herodotus; so I thought I'd bring it you."

"By Jove!" said Wilton, "talk of—"

"Herodotus, and he'll appear," said Kenrick; "how very odd. It's mine, sure enough. I lost it, as I was just telling Wilton, I don't know how long ago. Now, Raven, I'll find you all he says about crocodiles."

"Before you look, may I tell you something?" asked Tracy. "I wanted an opportunity to speak with you."

St. Winifred's, or The World of School

"Well?"

"Do you mind coming out into the court, then?" said Tracy, glancing at Wilton.

"Oh, never mind me," said Wilton; "I'll go out."

"I shan't be a minute," said Tracy, "and then you can come back. What I wanted to say, Kenrick, was only this, and it was a great shame of me not to tell you before; but I see now that I've been a poor tool in the hands of those fellows. Jones made you believe, you know, *that Evson had told him* all about your home affairs, and about the pony–chaise, and so on," said Tracy, hurrying over the obnoxious subject.

"Yes, yes," said Kenrick impatiently.

"Well, he never did, you know. I've heard Jones confess it often with his own lips."

"How can I believe him in one lie more than another, then? I believe the fellow couldn't open his lips without a lie flying out of them. How could Jones possibly have known about it any other way? There was only one fellow who could have told him, and that was Evson. Evson *must* have told me a lie when he said that he'd mentioned it to no one but Power."

"I don't believe Evson ever told a lie in his life," said Tracy. "However, I can explain your difficulty; Jones was in the same train as Evson; he saw you and him ride home; and, staying at Littleton, the next town to where you live, he heard all about you there. I've heard him say so."

"The black–hearted brute!" was all that Kenrick could ejaculate, as he paced up and down his study with agitated steps. "Oh, Tracy, what an utter, utter ass, and fool, and wretch I've been."

"So have I," said Tracy; "but I'm sorry now, and hope to improve. Better late than never. Good–morning, Kenrick."

When Wilton returned to the study a quarter of an hour after, he found Kenrick's attention riveted by a note which he held in his hand, and which he seemed to be reading with his whole soul. So absorbed was he that he was not even disturbed by Wilton's entrance. Listlessly turning over the pages of his Herodotus to divert his painful thoughts by looking for the passage about the crocodiles, Kenrick had found an old note directed to himself. Painful thoughts, it seems, were to give him no respite that day; how well he knew that handwriting, altered a little now, more firm and mature, but even then a good, though a boyish hand. He tore it open; it was dated three years back, and signed Walter Evson. It was the long-lost note in which Walter, once or twice rebuffed, had frankly and even earnestly asked pardon for any supposed fault, and begged for an immediate reconciliation;—the very note which Walter of course imagined that Kenrick had received, and from his not taking any notice of it, inferred that all hope of renewing their friendship was finally at an end. Kenrick could not help thinking how very different a great part of his school life would have been had that note but come to hand!

He saw it all now as clearly as possible—his haste, his rash and false inferences, his foolish jealousy, his impetuous pride, his quick degeneracy, all the mischief he had caused, all the folly he had done, all the time he had wasted. Disgraced, degraded, despised by the best fellows in the school, censured unanimously by his colleagues, given up by masters whom he respected, without a single true friend, grievously and hopelessly in the wrong from the very commencement, he now felt *bowed down and conquered*, and, to Wilton's amazement, he laid his head upon his arms on the table before him without saying a word, and broke into a heavy sob. If his conscience had not declared against him, he could have borne everything else; but when conscience is our enemy, there is no chance of a mind at ease. Kenrick sat there miserable and self-condemned; he had injured his friend, injured his fellows, and injured, most deeply of all, himself. For, as the poet sings—

> He that wrongs his friend,
> Wrongs himself more; and ever bears about
> A silent court of justice in his breast;
> Himself the judge and jury, and himself
> The prisoner at the bar, ever condemned,
> And that drags down his life.

St. Winifred's, or The World of School

CHAPTER THIRTY SIX. IN THE DEPTHS.

How easy to keep free from sin,
  How hard that freedom to recall!
For dreadful truth it is, that men
  Forget the heavens from which they fall.
    Coventry Patmore.

It may be thought strange that Kenrick did not at once, while his heart was softened, and when he saw so clearly how much he had erred, go there and then to Walter, confess to him that everything was now explained, that he had never received his last note, and that, for his own sake, he desired to be restored, as far as was possible, to his former footing. If that had not been for Kenrick a period of depression and ill-repute, he would undoubtedly have done so; but he did not like to go, now that he was in disgrace, now that his friendship could do no credit, and, as he feared, confer no pleasure on any one, and under circumstances which would make it appear that he had changed his views under the influence of selfish interest, rather than of true conviction or generous impulse. He thought, too, that friendship over was like water spilt, and could not be gathered up again; that it was like a broken thread which cannot again be smoothly reunited. So things remained on the same footing as before, except that Kenrick's whole demeanour was changed for the better. He bore his punishment in a quiet and manly way; took his place without a murmur below Henderson at the bottom of the monitors; did not by any bravado attempt to conceal that he felt justly humiliated, and gave Whalley his best assistance in governing the Noelites, and bringing them back by slow but sure degrees to a better tone of thought and feeling. Towards Walter especially his whole manner altered. Hitherto he had made a point of always opposing him, and taking every opportunity to show him a strong dislike. If Walter had embraced one opinion at a monitors' meeting, it was quite sufficient reason for Kenrick to support another; if Walter had spoken on one side at the debating society, Kenrick held it to be a logical consequence that, whatever he thought, he should speak on the other, and use his powers of speaking, which were considerable, to throw on Walter's illustrations and arguments all the ridicule he could. All this folly and virulence was now abandoned; the swagger which Kenrick had adopted was from that time entirely laid aside. At the very next meeting of the debating society he spoke, as indeed he generally thought, on the same side with Walter; and spoke, not in his usual flippant conceited style, but more seriously and earnestly, treating Walter's speech with approval and almost with deference. Every one noticed and rejoiced in this change of manner, and none more so than Walter Evson and Power.

Kenrick finished with these words—"Gentlemen, before I sit down I have a task to perform, which, however painful it may be to me, it is due to you that I should not neglect. I may do it now, because I see that none but the sixth-form are present, and because I may not have another early opportunity. I have incurred, as you are all well aware, a unanimous vote of censure from my colleagues—unanimous, although, through a delicacy which I am thankful to be still capable of keenly appreciating, the name of one,"—the word "friend" sprang to his lips, but humility forbade him to adopt it, and he said,—"the name of one monitor is absent from the appended signatures. Gentlemen, I do not like public recantations or public professions, but I feel it my duty to acknowledge without palliation that I feel the censure to have been deserved." His voice faltered with emotion as he proceeded. "I have been misled, gentlemen, and I have been labouring for a long time under a grievous mistake, which has led me to do much injustice and inflict many wrongs; for these errors I now ask the pardon of all, and especially of those who are most concerned. Your censure, gentlemen, concluded with a kind and friendly wish, and I cannot trust myself to say more now, than to echo that wish with all my heart, and to hope that ere long the efforts which I shall endeavour to make may succeed in persuading you to give me back your confidence and esteem, and to erase from the book the permanent record of your recent disapproval."

Every one present felt how great must have been the suffering which could wring such an expression of regret from a nature so proud as Kenrick's. They listened in silence, and when he sat down greeted him with an applause which showed how readily he might win their regard; while many of them came round him and shook hands with warmth.

"Gentlemen," said Power, rising, "I am sure we all feel that the remarks we have just heard do honour to the speaker. I hold in my hand the monitors' book, open at the page on which our censure was written. After what we have heard there can be no necessity why that page should remain where it is for a single day. I beg to move that leave may be given me to tear it out at once."

"And I am eager to second the motion," said Henderson, starting up at the same moment with several others, "and, Kenrick—if I may break through, on such an occasion as this, our ordinary forms, and address you by name—I am sure you will believe that though I have very often opposed you, no one will be more glad than myself to welcome you back as a friend, and to hope that you may soon be, what you are so capable of being, not only our greatest support, but also one of the brightest ornaments of our body." He held out his hand, which Kenrick readily grasped, whispering, with a sigh, "Ah, Flip, how I wish that we had never broken with each other!"

The proposal was carried by acclamation, and Power accordingly tore out the sheet and put it in the fire. And that night brightened for Kenrick into the dawn of better days. Twenty times over Walter thought that Kenrick was going to speak to him—for his manner was quite different; but Kenrick, though every particle of ill-will had vanished from his mind, and had been replaced by his old unimpaired affection, put off the reconciliation until he should have been able in some measure to recover his old position, and to meet his friend on a footing of greater equality.

Do not let any one think that his reformation was too easy. It took him long to conquer himself, and he found the task sorely difficult; but after many failures and relapses, the words of another who had sinned and suffered three thousand years ago, and who, after many a struggle, had discovered the true secret, came home to Kenrick and whispered to him the message—"Then I said, *it is mine own infirmity, but I will remember the years of the right hand of the Most Highest.*"

It was not long before one great difficulty confronted him, the consequence of former misdeeds, and put him under circumstances which demanded the whole courage of his character, and thoroughly tested the sincerity of his repentance.

After Mackworth's expulsion, and under Whalley's good government, the state of the Noelites greatly improved. Charlie Evson, for whom, now, by the bye, Kenrick always did everything that lay in his power, became far more a model among the younger boys than Wilton had ever been, and there was a final end of suppers, smoking parties, organised cribbing, and recognised "crams." But just as the house was recovering lost ground, and had ceased to be quite a byword in the school, it was thrown into consternation by a long-continued series of petty thefts.

Small sums were extracted from the boys' jacket pockets after they had gone to bed; from the play-boxes which were not provided with good locks and keys; from the private desks in the classrooms, from the dormitories, and from several of the studies. There was no clue to the offender, and first of all suspicion fell strongly on the new boy, little Elgood. A few trifling articles of circumstantial evidence seemed to point him out, and it began to be gradually whispered, no one exactly knew how or by whom, that he must be the guilty boy. Hints were thrown out to him to this effect; little bits of paper, on which were written the words "Thou shalt not steal," or, "The devil will have thieves," were dropped about in his books and wherever he was likely to find them, and whenever the subject was brought on the tapis his manner was closely watched. The effect was unsatisfactory; for Elgood was a timid, nervous boy, and the uneasiness to which this nervousness gave rise was set down as a sign of guilt. At length a sovereign and a half were stolen out of Whalley's study, and as Elgood, being Whalley's fag, had constant access to the study, and might very well have known that Whalley had the money, and in what place he kept it, the prevalent suspicions were confirmed. The boys, with their usual thoughtless haste, leapt to the conclusion that he must have been the thief.

The house was in a perfect ferment. However lightly one or two of them, like Penn, may have thought about taking trifles from small tradesmen, there was not a single one among them, not even Penn himself, whose morality did not brand this thieving from schoolfellows as wicked and mean. The boys felt, too, that it was a stigma on their house, and unhappily just at the time when the majority were really anxious to raise their corporate reputation. Every one was filled with annoyance and disgust, and felt an anxious determination to discover and give up the thief.

At last the suspicions against Elgood proceeded so far, that out of mere justice to him the heads of the house, Whalley, Kenrick, and Bliss, thought it right that he should be questioned. So, after tea, all the house assembled in the classroom, and Elgood was formally charged with the delinquency, and questioned about it, Wilton, in particular, urging him in almost a bullying tone to surrender and confess. The poor child was overwhelmed with terror—cried, blushed, answered incoherently, and lost his head, but would not for a moment confess that he had done it, and protested his innocence with many sobs and tears.

"Well, I suppose if he persists in denying it, we can't go any further," said Kenrick; "but I'm afraid, Elgood, that you must have had something to do with it, as every one seems to see ground for suspecting you."

St. Winifred's, or The World of School

"Oh, I hadn't, I hadn't; indeed I hadn't," wailed Elgood; "I wish you wouldn't say so, Kenrick; indeed I'm innocent, and I'd rather write home for the money ten times over than be suspected."

"So would any one, you little fool," said Wilton.

"Don't bully him in that way, Wilton," said Whalley; "it's not the way to get the truth out of him. Elgood, I should have thought you innocent, if you didn't behave so oddly."

"May I speak?" modestly asked a new voice. The speaker was Charlie Evson.

"Yes, certainly," said Kenrick in an encouraging tone.

"Well then, please, Kenrick, and the whole of you, I think you *have* had the truth out of him; and I think he *is* innocent."

"Why, Charlie?" said Whalley; "what makes you think so?"

"Because I've asked him, and talked to him privately about it," said Charlie; "when you frighten him he gets confused, and contradicts himself, but he can explain whatever looks suspicious if you ask him kindly and quietly."

"Bosh!" said Wilton; "who frightened him?"

"Silence, Wilton," said Whalley. "Well, Charlie, will you question him now for us?"

"That I will," said Charlie, advancing and putting his hand kindly round Elgood's shoulder, as he seated himself on the desk by which Elgood was standing. "Will you tell us, as I ask you, all you told me this morning?"

"Yes," said Elgood eagerly, while his whole manner changed from nervous tremor to perfect simplicity and quiet, now that he had a friend to stand by him.

"Well, now, about the money you've been spending lately?" questioned Charlie, with a smile. "You usen't to be so flush of cash, you know, a month ago."

St. Winifred's, or The World of School

"I can tell you," answered Elgood; "I had a very large present— large for me, I mean—three weeks ago. My father sent me a pound, because it was my birthday, and my big brother and aunt sent me each a pound too."

"I can answer for that being perfectly true," said Charlie, "for I went with my brother to the post-office this afternoon and asked, and found that Elgood had had three money-orders changed there. And now, Elgood, can you trust me with your purse?"

"Of course I can, Charlie," said Elgood, readily producing it, and almost forgetting that the others were present.

"Ah, well, now you see *I'm* going to rifle it. Ah! what have we here? why, here's a whole sovereign, and eight shillings; that looks suspicious, doesn't it?" said Charlie archly.

"No," said Elgood, laughing; "you went with me yourself when I bought my desk for eighteen shillings, and the rest—"

"All right," said Charlie. "Look, you fellows: Elgood and I put down this morning the other things he's bought, and they come to fourteen shillings. I know they're right, for I didn't like Elgood to be wrongly suspected, so Walter went with me to the shops; indeed it was chiefly spent at Coles',"—at which remark they all laughed, for Coles' was the favourite "tuck-shop" of the boys. "Well, now, 1 pound, 8 shillings, plus 18 shillings, plus 14 shillings makes 3 pounds, the sum which Elgood received from home. Is that plain?"

"As plain as a pike-staff," said Bliss; "and you're a little brick, Evson; and it's a chouse if any one suspects Elgood any more."

Wilton suggested something about Elgood being Whalley's fag.

"Shame, Raven," said Kenrick; "why, what a suspicious fellow you must be; there's no ground whatever to suspect Elgood now."

"I only want the fellow found out for the honour of the house," said Wilton, with a sheepish look at this third rebuff.

"Oh, I forgot about that for the moment," said Charlie; "Whalley, please, you know the time, don't you, when the money was taken from your desk?"

"Yes it must have been between four and six, for I saw it safe at four, and it was gone when I came back after tea."

"Then all right," said Charlie joyfully, "for at that very time, all of it, Elgood was in my brother's study with me, learning some lessons. Now then, is Elgood clear?"

"As clear as noonday," shouted several of them, patting the poor child on the head.

"And really, Charlie, we're all very much obliged to you," said Whalley, "for setting this matter straight. But now, as it *isn't* Elgood, who *is* the thief? We must all set ourselves to discover."

"And we *shall* discover," said Bliss; "he's probably here now. Who is it?" he asked, glancing round. "Well, whoever it is, I don't envy him his sensations at this minute."

The meeting broke up, and Kenrick accompanied Whalley to his study to concert further measures.

"Have you any suspicion at all about it, Whalley?"

"Not the least. Have you? No. Well, then, what shall we do?"

"Why, the thief isn't likely to visit *your* study again, Whalley; very likely he'll come to mine. Suppose we put a little marked money in the secret drawer. It's rather a joke to call it the *secret* drawer, for there's no secret about it: anyhow, it's an open secret."

"Very good; and then?"

"Why, you know the money generally goes at one particular time on half-holidays. I'm afraid the rogue, whoever he is, has got a taste for it by this time, and will come to money like a fly to a jam-pot. Now, outside my room, a few yards off, is the shoe-cupboard; what if you and I, and a few others, agree to shut ourselves up there in turns, now and then, on half-holidays between roll-call and tea-time?"

St. Winifred's, or The World of School

"I see," said Whalley; "well, it's horridly unpleasant, but I'll take my turn first. Isn't the door usually locked, though?"

"Yes, but so much the better; we can easily get it left open, and the thief won't suspect an ambuscade. He *must* be found out, for the sake of all the boys who are innocent, and to wipe out the blot against the house."

"All right; I'll ensconce myself there to-morrow. I say, Ken, isn't young Evson a capital fellow? how well he managed to clear Elgood, didn't he? I declare he taught us all a lesson."

"Yes," said Kenrick; "he's his brother all over; just what Walter was when he came."

"What, *you* say that?" said Whalley, smiling and arching his eyebrows.

"Indeed I do," said Kenrick, with some sadness; "I haven't always thought so, the more's the pity;" and he left the room with a sigh.

After his turn for incarceration in the shoe-cupboard, Bliss complained loudly that it wasn't large enough to accommodate him, and that it cramped his long arms and legs, to say nothing of the unpleasant vicinity of spiders and earwigs! But the others, laughing at him, told him that, if the experiment was to be of any use whatever, they must persevere in it, and Bliss allowed himself to be made a victim. For a time nothing happened, but they had not to wait very long.

One day, Kenrick had been mounting guard for about half an hour, and was getting very tired, when a light and hasty step passed along the passage, and into his room. The boy found the study empty, and proceeded noiselessly to open Kenrick's desk, and examine the contents. At length he pulled open the secret drawer; it opened with a little click, and *there* lay before him two half-sovereigns and some silver. He was a wary fellow, for he scrutinised these all over most carefully to see if they were marked, and finding no mark of any kind on them—for it almost required a microscope to see the tiny scratch between the w.w. on the smooth edge of the neck—he took out his purse, and was proceeding to drop them into it, when *a heavy hand was laid upon his shoulder*, and Kenrick and Wilton—the detected thief— stood face to face. The purse dropped on the floor.

St. Winifred's, or The World of School

For a moment they stood silent, staring at each other, and drawing quick breath. Wilton stood there pale as death, and looked up at Kenrick trembling, and with a frightened stare. It was too awful to be so suddenly surprised; to have had an unknown eye-witness standing by him all the while that, fancying himself unseen, he was in the very act of committing that secret deed of sin; to be arrested, detected, exposed, as the boy whose hidden misdoings had been, for so long, a source of discomfort, anxiety, and shame.

"*You*, Wilton—you, *you! you* the disturber of the house; *you*, who have so long been treated by me as a friend, and allowed at all times to use my study; *you*, the foremost to throw the suspicion on others!" He stopped, breathless, for his indignation was rushing in too deep and strong a torrent to find vent in words.

"Oh, Kenrick, don't tell of me."

"Don't *tell* of you! Good heavens! is *that* all you can find to say? Not one word of sorrow—not one word of shame? Abandoned, heartless, graceless fellow!"

"I was driven to it, Kenrick, indeed I was. I owed money to Dan, and to—to other places, and they threatened to tell of me if I didn't pay. Then Harpour and those fellows quite cleared me out at cards; I believe they did it by cheating. Oh, don't tell of me!"

"I cannot screen a thief," was the freezing reply; and the change from flame to ice showed into what commotion his feelings had been thrown.

"Well then, if it comes to that," said Wilton, turning sullen, " *I'll* tell of *you*. It'll all come out; remember it was you who first took me to Dan's, and that's not the only thing I could tell of you. Oh, Kenrick, don't tell, or it will get us all into trouble."

"This then is the creature whom I have suffered to call me friend!" said Kenrick; "for whom I have given up some of the best friends in the school! And this is your gratitude! Why, you worm, Wilton, what do you take me for? Do you think that fear of *your* disclosures will make me hush up twenty thefts? You enlist the whole strength of my conscience against you, lest I should seem to screen you for my own sake. Faugh! your very touch sickens me! —go!"

St. Winifred's, or The World of School

"Oh, Kenrick, don't be so angry; I didn't mean to say it; I didn't know what I was saying; I am driven into a corner by shame and misery. I know I have been a mean dog; but even if you tell of me, don't crush me so with your anger, for indeed, indeed, I *have* been grateful, and *have* loved you, Kenrick. But oh, don't tell, I implore, I entreat you, Ken. How little I thought that I should have to speak to you like this!"

But Kenrick could only say—"*You* the thief; *you*, the *last* fellow of all I should have suspected; *you* whom I have called friend, oh heavens! Yes, I know that I've done you harm by bad example, I know that I've much to answer for, but at any rate I never taught you to be a thief."

"But one thing comes of another, Ken; it all came of my being so much with those brutes, and going to Dan's; it all came of that. I shouldn't have thought myself that I could do it or do half the bad things I *have* done, two months ago. It all came of that; and you used to go with those fellows, Ken, and you went with me to Dan's;" and the boy wrung his hands, and wept, and flung himself on his knees. "I must tell all, if you tell of *me*."

"Say that again," said Kenrick, spurning him scornfully away, "say it once again, and I go straight to Dr Lane. Poor worm, you don't understand me, you don't seem to have the capability of a high thought in you. I tell you that nothing you can say of me shall shake my purpose. I am going now."

But before he could get his straw hat Wilton had clasped him by the knees, and in a voice of agony was beseeching him to relent.

"It's all true, Kenrick; I *am* base, I know it; I have quenched all honour in me. I won't say that again, but do, for God's sake, forgive me this once, and not tell of me. Oh, Kenrick, have *you* never had to say forgive? Do, do pity me, as you hope to be forgiven; don't ruin me, and give me a bad name; I am so young, so young, and have fallen into bad hands from the first."

He still knelt on the floor, exhausted with the violence of his passion, hanging his head upon his breast, sobbing as if his heart would break. It was sad to see him, a mere child still, who might have been so different, long a little reprobate, and now a convicted thief. His face bathed in tears, his voice choked with sobs, the memory of the past, consciousness that much which he said was only too true, touched Kenrick with compassion; the tears rolled down his own face fast, and he felt that, though personal fear could not influence him, pity would perhaps force him to relent, and wring from him in his weakness a reluctant promise not to disclose Wilton's discovered guilt.

"What can I say to you, Wilton? You know that I have liked you, but I never thought that you could act like this."

"Nor I, Kenrick, a short time ago: but the devil tempted me, and I have never learned to resist."

"From my very heart I *do* pity you; but I fear I *must* tell, I fear it's my duty, and I have neglected so many that I dare neglect no more; though, indeed, I'd rather have had any duty but this."

Wilton was again clasping his knees and harrowing his soul by his wild anguish, imploring to be saved from the horror of open shame; and, accustomed as Kenrick was to grant anything to this boy, he was reduced to great distress. Already his whole manner had relented from the loathing and anger he first displayed. He could stand no more at present.

"Oh, Wilton," he said, "you will make me ill if you go on like this. I cannot, must not, will not make you any promise now; but I will think what to do."

"I will go," said Wilton, deeply abashed; "but before I go, promise me one thing, Ken, and that is, even if you tell of me, don't quite cast me off. I shouldn't like to leave and think that I hadn't left *one* behind me to give me a kind thought sometimes."

"Oh, Ra, Ra, to think that it was *you* all the while who were committing all these thefts!"

"You *will* cast me off then?" said Wilton in a voice broken by penitence; "oh! what a bitter, bitter thing it is to feel shame like this."

"I have felt it too in my time, Raven. Poor, poor fellow! who am I that I should cast you off? No, you unhappy child, I may tell of you, but I will not cease to be fond of you. Go, Wilton; I will decide between this and tea–time;—you may come and hear about it after tea."

St. Winifred's, or The World of School

He was already outside the door when Kenrick called out, "Wilton, stop—"

"What is it?" asked Wilton, returning alarmed, for conscience had made him a coward.

"There!" Kenrick only pointed to the purse lying on the floor.

"Oh, don't ask me to touch it again, the money is in it;" said Wilton, hastily leaving the room. There was no acting here; it was plain that he was penitent—plain that he would have given worlds not to have been guilty of the sin.

Very sadly, and with pain and doubt, Kenrick thought the matter over, and thus much at least was clear to him: first, that the house must be informed, though not necessarily the masters or the other boys; secondly, that Wilton must make full and immediate restitution, to all from whom he had stolen; thirdly, there could be no doubt about it, that Wilton must get himself removed at once. On these conditions he thought it possible that the matter might be hushed up; but his conscience was uneasy on this point. That unlucky threat or hint of Wilton's, that he could and would tell some things of his wrong-doings, was his great stumbling- block; whenever extreme pity influenced him to screen the poor boy from full exposure, he began to ask himself whether this was a mere cowardly alternative suggested by his own fears. But for this, he would have determined at once on the more lenient and merciful course; but he had to face this question of self- interest very earnestly, nor could he come to any conclusion about it until he had determined to take a step in all respects worthy of the highest side of his character, by going, in any case, spontaneously to Dr Lane and laying before him a frank confession of past delinquencies, leaving him to act as he thought fit.

Having thus disentangled the question from all its personal bearings he was able to review it on its merits, and went to ask the counsel of Whalley, to whom he related, in confidence, the whole scene exactly as it had occurred. Whalley, too, on hearing the alternative conditions which Kenrick had planned, was fully inclined to spare Wilton as much as possible, but, as neither of them felt satisfied to do this on their own authority, they sought Power's advice, and, as he too felt very doubtful on the matter, he suggested that they should put it to Dr Lane, without mentioning any names, *as a hypothetical case*, and be finally guided by his directions.

St. Winifred's, or The World of School

Accordingly Kenrick sought Dr Lane's study, and laid the entire difficulty before him. He listened attentively, and said, "If the boy is so young, and has been, as you say, misled, and accepts the very sensible conditions which you have proposed, I am inclined to think that the course you have suggested will be the wisest and the kindest one. You have my full authority, Kenrick, to arrange it so, and I am happy to tell you that you have behaved throughout this matter in an honourable and straightforward way."

"I fear, sir, I very little deserve your approval," said Kenrick, with downcast eyes. "In coming to ask your advice in this case, I wanted also to say that I have gone so far wrong that I think you ought to be told how badly I have behaved. It may be that after what I say, you may not think right to allow me to stay here, sir; but at any rate I shall have disburdened my own conscience by telling you, and shall perhaps feel less wretched."

"My dear Kenrick," said Dr Lane, "it was a right and a brave thing of you to come here for this purpose. Confession is often the first, as it is one of the most trying parts of repentance; and I hail this as a new proof of your strong and steady desire to amend. But tell me nothing, my dear boy. It may be that I know more than you suppose; at any rate, I accept the will for the deed, and wish to hear no more, unless, indeed, you *desire* to consult me as a clergyman, and as your spiritual adviser, rather than as your master. I do not seek this confidence; only if there is anything on your conscience of which my advice may help to relieve you, I do not *forbid* you to proceed, and I will give you what help I can."

"I think it would relieve me, sir," said Kenrick; "I have no father; I have, I am sorry to say, no friend in the school to whom I could speak."

"Then sit down, Kenrick, and be assured beforehand of my real sympathy."

He sat down, and, twitching nervously at the ribbon of his straw hat, told Dr Lane much of the history of the last two years, confessing, above all, how badly he had behaved as head of the house, and how much harm he feared his example had done.

Dr Lane did not attempt to extenuate the heinousness of his offence, but he pointed to him what were the fruits and the means of repentance. He exhorted him to let the sense of his past errors stimulate him to double future exertions. He told him of many ways in which, by kindness, by moral courage, by Christian principle, he might be a help and a blessing to other boys. He earnestly warned him to look to God for strength, and to watch and pray lest he should enter into temptation. And then, promising him a full and free oblivion of the past, he knelt down with him and offered up from an overflowing heart a few words of earnest prayer.

"There is nothing like prayer to relieve the heart, Kenrick," said Dr Lane; "and now, good–night, and God bless you."

With a far lighter heart, with far brighter hopes, Kenrick left him, feeling as if a great burden had been rolled away, and inwardly blessing the Doctor for his comforting kindness. He found Wilton anxiously awaiting his arrival in his study; and thinking that their cases in some respects resembled each other, he strove not to be like the unforgiving debtor of the parable, and spoke to Wilton with great gentleness.

"Come here, my poor child; first of all, let me tell you that you shall not be reported." Wilton repaid him by a look of grateful joy.

"But you must restore all the stolen money, Wilton; the house must be told privately; and you must leave at once."

"Well, Kenrick, I ask only one favour," said Wilton, after a short pause.

"What is that?"

"That the house may not be told who stole the money until it is nearly time for me to go."

"No; it shall be kept close till then, otherwise the next fortnight would be too hard for you to bear."

"But *must* I leave?" asked Wilton appealingly.

"It must be so, Wilton; *I* shall be sorry for you, but it must be settled so. Can you manage it?"

"Oh yes," said Wilton, crying quietly; "I'll write home and tell my poor mother all about it, and then of course she'll send me some money and take me away at once, to save me from being expelled. My poor mother, how wretched it will make her!"

"Sin makes us all wretched, Raven boy. I'm sure it makes me wretched enough. And that you mayn't think that fear has had anything to do with our letting you off, I must tell you, Wilton, that I've been to Dr Lane himself and told him all the many sins I've been guilty of."

"Have you? Oh! I'm so sorry; it was all through me."

"Yes; but I'm not sorry; I'm all the happier for it, Raven. There's nothing so miserable as undiscovered sin;—is there?"

"Oh, indeed there isn't. I'm sure I feel happier now, in spite of all. No one knows, Ken, how I've suffered this last fortnight. I've been in a perpetual fright; I've had fearful dreams; I've felt ready to sink for shame; and I've always been fancying that fellows suspected me. Do you know, I am almost glad you caught me, Ken. I'm *very* glad it was you and no one else, though it was a *horrid, horrid* moment when you laid your hand on my shoulder. Yet even this isn't so bad as to have gone on nursing the guilt secretly, and not to have been detected."

Kenrick was musing; the boy who could talk like that was clearly one who *might* have been very unlike what Wilton then was.

"Wilton," he said, "come here, and draw your chair by mine while I read you a little story."

"Oh, Ken, I'm so grateful that you don't hate and despise me though I am a—;" he murmured the word "thief" with a shudder, and under his breath, as he drew up his chair, and Kenrick read to him in a low voice the story of Achan, till he came to the verses—

"And Achan, the son of Carmi, the son of Zabdi, the son of Zerah, of the tribe of Judah, was taken.

"And Joshua said, *My son, give, I pray thee, glory to the Lord God of Israel, and make confession unto Him*; and tell me now what thou hast done, hide it not from me.

"And Achan answered Joshua and said, Indeed I have sinned against the Lord God of Israel, and thus and thus have I done."

And there Kenrick stopped, while Wilton said, "My son! You see Joshua still called him `my son' in spite of all his sin and mischief."

"Yes, Raven boy, but that wasn't why I read you the story which has often struck me. What I wanted you to see was this:—The man was detected—the thing had been coming, creeping horribly near to him;—first his tribe marked by the fatal lot, then his family, then his house, then himself; and while he's standing there, guilty and detected, in the very midst of that crowd who had been defeated because of his baseness, and when all their eyes were scowling on him, and when he knows that he, and his sons, and his daughters, are going to be burned and stoned—at this very moment Joshua says to him, `My son, *give, I pray thee, glory to the God of Israel.*' You see he's to *thank God* for detecting him—thank God even at that frightful moment, and with that frightful death before him as a consequence. One would have thought that it wasn't a matter for much gratitude or jubilation; but you see it *was*, and so both Joshua and Achan seem to have admitted."

"Ah, Kenrick!" said Wilton sadly, "if you'd always talked to me like that, I shouldn't be like Achan now."

Kenrick said nothing, but as he had received infinite comfort from Dr Lane's treatment of himself, he took Wilton by the hand, and, without saying a word, knelt down. Wilton knelt down beside him, and he prayed for forgiveness for them both. A few broken, confused, uncertain words only, but they were earnest, and they came fresh and burning from the heart. They were words of true prayer, and the poor, erring, hardened little boy rose from his knees too overcome to speak.

CHAPTER THIRTY SEVEN. THE RECONCILIATION AND THE LOSS.

The few remain, the many change and pass,
Heaven's light alone remains, earth's shadows flee;
Life, like a dome of many coloured glass,

St. Winifred's, or The World of School

Stains the white radiance of eternity,
Until death shiver it to atoms.
Shelley's *Adonais*.

The termination of Wilton's sojourn at St Winifred's soon arrived. As yet none but the two head–boys in the house knew of his detection. The thefts indeed had ceased; but the name of the offender was still a matter of constant surmise, and it was no easy task for Wilton—conscious how soon they would be informed —to listen to the strong terms of disgust which were applied to the yet unknown delinquent. The barriers of his conceit, his coolness, his audacity, were all broken down; he was a changed boy; his manner was grave and silent, and he almost hid himself during those days in Kenrick's study, where Kenrick, with true kindness, still permitted him to sit.

Meanwhile it became generally known that he was going to leave almost immediately; and as boys often left in this way at the division of the quarter, his departure, though rather sudden, created no astonishment, nor had any one as yet the most distant conjecture as to the reasons which led to it. It is not too much to say, that Wilton was one of the last boys whom the rest would have suspected; they knew indeed that he never professed to be guided by any strong moral principles; but they thought him an unlikely fellow to be guilty of acts which sinned so completely against the schoolboy's artificial code, and which branded him who committed them with the charge of acknowledged meanness.

On the very evening of his departure, the house was again summoned by a notice from Whalley and Kenrick to meet in the classroom after preparation. They came, not knowing for what they were summoned. Whalley opened the proceedings by requesting that any boy who had of late had money stolen from him would stand up. Four or five of them rose, and on stating the sums, mostly small, which they had lost, immediately received the amount from Whalley, much to their surprise, and no less to their content.

The duty which still remained was far less pleasing and more delicate, and it was by Wilton's express and earnest request that it was undertaken by Kenrick and not by Whalley. It was a painful moment for both of them when Kenrick rose, and very briefly, with all the forbearance and gentleness he could command, informed the house that there was every reason to hope that, from that time forward, these thefts, which had caused them all so much distress, would cease. The offender had been discovered, and he begged them all, having confidence that they would grant the request, not to deal harshly with him, or think harshly of him. The guilty boy had done all that could be done by making full and immediate restitution, so that none of them now need remember any injury received at his hands, except Elgood, on whom suspicion had been unjustly thrown, and whose forgiveness the boy earnestly begged.

At this part of his remarks there arose in the deep silence a general murmur of, "Who is it? who is it?"

Wilton, trembling all over with agitation and excitement, was seated beside Kenrick, and had almost cowered behind him for very shame; but now Kenrick stood aside, and laying his hand on Wilton's head, continued, "He is one of ourselves, and he is sitting here," while Wilton covered his face with both hands, and did not stir.

An expression of surprise and emotion thrilled over all the boys present; not a word was spoken; and immediately after Kenrick said to them, "He is punished enough; you can understand that this is a terrible thing for him. He has made reparation as far as he can, and besides this, he is *on this account* going to leave us to-day. I may tell you all, too, that he is very, very, very sorry for what he has done, and has learned a lesson that he will carry with him to his grave. May I assure him that we all forgive him freely? May I tell him that we are grieved to part with him, and most of all grieved for this which has caused it? May I tell him that, in spite of all, he carries with him our warmest wishes and best hopes, and that he leaves no enemy behind him here?"

"Yes, yes!" was murmured on all sides, and while the sound of Wilton's crying sounded through the room, many of the others were also in tears. For this boy was popular; bad as he had been—and the name of his sins was Legion—there was something about him which had endeared him to most of them. Barring this last fault, they were generally proud of him; there had been a certain generosity about him, a gay thoughtlessness, a boyish daring, which won their admiration. He was a promising cricketer, active, merry, full of spirits: before he had been so spoiled by the notice of bigger fellows, there was no one who did not like him and expect that he would turn out well.

"Then my unpleasant task is over," said Kenrick, "and I have no more to say. Oh yes; I had forgotten, there was one very important thing I had to say, as Whalley reminds me. It is this: You know that the Noelites have kept other secrets before now, not always good secrets, I am sorry to say. But will you all now keep this honourable secret? Will you not mention, (for there is no occasion for it), to any others in the school, who it was that took the money? The matter will very soon be forgotten; do not let Wilton's sin be bruited through the whole school, so as to give him a bad name for life."

"Indeed we won't, not one of us will tell," said the boys, and they kept the promise admirably afterwards.

"Then we may all separate. You may bid Wilton good-bye now if you wish to do so, for he starts to-night, almost at once; the carriage is waiting for him now, and you will have no opportunity of seeing him again."

They flocked round him and said "good-bye" without one word of reproach, or one word calculated to wound his feelings; many of them added some sincere expressions of their good wishes for the future. As for Wilton himself, he was far too much moved to *say* much to them, but he pressed their hands in silence, only speaking to beg Elgood to pardon his unkindness, which the little fellow begged him not to think of at all.

Charlie Evson lingered among the last, and spoke to him with frank and genial warmth.

"How you must hate me, Charlie, for annoying you so, and trying to lead you wrong!" said Wilton penitently.

"Indeed I don't, Wilton," said Charlie; "I wish you weren't going to leave. I'm sure we should all get on better now."

"Don't think me as bad as I have seemed, Charlie. I was ashamed at heart all the time I was trying to persuade you to crib and tell lies, and do like other fellows. I felt all the while that you were better than me."

"Well, good-bye, Wilton. Perhaps we shall meet again some day, and be good friends; and I wish you happiness with all my heart."

Charlie was the last of them, and Kenrick and Wilton were left alone. For Wilton's sake Kenrick tried to show all the cheerfulness he could, as he went with him through the now silent and deserted court to the gate where the carriage was waiting.

St. Winifred's, or The World of School

"Have you got all your luggage, and everything all right, Raven?"

"Yes, everything," he said, taking one last long look at the familiar scene. It was dim moonlight; the lights twinkled in the studies where the upper boys were working, and in the dormitories where the rest were now going to bed. The tall trees round the building stood quite black against the faintly lighted sky, waving their thinned remnant of yellow leaves in the November air. In the stillness you heard every slight sound; and the murmur of boys' voices came mingled with the plashing of the mountain stream, and the moaning of the low waves as they broke upon the shore. A merry laugh rang from one of the dormitories, jarring painfully on Wilton's feelings, as he stood gazing round in silence.

He got into the carriage, sighing heavily and grasping Kenrick's hand.

"Well, good-bye, Ken; it *must* be said at last. May I write to you?"

"I wish you would. I shall be so glad to hear of you."

"And you will answer me, Ken?"

"Of course I will, my poor child. Good-bye. God bless you." They still lingered for a moment, and Kenrick saw in the moonlight that Wilton's face was bathed in tears.

"All right, sir?" said the driver.

"Yes," said Wilton; "but it's all wrong, Ken, I think. Good-bye." He waved his hand, the carriage drove off into the darkening night with the little boy alone, and Kenrick with a sinking heart strolled back to his study. Do not pry into his feelings, for they were very terrible ones, as he sat down to his books with the strong conviction that there is nothing so good as the steady fulfilment of duty for the driving away of heavy thoughts.

All his time was taken up with working for the scholarship. It was a scholarship of ninety pounds a year for four years, founded by a princely benefactor of the school, but only falling vacant biennially. There were other scholarships besides this, but this was by far the most valuable one at St Winifred's; the tenure of it was circumscribed by no conditions, and it was therefore proportionably desirable that Kenrick, who was poor, should obtain it. He had, indeed, hardly a chance, as he well knew; for even if he succeeded in beating Walter, he could not expect to beat Power. But Power, though a most graceful and finished scholar, was not strong in mathematics, and as they counted something in the examination, Kenrick's chief chance lay in this, for as a scholar he was by no means to be despised; and with a just reliance on his own abilities, he hoped, if fortunate, to make up for being defeated in classics, by being considerably ahead in the other branches of the examination. How he longed now to have at his command the time he had so largely wasted! had he but used that aright he might have easily disputed the palm in any competition with Power himself. Few boys had been gifted with stronger intellects or clearer heads than he. But though *fresh* time may be carefully and wisely used, the *past* time that has once been wasted can never be recovered or redeemed.

And as he worked hard day by day the time quickly flew by, the scholarship examination took place, and the Christmas holidays came on. The result of the competition could not be known until the boys returned to school.

Mrs Kenrick thought that this Christmas was the happiest she had known. They spent it, of course, very quietly. There were for them none of those happy family gatherings and innocent gaieties that made the time so bright for others, yet still there was something peaceful and something brighter than usual about them. Harry's manner, she thought, was more affectionate, more tenderly respectful, than it often was. There seemed to be something softer and more lovable about his ways. He bore himself with less haughty indifference towards the Fuzbeians; he entered with more zest into such simple amusements as he could invent or procure; he condescended to play quite simply with the curate's little boys, and seemed to be more humble and more contented. She counted the days he spent with her as a miser counts his gold; and he, when he left her, seemed more sorry to leave, and tried to cheer her spirits, and did not make so light, as his wont had been, of the grief which the separation caused.

The first event of importance on the return of the boys to school was the announcement of the scholarship. The list was read from the last name upwards; Henderson stood sixth, Kenrick third, Evson second, *Power first*. "But," said Dr Lane, "Power has communicated to me privately that he does not wish to receive the emoluments of the scholarship, he will therefore be *honorary* scholar, while the scholarship itself will be held by Evson."

St. Winifred's, or The World of School

Disappointed at the result, as he undoubtedly was, yet Kenrick would have been glad at that moment to be able to congratulate Walter. He took it very quietly and well. Sorrow and failure had come on him so often lately, that he hardly looked for anything else; so, when he had heard the result announced, he tried to repress every melancholy thought, and walking back to his study, resumed his day's work as though nothing had happened.

And as he sat there, making believe to work, but with thoughts which, in spite of himself, sadly wandered, there was a knock at the door, and to his great joy, no less than to his intense surprise, Walter Evson entered.

"Oh, Evson," he said, blushing with awkwardness, as he remembered how long a time had passed since they had exchanged a word; "I'm glad you've come. Sit down. Let me congratulate you."

"Thanks, Kenrick," said Walter, holding out his hand; "I thought we had gone on in this way long enough. I have never had any ill-feeling for you, and I feel sure now from your manner that you have none towards me."

"None, Walter, none; I *had* at one time, but it has long ceased: my error has long been explained to me. I have done you wrong, Walter, for two years and more; it has been one of my many faults, and the chief cause of them all. Can you forgive me?"

"Heartily, Ken, if I have anything to forgive. We have both been punished enough, I think, in losing the happiness which we should have been enjoying if we had continued friends."

"Ah, Walter, it pains me to think of that irrevocable past."

"But, Ken, I have come now for a definite purpose," said Walter. "You'll promise me not to take offence?"

"Never again, Walter, with you."

"Well, then, tell me honestly, was it of any consequence to you to gain this scholarship, in which, so unexpectedly to myself, some accident has placed me above you?"

St. Winifred's, or The World of School

Kenrick reddened slightly, and made no answer, while Walter quickly continued—"You know, Ken, that I am going to stay here another year: are you?"

"I'm afraid not; my guardian does not think that we can afford it."

"Well, then, Ken, I think I may say, without much presumption, that, as I stay here for certain, I may safely reckon on getting a scholarship next year. At any rate, even if I don't, my father is quite rich enough to bear my university expenses unaided without any inconvenience. It would be mere selfishness in me, therefore, to retain this scholarship, and I mean to resign it at once; so that let me now congratulate *you* heartily on being Marsden scholar."

"Nay, Walter, I can't have you make this sacrifice for my sake."

"You can't help it, Ken; for this is a free country," said Walter, smiling, "and I may waive a scholarship if I like. But it's no sacrifice whatever, my dear fellow; don't say anything more about it. It gives me ten times the pleasure that you should hold it rather than I. So again I congratulate you; and now, as you must have had enough of me, I'll say good-morning."

He rose with a smile to leave the room, but Kenrick, seizing him by the hand, exclaimed:

"Oh, Walter, you heap coals of fire on my head. Am I never to receive anything from you but benefits which I can never return?"

"Pooh, Ken, there are no benefits between friends; only let us not be silent and distant friends any longer. Power is coming into my study to tea to-night; won't you join us as in old days?"

"I will, Walter; but can the ghost of old days be called to life?"

"Perhaps not; but the young present, which is no ghost, shall replace the old past, Ken. At six o'clock, mind. Good-bye."

"Don't go yet: do stay a little. It is a greater pleasure than I can tell you to see you here again, Walter. I want to have a talk with you."

St. Winifred's, or The World of School

"To make up for two years' arrears, eh, Ken? Why, what a pretty little study you've got! Isn't it odd that I should never have been in it before? It seems quite natural to me to be here somehow. You must come and see mine this evening; I flatter myself it equals even Power's, and beats Flip's in beauty, and looks out on the sea: such a jolly view. But you mustn't see it till this evening. I shall make Charlie put it to rights in honour of your visit. Charlie beats any fag for neatness; why did you turn him off, eh? I've made him my fag now, to keep his hand in."

"Let him come back to me now, Walter; I'm sadder and wiser since those days."

"That I will, gladly. I know, too, that he'll be delighted to come. Ah, Wilton's photograph, I see," said Walter, still looking about him; "I thought him greatly improved before he left."

Kenrick was pleased to see that Walter had no suspicion *why* he left, so that the secret had been kept. They talked on very pleasantly, for they had much to say to each other, and Walter had, by his simple, easy manner, completely broken the ice, and made Kenrick feel at home with him again. Kenrick was quite loth to let him go, and kept detaining him so eagerly that more than half an hour, which seemed like ten minutes, had slipped away before he left. Kenrick looked forward eagerly to meet him again in the evening, with Power, and Henderson, and Eden; their meeting would fitly inaugurate his return to the better feelings of past days;—but it was not destined that the meeting should take place; nor was it till *many* evenings afterwards that Kenrick sat once more in the pleasant society of his old friends.

When Walter had at last made good his escape, playfully refusing to be imprisoned any longer, Kenrick rose and paced the room. He could hardly believe his own happiness; it was the most delightful moment he had experienced for many a long day; the scholarship, so long the object of his hope and ambition, was now attained; impossible as it had seemed, it was actually his, and, at the same moment, the truest friend of his boyhood—the friend for whose returning respect and affection he so long had yearned—was at last restored to him.

With an overflowing heart he sat down to write to his mother, and communicate the good news that he was reconciled to Walter, and that Power and Walter had resigned the scholarship in his favour. He had never felt in happier spirits than just then;—and then, even at the same moment, the cup of sincere and innocent joy, so long untasted, was, with one blow, dashed away from his lip.

For at that moment the post came in, and one of his fags, humming a lively tune, came running with a letter to his door.

"A letter for you, Kenrick," the boy said, throwing it carelessly on the table, and taking up his merry song as he left the room. But Kenrick's eyes were riveted on the letter: it was edged with the deepest black, and bore the Fuzby postmark. For a time he sat stupidly staring at it: he dared not open it.

At length he made an effort, and tore it open. It was a rude, blurred scrawl from their old servant, telling him that his mother had died the day before. A brief note enclosed in this, from the curate of the place, said, "It is quite true, my poor boy. Your mother died very suddenly of spasms in the heart. God's ways are not as our ways. I have written to tell your guardian, and he will no doubt meet you here."

Kenrick remained stupefied, unable to think, almost unable to comprehend. He was roused to his senses by the entrance of his fag to remove his breakfast things, which still lay on the table; and with a vague longing for some comfort and sympathy, he sent the boy to Walter with the message that Kenrick wanted him.

Walter came at once, and Kenrick, not trusting his voice to speak, pushed over to him the letter which contained the fatal news. In such a case human consolation cannot reach the sorrow. It passes like the idle wind over the wounded heart. All that *could* be done by words, and looks, and acts of sympathy, Walter did; and then went to arrange for Kenrick's immediate journey, not returning till he came to tell him that a carriage was waiting to take him to the train.

That evening Kenrick reached the house of death, which was still as death itself. The old faithful servant opened the door to his knock, and using her apron to wipe her eyes, which were red with long weeping, she exclaimed:

"Oh, Master Harry, Master Harry, she's gone. She had been reading and praying in her room, and then she came down to me quite bright and cheerful, when the spasms took her, and I helped her to bed, and she died."

St. Winifred's, or The World of School

Harry flung down his hat in the hall, and rushed upstairs to his mother's room; but when he had opened the door he stood awestruck and motionless;—for he was alone in the presence of the dead.

The light of winter sunset was streaming over her, whose life had been a winter day. Never even in life had he seen her so lovely, so beautiful with the beauty of an angel, as now with the smiling never-broken calm of death upon her. Over the pure pale face, from which every wrinkle made by care and sorrow had vanished, streamed the last cold radiance of evening, illuminating the peaceful smile, and seeming to linger lovingly as it lit up strange glories in the golden hair, smoothed in soft bands over her brow. There she lay with her hands folded, as though in prayer, upon her quiet breast; and the fitful fever of life had passed away. Dead—with the smile of heaven upon her lips, which should never leave them more!

Hers had been a hard, mysterious life. In all the sweet bloom of her youthful beauty she had left her rich home, not, indeed, without the sanction, but against the wishes of her relatives, to brave trial and poverty with the man she loved. How bitter that poverty, how severe, how unexpected those trials had proved to be, we have seen already; and then, still young, as though she were meant to tread with her tender feet the whole thorny round of human sorrow, she had been left a widow with an only son. And during the eight years of her widowed loneliness, her relatives had neglected with cold pride both her and her orphan boy; even that orphan boy, in the midst of all his love for her, had by his pride and waywardness caused her many an anxious hour and many an aching heart, yet she clung to him with an affection whose yearning depth no tongue can utter. And now, still young, she had died suddenly, and left him on the threshold of dangerous youth almost without a friend in the wide world; had passed, with a silence which could never more be broken, into the eternal world; had left him, whom she loved with such intensity of unspeakable affection, without a word, without a look, without a sign of farewell. She had passed away in a moment to the far-off untroubled shore, whence waving hands cannot be seen, and no sounds of farewell voices heard. How must that life expand in the unconceived glory of that new dawn—the life which on earth so little sunshine visited!

She was one of the most sweet, the most pure, the most unselfish, the most beautifully blameless of all God's children; and she had lived in hardship, in neglect, in anxiety, in calumny; she had lived among those mean and wretched villagers, and an angel was among them, and they knew it not; she had tasted no other drink but the bitter waters of affliction; no hope had brightened, no love sustained her earthly course. And now her young orphan son, his heart dead within him for anguish, his conscience tortured by remorse, was kneeling in that agony which no weak words can paint, was kneeling for the last time, *too late*, beside her corpse.

Truly life is a mystery, which the mind of man cannot fathom till the glory of eternal truth enlighten it!

CHAPTER THIRTY EIGHT. THE STUPOR BROKEN.

Hon thymon katedoon, paton anthroopoon aleeinoon.
Homer, *Iliad*, 6, 202.

The white stone, unfractured, ranks as most precious;
The blue lily, unblemished, emits the finest fragrance;
The heart, when it is harassed, finds no place of rest;
The mind, in the midst of bitterness, thinks only of grief.
The Sorrows of Han, a Chinese Tragedy.

After these days Kenrick returned to St Winifred's, as he supposed, for the last time. His guardian, a stiff, unsympathising man, had informed him, that as his mother's annuity ceased with her life, there was very little left to support him. The sale, however, of the house at Fuzby, and the scholarship which he had just won, would serve to maintain him for a few years, and meanwhile his guardian would endeavour to secure for him a place in some merchant's office, where gradually he would be able to earn a livelihood.

It was a very different life from that which this fine, clever, high-spirited boy had imagined for himself, and he looked forward to the prospect with settled despair. But he seemed now to regard himself as a victim of destiny, regretting nothing, and opposing nothing, and caring for nothing. He told Walter with bitter exaggeration, "that he must *indeed* thank him for giving up the scholarship, as he supposed that it had saved him from starvation. His guardian, who had a family of his own, didn't seem to care a straw for him; and he had no friend in the world besides."

And as, for days and weeks, he brooded over these gloomy thoughts and sad memories, he fell into a weary, broken, aimless kind of life. Many tried to comfort him, but they could not reach his sorrow; in their several ways his school-friends did all they could to cheer him up, but they all failed. He grew moody, solitary, silent. Walter often sought him out, and talked in his lively, cheerful, happy strain; but even *his* society Kenrick seemed to shun. He was in that morbid unhealthy state when to meet others inspires a positive shrinking of mind. He seemed to have no pleasure except in shutting himself up in his study, and in taking long lonely walks. He performed his house duties mechanically, and by routine; when he read the lessons in chapel, his voice sounded as though it came from afar, like the voice of one who dreamed; he sat with his books before him for long hours, and made no progress, hardly knowing the page on which he was employed. In school, he sat listlessly playing with his pen, taking no notes, seeming as though he heard nothing, and was scarcely aware of what was going on. His friends could not guess what would come of it, but they grew afraid for him when they saw him mope thus inconsolably, and pine away without respite, till his eyes grew heavy, and his face pale and thin. He had changed all his ways; he seemed to have altered his very nature; he played no games, took no interest in anything, and dropped all his old pursuits. His work was quite spiritless, and he grew so absent, that he forgot the commonest occupations of every day— living as in a waking sleep.

Power and Walter, in talking of him, often wondered whether it was the uncertainty of his future prospects which had thus affected him; and in the full belief that this must have something to do with his morbid melancholy, Power mentioned the matter to Dr Lane as soon as he had the opportunity.

Dr Lane had observed, with much pity, the depression which had fastened on Kenrick like a disease. He was not surprised to see him come back deeply affected; but if "the thoughts of youth are long, long thoughts," its sorrows are usually short and transient, and he looked upon it as unnatural that Kenrick's grief should seem thus incurable, and that a young boy like him should thus refuse to be comforted. It was not long before he introduced the subject, while talking to Power after looking over his composition.

"Kenrick has just been here, Power," he said; "it pains me to see him so sadly altered. I can hardly get him to speak a word; all things seem equally indifferent to him, and his eyes look to me as though they were always ready to overflow with tears. What can we manage to do for him? Would not a little cheerful society brighten him up? We had him here the other day, but he did not speak once the whole evening. Can't even Henderson

St. Winifred's, or The World of School

get him to smile somehow?"

"I'm afraid not, sir," said Power. "Henderson and Evson and I have all tried, but he seems to avoid seeing any one. It makes him ill at ease apparently. I am afraid, for one thing, that he is vexing himself about not being allowed to return, and about being sent into a merchant's office, which he detests."

"If that is all, there can be no difficulty about it," said the Doctor; "we have often kept deserving boys here, when funds failed, and I can easily assure his guardian, without his knowing it, that the expense need not for a moment stand in the way of his return."

These generous acts are common at St Winifred's, for she is indeed an *alma mater* to all her children; and since Kenrick had confided this particular sorrow to *Walter*, Walter undertook to remove it by telling him that Dr Lane would persuade his guardian to let him return. Kenrick appeared glad of the news, as though it brought him a little relief, but it made no long change in his present ways.

Nor even did a still further piece of good fortune, when his guardian wrote and told him that, *on condition of his being sent to the University*, an unknown and anonymous friend had placed at his disposal 100 pounds a year, to be continued until such time as he was able to maintain himself; and that this generous gift would of course permit of his receiving the advantage of an Oxford training, and obviate the necessity of his entering an office, by clearing for him the way to one of the learned professions. This news stirred him up a little, and for a time;— but not for long. He looked upon it all as destiny: he could not guess, he hardly tried to surmise, who the unknown friend could be. Nor did he know till years afterwards that the aid was given by the good and wealthy Sir Lawrence Power, at his son's earnest and generous request. For Power did this kind deed by stealth, and mentioned it to no one, not even to Walter; and Kenrick little thought when he told the good news to Power, and received his kind congratulations, that Power had known of it before he did himself. But still, in spite of all, Kenrick seemed sick at heart, and his life crept on in a sluggish course, like a river that loses its bright stream in the desert, and all whose silver runnels are choked up with dust and sand.

The fact was, that the blows of punishment had fallen on him so fast and so heavily that he felt crushed to the very earth. The expulsion of the reprobates with whom he had consorted, his degradation and censure, Wilton's theft and removal, the violent tension and revulsion of feeling caused by his awakened conscience, his confession, and the gnawing sense of shame, the failure of his ambition, and then his mother's death coming as the awful climax of the calamities he had undergone, and followed by the cold, unfeeling harshness of his guardian, and the damping of his hopes—all these things had broken the boy's spirit utterly. Disgrace, and sorrow, and bereavement, and the stings of remorse, and the suffering of punishment—the forfeiture of a guilty past, and the gloom of a lonely future—these things unmanned him, bowed him down, poisoned his tranquillity of mind, unhinged every energy of his soul, seemed to dry up the very springs of life. The hand of man could not rouse him from the stupor caused by the chastisements of God.

But the rousing came at last, and in due time; and it all came from a very little matter—so slight a matter as a little puff of seaward air. A trivial accident, you will say; yes, one of those very trivial accidents that so often affect the destinies of a lifetime, and

> Shape our ends,
> Rough–hew them how we will.

Kenrick, as usual, was walking along the top of the cliffs alone —restless, aimless, and miserable—"mooning," as the boys would have called it—unable even to analyse his own thoughts, conscious only that it was folly in him to nurse this long- continued and hopeless melancholy, yet quite incapable of making the one strong effort which would have enabled him to throw it off. And in this mood he sat down near the cliff, thinking of nothing, but watching, with idle guesses as to their destination and history, the few vessels that passed by on the horizon. The evening was drawing in, cold and windy; and suddenly remembering that he must be back by tea–time, he rose up to return. The motion displaced his straw hat, and the next moment the breeze had carried it a little way over the edge of the cliff, where it was caught in a low bush of tamarisk. It rested but a few feet below him, and the chalky front of the cliff was sufficiently rough to admit of his descent. He climbed to it, and had just succeeded in disengaging it with his foot, when, before he had time to seize it, it again fell, and rolled down some thirty feet. Kenrick, finding that he had been able to get down with tolerable ease, determined to continue his descent in order to secure it. It never occurred to him that the hat was of no great importance, and that it would have been infinitely less trouble to walk home without it, and buy a new one, than to run the risk and encounter the trouble of his climb. However, he *did* manage to reach it, and put it on with some satisfaction, when, as he was beginning to remount, a considerable mass of chalk crumbled away under his feet, and made him cling on with both hands to avoid being precipitated. He had been able to get down well enough, because, if the chalk slipped, he glided on safely with it, but in climbing up he was obliged to press his feet strongly downwards in order to gain his spring; and every time he did this, he found that the chalk kept giving way, exhausting him with futile efforts, filling his shoes with dust and pebbles, slipping into his clothes, and blinding his eyes. Every person who has climbed at all, whether in the Alps or elsewhere, knows that it is easy enough to get down places which it is almost impossible to mount again; and Kenrick, after many attempts, found that he had been most imprudent, and becoming seriously alarmed, was forced, when he had quite tired himself with fruitless exertions and had once or twice nearly fallen, to give up the attempt altogether, and do his best to secure another way of escape.

This was to climb down quite to the bottom of the cliff, and make his way, as best he could, over rocks and shingle round the bluff which shut in one side of the little bay, on which he stood, and along the narrow line of beach, to St Winifred's Head. This was possible sometimes, and he fancied that the tide was sufficiently far out to enable him to do it now. At any rate herein lay, so far as he saw, his only chance of safety.

Down the cliff then he climbed once more, and though it was some ninety feet high he found no difficulty in doing this, with care, till he came to a place where its surface was precipitous for a height of some ten feet, worn smooth by the beating of the waves. Holding with his hands to the edge, he let himself fall down this height, and found himself standing, a little shaken though unhurt, in a small pebbly bay or indentation of the shore formed by a curve in the line of cliffs, with a series of headlands and precipices trending away on one side far to his right, and with the Ness of St Winifred's reaching out to his left. Once round that headland he would be safe, and indeed if he once got beyond the little pebbly inlet where he stood, he hoped to find some place where he might scale the rocks, and so cross the promontory and get home.

There was no time to be lost, and he ran with all his speed over the loose stones towards the bluff, letting the unlucky straw hat drop on the shore, as it had no string, and it impeded him to be obliged to hold it on with one hand. Reaching the end of the shingle, he stumbled with difficulty over some scattered rocks slimy with ooze and seagrass, hoping with intense hope that when he rounded the projection of cliff, he would see a line of beach, narrow indeed, but still wide enough to allow of his running along it before the tide had come in, and reaching some part of St Winifred's Head which he might be able to scale by means of a sheep-path, or with the help of hands and knees. Very quickly he reached the corner, and hardly dared to look; but when he *did* look, a glance showed him that but slender hope was left. At one spot the tide had already reached the foot of the cliffs; but if he could get to that spot while the water was yet sufficiently shallow to allow him to run through it, he trusted that he might yet be saved. The place was far-off, but he ran and ran; and ever as he ran the place seemed to get farther and farther, and his knees failed him for fatigue, as he sank at every step in the noisy and yielding mixture of sand and pebbles.

Reader, have you ever run a race with the sea? If not, accept the testimony of one who has had to do it more than once, that it is a very painful and exciting race. I ran it once successfully with one who, though we then escaped, has since been overtaken and swallowed up by the great dark waves of that other sea, whose tides are ever advancing upon us, and must sooner or later absorb us all—the great dark waves of Death. But to take your life in your hand, and run, and to know that the sea is gaining upon you, and that, however great the speed with which fear wings your feet, your subtle hundred-handed enemy is intercepting you with its many deep inlets, and does not bate an instant's speed, or withhold itself a hair's-breadth for all your danger,—is an awful thing to feel. And then to see that it *has* intercepted you is worst of all;—it is a moment not to be forgotten. And all this was what Kenrick had to undergo. He ran until he panted for breath, and stumbled for very weariness;—but he was too late. A broad sheet of water now bathed the bases of the cliff, and the waves, as though angry with the opposing breeze, were leaping up with a frantic hiss, and deluging the rocks with sheets of spray and foam.

Experience had taught him with what speed and fury on that dangerous coast the treacherous tide came in. There was not a moment to spare, and as he flew back to the small shelter of the pebbly cove, the water was already gliding close to him, and stretching its arms like a hungry medusa round the seaweed-matted lumps of scattered rock, over which he trod.

His face wetted with the salt dew, his brown hair scattered on the rising wind, he flew rather than ran once more to the place where he had descended, to renew the wild attempt to scale the cliff which seemed to afford him the only shadow of a hope. Yet a mere glance might have been enough to show him that this hope was vain. Both at that spot, and as far as he could see, the sheer base of the cliff offered him no place where it was possible to rest a foot, no place where he could mount three feet above the shingle. But his scrutiny brought home to him another appalling fact,—namely, that the sea-mark where the highest tide fringed its barriers with a triumphal wreath of hanging seaweed, and below which no foliage grew, was high up upon the cliff, far above his head.

It was too late to curse his rashness and folly, nor would he even try to face his frightful situation, till he had thought of every conceivable means by which to escape. A friend of mine had, and I suppose still has, a pen-and-ink sketch which made one shudder to look at it. All that you see is a long sea-wall, apparently the side of some stone pier, so drawn as to give the impression of great height, and the top of it not visible in the picture; by the side of this ripples and plashes a long dark reach of sea-water, lazily waving the weeds which it has planted in the crevices of stone, and extending, like the wall itself, farther than you can guess. The only living thing in the picture is a single, spent, shaggy dog, its paws rested for a moment on a sort of hollow in the wall, and half its dripping body emergent from the dark water. It is staring up with a look of despondent exhaustion, yet mute appeal. The sketch powerfully recalls and typifies the exact position in which poor Kenrick now found himself placed;—before him the hungry, angry, darkening sea, behind him the inaccessible bastions of forbidding cliff. It is a horrible predicament, and those can most thrillingly appreciate it who, like the author, have been in it themselves.

There was yet one thing, and one thing only, to be tried, and it was truly the refuge of desperation. Kenrick was an excellent swimmer; many a time in bathing at St Winifred's, even when he was a little boy, he had struck out boldly far into the bay, even as far as the huge tumbling red buoy, that spent its restless life in "ever climbing with the climbing wave." If he could swim for pleasure, could he not swim for life? It was true that the swim before him was, beyond all comparison, farther and more hazardous than he had ever dreamt of. But swimming is an art which inspires extraordinary confidence; it makes us fancy that drowning is impossible to us, because we cannot imagine ourselves so fatigued as to fail in keeping above water. Kenrick knew that the attempt was only one to be undertaken at dire extremity but that extremity had now arrived, and it was literally the last chance that lay between him and—what he would not think of yet.

So, in the wintry air, with the strong wind blowing keenly, and the red gleam of sunset already beginning to fail, he flung off his clothes on the damp beach, and as one who rushes on a forlorn hope in the teeth of an enemy, he ran down the rough uneven shore, hardly noticing how much it hurt his feet, and plunged boldly into the hideous yeast of seething waves. The cold made him shiver and shiver in every limb; his teeth chattered; he was afraid of cramp; the slimy seaweeds that his feet touched, the tangled and rotting strings of sea-twine that waved about his legs, sent a strong shudder through him; and there was a sick clammy feeling about the frothy spume, through which he had to plunge. But when he had once ploughed his way through all this, and was fairly out of his depth, the exercise warmed him, and he rose with a swimmer's triumphant motion over the yielding waves. On and on he swam, thinking only of that, not looking before him; but when he began to feel quite tired, and *did* look, he saw that he was not nearly half-way to the headland. He saw, too, how the breakers were lashing and fighting with the iron shore which he was madly striving to reach. Even if he could swim so far,— and he now *felt* that he could not,—how could he ever land at such a spot? Would not one of those billows toss him up on its playful spray, and dash him as it dashed its own unpitied offspring, dead upon the rocks? And as this conviction dawned on him, withering all his energy of heart, the wind wailed over him, the water bubbled in his ears, and the sea-mew, flapping as it flew past him, uttered above his head its plaintive scream. His heart sank within him. With a quick motion he turned in the water, and with arms wearied out he swam back again, as for dear life, towards the little landing-place which alone divided him from instant death; struggling on heavily, with limbs so weary that he could barely move them through the waves, whose increasing swell often broke around his head. Already the tide had reached the spot where he had let his straw hat drop on the beach; the sea was scornfully playing with it, tossing it up and down, whirling it round and round like a feather; the wind blew it to the sea, and the sea, receiving no gifts from an enemy, flung it back again; but the wind carried the day, and while Kenrick was wringing the brine out of his dripping hair, and huddling his clothes again over his wet, benumbed, and aching limbs, he saw the straw hat fairly launched, and floating a way over the waves.

And then it was that, as the vision of Sudden Death glared out before his eyes, and the Horror of it leapt upon him, that a scream—a loud, wild, echoing scream, which sounded strange in that lonely place, and rose above the rude song that the wind was now singing—broke from his blanched lips. And another, and another, and then silence; for Kenrick was now crouching at the cliff's foot farthest off from the swelling flood, with his eyes fixed motionless in a wild stare on its advancing line of foam. He was conjuring up before his imagination the time when those waves should have reached him; should have swept him away from the shelter of the shore, or risen above his lips; should have forced him again to struggle and swim, until his strength, already impaired by hunger, and thirst, and cold, and fatigue, should have failed him altogether, and he would sink, and the water gurgle wildly in his ears, and stop his breath,—and all would be still. And when he had pictured this scene to himself with a vividness which made him experience all its agony, for a time his mind flew back through all the faultful past up to that very day; memory lighted her lantern, and threw its blaze on every dark corner, on every hidden recess, every forgotten nook, —left no spot unsearched, unilluminated with sudden flash;—all his past sins were before him, words, looks, thoughts, everything. As when a man descends with a light in his diving- bell into the heaving sea, the strange monsters of the deep, attracted by the unknown glimmer, throng and wallow terribly around him, so did uncouth thoughts and forgotten sins welter in fearful multitudes round this light of memory in the deep sea of that poor human soul. And finally, as though in demon voices, came this message whispered to him, shouted to him tauntingly, rising and falling with maddening alternation on the rising and falling of the wind,—"You have been wasting your life, moodily abandoning yourself to idle misery, neglecting your duties, letting your talents rust,—God *will take from you the life you know not how to use*." And then, as though in answer to this, another voice, low, soft, sweet, that his heart knew well,— another voice filling the interspaces of the others with unseen music, whispered to him soothingly,—"It shall be given you again, use it better, use it better; awake, use it better, *it shall be given you again*."

Those three wild shrieks of his had been heard; he did not know it, but they had been heard. The whole coast was in general so lonely that you could usually pace it for miles without meeting a single human being, and it never even occurred to him that some one might pass that way. But it so happened that the boisterous weather of the last few days had cast away a schooner at a place some five miles from St Winifred's, and Walter Evson had walked with Charlie to see the wreck, and was returning along the cliff. As they passed the spot where Kenrick was, they had been first startled and then horrified by those shrieks, and while they stood listening another came to their ears, more piercing, more heartrending than the rest.

"Good heavens, there *must* be some one down there!" exclaimed Walter.

"Why, how could any one have got there?" asked Charlie.

"Well, but didn't you hear some one scream?"

"Yes, several times. Oh, Walter, do look here." Charlie pointed to the traces on the cliff that some one had descended there.

"Who could have wanted to get down *there*, I wonder; and for what possible purpose?"

"Do you see any one, Walter?"

"No, I don't; there's nothing but the sea,"—for Kenrick, crouching under the cliff, was hidden from sight, and now the tide had come up so far that, from the summit, none of the shingle was visible,—"but what's that?"

"Why, Walter, *it's a straw hat*, it must be one of our fellows down there; I see the ribbon distinctly, dark blue and white twisted together."

"*Dark blue and white*! why, then, it must be some one in the football eleven: Charlie, it must be Kenrick! Heavens, what can have happened?"

"Kenrick!" they both shouted at the top of their voices. But the cliff was high, and the wind, momently rising to a blast, swept away their shouts, and although Kenrick might have heard them distinctly under ordinary circumstances, they now only mingled with, and gave new form and body to, the wild madness which terror was beginning to kindle in his brain. So they shouted, and no answer came.

"No answer comes, Charlie; but there's some one down there as sure as we are here," said Walter. Charlie had already begun to try and descend the face of the cliff. "Stop, stop, Charlie," said Walter, seizing him and dragging him up again, "you mustn't try that;—nay, Charlie, you really *must not*. If it's possible, *I* will." He tried, but three minutes showed him that, however practicable a descent might be, an ascent afterwards would be wholly beyond his power. Besides, if he did descend, what could he do? Clearly nothing; and with another plan in view, he with difficulty reached his former position.

"Nothing to be done that way, Charlie." At that moment another cry came, for Kenrick, in a momentary lull of the wind, had fancied that he had heard sounds and voices other than those of his perturbed and agitated fancy. "Ha! you heard that?" said Walter, and he shouted again, but no sound was returned.

St. Winifred's, or The World of School

"We must fly to St Winifred's, Charlie; there's a boy down on the shore beyond a doubt. You stay behind if you like, for you can't run as fast as me. I'm afraid, though, it's not the least good. St Winifred's is three miles from here, and long before I've got help and come three miles back, it's clear that no one can be alive down there; still we must try," and he was starting when Charlie seized his arm.

"Don't you remember, Walter, the hut at Bryce's cove? there's an old boat there, and it's a mile and a half nearer than St. Win's."

"*Capital* boy, Charlie," said Walter; "how good of you to think of it;—it's the very thing. Come."

They flew along at full speed, Walter taking Charlie's hand, and saying, "Never mind stretching your legs for once, even if you *are* tired. How well you run! we shall be there in no time."

They gained the cove, flew down the steep narrow path, and reached the hut door. Their summons was only answered by the furious barking of a dog. No one was in.

"Never mind; there's the boat; we must take French leave;" and Walter, springing down, hastily unmoored it.

"Wah! what a horrid old tub, and it wants baling, Walter."

"We can't stay for that, Charlie boy; it's a good thing that Semlyn Lake has taught us both to row, isn't it?"

"Oh yes; don't you wish we had the little *Pearl* here now, Walter? Wouldn't we make it fly, instead of this cranky old wretch?"

"Well, we must fancy that this is the *Pearl*, and this Semlyn Lake," said Walter, wading up to the knees to launch the boat, and springing in when he had given it the final shove.

They were excellent rowers, but Charlie had never tried his skill in a sea like that, and was timid, for which there was every excuse.

"How very rough it is, Walter," he said, as the boat tossed up and down like an egg-shell on the high waves.

"Keep up your heart, Charlie, and row steadily; don't be afraid."

"No, Walter, I won't, as you're with me; but—Walter?"

"Well?"

"It'll be dark in half an hour."

"Not quite, and we shall be there by that time; we needn't go far out, and the tide's with us." So the two brave brothers rowed steadily on, with only one more remark from Charlie, ushered in by the word—

"Walter!"

"Anything more to frighten me with, Charlie?" he answered cheerily; "you shan't succeed."

"Well, Walter," he answered, with a little touch of shame, "I was only going to say that, if you look, you'll see that your oar's been broken, and is only spliced together."

"I've seen it all along, Charlie, and will use the oar gingerly; and now, Charlie, I see you're a little frightened, my boy. I'm going to brace you up. Rest on your oar a minute."

He did so. "Now turn round and *look*."

He pointed with his finger to a dark figure, now distinctly seen, cowering low at the white cliff's foot.

"Oh, Walter, I'm ready; I won't say a word more;" and he leant to his oar, and plied it like a man.

It is a pretty, a delightful thing, in idle summer-time, to lie at full length upon the beach on some ambrosial summer evening, when a glow floats over the water, whose calm surface is tenderly rippled with gold and blue. And while the children play beside you, dabbling and paddling in the wavelets, and digging up the ridges of yellow sand, which take the print of their pattering footsteps, nothing is more pleasant than to let the transparent stream of the quiet tide plash musically with its light and motion to your very feet; nothing more pleasant than to listen to its silken murmurs, and to watch it flow upwards with its beneficent coolness, and take possession of the shore. But it is a very different thing when there rises behind you a wall of frowning cliff, precipitous, inaccessible, affording no hope of refuge; and when, for the golden calm of summer eventide, you have the cheerless drawing in of a loud and stormy February night; and when you have the furious hissing violence of rock-and- wind-struck breakers for the violet-coloured margin of rippling waves,—knowing that the wind is wailing forth your requiem, and that, with the fall of every breaker, unseen hands are ringing your knell of death.

The boy crouched there, his face white as the cliffs above him, his undried limbs almost powerless for cold, and his clothes wetted through and through with spray,—pushing aside every moment the dripping locks of hair which the wind scattered over his forehead, that he might look with hollow staring eyes on the Death which was advancing towards him, wrapping him already in its huge mantlefolds, calling aloud to him, beckoning him, freezing him to the very bone with the touch of its icy hand.

And the brutal tide coming on, according to the pitiless, irreversible certainty of the fixed laws that governed it,— coming on like a huge, wallowing monster, dumb and blind,—knew not, and reeked not, of the young life that quivered on the verge of its advance,—that it was about to devour remorselessly, with no wrath to satiate, with no hunger to appease. None the less for the boy's presence, unregardful of his growing horror and wild suspense, it continued its uncouth play,—leaping about the rocks, springing upwards and stretching high hands to pluck down the cliffs, seeming to laugh as it fell back shattered and exhausted, but unsubdued;—charging up sometimes like a herd of wild white horses, bounding one over the other, shaking their foamy manes;—hissing sometimes like a brood of huge sea- serpents, as it insinuated its winding streams among the boulders of the shore.

It might have seemed to be in sport with *him* as it ran first up to his feet, and playfully splashed him, as a bather might splash a person on the shore from head to heel, and then ran back again for a moment, and then up again a little farther, till, as he sat on the extreme line of the shore and with his back huddled up close against the cliff, it first wetted the soles of his feet, and then was over his shoes, then ankle–deep, then knee–deep, then to the waist. Already it seemed to buoy him up;—he knew that in a few moments more he would be forced to swim, and the last struggle would commence.

His brain was dull, his senses blunted, his mind half idiotic, when first, (for his eyes had been fixed downwards on the growing, encroaching waters), he caught a glimpse, in the failing daylight, of the black outline of a boat not twenty yards from him, and caught the sound of its plashing oars. He stared eagerly at it, and just as it came beside him he lost all his strength, uttered a faint cry, and slipped down fainting into the waves.

CHAPTER THIRTY NINE. ON THE DARK SEA.

paides d' eretmois eemenoi glaukeen ala
rhothioisi leukainontes, ezeetoun s'.
Euripides, Cyclops 16.

>   Boys
> Leaning upon their oars, with splash and strain,
> Made white with foam the green and purple sea.
> *Shelley.*

In a moment Walter's strong arms had caught him, and lifted him tenderly into the boat. While the waves tossed them up and down they placed him at full length as comfortably as they could,— which was not very comfortably,—and though his clothes were streaming with salt–water, and his fainting–fit still continued, they began at once to row home. For, by this time, it was dim twilight; the wind was blowing great guns, the clouds were full of dark wrath, and the stormy billows rose higher and higher. There was no time to spare, and it would be as much as they could do to provide for their own safety. The tide was already bumping them against the cliff at the place where, just in time, they had rescued Kenrick, and, in order to get themselves fairly off, Walter, forgetting for a moment, pushed out his oar and pressed against the cliff. The damaged oar was weak enough already, and instantly Walter saw that his vigorous shove had weakened and displaced the old splicing of the blade. Charlie too observed it, but neither of them spoke a word; on the contrary, the little boy was at his place, oar in rowlock, and immediately smote lightly and in good time the surface of the water, splashed it into white foam, and pulled with gallant strokes.

They made but little way; the waves pitched them so high and dropped them with such a heavy fall between their rolling troughs, that rowing became almost impossible, and the miserable old boat shipped quantities of water. At last, after a stronger pull than usual, Walter's oar creaked, snapped, and gave way, flinging him on his back. The loosened twine with which it had been spliced was half rotten with age; it broke in several places, the oar blade fell off and floated away,—and Walter was left holding in both hands a broken and futile stump.

"My God, it is all over with us!" was the wild cry that the sudden and awful misfortune wrung from his lips; while Charlie, shipping his now useless oar, clung round his brother's neck and cried aloud. The three boys—one of them faint, exhausted, and speechless—were in an unsafe and oarless boat on the open tempestuous sea, weltering hopelessly at the cruel mercy of winds and waves; a current was sweeping them they knew not whither, and the wind, howling like a hurricane, was driving them farther and farther away from land.

"Oh, Walter, I can't die, I can't die yet; and not out on this black sea, away from every one!"

"From every one but God, Charlie; and I am with you. Cheer up, little brother, God will not desert us."

"Oh, Walter, pray to God for you and me and Kenrick; pray to Him for life."

"We will both pray, Charlie;" and folding his arms round him, for now that the rowing was over and there was nothing left to do, the little boy was frightened at the increasing gloom, Walter, calm even at that wild moment, with the calm of a clear conscience and a noble heart, poured forth his soul in words of supplication, while Charlie, his voice half stifled with tears, sobbed out a terrified response and echo to his prayer.

And after the prayer Walter's heart was lightened and his spirit strengthened, till he felt ready in himself to meet anything and brave any fate; but his soul ached with pity for his little brother and for his friend. It was his duty to cheer them both and do what could be done. Kenrick had so far recovered as to move and say a few words, and the brothers were by his side in a moment.

"You have saved my life, Walter, when I had given it up; saved it, I hope, to some purpose this time," he whispered, unconscious as yet of his position; and he dragged up his feet out of the pool of water, in which they were lying at the bottom of the boat. But gradually the situation dawned upon him. "How is it you're not rowing?" he asked; "are you tired? Let *me* try; I think I could manage."

"It would be of no use, Ken," said Walter; "I mean that we can't row," and he pointed to the broken oar.

"Then you have saved me at the risk, perhaps at the cost, of your own lives. Oh, you noble, noble Walter!" said Kenrick, the tears gushing from his eyes. "How awfully terrible this is! I seem to be snatched from death to death. Life and death are battling for me to–night; yes, eternal life and death too," he whispered in Walter's ear, catching him by the wrist. "All this danger is for me, Walter, and for my sin. I am like Jonah in the ship; I have been buffeting Death away for hours, but he has been sent for me, he must do his mission. I see that *I* cannot escape, but, O God, I hope that *you* will escape, Walter. Your life and Charlie's must not be spilt for mine."

It was barely light enough to see his face, hut it looked wild and haggard in the ragged gleams of moonlight which the black flitting clouds suffered to break forth at intervals; and his words, after this, were too incoherent to understand. Walter saw that the long intensity of fear had rendered him half delirious and not master of himself. Soon after he sank into a stupor, half sleep, half exhaustion, and even the lurching of the boat did not rouse him any more.

"Walter, he's asleep, or—oh! is he dead, Walter?" asked Charlie in horror.

"No, no, Charlie; there, put your hand upon his heart. You see it beats; he is only exhausted, and in a sort of swoon."

"But he will be pitched over, Walter."

St. Winifred's, or The World of School

"Then I'll show you what we'll do, Charlie. We must make the best of everything." Walter lifted up the useless rudder, pulled out the string of it, to lash Kenrick safely to the stern bench by which he lay, and took off his own coat in order to cover him up that he might sleep; and then, anxious above all things to relieve Charlie's terror, the unselfish boy, thinking only of others, sat beside him on the centre bench, and encircled him with a protecting arm. And, as though to increase their misery, the cold rain began to fall in torrents.

"Oh, Walter, it's so cold, and wet, and stormy, and pitch dark. I'm frightened, Walter. I try not to be, but I can't help it. Take me on your knees and pray for us again."

Walter took him on his knees, and laid his head against his own breast, and folded him in his arms, and wiped his tears; and the little boy's sobs ceased as Walter's voice rose once more in a strain of intense prayer.

"Walter, God *must* grant that prayer; I'm sure he must; he can't reject it," said Charlie simply.

"He will answer it in the way best for us, Charlie, whatever that is."

"But shall we die?" asked his brother again, with a cold shudder at the word.

"Remember what you said just now, Charlie, and be brave. But even if we were to die, could we die better, little brother, than in doing our duty, and trying to save dear Ken's life? It isn't such a very terrible thing, Charlie, after all. We must all die some time, you know, and boys have died as young and younger than you or me."

"Ay, but not like this, Walter: out in these icy, black, horrid waters."

"Yes, they have indeed, Charlie;—little friendless sailor-boys dashed on far away rocks that splintered their ships to atoms, or swallowed up when their vessels foundered in great typhoons, thousands of miles away from home and England, in unknown seas;— little boys like you, Charlie; and they have died bravely, too, though no living soul was near them to hear their cries, and nothing to mark their graves but the bubble for one minute while they sank."

St. Winifred's, or The World of School

"Have they, Walter?"

"Ay, many and many a time they have; and the same God who called for their lives gave them courage and strength to die, as He will give us if there is need."

There was a pause, and then Charlie said, "Talk to me, Walter; it prevents my listening to the flapping and plunging of the boat, and all the other noises. Walter, I think—I think we shall die."

"Courage, brother, I have hope yet, and if we die we will die like this together—I will not let you go. Our bodies shall be washed ashore together—not separated, Charlie, even in death."

"You have been a dear, dear good brother to me. How I love you, Walter!" and as he pressed yet closer to him, he said more bravely, "What hope have you then, Walter?"

"Look up, Charlie; you see that light?"

"Yes; what is it?"

"Sharksfin Lighthouse; don't you remember seeing it sometimes at night from St Win's? Yes; and those lights twinkling far-off are St Win's. Those must be the school lights; and those long windows you can just see are the chapel windows. They are in chapel now, or the lights wouldn't be there. Perhaps some of our friends—Power, perhaps, and Eden—are praying for us; they must have missed us since tea-time."

"How I wish we were with them!"

"Perhaps we may be again; and all the wiser and better in heart and life for this solemn time, Charlie. If we are but carried by this wind and current within hearing of the lighthouse!"

The Sharksfin Lighthouse is built on a sharp high rock two miles out at sea. I have watched it from Bleak Point on a bright, warm summer's day, when the promontory around me was all ablaze with purple heather and golden gorse, and there was not breeze enough to shake the wing of the butterfly as it rested on the bluebell, or disturb the

St. Winifred's, or The World of School

honey-laden bee as it murmured in the thyme. Yet even then the waters were seething and boiling in never-ended tumult about those hideous sunken rocks; and the ocean all around was hoary as with the neezings of a thousand leviathans floundering in its monstrous depths. You may guess what they are on a wild February night;—how, in the mighty rush of the Atlantic, the torn breakers beat about them with tremendous rage, till the whole sea is in angry motion like some demon caldron that seethes over roaring flame.

Drifting along, or rather flung and battered about on the current, they passed within near sight of the lighthouse, and they might have thanked God that they passed no nearer, for to have passed nearer would have been certain death. The white waves dashed over it, enveloped its tall, strong pillar that buffeted them back, like a noble will in the midst of calumny and persecution; *they* fell back hissing and discomfited, and could not dim its silver or quench its flame; but it glowed on with steady lustre in the midst of them—flung its victorious path of splendour over their raging motion, warned from the sunken reef the weary mariner, and looked forth untroubled with its broad, calm eye into the madness and fury of the tempest-haunted night.

Through this broad track of light the boat was driven, and Walter shouted at the top of his voice with all his remaining strength. The three men in the lighthouse fancied indeed, as they acknowledged afterwards, that they had heard some shouts; but strange, mysterious, inarticulate voices are often borne upon the wind, and haunt always the lonely wastes of foamy sea. The lighthouse men had often heard these unexplained wailings and weird screams. Many a time they had looked out, and been so continually deceived, that unless human accents were unmistakable and well-defined, they attribute these sounds to other agencies, or to the secret phenomena of the worst storms. And even if they *had* heard, what could they have done, or how have launched their boat when the billows were running mountain-high about their perilous rock?

Charlie had been quiet for a long time, his face hidden on Walter's shoulder; but he had seen the glare which the light threw across the waves, and had observed that they had gradually been driven through it into the blackness again, and he asked, "Have we passed the lighthouse, Walter?"

"We have."

"Oh, I am so hungry and burning with thirst! Oh, what shall we do?"

"Try not to think about it, Charlie;—a little fasting won't hurt us much."

Another long pause, during which they clung more closely to each other, and their hearts beat side by side, and then Charlie said, in a barely articulate whisper:

"Walter!"

"I know what you are going to say, Charlie."

"The water in the boat is nearly up to my knees."

"We have shipped a great deal, you know."

"Yes; and besides that—"

"Yes, it is true; there is a leak. Do you mind my putting you down and trying what I can do to bale the water out?"

"Oh, Walter, don't put me off your knee;—don't let go of me."

"Very well, Charlie; it wouldn't be of much use."

"Good God!" cried the little boy in a paroxysm of agony, "we are sinking—we are foundering!"

They wound their arms round each other, and Walter said, "It is even so, my darling brother. Death is near, but God is with us; and if it is death, then death means rest and heaven. Good-bye, Charlie, good-bye; we will be close together till the end."

CHAPTER FORTY. WHAT THE SEA GAVE UP.

>The sands and yeasty surges mix
>   At midnight in a dreary bay;

St. Winifred's, or The World of School

And on thy ribs the limpet sticks,
 And o'er thy bones the scrawl shall play.
  Tennyson.

Anxiety reigned at St Winifred's, succeeded by consternation and intense grief. Little was thought of the absence of the three at tea-time, but when it came to chapel-time and bedtime, and they had not yet appeared, and when next morning it was found that they had not been heard of during the night, every one became seriously alarmed, and all the neighbouring country was searched for intelligence.

The place on the cliff where Kenrick had descended was observed, but as the traces showed that only *one* boy had gone down there, the discovery, so far from explaining matters, only rendered them more inexplicable. Additional light was thrown on the subject by the disappearance of Bryce's boat, and the worst fears seemed to be confirmed by his information that it was a rickety old concern, only intended to paddle in smooth weather close to the shore. But what earthly reason could have induced three boys to venture out in such a tub on so wild a night? That they did it for pleasure was inconceivable, the more so as rowing was strictly forbidden; and as no other reason could be suggested, all conjecture was at fault.

The fishermen went out in their smacks, but found no traces, and gained no tidings of the missing boys; and all through that weary and anxious day the belief that they had been lost at sea gained ground. Almost all day Power, and Eden, and Henderson had been gazing out to sea, or wandering on the shore, in the vain hope of seeing them come rowing across the bay; but all the sailors on the shore affirmed that if they *had* gone out in an open boat, and particularly in Bryce's boat, it was an utter impossibility that they could have outlived the tempest of the preceding night.

At last, towards the evening, the sea gave up, not indeed her dead, but what was accepted as a positive proof of their wretched fate. Henderson, who was in a fever of excitement, which Power vainly strove to allay, was walking with him and Eden, who was hardly less troubled, along the beach, when he caught sight of something floating along, rising and falling on the dumb, sullen swell of the advancing tide. He thought and declared at first, with a start of horror, that it was the light hair of a drowned boy; but they very soon saw that it could not be that, and dashing in waist-deep after it, Henderson brought out *the torn and battered fragments of a straw hat*. The ribbon, of dark blue and white, though

St. Winifred's, or The World of School

soaked and discoloured, still served to identify it as having belonged to a St Winifred's boy; and, carefully examining the flannel lining, they saw on a piece of linen sewn upon it—only too legible still—the name "H. Kenrick." Nor was this all they found. The discovery had quickened their search, and soon afterwards Power, with a sudden suppressed cry, pointed to something black, lying, with a dreadful look about it, at a far part of the sand. Again their hearts grew cold, and running up to it they all recognised, with fresh horror and despair, *the coat which Walter had last worn*. They recognised it, but besides this, to place the matter beyond a doubt, his name was marked on the inside of the sleeve. In one of the pockets was his school notebook, with all the notes he had taken, and the playful caricatures which here and there he had scribbled over the pages; and in the other, stained with the salt- water, and tearing at every touch, were the letters he had last received.

All the next day the doubt was growing into certainty. Mr and Mrs Evson were summoned from Semlyn, and came with feelings that cannot be depicted. Power gave to Mrs Evson the coat he had picked up, and he and Henderson hardly ever left the parents of their friend, doing all they could to cheer their spirits and support in them the hopes they could hardly feel themselves. To this day Mrs Evson cherishes that coat as a dear and sacred relic, which reminds her of the mercy which sustained her during the first great agony which she had endured in her happy life. Power kept poor Kenrick's hat, for no relation of his was there to claim it.

Another day dawned, and settled grief and gloom fell on all alike at St Winifred's—the boys, the masters, the inhabitants. The sight of Mr and Mrs Evson's speechless anguish oppressed all hearts, and by this time hope seemed quenched for ever. For now one boy only—though young hearts are slow to give up hope—had refused to believe the worst. It was Eden. He *persisted* that the three boys must have been picked up. The belief had come upon him suddenly, and grown upon him he knew not how, but he was *sure* of it; and therefore his society brought most relief and comfort to the torn heart of the mother. "What made him so confident?" she asked. He did not know; he had seen it, or dreamt it, or *felt* it somehow, only he felt unalterably convinced that so it was. "They will come back, dear Mrs Evson, they will come back, you will see," was his repeated asseveration; and oppressed as her heart was with doubt and fear, she was never weary of those words.

And on the fourth day, while Mr Evson was absent, having gone to make inquiries in London of all the ships which had passed by St. Winifred's on that day, Eden, radiant with joy, rushed into Dr Lane's drawing-room, where Mrs Evson was sitting, and utterly regardless of *les convenances*, burst out with the exclamation, "Oh, Mrs Evson, it is true, it is true what I always told you. Didn't I say that I knew it? They *have* been picked up."

"Hush, my boy; steady," whispered Mrs Lane; "you should have delivered the message less suddenly. The revulsion of feeling from sorrow to joy will be too much for her."

"Oh, Eden, tell me," said the mother faintly, recalling her senses bewildered by the shock of intelligence; "are you certain? Oh, where are my boys?"

"You will see them soon," he said very gently; and the next moment, to confirm his words, the door again flew open, and Charlie Evson was wrapped in his mother's arms, and strained to her heart, and covered with her kisses, and his bright young face bathed in her tears of gratitude and joy.

"Charlie, darling Charlie, where is Walter?" were her first words.

"What, don't you know me then, mother; and have you no kiss to spare for me?" said the playful voice of a boy enveloped in a sailor's blue shell-jacket; and then it was Walter's turn to feel in that long embrace what is the agonising fondness of a mother's love.

Kenrick was looking on a little sadly,—not envious, but made sorrowful by memory. But the next moment Walter, taking him by the hand, had introduced him to his mother, and she kissed him too on the cheek. "Your name is so familiar to me, Kenrick," she said; "and you have shared their dangers."

"Walter has twice saved my life, Mrs Evson," he answered; "and this time, I trust, he has saved it in more senses than one."

The boys' story was soon told. Just as their boat was beginning to sink, and the bitterness of death seemed over, Walter caught sight of the lights of a ship, and saw her huge dark outline looming not far from them, and towering above the waves. Instantly he and Charlie had shouted with all the frantic energy of reviving hope. By God's mercy their shouts had been heard; in spite of the risk and difficulty caused by the turbulence of the night, the ship hove to, the long-boat was manned, and the amazed sailors had rescued them not ten minutes before their wretched boat swirled round and sank to the bottom.

St. Winifred's, or The World of School

Nothing could exceed the care and tenderness with which the sailors and the good captain of the *Morning Star* had treated them. The genial warmth of the captain's cabin, the food and wine of which they stood so much in need, the rest and quiet, and a long, long sleep, continued for nearly twenty-four hours, had recruited their failing strength, and restored them to perfect health. Past St Winifred's Bay extends for miles and miles a long range of iron-bound coast, and this circumstance, together with the violence of the breeze blowing away from land, had prevented the captain from having any opportunity of putting them ashore until the morning of this day, when, with kind-hearted liberality, he had also supplied them with the money requisite to pay their way to St Winifred's.

"You can't think how jolly it was on board, mother," said Charlie. "I've learnt all about ships, and it was such fun; and they were all as kind to us as possible."

"You mustn't suppose we didn't think of you, mother dearest," said Walter, "and how anxious you would be; but we felt sure you would believe that some ship had picked us up."

"Yes, Walter; and to taste this joy is worth any past sorrow," said his mother. "You must thank your friend Eden for mainly keeping up my spirits, for he was almost the only person who maintained that you were still alive."

"And now, Mrs Evson," said Power, "you must spare them for ten minutes, for the masters and all the school are impatient to see and congratulate them."

The whole story had spread among the boys in ten minutes, and they were again proud to recognise Walter's chivalrous daring. When he appeared in the blue jacket with which Captain Peters had replaced the loss of his coat, with Kenrick's arm in his, and holding Charlie's hand, cheer after cheer broke from the assembled boys; and finally, unable to repress their joy and enthusiasm, they lifted the three on their shoulders and chaired them all round the court.

You may suppose that it was a joyful dinner-party that evening at Dr Lane's. Mr Evson, as they had conjectured, had heard of his sons' safety in London from the captain of the *Morning Star*, to whom he had tendered his warmest and most grateful thanks, and to whom, before leaving London, he had presented, in testimony of his gratitude, an exquisite chronometer. Returning to St. Winifred's, he found his two boys seated happily

St. Winifred's, or The World of School

in the drawing- room awaiting him, each with their mother's hand in theirs, and in the company of their best boy-friends. Walter was still in the blue shell-jacket, which became him well, and which neither Mrs Lane nor the boys would suffer him to change. It was indeed an evening never to be forgotten, and hardly less joyous and rememberable was the grand breakfast which the Sixth gave to Walter and Kenrick in memory of the event, and to which, by special exception, little Charlie was also invited.

Rejoicings are good, but they were saved for greater and better things. These three young boys had stood face to face with sudden death. Death, as it were, had laid his hand on their shoulders, had taken them by the hair and looked upon them, and bade them commune with themselves; and, when he released them from that stern cold grasp, it gave to their lives an awful reality. It did not quench, indeed, their natural mirthfulness, but it filled them with strong purposes and high thoughts. Kenrick returned to St Winifred's a changed boy; long-continued terror had quite altered the expression of his countenance, but, while this effect soon wore off, the *moral* effects produced in him were happily permanent. He began a life in earnest; for him there was no more listlessness, or moody fits of sorrow, or bursts of wayward self- indulgence. He became strenuous, diligent, modest, earnest, kind; he too, like Walter and Charlie, began his career *"from strength to strength."* Under him, and Power, and Walter, and others, whom their influence had formed or who had been moulded by the tradition they had left behind them, St Winifred's flourished more and more, and added new honours and benefits to its old and famous name. At the end of that half-year Power left, but not until he had won the Balliol scholarship and carried off nearly all the prizes in the school. Walter succeeded him as head of the school; and he and Kenrick, (who was restored to his old place on the list), worked heart and soul together for the good of it. In those days it was indeed in a happy and prosperous state— renowned and honoured without, well governed and high toned within. Dr Lane felt and acknowledged that much of this success was due to the example and to the vigour of these head-boys. Power, when he left, was beloved and distinguished; Walter and Kenrick trod in his steps. To the boundless delight of the school they too carried off in one year the highest open scholarship at each University; and when they also left, they had been as successful as Power, and were, if possible, even more universally beloved. Whalley carried on for another year the high tradition, and, in due time, little Charlie also attained the head place in the school, and so behaved as to identify his name and Walter's with some of its happiest and wisest institutions for many years.

St. Winifred's, or The World of School

CHAPTER FORTY ONE. L'ENVOI.

> Is not to-day enough? why do I peer
> Into the darkness of the day to come?
> Is not to-morrow e'en as yesterday?
> *Relics of Shelley.*

May I not leave them here? Where could I leave them better than on this marble threshold of a promising boyhood; still happy and noble in the freshness of their feelings, the brightness of their hopes, the enthusiasm of their thoughts? Need I say a word of after-life, with the fading of its earlier visions, and the coldness and hardness of its ways? I should like to linger with them here; to shake hands here in farewell, and leave them as the boys I knew. They are living still, and are happy and highly honoured in the world. In their case "the boy has been father to the man"; and the reader who has understood and sympathised with them in their early life will not ask me to draw aside the curtain, even for a moment, to show them as they appeared when a few more summers had seen them grow to the full stature of their manhood.

I said that they were living still; but it is not so with all of them.

Charlie Evson alone, of the little band who have been amongst the number of our friends at St Winifred's,—alone, though the youngest of them all,—is now dead. He died a violent death. Filled with a missionary spirit, and desirous, like Edward Irving, of "something more high and heroical in religion than this age affecteth," he joined a mission to one of the great groups of Pacific Islands. And there, many a time, in the evening, after a day spent in teaching the natives how to plant their fields and build their houses, he would gather them round him in the twilight, and, while the cool wind wandered over his hair and brow, and shook overhead the graceful plumes of the cocoa-palm, he would talk to them in low sweet tones, until the fireflies were twinkling in the thicket and the stars stole out one after another in their silent myriads, of One who came from the highest Heaven to redeem them from savagery and degradation, and to make them holy as He was holy, and pure as He was pure. He was eminently successful; but when he had planted in some islands the first seeds of a fruitful Christianity, he sailed to other reefs, still carrying the everlasting gospel in his hands. One evening as the little missionary ship, which Charlie himself had built, drew near the land, they saw that the natives were drawn up in a threatening attitude on the beach. Trusting to conciliate them by kindness and by presents, the young missionary, taking with him a few glittering trifles to attract their notice, proceeded with a small band of followers towards the shore. At first the natives seemed inclined to receive them well, but suddenly, by the wild impulse to which barbarians are so liable, one of the savages pierced a sailor with his spear. Evson, by an effort of strength, wrenched the weapon out of his hand and told his men to take up the wounded sailor and retreat. This they effected in safety, for the islanders were struck and awed by the young Englishman's high bearing and firm attitude; and his eye fixed quietly upon them kept them back. He was himself the last to step into the boat, and, as he turned to do so, one of the wretches struck him on the head with his accursed club. He fell stunned and bleeding upon the beach, and in an instant was despatched by the spears and clubs of a hundred savages, while the boat's crew barely escaped with their lives, and the little mission vessel, spreading all her sails, could with difficulty elude the pursuit of the canoes, which swarmed out of the creeks to give her chase. The corpse lay bleeding upon a nameless strand, and the soft fair hair that a mother's hand had fondled and a mother's lips had kissed, dangled as a trophy at the girdle of a cannibal. Thus it was that Charlie died; and a marble tablet in Semlyn Church, ornamented with the most delicate and exquisite sculpture, records his tragic fate, and stands as a monument of his parents' tender love. As a boy he had shown a martyr's dauntless spirit; as a man he was suffered to win the rare and high glory of a martyr's crown.

Of Walter, and Henderson, and Sir Reginald Power—for Power has succeeded only too early to his father's title and estates—I need say no more. Their days from youth to maturity were linked together by a natural progress in all things charitable, and great, and good. They did not belie their early promise. The breeze of a happy life bore them gently onward, and they cast no anchor in its widening stream. They were brave and manly and honourable boys, and they grew up into high-minded and honourable men.

I do not wish you to suppose that they had not their own bitter trials to suffer, or that they were exempt in any degree from our common sorrows. In that turbulent and restless period of life when the passions are strong and the heart wild and wilful and full of pride, while, at the same time, the judgment is often weak and the thoughts are immature and crude, they had, (as we all have), to purchase wholesome experience at the price of suffering; to remember with shame some follies, and mourn over some mistakes. In saying this, I only say that they were not faultless; which of us is? But, at the same time, I may fairly say that we do not often meet with nobler or manlier boys and youths than these; that the errors which they committed they humbly endeavoured by patience and carefulness to amend; that they used their talents well and wisely, striving to live in love and charity with all around them; that above all they kept the fear of God before their eyes, and never lost the freshness and geniality of early years, but kept

   The young lamb's heart amid the full-grown flocks;

—kept the heart of boyhood taken up and purified in the powers of manhood. And this is the reason why the eye that sees them loves them, and the tongue that speaks of them blesses them. And when the end comes to them which comes to all; when—as though a child should trample out the sparks from a piece of paper—death comes upon them and tramples out for ever their joys and sorrows, their hopes and fears; then, sure I am, that those who mourn for them, that those who cherish their memory and regret their loss, will neither be insincere nor few, and that they themselves will meet calmly and gladly that Great Shadow, waiting and looking sure though humble hope to a better and less transient life; to a sinless and unstained world; to the meeting with long-lost Friends; to the REST WHICH REMAINETH FOR THE PEOPLE OF GOD.

And here, gentle reader, let us bid them all farewell.

DOXA TOO THEOO.

Printed in the United States
65395LVS00003B/16